Either/Or

ALSO BY ELIF BATUMAN

The Possessed
The Idiot

Either/Or

Elif Batuman

JONATHAN CAPE
LONDON

1 3 5 7 9 10 8 6 4 2

Jonathan Cape is part of the Penguin Random House group of companies
whose addresses can be found at global.penguinrandomhouse.com.

Penguin
Random House
UK

First published by Jonathan Cape in 2022

penguin.co.uk/vintage

A CIP catalogue record for this book is available from the British Library

HB ISBN 9781787333864
TPB ISBN 9781787333871

Printed and bound in Great Britain by Clays Ltd, Elcograf S.p.A.

The authorised representative in the EEA is Penguin Random House Ireland,
Morrison Chambers, 32 Nassau Street, Dublin D02 YH68

Penguin Random House is committed to a sustainable future
for our business, our readers and our planet. This book is made
from Forest Stewardship Council® certified paper.

And is it not a pity and a shame that books are written which confuse people about life, make them bored with it before they begin, instead of teaching them how to live?

—SØREN KIERKEGAARD, *Either/Or*

PART ONE

September 1996

THE FIRST WEEK

It was dark when I got to Cambridge. I pulled my mother's suitcase over the cobblestones toward the river. Riley had been really mad when we were assigned to Mather, and not to one of the historic ivy-covered brick buildings where young men had lived in ancient times with their servants. But I wasn't into history, so I liked that the rooms in Mather were all singles, and nobody had to figure out how to share an irregularly sized suite where people had lived with their servants.

I hadn't spoken to Ivan since July, when we said goodbye in a parking lot on the Danube. We hadn't exchanged phone numbers, since we were both going to be traveling, and anyway we never had talked much on the phone. But I had never doubted that, when I got back to school, I would find an email from him, explaining everything. It was not, after all, conceivable that there was no explanation, or that the explanation could come from anyone else, or that it could come in any way other than email, since that was how everything had always happened between us.

Mather resembled an alien starship: impregnable, simultaneously ancient and futuristic, gathering its powers. I held my ID card in front of the reader, and the door to the computer room clicked open. I found myself remembering a book I'd read where a woman looked in a mirror for the first time after seven years in a gulag, and the face looking back wasn't her own, but that of her mother. I immediately recognized how shameful, self-important, and obtuse it was for me, an American college student who hadn't checked email for three months, to compare herself to a political prisoner who had spent seven years in a gulag. But it was too late—I had already thought of it.

I mistyped my password twice before I got it right. Information started cascading down the screen, first about the computer itself and the different protocols it was using, then about when and where it had last seen me, and finally the sentence that sent a jolt to my heart: You have new mail.

Ivan's name was there, just like I had known it would be. Before reading the message through, I looked at it all at once, to see how long it was and what it was like. Right away, I could tell something was wrong. So something is wrong, I read. I saw the words "shocked" and "monster": "I am very shocked that you see me as such a monster," it said. "I know you won't believe anything I say." And: "I hope you will tell me why I am so horrible, so that I can defend myself."

I had to reread the whole message twice before I understood that it was three months old. Ivan had sent it in June, in response to an angry email I had sent him before leaving campus. Technically, his reply had been invalidated by all the things that had happened between us in the intervening months. But it still felt like a new and final word from him, because, although there were several other messages in the inbox, none was from Ivan. He hadn't written anything to me at all since

4

that day in the parking lot—since he had held me so close to him, and then gotten in his car and driven away.

Most of the other emails were also months old and out-of-date. There was one from Peter that said, I desperately need to know your flight arrival time in Budapest, and another from Riley asking if it was OK to apply to overflow housing so we wouldn't have to live in Mather. Only two messages were from the past couple of days. One said that I had to see my financial aid officer at the earliest opportunity. The other, from the new president of the Turkish Students Association, said that somebody had found a store in Brookline that sold Kayseri-style *pastırma*: a kind of cured meat that some people said was etymologically related to pastrami. So if you like Kayseri-style pastirma, you can go there, his message concluded.

I exited the email program and used the terrible "finger" command, to see where Ivan was. He had logged on from Berkeley two hours earlier. So he was there. He just wasn't writing to me.

———

Svetlana got to campus the day after me, though it felt like years. I had already slept the night in my new room, eaten breakfast and lunch in the cafeteria, and made numerous trips back and forth to the storage facility, having the same conversation over and over. "How was your summer?" "How was your summer?" "How was Hungary?" I was dissatisfied by the vagueness of my own answers. I still hadn't figured out the right angle.

"How was Hungary?" Lakshmi asked at lunch, with a conspiratorial sparkle. "Did anything happen?" Notwithstanding my strong feeling that a lot of things had happened, I answered the question truthfully in the sense that I knew Lakshmi intended it. Nothing had happened.

Svetlana asked me the same question that evening, when we met at her warehouse-like suite in new Quincy, and sat on bean-bag chairs under an Edward Hopper poster, and talked about everything that had happened since the last time we had spoken—when I had been in a phone booth in the Kál train station, and Svetlana had been at her grandmother's house in Belgrade. I told her how I had finally called Ivan in Budapest, how he had showed up with a canoe, and we had sat up all night at his parents' house.

"Did anything happen?" she asked, in a lazier, more amused voice than Lakshmi's, but meaning the same thing.

"Well, like, *that one thing* didn't happen," I said.

"Oh, Selin," Svetlana said.

When Ivan first told me about the summer program in Hungary, he said I should take my time to think about it, because he didn't want to force me into anything. Svetlana said that, if I agreed to go, Ivan was going to try to have sex with me. This was a possibility I had never previously considered. I daydreamed about Ivan all the time, imagining different conversations we might have, how he might look at me, touch my hair, kiss me. But I never thought about having sex. What I knew about "having sex" didn't correspond to anything I wanted or had felt.

I had tried, on multiple occasions, to put in a tampon. Tampons were spoken of by older or more sophisticated girls as being somehow more liberated and feminist than maxi pads. "I just put one in and forget about it." I felt troubled by the implication that a person was constantly thinking about their maxi pad. Nonetheless, every few months I would give tampons another shot. It was always the same. No matter what direction I pushed the applicator, however methodically I tried all the different angles, the result was a blinding, electric pain. I read and reread the instructions. Clearly I was doing something wrong, but what? It was worrisome, especially since I was pretty sure that a guy—that Ivan—would be bigger than a tampon. But at that point my brain stopped being able to entertain it, it became unthinkable.

Svetlana said I had better think about it. "You wouldn't want to end up in that situation and not have thought about it," she said, reasonably. And yet, it turned out there wasn't much to think about. It was immediately obvious that if Ivan tried to have sex with me, I would let him. Maybe he would be able to tell me what I had been doing wrong, and it wouldn't be as terrible as trying to put in a tampon.

But he hadn't tried, and all the nights we sat up late together, all we did was talk. Then he left for Thailand, at the end of July, and I still had another ten days in the village, surrounded by people who weren't him. A strange thing: I had gone to Hungary in some way to understand Ivan better, because being Hungarian was such a big deal for him—and it was only in the villages that I had realized, with a certain shock, that, although Hungarianness was a big part of Ivan, Ivan himself was only a very small part of Hungary. On some level, I had always known that Hungary was a whole country, home to millions of people who had never met Ivan, and didn't know or care about him. But apparently I hadn't completely thought it through, because it still felt like a surprise.

Had that been when I lost the thread of the story I was telling myself—the thread of the story about my life?

Svetlana's trip to Belgrade—her first time back since the war—had gone well, maybe thanks to all the preparation she had done with her shrink. There had been only one moment, at the store downstairs from her grandmother's apartment, when she had dropped a coin and bent over to pick it up, and suddenly remembered with horror how a milk bottle had once smashed on those particular floor tiles. She didn't remember what else had happened, or what had been so horrible. There was just the image of the glass splintering irretrievably in all directions, the blob of milk spreading over the dingy tiles like a diabolical hand.

"Spilled milk." Svetlana sighed. "Sometimes I wish my subconscious would be a little more original."

I wanted to hear more about it, but Svetlana was already thinking less about Belgrade than about the wilderness, where she had just come back from being a leader on a freshman pre-orientation program. I kept forgetting about the existence of the freshman pre-orientation programs. In addition to the outdoors one, there was an arts one, and a community-service one where you built houses for underprivileged people. You had to pay extra to do them—even the one where you built houses—so it had never occurred to me to apply. But Svetlana had done the outdoors one as a freshman, and had had a profound experience that was related to the sublime.

Listening to Svetlana talk, I fluctuated between believing that something really good had happened to her, and experiencing a profound sense of alienation. She described the intense relationships that she had formed with boring-sounding freshmen through trust exercises, games, and activities that had been devised, over the years, for just this purpose. She didn't seem disturbed, as I would have been, by the idea that it was an experience designed *for* you, to make you feel a certain way.

An increasingly important role was played in Svetlana's narration by her co-leader, Scott. Each group had two leaders, a guy and a girl. I understood that it must have been exciting to have a shared mission with a guy, requiring coordination and discussions and responsibility. At the same time, there was something sinister about everyone being really into this camping-themed mom-and-dad dress-up. Did I only feel that way because my parents were divorced?

Scott, who was into bluegrass and Zen, sounded like the kind of bland super-American dude who invariably found Svetlana hilarious. For some reason, guys like that always seemed negatively disposed toward me. When she got to the part about how Scott was a senior and had a girlfriend, Svetlana's tone implied that she was either steering away from, or ironically referring to, the comparison, immediately obvious to both of us, to Ivan. She kept emphasizing how specific her relationship to Scott was to the circumstances, because of how completely they had to trust each other, how they had to know each other's bodies, how they had to help each other to climb different natural and man-made obstacles, and to carry the things their bodies needed to survive out there, enveloped day and night in the fathomless beauty of nature.

"How am I ever going to give you up from my life?" Scott had asked Svetlana, on their last night together. Svetlana had told him that maybe it was for the best that their closeness was coming to an end there, since she was never so alive and intense as she was in the woods. "I told him, 'I can be pretty *lackluster* in the winter,'" she said, leaning characteristically into the unusual word choice, "'and I wouldn't want to disappoint you.'"

"You don't have to talk like that, about disappointing me," Scott had replied. "It's not like we're going out."

Why did I feel crushed? Svetlana was only quoting something Scott had said to her. It had nothing to do with me, and Svetlana herself didn't seem upset.

Svetlana and I were sitting in her room reading the course catalog. It was a magical book. All human knowledge was in it, hidden in the form of its classification. It was like *From the Mixed-Up Files of Mrs. Basil E. Frankweiler*, where the answer to whether the statue was really by Michelangelo—the answer that would determine the meaningfulness of everything else that had happened—was right there in the

9

filing cabinets, and the children had only to find it, but first they had to guess what it was filed under.

I thought there was something wrong with the way the departments and majors were organized. Why were the different branches of literature categorized by geography and language, while sciences were categorized by the level of abstraction, or by the size of the object of study? Why wasn't literature classified by word count? Why wasn't science classified by country? Why did religion have its own department, instead of going into philosophy or anthropology? What made something a religion and not a philosophy? Why was the history of non-industrial people in anthropology, and not in history? Why were the most important subjects addressed only indirectly? Why was there no department of love?

I knew, even before I asked her, that Svetlana would defend the system of departments—but how? They were so clearly arbitrary categories that some guy had thought of.

"Well, of course they're arbitrary," Svetlana said, "but it's because they're historical categories, not formal categories." She said the course catalog was a relic of how human knowledge had been split into disciplines since Ancient Greece. You couldn't actually separate the knowledge from the history of how it had been conceived and organized, so that was the most meaningful way to study it: divided into historically determined categories. I was impressed by how smart Svetlana was, but I didn't agree. I thought we should be rewriting the categories and trying to think of a better organization than whichever one we happened to have inherited.

In general, I mistrusted Svetlana's attitude toward historical influences, and other influences. She was constantly thinking about the influence of her parents. Nor was she unique in this respect. Half the people at Harvard, within five minutes of meeting you, they were telling you about the influence of their parents.

People said it was universal to be obsessed with your parents, but I didn't feel that way. When we read *Hamlet* in high school I almost died of impatience. All I thought about at that time was getting out— and Hamlet had done it, he was in college, and then he came *back* to get entangled in a gross drama related to his mother's sex life? Because his father told him to, in a pages-long outpouring of moralizing self-pity, where he didn't say anything to or about Hamlet, and just droned on about how lust was preying on garbage? And then Hamlet went around making cutting remarks to people about his mom? I had no patience for such a person.

Last spring, months before we had to declare our majors, Svetlana had started soliciting advice from her parents and other old people. Her father had perversely withheld guidance, saying, "I can't possibly know you any better than you know yourself." That was classic Svetlana's dad. He clearly thought he knew what she should do, but was teaching her a lesson. Her mother told her, "Ask Gould," meaning that she should ask Stephen Jay Gould, because she had gone to his office hours once and they had had a two-hour conversation about the descent of man. "How I envy you in this sea of choices," Svetlana's mother said. "I wish I was you. I'm so happy for you that sometimes I weep."

Svetlana was pretending she hadn't chosen all her classes yet, but it was clear that she had. We were both taking accelerated Russian, which you had to do if you wanted to have any hope of reading an actual book in Russian before your four-year college education ran out. It counted as two classes. Once you added in a Core class, and a tutorial in your major, that was four classes, a full courseload.

I was taking an extra class, though, so I could actually pick one that wasn't some kind of requirement. I didn't get why more people didn't take a fifth class. It didn't cost extra. All you had to do was fill out a "petition" and meet with a dean. Granted, such meetings were never pleasant. Behind a dean's strained expression, you could glimpse some hidden mechanism ceaselessly translating everything you said into an expression of unreasonableness or immaturity. But, for some reason, the laws of their universe didn't allow them to openly oppose you. All they would do was smile fixedly and try to tell you not to take so many classes and, if you smiled fixedly back for long enough, they would eventually sign the petition.

I opened the catalog to a random page.

COMP LIT 140: CHANCE

"An incalculable amount of human effort is directed to combating and restricting the nuisance or danger represented by chance," Carl Jung writes in his foreword to the *I Ching*. We will consider attempts by modern artists and thinkers to redirect this effort, to use chance as an artistic praxis, a conduit to the subconscious, an egress from the constraints of memory and imagination. . . .

My heart jumped when I learned that there was a literature class about chance, especially when I got to "topics include the flâneur and the random walk as the paradigmatic site of urban experience." Chance, probability, was what Ivan had gone to California to study, and his thesis had been about random walks! And flâneurs were something that literature people talked about. I had never understood why; they would just say that someone was a flâneur, or a voyeur, and seem satisfied. I knew that flâneurs walked around, and voyeurs looked at things. This in itself did not seem interesting; nor was I sure why a random walk was a worthy object of study. Was it possible that these things were related?

At the bottom of the description, it said that topics discussed would include "André Breton's Surrealist strategies in *Nadja*," and this, too, felt like a sign, because the book *Nadja* had so often caught my eye in Svetlana's room: lightweight, with a striking minimalist cover, and numbered black-and-white photographs interspersed in the text. Once, while I was waiting for Svetlana to get out of the shower, I had read the first lines. "Who am I? If this once I were to rely on a proverb, then perhaps everything would amount to knowing whom I 'haunt.'" The rest of the paragraph went on for pages. It seemed less interesting than wondering whom I haunted.

"Is this good?" I asked, holding up the book, when the door opened and Svetlana came in, totally pink, with her hair up in a towel.

She looked thoughtful. "I don't know if you would like it. You can borrow it if you want."

I turned to the last page. It said: "Beauty will be CONVULSIVE or will not be at all."

"Maybe another time," I said, replacing the book on the shelf.

Months later, Ivan had written me a long email about Fellini and clowns, and the last line had been: Beauty, Breton says, will be convulsive or will not be at all. I had resolved to look again at *Nadja*, the next time I was in Svetlana's room, to see if there were any context clues that might help with the clowns. But the school year had somehow ended without my ever again waiting for her in her room with time to spare, looking at her books.

Now we already lived in different buildings, and soon we would live even farther away from each other, and she would be married, and I would never wait for her in her bedroom again. How brief and magical it was that we all lived so close to each other and went in and out of each other's rooms, and our most important job was to solve mysteries. The temporariness made it all the more important to do the right thing—to follow the right leads.

It was exciting to turn the corner in the bookstore from Computer Science to Comparative Literature—to see the fat textbooks give way to normal-sized books with interesting covers that looked like a person might actually read them in the course of normal life. The books for the Chance class, however, had an off-putting coolness. Would I enjoy them? The books I enjoyed were usually long, containing descriptions of furniture and of somebody falling in love, and often had ugly nineteenth-century paintings on the cover. The Chance books were the kind of slim attractive books with wide margins, that I never actually felt like reading: books that were experimental or hybrid or post-modern or lyrical. Why were poems so expensive, when they had so few words? That *Flowers of Evil* cost thirty dollars! I opened to a random page: "Don Juan in Hell." "Women, their open dresses exposing pendant breasts, writhed under a dark sky and, like a herd of sacrificial victims, let trail behind a long drawn-out moan." What? Why were the *women* in hell? Thirty dollars?

Then I noticed a fat Penguin Classics volume with a poorly reproduced nineteenth-century painting on the cover, and the white-on-black medallion read:

SØREN KIERKEGAARD

EITHER/OR
A Fragment of Life

I picked up a secondhand copy—$7.99—and read the text on the back: "Either, then, one is to live aesthetically or one is to live ethically."

My heart was pounding. There was a book about this?

I had first heard the phrase "aesthetic life" last year, in a class called Constructed Worlds. We were reading a French novel called *Against Nature*—about the degenerate scion of a noble family who retired to the country and devoted himself to "decadent" projects, like growing orchids that resembled meat, or more generally trying to get organic and inorganic objects to resemble each other. By the end of the book, I didn't think much of what that guy had accomplished. Still, I found the *idea* of an aesthetic life to be tremendously compelling. It was the first time I had heard of an organizing principle or goal you could have for your life, other than making money and having kids. Nobody ever said that that was their organizing principle, but I had often noticed it, when I was growing up: the way adults acted as though trying to go anywhere or achieve anything was a frivolous dream, a luxury, compared to the real work of having kids and making money to pay for the kids.

Nobody ever explained what was admirable about having the kids, or why it was the default course of action for every single human being. If you ever asked why any particular person had had a kid, or what good a particular kid was, people treated it as a blasphemy—as if you were saying they should be dead, or the kid should be dead. It was as if there was no way to ask what the plan had been, without implying that someone should be dead.

One day, early in our friendship, Svetlana had spontaneously told me that she thought I was trying to live an aesthetic life, and that it was a major difference between us, because she was trying to live an ethical life. I wasn't sure why the two should be opposed, and worried for a moment that she thought that I thought that it was OK to cheat or steal. But she turned out to mean something else: that I took more risks than her and cared more than she did about "style," while she cared more about history and traditions.

Soon, the "ethical and the aesthetic" was the framework we used to talk about the ways we were different. When it came to choosing friends, Svetlana liked to surround herself with dependable boring people who corroborated her in her way of being, while I was more interested in undependable people who generated different experiences or impressions. Svetlana liked taking introductions and survey classes, "mastering" basics before moving to the next level, getting straight A's. I had a terror of being bored, so I preferred to take highly specific classes with interesting titles, even when I hadn't taken the prerequisites and had no idea what was going on. I could see how my way might be called aesthetic. It was less clear to me why Svetlana's way was ethical, though it did seem "responsible" and obedient.

It felt related, somehow, that Svetlana was so close to her father, and that it was from her father that she had first gotten into reading and debating philosophical and ethical questions. I could relate to this. When I was little, my father and I spent whole weekends driving around the countryside in New Jersey, just the two of us, stopping sometimes to pick apples at farms, or to watch birds in the nature preserve—but mostly driving, listening to classical music, and talking about ethics, morality, and the meaning of life. I had loved those conversations. Yet, now, the word "ethics" made me impatient.

When I tried to pinpoint when things had changed, I found myself remembering one evening when I was ten. I was doing homework in my room when my father knocked on the door and proposed going out on one of our long drives, even though it was a weeknight. In the car, my father asked if I agreed with him that there was nothing worse, ethically, than betrayal, and that women were particularly prone to betraying people. Clytemnestra, for example, had betrayed Agamemnon when he had one foot out of the bath, fulfilling the prophecy that Agamemnon would die neither on land nor at sea.

I didn't know, until Svetlana told me, that Agamemnon had murdered his daughter as a sacrifice to the Trojan War. That's what Clytemnestra was even mad about. None of this was anything I wanted to think about, or model my life on.

According to the back cover, the first half of *Either/Or* was about the aesthetic life, and included a novella called "The Seducer's Diary," while the second half was about the ethical life, and consisted of some letters from a judge about marriage.

So, the ethical life *was* related to getting married. It was somehow implicit in my friendship with Svetlana that she wanted to be in "a stable relationship" and to someday have children, while I wanted to have interesting love experiences that I could write about. Svetlana didn't seem to have enjoyed family life more than I had, but in her case it had made her want to have a do-over, to do well herself all the things that her parents had done badly. I, on the other hand, thought that my parents had been doomed; I didn't see how I could do any better than they had.

Unsurprisingly, the back of *Either/Or* didn't say which kind of life was better. All it said was: "Does Kierkegaard mean us to prefer one of the alternatives? Or are we thrown back on the existentialist idea of radical choice?" That had probably been written by a professor. I recognized the professors' characteristic delight at not imparting information. Still, I bought a copy—along with a secondhand *Nadja*. It seemed possible that one or both of these books might change my life.

Sometimes it still felt weird that Svetlana and I weren't rooming together. We had talked about it in the spring. "Ours is definitely my most stimulating friendship," she had said, "but I might feel threatened to live with someone who doesn't have a weaker personality than I do." Svetlana was the only person I knew who spoke so candidly. I would have been embarrassed to think, let alone say, that I felt threatened by other people's strength of personality. I wouldn't even have admitted that I didn't think that all people were somehow equal in this respect. Once Svetlana said it, though, it seemed obvious and noncontroversial. Svetlana herself had the strongest personality of anyone I had ever met—way stronger than mine. She would never have spent the summer in such a peripheral European nation, with so little connection either to her own past or to the great edifices of Western history and culture. Why, then, had she said that my personality was stronger? I decided that she was trying to be polite—to make me feel less badly that she didn't want to live with me.

On the other hand, when I thought about her freshman-year roommates, who were in her new housing block, their dynamic with Svetlana did seem to depend on a shared consensus about Svetlana's stronger personality. They were Svetlana's encouraging spectators, in sort of a feudal exchange for protection, tutelage, and entertainment. Where would I fit in? I couldn't imagine recruiting Dolores and Valerie to root for me, any more than I could imagine joining them to root for Svetlana. I couldn't imagine referring to each other's stuffed animals by name, or taking turns bringing Guthrie, the platypus, to exams. Why did Svetlana want to do those things more than she wanted to spend time with me?

When Riley asked me to room with her, I immediately agreed, even though I didn't know her that well. Riley was the most intransigent person I knew, and the funniest. Her closest friends—Oak, Ezra, and Lucas—were guys, and were "serious about comedy." Telling jokes—like getting in arguments, or playing ping-pong—was one of the many seemingly casual and non-professional human activities that turned out, in college, to be a rigorous, technical discipline that some people studied day and night, and pursued to a competitive career path.

When I sat with them in the cafeteria—Riley, upright and self-contained like a cat, the three others with their long limbs extending variously over and under the table, and all of them shooting a joke back and forth, escalating for more steps than I thought possible, prosecuting its ramifications like fine points of the law—it seemed to me imperative to keep such people close to me, both to be cushioned against the vicissitudes of life, and to learn how they did it.

It was hard to imagine Svetlana even having a conversation with Riley, let alone living with her. It was even harder to imagine Ivan talking to Riley, although this had actually happened once, in the spring, when Ivan had mysteriously turned up at the freshman cafeteria. It was one of many things he seemed to have done only to confound me.

"How are you even here?" I asked.

"I was in the Science Center and didn't have time to get to my house. So I thought I'd see if *you* were here."

"But I'm meeting my friend."

"So can I eat with you and your friend?"

I led him to our table with mounting despair. "This is my friend Riley," I said. "This is Ivan."

"Hey," Riley said.

"Hey," Ivan said.

I sat across from Riley and Ivan sat next to me. Riley glanced at Ivan, who was vigorously cutting up a Salisbury steak: something Riley would never have eaten. Then Oak, Ezra, and Lucas turned up, managing to seem like at least five people. They kept sitting down and jumping up and going to get things and changing seats. Everyone was joking about this other guy, Morris. Riley told a story about how she had once picked up a comb belonging to Morris, and it had broken in two, so she had bought him a new comb. She had felt that she was acting in a responsible and generous way, since she hadn't done anything to the first comb, it had just broken. But Morris hadn't accepted the new comb and said, angrily: "I had that comb for fifteen years!" Everything in this story, including the spontaneous rupture of the comb, was highly characteristic of Morris.

"Fifteen years ago you were three. You barely had hair," Riley said, addressing imaginary Morris.

"Maybe the comb is like the watch in *Pulp Fiction*," suggested Ivan.

Oak, the child of hippies, stared at Ivan with his round blue insane-looking eyes, and said: "My father had this comb up his ass for fifteen years!"

This new development, about Morris's father having the comb up his ass for fifteen years, was absorbed without further comment into the consensus. I admired Ivan for being able to contribute a joke close enough to the spirit of Riley and her friends to be assimilated in this way.

Svetlana's housing block ended up having six Orthodox Jewish guys in it, because Svetlana had been in a Moral Reasoning section with the alpha Orthodox guy, Dave. The two had merged their blocks together, like a dynastic wedding. Dave was our age, but had a rich, chestnut-colored beard, and a voice like a radio announcer's. He and Svetlana had been the two most outspoken people in their class, and had often continued their debates for hours, with what Svetlana called "an almost sexual intensity." Svetlana said that she thought of herself as formed by classical thought as rediscovered by Christian people in the Renaissance, while Dave had a Talmudic system of interrogation and commentary, but they were able to meet on a certain plane, because their systems had a common origin in the Hebrew Bible.

The Moral Reasoning class had been called "If There Is No God, Then All Is Permitted." I didn't understand how people living in 1996 could have a huge debate about something like that. Someone whose only reason for *not* acting in an antisocial way was that they were scared of getting in trouble with God . . . where did you even start with such a person?

Riley's system of patronage was less oppressive than Svetlana's, but also somehow less benevolent. Maybe you couldn't really be benevolent unless you were up in everyone's business. Svetlana said her block was more nurturing, and my block was cooler; whereas proximity to such coolness would have prevented her, Svetlana, from being her authentic self, I didn't need as much nurturing. Was that true? Definitely, the word "nurturing" made my chest tighten.

My block had been assigned to Mather, which was where the guys now lived: Oak, Ezra, Lucas, Morris, and some friendly geologists who were somehow attached to Oak. But Riley hated Mather so much that she got the rest of us—me, Riley, Riley's premed classmate Priya, and Priya's roommate Joanne—transferred to overflow housing. We still used the Mather facilities, but our rooms were in this other building: a red brick medium-rise full of two-bedroom units, with dishwashers, microwaves, garbage disposals, wall-to-wall carpet, and central heating. It was like an ordinary apartment building, except each bedroom had a metal bunk bed and two dorm-issue desks. I thought there was something spooky about the presence of a dormitory inside a building that seemed like normal people might live in it.

Even in shopping week, accelerated Russian already met for the full two hours. Everyone complained, but I was secretly pleased. I didn't like when people acted as if nothing we did was time-sensitive. "You have *a lot* of time, you don't need to be in a hurry." That's what the deans said, when you tried to take five classes. Easy for them: they were already deans. Either that was something they wanted to be doing, in which case they could afford to relax; or it *wasn't* what they had wanted to be doing, and now they were invested in preventing anyone else from accomplishing anything, either.

That had been the worst part of childhood: people telling you how lucky you were to live in a carefree time with no responsibilities. This was a point on which my mother and I had differed. She said that one of the most wonderful things about America was how children were allowed to be children, whereas in other countries, children had to become adults before they were ready; they were sexualized, or put to work. In America, childhood was a time to play and be innocent, to not have to make money or do anything that counted for anything. When I was little, whenever I heard of children who were distinguishing themselves in any field of art or science or sports, I was filled with longing and a deep sense of failure. But my mother viewed such prodigies with pity and sorrow: they hadn't been allowed to be children.

After Russian, I had a meeting with Bob, my financial aid officer. As I was walking through the square, I felt a grown man trying to get my attention. Doom washed over me. He could only be asking for money. If I gave him anything, I was frivolously disposing of my mother's hard-won earnings—just to feel better about myself, in the eyes of some man. If I didn't give him anything, then I was a hypocrite, because I regularly used my mom's money to buy stuff that I didn't really need, like seven-dollar pore-refining skin cleanser from CVS.

I tried to pretend I didn't see him, but I could feel him trying harder, with a righteous energy that came from knowing that I had more money than him and that it wasn't fair. I gave up, and did what he was trying to force me to do: look at him. Then I saw that he was selling *Real Change*, the street paper, and felt relieved, because *Real Change* was technically a newspaper—a legitimate expenditure—and was both cheaper and more interesting than other newspapers. I knew that my mother would have found it interesting, too.

"I love *Real Change*," I told the guy, giving him a dollar. He handed me the paper with a flourish. As I walked, I scanned the front page. The "CONSPIRACY CORNER" by John Doe—"my real name will be concealed for security reasons"—delighted me with its jaunty tone and abrupt ending: "Anyway, I'm off to go hide. Talk to you never!" And why didn't more newspapers have a poetry section?

The poems in *Real Change* were no worse, in any way that I could see, than the ones in the student literary magazine. Were the street people really good at poetry, or were we really bad? In "We Masses Don't Want Tofu," "tofu" had been rhymed with "opposed to." Another poem began: "We live in a world where toddlers stake virgins. / Cuddling and cuteness are their diversions." Farther down, it turned out that the toddlers actually held some kind of elected office. I could cut that one out to make a collage for Riley. We had started making collages for each other and taping them to the bathroom mirror.

In the waiting room at the financial aid office, I contemplated a poem called "Hate."

> None of this to me seems real.
> I have no soul left to steal.
> My heart is now made of stone.
> Please don't leave me all alone.

Was that poem good? It sounded like a Nine Inch Nails song. Was Nine Inch Nails good? I felt annoyed when people showed you a photograph of a urinal and tried to make you debate whether it was art. Nonetheless, I wanted to know whether a poem was good. "Please don't leave me all alone." Was that what I, too, was afraid of? And maybe not just me, but everyone? I glanced around the waiting room, taking in various paintings of sailboats. The boy two chairs over from me was leaning down in his chair with his legs stretched out; his backpack had fallen over on the floor in front of him and looked like it had been shot. Something about the scene made me wonder whether that poem, and all the other poems, and the rest of the newspaper, and maybe other newspapers, were an expression of suffering that it was obscene to print and publish and distribute and read.

Well, that's just it, I thought: you didn't just *write down* a raw cry of suffering. It would be boring and self-indulgent. You had to disguise it, turn it into art. That's what literature was. That was what required talent, and made people want to read what you wrote, and then they would give you money.

My financial aid officer, Bob, said that discrepancies involving my mother's reported assets were interfering with my federal loan eligibility. He showed me a credit report that said that my mother had taken out a mortgage on a home in Louisiana. The credit report seemed to be written in a way that was deliberately confusing, but eventually I understood what had happened: the reporting agency had confused my mother and my stepmother, who shared the same first name, and also the same last name. (My mother still used her married name, because it was on all her scientific papers.) My stepmother's middle name even started with the same letter as my mother's maiden name.

"It's kind of a funny coincidence," I said, "because their name isn't actually that common. I mean it's not a super-common Turkish name."

Bob looked like he was in pain. "So you're saying that Nurhan M. Karadağ and Nurhan M. Karadağ are two different people." I felt sorry for him. Every time I saw this guy, I ruined his day.

I was already ineligible for any financial aid other than loans, because my parents' combined income was more than a hundred thousand dollars. It didn't matter that they were in debt, having given all their money to lawyers during the custody suit when I was fourteen. My mother had eventually won the suit, on the condition that she move back to New Jersey. She sold her apartment at a loss, quit the job she loved in Philadelphia, and found a lower-paying position in Brooklyn, where she had to commute every day. We rented half a house in Essex County from two elderly Italian sisters who lived in the other half. It ended up being fun. Whenever the electricity or the gas was cut off, it felt like an adventure. My mother was sure I was going to become a great writer. Then I got into Harvard, like we had always wanted. My mom said that my getting in proved that *she* could have gotten in.

Still, when Harvard said I wasn't eligible for financial aid, and another university offered me a full scholarship, I thought I should go there. My mother became furious and said I was always sabotaging myself. She was proud of being able to borrow money at a loss from her own retirement fund, and give it to Harvard. I felt proud of her, too. But I did not feel proud of myself. It made the college application process feel, in retrospect, somehow hurtful and insulting: all the essays and interviews and supplements and letters *seemed* to be about you, about your specialness—but actually it was all about shaking your parents down for money.

Harvard seemed really proud of its own attitude toward financial aid. You were always hearing about how "merit-based aid," which was fine for other schools, didn't work here, where everyone was so full of merit. When your parents paid full tuition, part of what they were paying for was the benefit you derived from being exposed to people who were more diverse than you.

"My parents are paying for him to be here, so I can learn from him," my friend Leora said once, about a homeschooled guy from Arkansas in her history section who started talking about how the Jews killed Jesus. Leora had been my best friend when we were little, and then we went to different middle schools and high schools, but now we were at college together. She already thought every single person on earth was anti-Semitic, so she definitely hadn't learned anything from that guy.

To me, the part of financial aid that made the least sense was that *all* the international students got full scholarships, regardless of how much money their parents had. The son of the prince of Nepal was in our class, and didn't pay tuition. Ivan had once caused me pain by saying something deprecating about "people whose parents paid a hundred thousand dollars for them to be here." Did he not know that my parents were paying a hundred thousand dollars for me to be there? The thought that really made me crazy was that my parents had paid for *Ivan* to be there. It was another experience they had paid for me to have.

I went to the student center to check email. Ivan still hadn't written. Today, I didn't feel that badly about it. He had been the last one to write, so wasn't it technically my turn to write to him? When I checked voice mail, I found a message from my mom, so I called her back at her lab. She answered on the second ring. I told her about the mix-up with Bob and Nurhan the Second. I thought she would think it was funny, but instead she sounded annoyed.

"I will speak to Bob," she said.

"I don't think you have to," I said.

"If they bother you again, let me know and I'll call them. They shouldn't be bothering you about this."

My mother said she had gone to the doctor and wanted to ask me for my opinion. She said she had a minor issue, like a cyst. Either she could get surgery and have it removed and it would be gone, or she could do a non-surgical treatment and go back for check-ups every six months.

I wasn't sure what my opinion could be based on, or what value it could have, since I wasn't a doctor, and she was. My mother said, a bit coldly, that she realized that I wasn't a physician, but that she had told me all the relevant information; she wasn't asking a medical question, but a question about personal preference. I understood I had said the wrong thing. I asked about how dangerous the surgery was, and what happened if you forgot to get one of the check-ups. She said the surgery needed general anesthesia, but it was a commonly performed procedure and wasn't considered high-risk. But you couldn't forget the check-ups; that *was* high-risk.

I thought my mom already had too much stuff to remember, so I said I thought she should get the surgery and not bother with check-ups.

"That's my feeling, too," my mother said in a warm voice.

After we hung up, I realized that I now felt anxious about Ivan not having written. It was weird: nothing external had changed, but I felt differently. I ended up back at the computers, using the "finger" command, even though it always made me feel worse.

Login name: ivanv In real life: Ivan Varga

On since Tue Sep 3 10:24 (PDT) on pts/7

28 seconds Idle Time

Mail last read Tue Sep 3 09:41 (PDT)

Plan: "Thou, nature, art my goddess; to thy law/ My services are bound." (KL I.ii.1-2)

27

He was online, right now, looking into a screen just like I was. He had been sitting there thinking about something for twenty-eight seconds. And he had added a "plan."

I had learned from Riley what a plan was. It was a file where you could enter any text you wanted, and it would show up whenever someone fingered you. If you hadn't entered anything, it said No plan. Professors usually had No plan, because they didn't know how to change it, or didn't care. Grad students sometimes put their office hours. Freshmen sometimes put World domination or Taking over the universe. Otherwise, the most common thing to put was some kind of a quote or maxim. Riley's said: The quickest way to a man's heart is through his chest, with an axe.

I didn't recognize Ivan's quote, but assumed from the annoying-looking citation that it was from Shakespeare. Someone at MIT had put all Shakespeare's plays online, and I found it in a soliloquy in *King Lear*. The last line was: "Now, gods, stand up for bastards!"

Although I planned to read *King Lear* someday, I didn't feel like reading it right now, and anyway I didn't have time. I decided to stop by the liquor store where they sold CliffsNotes.

In the liquor store, I learned that the soliloquy "Thou, Nature, art my goddess" was spoken by Edmund, the illegitimate son of the Earl of Gloucester. Edmund, a Machiavellian character, rejected conventional morality, authority, and legitimacy, in favor of "the law of nature." This involved a play on the term "natural child," which also meant "bastard." We didn't despise Edmund for plotting to usurp rightful power, because Shakespeare made Edmund speak directly to us, drawing us into his dangerous but exciting adventures, including his promiscuous sexual conquest of Goneril and Regan.

Nothing I learned about Edmund made me feel better.

Svetlana and I went to a lecture about *Mrs. Dalloway* and time. Apparently, *Mrs. Dalloway* illustrated a theory by Henri Bergson about two different kinds of time: the kind that could be measured by clocks, and another kind.

At some point, a professor stood up and said in a tone of irritation that Virginia Woolf had never read Henri Bergson. The atmosphere in the room turned against the speaker, who said, lamely, that Woolf had once attended a public lecture by Bergson. Then a genial Italian-sounding man stood up and proposed that Bergson's ideas had been "in the air." This utterance mended some tear in the social fabric to the extent that the talk could continue—but it was somehow clear, even to me, that what we were hearing was fanciful, ahistorical, and not "rigorous."

I felt outraged. So one writer hadn't read another writer: how was that proof that what they were saying wasn't related? Wasn't a theory of time *more* likely to be true if two people had come up with it independently? What kind of cretins cared more about hammering out a string of inheritance than about discovering universal truths? Historians, that was what kind. They would only be happy when they had translated every miraculous book into a product of its historical moment.

Svetlana thought it made a miraculous book *more* miraculous to learn the writer's historical influences: that way you could identify the miracle more precisely. To me, it seemed frivolous to waste time celebrating the circumstances under which someone had discovered some phenomenon. Wasn't it more important to try to apply the phenomenon to more different historical circumstances?

In the end, Svetlana chose the major called History and Literature. But I didn't care about history so I chose the major that was just called Literature.

THE SECOND WEEK

All the literature majors had to take a "tutorial," where you read books and talked about them. My tutor, Judith, had a young face and white hair, and spoke in a knowing voice, occasionally bursting into high-pitched laughter. The subjects that most excited her—how *Star Wars* had the same narrative arc as *The Iliad*; how, if you looked up "fix" in the *Oxford English Dictionary*, the different definitions "subverted" each other—while not exactly uninteresting, were things I had nothing to say about. Once or twice, I made up some kind of opinion and said it anyway. It felt both boring and depressing.

Most of the other people in my tutorial also said boring and depressing things. There were only two people, Allie and Jason, who ever said anything interesting. Allie had a New York accent and wore cat-eye eyeliner. Jason always looked mussed and half-asleep. I listened carefully to everything they said, to try to figure out what made it interesting.

After tutorial, I went to the undergraduate library to try to read *Either/ Or*. I stopped in front of the bookshelves in the foyer, where they displayed bound copies of all the senior honors theses that had won prizes last year. Mechanically I scanned the gold-lettered spines for Ivan's name. When I found it, it felt like a dream. The name I thought about all the time, but never said—embossed on a library binding—as if there was already a book about it.

I took the thesis down from the shelf. It was really thin, like all the math theses. To my surprise, it started with a story. "A girl and her parents are visiting the Museum of Very Modern Art. In the Cubism exhibit, the little girl wanders away and starts taking a random walk in three dimensions. How many rooms will she pass through before she finds her parents again?"

The rest of the thesis was symbols and equations. I replaced it on the shelf, wondering why I had such an uneasy feeling. Was it just the effect of seeing something Ivan had written that had nothing to do with me, and that I hadn't known about? The idea of a person finding their parents again, by random chance, felt like a Greek tragedy. And why was it a little girl? What was it with girls—why was he so interested? I realized that I envied her—because of her curiosity and fearlessness, and because Ivan had written a whole book about her. I wondered if anything I wrote would ever become a library book, with my name in gold letters.

I usually skipped introductions, but I read the one in *Either/Or*, just to figure out what kind of book it was. Though classified as philosophy, it had different narrators, like a novel, and had originally been published as two volumes: the collected papers of A, who lived aesthetically, and B, who lived ethically. The papers, which had supposedly been found in an old desk, included essays, aphorisms, sermons, letters, music criticism, a play, and the novella "The Seducer's Diary," attributed to A's friend, Johannes.

According to the introduction, lots of people skipped the "ethical" half, and even most of the "aesthetic" half, and just read "The Seducer's Diary." Kierkegaard himself had said of *Either/Or* that you had to *either* read the whole book, *or* just not read it at all. Kierkegaard was funny! Nonetheless, I too flipped forward to "The Seducer's Diary."

It started with a description of Johannes, the seducer—about how he was able, using his "mental gifts," to make a girl fall in love with him, "without caring to possess her in any stricter sense":

> I can imagine him able to bring a girl to the point where he was sure she would sacrifice all, but when matters had come that far he left off without the slightest advance having been made on his part, and without a word having been let fall of love, let alone a declaration, a promise. Yet it would have happened, and the unhappy girl would retain the consciousness of it with double bitterness . . . she would constantly have to contend with the doubt that the whole thing might only have been imagination.

When I read that, I almost threw up. Wasn't that what had happened to me? Hadn't I been brought to the point where I would sacrifice everything—only for him to leave off without the slightest advance having been made? Wasn't I always asking myself—hadn't other people, including a psychologist at the student center, repeatedly asked *me*—whether the whole thing was in my imagination? "As soon as she wanted to speak of it to another," Kierkegaard wrote, "it was nothing." The extent to which he left a girl with nothing was the very mark of his artistry. It meant having the self-control to not get her pregnant or abandon her at the altar. It meant no spectators, no proof.

The more I read, the more parallels I found to my own experience. The emails Ivan and I had exchanged, which had felt like something new we had invented, now seemed to have been following some kind of playbook. The seducer explained the importance of alternating between anguished or ambiguous love letters and ironic in-person meetings. In person, you could never explicitly mention the letters, or say, "Did you get my letter," but you had to always be alluding to them, reinforcing or undercutting their message.

The reason he had such good techniques, the seducer explained, was because he had learned them from the best teachers: young girls themselves. The idea that Ivan could have written letters with other girls—that he could have done that whole thing before, multiple times, on purpose—was new, painful, and baffling.

At five I had to go back to the literature department to watch *The Usual Suspects*. It was for tutorial, for a unit on genre theory. Kevin Spacey, that bland-looking man who always played sociopaths, apparently used genre theory to trick the detective into thinking he was a small-time crook who had been duped by a Turkish master criminal. The Turkish master criminal—whose name, Keyser Söze, was not an actual Turkish name—had murdered his own family, and also the families of some Hungarians.

"Selin, was that what your summer was like?" asked Jason.

"Yeah, it's an exact transcript," I said. "I guess they had a secret camera."

At the end of the movie, Kevin Spacey limped out of the detective's office, seemingly broken by the discovery of how he had been manipulated by Keyser Söze. Then, the detective noticed that the bulletin board in his office was manufactured by a company called Quartet, in Skokie, Illinois. Kevin Spacey's story had involved a barbershop quartet in Skokie, Illinois. Looking around the room, the detective recognized more words and details from Kevin Spacey's story. In this way, he understood that the story had been false, and that Kevin Spacey himself was Keyser Söze.

The sense of discovering a total deception, in the absence of the person who had created it; the fact that the deception itself was specially tailored for one other person, using words that seemed meaningful but had actually occurred randomly in the environment; the confusing fact that the random words in the environment thus *did* have a special meaning, though they got it somehow retrospectively: all rose in my chest and prevented me from breathing.

Someone turned on the lights. The VCR machine started shrieking as it reverse-digested the tape. Jason and Allie were talking about whether something had been exploitative. It sounded interesting, but I couldn't concentrate. After a while I stood up and left without saying anything, as if I was just going to the bathroom. I went downstairs and sat in an empty classroom, remembering one thing after another that Ivan had written or said, things that hadn't seemed important at the time. Once, he had told me that strawberries grew on trees. I had contradicted him, citing my memory of an actual strawberry plant I had seen once—and yet, when he had held his ground, I had backed down: it hadn't seemed important, and my memory itself hadn't seemed to prove anything. "You're easy to convince," he had said.

"I was wondering when you were going to stop me," he had said, another time. "I was wondering how long you would let me keep going."

I felt the same horror I had felt when I was reading Kierkegaard—the same sense that Ivan's actions had been following a playbook that I hadn't known existed. However I felt right now, had Ivan planned for me to feel that way? The thought was terrifying but somehow sexually magnetic.

In the Quincy dining hall, the meal service was over, but almost half the tables were still occupied. Svetlana had seen me and was waving. She was methodically making her way through a plate of cottage cheese and raw vegetables. This was a new development. She said it wasn't a diet, because the idea wasn't to diminish herself, but, rather, to reveal her real, stronger body. I was still the kind of person who thought it was interesting to see what happened if you only ate cashews for a week.

Svetlana and her roommates were talking about a junior on their floor who had been named one of *Glamour* magazine's top ten promising college women and who, in addition to having perfect classical features, a sexy mole, and lustrous hair, was the co-author of three peer-reviewed papers on genetics, ran a science program for under-privileged teens, vice-chaired a committee on intercultural and race relations, and held "a black belt in tai chi." It was objected that it wasn't possible to have a black belt in tai chi.

"If anyone could have one, it would be Ayesha," Svetlana said.

I had been hoping to talk to Svetlana about Kierkegaard and *The Usual Suspects*, but she and her roommates were going to their friend Patience's birthday party. Everyone had chipped in for a cake that Svetlana wasn't going to eat.

"Why don't you come?" Svetlana said, and Valerie added, "You should come! You can eat Svetlana's cake!" Svetlana's roommates really were nice. But there was no way I was going to that birthday party.

Late at night, I wrote Ivan an email listing everything he had done that I didn't understand. I put in all the contradictions and the things that seemed like lies—so he could "defend himself," like he had said. It came out really long.

By the time I got to breakfast the next morning, Svetlana was already almost done with her yogurt. I barely had time to gulp down half a bowl of Cracklin' Oat Bran—the most filling cereal, in almost a sinister way—before she made us leave for Russian. We were the first people there. At first it seemed like I might have time to tell her about Kierkegaard, but I had barely gotten started when our classmate Gavriil came in. Gavriil had a wiry build and fluffy hair resembling that of Mozart in the movie *Amadeus*, and was always climbing things. You might look at a library or a church and see something on the wall, and it would be that guy, Gavriil.

"Check it out," Gavriil said, proudly unzipping his backpack. It was full of broccoli and cabbage.

"Looks like you have some healthful vegetables there," Svetlana said.

"Let's just say they fell off the back of a truck," he said, zipping the bag and depositing it on the floor. "So how's it going?"

"Selin could be better," Svetlana said.

"Oh? Who do I have to beat up?"

Svetlana rolled her eyes. "He's much bigger than you, *and* he's in California."

"Wait, it's really a guy? Do I know him?"

"He was in our Russian class part of last year," Svetlana said. "Remember that really tall guy, Ivan?"

"Oh, yeah, the guy nobody ever talked to! He's Hungarian. I talked to him once. He was really nice."

"Well, Selin talked to him too, and then he terrorized her with ambiguous emails about sex, even though he already had a girlfriend, and led her on a wild-goose chase to a Hungarian village, and then he disappeared, and now he won't talk to her."

"Really?" Gavriil looked impressed.

"Not exactly," I said, at the same time as Svetlana said, "Yes."

Gavriil furrowed his brows. "Do you think he went through a process of ideological formation under the Warsaw Pact? Do you think he was specially created to destroy women? Like they send him to the West to meet women who might have become famous engineers or professors, but they don't, because of him?"

"That must be really comforting for Selin," Svetlana said.

"I'm going to become whatever I was going to become," I said.

"Oh definitely, you got out of it in time," Gavriil said, looking satisfied. He tipped his chair back against the wall, leaning his feet on the backpack full of stolen vegetables.

I couldn't talk to Svetlana after class, because I had a lunch meeting with Peter and the other English teachers from the Hungary program. Peter had set the date in July, in the town square in Eger: noon, the second Wednesday of September, outside the Science Center. I got there a few minutes early and went inside to check my email at a terminal.

There was a new message from Ivan.

In response to everything I had written, he had composed a poem. It was a truly awful poem—way worse than the ones in *Real Change*. "Let's eat some dirty strawberries" rhymed with "This psychologist is smart, I'm just a mass of dishonesties." "I don't love you, you hate me." "Come dance with me again." "Writer queen whom I admire, fallen analyst"—I logged out, my heart pounding. He hadn't refuted anything, or reassured me about anything. Was he saying I was *right*?

The English teachers were standing in the sun. Everyone looked a little bit different than I remembered, especially their hair. Peter turned up with a girl I had never seen before, from his Korean program. She was wearing perfect neutral makeup and kept talking about the genius of Johannes Kepler. "That's the genius of Johannes Kepler," she said, more than once. We went to a Spanish restaurant. Peter ordered sangria for the table. Nobody checked ID.

"Whatever happened to Ivan?" asked the girl who loved Kepler. "I never see him anymore."

"He graduated," Peter said. "He went out to California."

"Does he have a new email address?"

"He must," Peter said, and looked at me.

I studiously fished an apple slice out of my sangria. Everyone else was talking about how some guy had brained a feral dog with a rock in Romania. "I will definitely find out and let you know," Peter told the girl.

Afterward, we all walked back toward campus. The world looked particularly crisp and etched-out in the sunlight. I became aware of Peter walking in step with me.

"Hey, Selin," he said. "How's it going."

"Fine," I said. "How are you?"

"Oh, excellent. Classes going OK?"

"Yeah."

"Splendid. Selin, I have a quick question for you. Would you happen to know Ivan's new email address at Berkeley?"

I didn't really want to tell him, but there didn't seem to be any other option. He spelled it back, to make sure he'd gotten it right. "You know, Ivan and I have been out of touch lately," he said. "How's he doing anyway?"

"I don't know," I said.

"Oh, you haven't heard from him since the summer either?"

"Well . . . he didn't say how he was doing."

"But we do know at least he's alive and breathing."

"Right," I said, unable to return his smile. "What's the deal with Ivan?" I blurted, without having meant to.

"What's . . . the deal?"

"Is he . . . an evil person?"

A series of expressions passed over Peter's face. I could see right away that he wasn't going to say anything useful.

"Never mind," I said.

"Some people say he is," Peter said. I felt my heart pounding.

"They do?"

"I suppose you ran into Zita."

"Sorry?"

"Zita is going through a difficult time right now," Peter said, in a careful, quiet tone, like somebody explaining racism to a child. "There's a lot going on. She isn't seeing things clearly. She's saying things she doesn't really mean. Ivan's ex-girlfriends may badmouth him, but they would take him back in a heartbeat."

Everything went black. So I was part of a larger group of ex-girlfriends: girls who had never gotten, would never get, over him. Worse than that: I wasn't even an ex-girlfriend. I didn't have the dignity of having once been a girlfriend.

I gradually became aware of Peter, who seemed to be waiting for me to say something.

"Please forget I said anything. I don't know who Zita is. Nobody said anything bad about Ivan to me."

"This isn't coming from Zita?"

"I literally don't know who that is."

"Then where is it coming from?"

I felt a pang of irritation. "My own life experiences."

There was a pause. "And what experiences were these?" Peter asked, in a gentler voice.

"Well, there were kind of a lot of them."

"Perhaps I can help elucidate."

I glanced at his face—at his concerned, adult expression. I meant to tell him to forget it, but instead I heard myself say: "He didn't tell me about his girlfriend."

"He didn't tell you about Zita?"

"He didn't tell me about his current girlfriend."

"Eunice? He didn't tell you about Eunice?"

"I think it was a misunderstanding."

Peter was quiet for a moment. "Ivan does strange things sometimes, but he's a good person. I really believe that. If there's a misunderstanding, you should talk to him about it. I know he really cares about you. He's told me so. You should let him explain."

I could hear the creaking sound behind my eyes that meant tears were forming.

Feeling unable to walk, I sat on a rock and stared at the advice column of *Real Change*. Three different people, Carol, Rich, and Tammi, answered all the letters, often contradicting each other.

"There is no hard-and-fast rule," Carol told Single in Somerville, who had a one-year-old son, and wanted to know when to start dating again. It was unclear whether she wanted to start dating, or whether she viewed it as some kind of requirement.

Rich thought that Single's one-year-old son deserved a male role model, but only as long as Single was "prepared for a mature relationship."

Tammi's advice was: "Honestly you have to put yourself out there, or you will never move on."

The next letter writer, Riled by Rumors, had an issue with people who wouldn't keep their noses and mouths in their own business. "Half of these are people I have never even done anything to," Riled wrote. "The only reason they don't like me is because of rumors they heard."

"Rumors always occur," Carol observed, with her typical lack of content. "If you want to stop them, there is no proven way."

"Avoid other people and tell them to avoid you," Rich advised. "If that doesn't work, reluctantly resort to physical violence."

According to Tammi, the best way to stop rumors was to keep your mouth shut. "You say that half of these are people you've never even done anything to, and that they don't like you because of rumors. Well, I don't like you already, and I've never even met you."

Why wasn't I better at keeping my mouth shut? I knew Peter would tell Ivan what I had said.

The actual diary part of "The Seducer's Diary" started on April 4. The seducer saw a seventeen-year-old girl go into a department store. He followed her around, trying to figure out who she was and how he could meet her. He basically kept stalking her for all of April.

By May 5, the seducer still hadn't managed to learn the girl's name, and started railing against chance. ("Damned chance! I am waiting for you. I do not wish to defeat you with principles. . . .") He talked about being worthy of serving chance—worthy of being a servant. Ivan, too, had expressed rhetorical anger at abstract concepts, and seemed to think in terms of being worthy and unworthy. The way the guy was sort of bragging about being both a colleague and a servant of chance reminded me of that line in *King Lear*. It occurred to me to wonder whether nature was *my* goddess. Somehow I felt like she wasn't.

On May 19, the seducer finally found out the girl's name: Cordelia, "like the third of King Lear's daughters." (Wait—so *King Lear* was part of it?)

Cordelia's father, a naval captain, had been strict. Now, both her parents were dead. She lived alone with her paternal aunt. It occurred to me that I, too, had once lived alone with my paternal aunt, for a couple of months during the custody suit.

"She has, then, some conception of life's pains, of its darker side," the seducer wrote. But how did he know? Wasn't it possible that none of it had really bothered her?

The seducer said it was good that Cordelia had suffered so early in life. On the one hand, her womanliness was still intact, and she wasn't "crippled." On the other, the fact that she *had* suffered could be "useful" to him. (Had my family background been useful to Ivan?) The seducer also noted with approval that Cordelia had always been alone. Isolation, though detrimental for a young man, was essential for a girl. This was because a girl should "not be interesting." The seducer didn't explain the connection between being isolated and being uninteresting, remarking only: "A young girl who wants to please by being interesting really only succeeds in pleasing herself." All my effort to be interesting: was that, too, something I had to be ashamed of?

"Her father and mother had not lived happily together; what usually beckons, more or less clearly or vaguely, to a young girl does not beckon to her." That was true of me, as well: both the part about my parents not living happily together, and the part about what beckoned to other girls—to Svetlana, for instance—not beckoning to me. Were the two things connected?

"Although she is quiet and modest, undemanding, there is an immense demand lying there unconsciously": why was that line so exciting, and so troubling? The seducer went on to say that he couldn't let Cordelia rest on him too heavily, like a burden. She had to be so light that he could take her on his arm. I immediately felt that I had rested on Ivan too heavily, like a burden. I wondered whether I had to go on a diet, like Svetlana was doing, even if she didn't call it that. Of course,

I knew he meant "light" figuratively. But didn't he also mean it literally? You couldn't imagine Cordelia being fat.

When the seducer proposed marriage, he did it as confusingly as possible, so that Cordelia would have no idea what she had agreed to: "If she can predict anything, then I have gone wrong and the whole relationship loses its meaning." It was just how I had felt, going to Hungary.

Once they were engaged, he put on a whole campaign to persuade Cordelia that engagements were dumb, and got her to break it off. It had to be her decision, because he was too proud to vulgarly deceive a girl with false promises. He also looked down on raping people, and thought it was unaesthetic to use "money, power, influence, sleeping draughts, and so on." And yet, wasn't he using money and power? He had servants and stagecoaches and all kinds of diversions—while Cordelia was stuck in that house with her aunt.

After Cordelia broke off the engagement, she was sent to the country to stay with "a family." The seducer sent her anguished letters, while secretly preparing a house where he micromanaged every detail: the views from the windows, the furniture and layout of the rooms, the music that lay open on the piano.

"Why can't a night like that be longer?" the seducer wrote, in the final diary entry, after they spent their first and last night together. He left before she woke up—because of how disgusted he was by women's tears and prayers, "which change everything yet are really of no consequence." I thought about that a lot: about what she could have said that would have been of consequence.

What to make of this chilling tale? Clearly, it wasn't true. Kierkegaard hadn't done those things, and didn't believe in them. He had made them up, to illustrate an impossibly villainous person. How was it, then, that "The Seducer's Diary" corresponded so closely to what felt like the most meaningful thing that had ever happened to me?

Was there a way of viewing Cordelia's situation as not bad, or as bad for only historically contingent reasons? Cordelia had lived in the nineteenth century, and couldn't go to college or have an interesting job, so she had to get married. But I didn't want to get married—not even to Ivan. It was true that I had daydreamed about taking his name—about having a new name—about feeling chosen and special. The phrase "have his baby"—like in the Alanis Morissette song, where she said "Would she have your baby"—was electrifying: to think of being weighted in that way, by him. But the thought of having an actual baby, like my aunts and my stepmother, was the opposite of electrifying.

Was there a version of "The Seducer's Diary" where they were equal—where he wasn't tricking her into doing something she didn't want? Or was that what seduction *was*?

—

When Svetlana came to pick me up at my suite, Priya was passing through the common room wearing a floaty dress. "I just wonder how much of wanderlust is just regular lust," she was saying into the cordless phone. We exchanged waves as she drifted into her bedroom.

Priya was a year younger than the rest of us, spoke in a lilting voice, and was so cartoonishly beautiful that you had to keep staring at her to be sure she was real.

"Who's the apparition of beauty?" Svetlana asked afterward, in the stairwell.

"That's Priya," I said. "Riley's friend."

"Riley has friends, other than those guys? What's her deal?"

"Well, I don't rightly know."

Svetlana nodded. "She probably can't have a strong personality because of her appearance. I don't mean only that she doesn't need one. Whatever personality she did have would end up being incidental to her beauty, so it couldn't be strong. I almost feel sorry for her, but I don't, because she doesn't seem sorry, and because she must go through life surrounded by a cushion of love. Everyone loves to be near beauty. Even Riley, who is so critical, isn't immune to it."

I told Svetlana everything I had thought about after watching *Usual Suspects* and reading Kierkegaard. It took a long time. At some point, I noticed Svetlana's expression.

"What," I said.

"I was just suddenly so glad I wasn't you," she said. "I'm sorry if that sounds mean. I used to envy your situation last year, but now I don't anymore."

She seemed to be growing smaller, like I was looking at her from the bottom of a deep pit.

"Oh," I said.

"I just really think you should be seeing someone," Svetlana said.

This was an unforeseen level of perfidy. "Seeing someone" was how people talked about having a boyfriend—about having "a relationship" that wasn't all in your head—about being healthy and self-respecting enough to be with someone who really cared about you.

"I mean a therapist," she said. And, when she saw my expression: "I think you aren't seeing things clearly."

How was a therapist going to help me see things more clearly, when he didn't know any of these people, and couldn't know anything other than what was told to him, by me: a person who apparently didn't see things clearly?

The first time I talked to a psychologist was when I was fourteen. The judge in the custody suit had decided that we all had to be psychologically evaluated: me, my parents, my stepmother, my aunts, even my mother's new boyfriend, who was identified in the records as "Paramour of the mother." The lawyers said that the judge seemed to be going out of his way to prolong the case. Some people in my family said it was because the judge was Greek, but I thought it was wrong to believe in something so prejudiced.

Everyone had been assigned to a different psychologist. Mine talked in a little-girl voice, and told me that when she thought of Turkey she imagined camels, and asked if I had to wear a veil when we went there. Sensing how hurt my mother would have been if she had heard those questions, I did my best to explain to the social worker how important secularism and science were in the Turkish national identity.

I went to three or four such meetings, at night, after I got off the bus from cross-country practice. I nearly wept from fatigue and annoyance. But the worst part was after it seemed to be over, when the psychologists wrote up reports of what we had all said, and circulated them to everyone involved. I hadn't known that everything we said would be circulated to everyone else.

I learned a lot from that, like how much it hurt to see how other people described you, and how things that you said about another person, especially your parents, seemed neutral when addressed to a third party, but lethal when you thought about your parents reading it.

Last year, when I almost got a C in Russian, I had tried talking to a psychologist at the student health center. He became visibly impatient whenever I mentioned Ivan, who was the reason I had gone there in the first place. All he wanted to talk about was my parents' divorce. Like all adults, he thought everything was always about my parents—about how I was affected by them, or reacting to them.

When I persisted in talking about Ivan, the psychologist said that I was in an imaginary relationship with an unavailable person, because I was afraid to be in a real relationship with an available person. This struck me as a statement devoid of meaning. What "available person" was he talking about? Where was that person? He didn't answer and only sat there, his left hand holding his right in a way that displayed his wedding band, in case I had missed the photo on his bookshelf. Obviously I knew that Ivan wasn't "available." That was how *he*, the therapist, knew it: because I had just told him. Obviously I knew that my position was humiliating. I didn't need some underachiever with a master's degree to tell me how my problem was that nobody loved me the way he loved his defeated conformist-looking wife.

Svetlana said that being evaluated by court psychologists didn't count as trying therapy, and neither did going once to the student health center. Therapy didn't work unless you found the right person, and went lots of times. She said she would ask her therapist to write me a referral. I recognized this mania for referrals from people our parents' age: the way they thought that the most difficult problems could only be solved by special insider information that you had coaxed out of some guy with a name like Chuck.

From everything I knew about Svetlana's therapist, he was just the kind of jocular Socratic advice-implier I didn't want to hear from. Svetlana had once told me, as if it was a funny story, about the time when he had asked her why she didn't have pierced ears, and she had explained that she didn't want to be punctured, considering it a violation of her bodily integrity. Her therapist started laughing, and then she laughed, too, because she realized she had been talking about her fear of sex. All I needed was some grown man guffawing at me about sex.

Furthermore, I knew that Svetlana paid her therapist, on top of what the insurance covered, because he wasn't at the student health center. For her, it wasn't a big deal, because her parents always sent her more money than she knew what to do with. But I didn't want to ask my parents for more money.

Anyway, how could therapy even work on me, when I was so far from sharing Svetlana's therapist-like belief that people should be healthy and well-adjusted, that they should go to bed at the same time every night, even if they were reading or having an interesting conversation, or that it was great and life-affirming to go hiking with some guy, or to get married? Of course therapy worked for someone who believed those things. Furthermore, Svetlana had actual psychological problems, like post-traumatic stress from the war in Yugoslavia. I hadn't been in a war, or had to leave the country. Everything had been rearranged so that I would stay in the same place. Nobody in my family had ever given me diet pills: something that had also befallen Svetlana. For Svetlana, therapy was a good solution, but my case was completely different. Whatever problems I had were of my own making—and that meant I was going to have to solve them myself.

Some Things Svetlana and I Talked About

What was an orgy like? I thought slow and languorous; Svetlana thought fast and frenetic. "Nobody would know who was who."

What was charisma: a content or a form? (We talked a lot about whether different things were a content or a form.) We thought charisma was probably more like a form: less a matter of saying or doing

48

particular charismatic things, than of saying or doing things in a charismatic way. We discussed which of the people we knew had charisma, whether it could be acquired, whether it was desirable. Svetlana said that she used to have it, but got freaked out by how much she enjoyed it, and forced herself not to have it. She thought I had it in a specific way but pretended not to have it.

Were we really more interesting than other people, or did we only seem that way to ourselves? I thought that we only seemed more interesting to ourselves. A corollary of this belief was that we had no particular responsibility to think about other people. They found themselves interesting, they could think about themselves. Svetlana thought that we really were more interesting, and thus had certain responsibilities.

Was an equal relationship possible, or did one person always like the other person more? Which of us, me or Svetlana, liked the other more? "I feel like it's different at different times," I said. Svetlana said she agreed.

Could friendships reach a stable point and stay there, or were they always either growing or shrinking? Svetlana thought they grew and shrank.

What was the worst cruelty: personal or political? Svetlana thought political: denying a person's personhood and turning them into a number. I thought it was just as bad to be tormented to death by a relative or a landlord as to be shot in a death camp.

Was every smart person funny? I thought humorlessness was the essence of stupidity. Svetlana thought she knew some genuinely smart people who happened not to be interested in whether things were funny. We agreed that Susan Sontag was not funny.

The quality of knowing what one wanted and how to get it: Svetlana had it more than I did, but the person who had it the most was this girl Misty who sang in operas and was a Mormon.

What was more pure: vocal or instrumental music? Svetlana said vocal, because everything else was an imitation of the human voice. I thought instrumental, because a violin had more range and fewer limitations than a person's voice.

Was it necessary to be cruel to be great or a genius or an effective person? I said no. Svetlana said yes. She said you had to have an "edge." She implied that I was tricking myself or being hypocritical, if I thought I disagreed. I felt uneasily flattered.

What is style, what is taste; how do you develop a style, how do you develop a taste? Who that we knew had one, how did they get it?

In Paris we had stayed for a few days in an apartment belonging to this girl Jeanne, the daughter of Svetlana's friend's family's friend. Jeanne was staying with her boyfriend the whole time, so we never met her.

Everything about her apartment—the chunky ashtrays and stacked *Cahiers du Cinéma*, the low Japanese-looking double bed, the kitchen with its aperitif bottles and espresso machine—all conveyed a level and granularity of style that we could not aspire to, living, as we did, in dormitories full of institutionalized furniture and schoolbooks.

"I find this apartment very intimidating," Svetlana had said, voicing what we had both been thinking. "Jeanne is only twenty but she already has a taste."

"What makes you say that?" Svetlana's friend Bill had said. "The fact that she has a boyfriend and you don't?"

I knew that he had brought up her lack of a boyfriend to make her feel bad, because a few sentences earlier she had upset him by using a word he didn't know. And yet, I felt in some sense that he was right: that the thing that intimidated us, "a style," "a taste," *was* related to having a boyfriend.

Was that why Svetlana put up with Bill—why boors, in general, were widely tolerated and promoted to high social positions: because they accurately gauged and reflected "the way of the world"? Or did the boors *determine* the ways of the world, from the positions they were put into? Was there another way things could be? Or was it, to use one of the boors' favorite phrases, cognitively hardwired?

I couldn't really ask Svetlana; whenever I criticized Bill in any detail, she started defending him and listing good things he had supposedly done that I didn't know about.

Was a style what you needed to make someone fall in love with you?

The other subject we talked about was whether men were less affected by love than women—whether they suffered less from heartbreak. Even if suffering was, as Svetlana insisted, universally human, and thus also befell men, it seemed inarguable that men were better at compartmentalizing, and less easily distracted from their intellectual goals. Was this because their neurological hardwiring made them better at systems, while women were better at empathy—because men valued abilities and things, while women valued feelings and people? How could we learn to place less value on feelings and people?

Svetlana liked to think of exceptions: cases of men whose hearts had been broken by women, who couldn't forget the women, even though the women could forget. I felt obliged to mention that it had been my mother who had left my father, and my father had been really upset and had cried. On the other hand, my mother had left because she thought she had always loved my father more than he loved her, and, before she left, *she* had been the one who cried. Furthermore, my father had soon remarried and became cheerful again, while my mother's boyfriend caused her suffering.

Svetlana brought up our friend Jeremy, a philosophy major, who was in love with two different girls named Diane, neither of whom loved him. But even though he talked about the Dianes constantly, he didn't seem incapacitated; he always had the strength to pivot to his other favorite topic, which was the works of Thomas Pynchon. You couldn't imagine him unable to stop crying. Was it possible that he was protected somehow by the fact that there were two of them?

Our other friend, Chris, *did* seem to become incapacitated by love—but Chris was gay, and that somehow made it different.

Svetlana pointed out that Young Werther, who was not gay, had killed himself for love. Furthermore, after Goethe wrote about Werther, lovesick youths all over Europe also started killing themselves.

The Sorrows of Young Werther was shorter than I had expected, under a hundred pages, and mostly in letters. I sat on one of those round step stools at the bookstore and skimmed just the parts about Werther's love life.

I realized, as I read, that I had wanted the girl to turn out to be less interested in Young Werther than in her own goals and activities, and for that to be why he had to kill himself. This was not the case. In fact, the girl, Charlotte, *had* no goals or activities, other than nursing sick people. You never found out if she even liked Werther, because she had already promised her sick mother that she would marry some other guy, and because she was "virtuous," meaning that Werther himself didn't expect or want her to change her mind.

Werther decided that the only way forward was for someone to die: either him, Charlotte, or the other guy. Because murder went against his moral code, he opted for suicide. First, he tricked Charlotte into giving him pistols, so he could say he was "dying by her hand." Then, he did such a crappy job of shooting himself that everyone had to watch him spurting blood for twelve hours. That part was narrated by an editor, because Werther couldn't write it himself. The last lines were: "Charlotte's life was despaired of. The body was carried by laborers. No priest attended."

It sounded to me as if Werther's suicide was less an expression of a rejection-induced loss of self-worth or cognitive capacity, than a practical work-around to his "no murder" rule. His self-worth had never been on the line. He hadn't been rejected, after careful consideration, on account of having an insufficiently impressive soul. For this reason, I didn't count *The Sorrows of Young Werther* as a book about how men were just as incapacitated by heartbreak as women.

THE THIRD WEEK

Almost overnight, the weather stopped feeling like summer. I was able to wear the new boots I had bought over the summer at the Payless across from Penn Station. Zip-up, chestnut-colored, with block heels, they not only came in women's eleven but ran large enough that they fit onto my feet, which were size eleven and a half: a conceptual category that was rarely realized, since half-sizes stopped at ten, in the form of any actual shoes. It felt exciting to wear shoes that weren't "unisex"—the way they rang out on the stones.

Because a Diet Coke can had exploded in my backpack, I also had a new bag: a canvas army surplus bag, with a shoulder strap. It made me feel grown-up and jaunty, the way it hit below my hip, and it wasn't a huge production to get things out, like it was from a backpack. If I happened to be carrying an object that felt talismanic, like my copy of *Either/Or*, I could feel it close at hand.

The Chance professor was wearing an expensive-looking shapeless dress with a collar that stood up like the mouth of a vase. I didn't understand everything she was saying, but every now and then a sentence jumped out and seemed to sparkle midair.

What was the role of chance in literature? The realist novel was predicated on the contingency of everyday life, laying out in its opening pages the accidents of the characters' birth to a particular historical, geographic, and social milieu. Characters were no longer allegorical, or social types. They were doomed to have "personalities."

Balzac called chance "the greatest novelist in the world." How was one to be so artful that the end product seemed to be free of art? The social novel gave meaning to chance events, by embedding them in a historical order. Baudelaire wrote something about flâneurs, and Walter Benjamin wrote something about Baudelaire. The flâneur on his walk both observed and constituted urban life. This was Hegelian.

Freud, Darwin, and Conan Doyle elevated chance to a new status. Dreams, fossils, clues: all were the accretions of chance, randomly piled up, like the cigar ashes that only Sherlock Holmes could parse. Proust's narrator couldn't write his book until a chance encounter with a specific kind of cookie.

André Breton, a Surrealist, not only documented but provoked coincidences, viewing them as "the royal road to the unconscious": that's what Freud called dreams. Louis Aragon described Paris as a palimpsest of chance encounters. Of Aragon's volume about Paris, Walter Benjamin said: "Evenings in bed I could not read more than a few words of it before my heartbeat got so strong I had to put the book down."

At that point in the lecture, I felt too excited to sit still, so I left, trying not to make any noise.

At dinner, I explained how I had gone to a literature class where the professor had read a quote from Walter Benjamin about how he could only read a few words of a book by Louis Aragon before he got too excited to read any more, and that then I myself had gotten so excited that I had to leave the lecture.

"What class was that? The Literature of Short Attention Spans?" Lucas asked.

"I'm pretty sure I already took that," Oak said thoughtfully. "Several times."

———

In the kitchen of our suite, I noticed a dark-colored cord draped over the edge of the sink. On inspection, it proved to be the tail of a square aquatic creature with eyes in the top of its head. It was big and flat, taking up nearly the whole basin, and resembled a flag that had been made out of a shark.

Scanning the environment for some sign as to why it was there, I noticed KC, a member of the Singaporean club, sitting at the heavy round oak table that our block had voted to steal from an atrium somewhere, where we thought it looked neglected. Lucas and Oak had just picked it up and carried it down the street, and nobody had stopped them.

"Hey, KC," I said.

"Hey," she said, barely looking up from her book.

"So . . . who's that in the sink?"

"It's a stingray."

Several questions came to my mind, like whose stingray it was, why it was in the sink, how KC had gotten into our apartment, and where

Joanne was. On reflection, though, I realized none of these things was actually a problem for me, so I just went to the library.

I tried to read the rest of *Either/Or*, but nothing in it felt as meaningful as "The Seducer's Diary." The ethical half, the one written by the judge, was not only more boring than the aesthetic half, but it also made less sense. In the first letter, titled "The Aesthetic Validity of Marriage," the judge tried to prove that a series of love affairs was objectively less interesting than one long painful boring marriage.

The last time I had read anything talking up marriage like that had been the report of my father's meetings with the court psychologist, where I first saw the phrase "nuclear family." My father had talked about the stabilizing influence of the nuclear family, which my mother couldn't offer, but he could, because he had gotten remarried, and my stepmother had gotten pregnant. My father said that he had done those things for me. But it wasn't clear to me how I immediately benefited. The dog had disappeared, as had all my mother's plates and towels, and my paternal aunt. The plates and towels were replaced by plates and towels with gold trim. Thenceforth, on drives, I sat in the back, with the baby. My father periodically looked in the rearview mirror and asked, "How's it going back there?" I tried my hardest to smile, knowing that, when I couldn't, I was going on the record as a sulky, difficult teen—or, worse yet, jealous of my father, of his attention.

By the time I got to dinner, I could see only two empty seats in the dining hall. The first was directly across from one of the house tutors: a grown man who, having attended Dalton, always asked what high school you had gone to, in the hope that it had been Dalton. The other seat was across from a blond cherubic-looking guy with a laptop. He was eating toast, and looked identical to Ivan's unpleasant friend, Imre. Imre had graduated and was supposed to be at Caltech, so probably it wasn't him. Even if it *was* him, though, I decided I would still rather sit there than across from the Dalton guy.

"Is it OK if I sit here?" I asked, in what came out as kind of an angry voice, setting my tray on the table.

"Ye-es," the blond guy said, pushing aside his computer. His eyes were a shockingly pale blue that I had never seen before.

"Sorry, I think I thought you were someone else," I said. "We haven't met before, right?"

"No. But we can meet now." His excessively correct posture and intonation, together with the slight lag in his replies, contributed to the impression that he was responding to directions that were being beamed to him from a great distance. He asked where the name Selin was from. It was a question I had to answer ten times every day, and yet, coming from this guy, who had such unusual mannerisms and who gave his own name as "Juho," it didn't really bother me.

"It's Turkish," I said. "What about Juho?"

"Can you guess?"

"Oh, wow. Um. Probably not."

"You could try, though."

"Greenland," I said, realizing, as I said it, that he was wearing an emerald-green sweatshirt and matching emerald-green pants.

He sat up even straighter than he had been. "This is a very surprising guess," he said. "Greenland has the lowest population density of the world. Even the Sahara is more densely populated than Greenland. The probability that I am from Greenland is very small. If you have to guess someone's nationality in the future, Greenland should probably be your last guess."

I looked at him closely, trying to judge if he was some kind of asshole. I hadn't even wanted to guess his nationality. "Iceland," I said.

"That is warmer, not just because Iceland is warmer than Greenland, but because it is closer to where I am from."

"Oh. Cool." I turned my attention to a bread bowl of Yankee bean soup. I was done trying to guess where this guy was from.

"I will give you a hint," he said. "In my country, we also speak an agglutinative language."

Then I knew he was Finnish, and was interested. I asked if he believed in the Ural-Altaic language family: a theory about how Finnish, Hungarian, Turkish, Korean, and Japanese were related to each other. Linguists stopped believing it in the 1960s, but I thought it might be true, because of all the similarities I had noticed between Hungarian and Turkish grammar. Juho said that he had had a similar experience when he studied Japanese. He asked whether it was theoretically possible in Turkish, as in Finnish and Japanese, to make an infinitely long nested word expressing an infinitely long delegation of command—for example, a single word that meant: "I ordered him to order him to order him to order him to order him to order him to do it." I thought about it and realized that you could make such a word.

Juho was twenty-three, like Ivan, but already had a Ph.D., in both chemistry and physics. He belonged to a society of fellows, who all lived here for three years, and were paid to do whatever they wanted. One fellow was working on a new classification of mammals. He thought mammals were classified wrong. Another was trying to use weather patterns to predict when the national soccer coach would be fired in Brazil.

"Wait, does that work?"

"I think all he has to prove is that the weather isn't *worse* than the other existing means of prediction."

I asked what Juho's project was. First he said something about trying to "build a clavichord." Then he said he was teaching his computer to recognize the concept of a chair. He turned his computer to face me, displaying one window full of illegibly tiny lines of code, and another window with a grid of photographs of chairs. He wasn't sure if he wanted to include armchairs and stools. "Or this," he said, clicking on a photo of a plastic child's "chair" in the shape of the purple animated lump—could its name really have been "Grimace"?—that was friends with Ronald McDonald.

Juho said that his favorite Finnish candy was called *turkinpippuri*, which meant "Turkish peppers," and contained sal ammoniac, which was the product of hydrochloric acid and ammonia. "Do they have these in Turkey?" he asked.

"I don't think so," I said.

"You have to try them," he said. "Someday I will give you some."

I audited a few meetings of an ethics seminar taught by a famous philosophy professor from Oxford. He had wire-rimmed glasses and wild white hair, and used a lot of overhead transparencies, usually putting them on upside-down or backward. The transparencies were charts and graphs, about the quality of life for different populations.

One question in the ethics seminar was how to weigh the benefit of a slight improvement in the present quality of life for millions of people, against a risk of great harm to millions of people who hadn't been born yet. It was complicated because, if you improved the present quality of life, then more people would have children—meaning that the people you were potentially harming in the future were people who might not otherwise have been born, so maybe you had still done them a favor.

A lot of ethical questions were related to failing to cause people to be born. Was it morally wrong to not have a child, if you knew she would be happy? Was it morally wrong to have a child when you were fourteen, instead of later, if you knew that the later child would be happier? What if you knew that most of her life would be happy, but the last five years would be extremely unhappy? I didn't get why the extremely unhappy person wasn't allowed to kill herself before she messed up her average.

I wished there was a class where they could teach you how to calculate the right time to die. The current arrangement—for everyone to sit there piously waiting for whenever their body happened to shut down—seemed so far from ideal. My grandmother often said that she had lived too long, because she was in constant pain and had outlived her husband and friends. Far from being taken at its face value, this statement was treated as a kind of bon mot demonstrating my grandmother's love of debate. My mother said that my grandmother was feisty and enjoyed life. She said that she enjoyed eating soft-boiled eggs.

The ethics professor was smart. When anyone made a suggestion or asked a question, he half smiled and immediately rattled off all kinds of implications that a normal person wouldn't have thought of if they had sat there for years. He was kind, too, never saying anything to make anyone feel dumb. The one time I asked a question, he jumped up and down, and even drew a picture. It was a relief that the person they sent to teach you ethics wasn't some kind of asshole.

Nonetheless, the ethics seminar always left me feeling dissatisfied and anxious. "Quality of life": as if we knew it, and could measure it. I wanted to know what it was: the quality of life.

Lakshmi said it was weird that I wasn't on the literary magazine, like everyone else who wanted to be a writer, or like Lakshmi herself, who "wasn't a writer" but cared about writing. I didn't get what Lakshmi meant when she said she "wasn't a writer."

"I'm rubbish at it," she said.

"Well, none of us are *good*."

"No, it's different. I used to write poems. . . ." Horror flickered over her face and I dropped the subject.

Joining the literary magazine hadn't previously occurred to me. I didn't want to be an editor, or run a magazine, so why would I want to do a fake version of those things in college? Also, the people who were the most into the literary magazine were the kind of guys who seemed unable to conceal their glee about all the famous writers who had been there a hundred years ago, or fifty years ago. It wasn't that I had any particular problem with Wallace Stevens or John Ashbery, but I wasn't about to join a club to chortle about them. But now it turned out that Lakshmi and other people I knew were actually already on the literary magazine, and I understood from what they said that *not* joining was making some kind of statement, so I decided to apply.

Everyone was randomly assigned to a "tutor": someone already on the literary magazine who was supposed to help with your application essay. My tutor was Riley's friend, Lucas. I felt a kinship with Lucas, because he read as much as I did, and because his parents had grown up on different continents and now lived separately. Lucas had gone to school in New York but spent all his vacations overseas, and was neither as impermeably American as Riley, who had never left the United States, nor as confidently international as Joanne or Lakshmi. He had a familiar air of displaced embarrassment, an anxiety about speaking languages poorly, which one didn't encounter in people who had done any of their schooling in the same country where most of their relatives lived.

For the application essay, you had to read a short story, describe its strengths and weaknesses, and say what revisions you would ask for if you were going to publish it. I met Lucas for lunch, so he could give me a photocopy of the story. I kept waiting for him to give me advice, but he didn't. When I brought it up, he acted as if I was joking. We ended up just talking about books, as usual.

Lucas had a way of talking about writing that seemed to hint at some previously unsuspected world of competence and collegiality. It was from Lucas that I first heard the phrase "good on a sentence level." He said it in a self-deprecating tone, indicating that he was attributing it to other people. To think that not only Lucas himself, but also other people, had also had the experience of reading a book where the individual sentences had delightful rhythm and word choices, but some other part of it gave you a bad feeling. To think there was a name for that feeling of mixed gratitude and disappointment that I had dismissed as too private to name.

The short story for the application was about a plumber who had sex with a housewife whose toilet he was fixing. I wrote down some ways that I thought the story could be less dumb than it was, and gave them to Lucas.

I got onto the literary magazine. Lakshmi was voted in charge of parties: an area in which her expertise was widely recognized.

Recently, on leaving a party in Boston, Lakshmi and her friends had run into some people who had graduated last year, one of whom had somehow attached herself to Lakshmi and asked her if she knew "a Turkish girl named Selin."

"It was bizarre," Lakshmi said. "I forget her name. Zina, Zelda, something like that."

I gaped. "Zita?"

"That's it. Who is she?"

"Ivan's ex-girlfriend."

"His ex? Why is she so keen to talk to you? She asked for your number. Should I have given it to her? I wasn't sure if you'd been avoiding her. What does she want?"

"I don't know. What was she like?"

"Very interested in you. Short. Not smartly dressed. Did he dump you for her, or her for you?"

"I think they had broken up before I met him," I said.

"It figures," she said. I didn't ask what she meant.

I had always assumed that Lakshmi's family was rich, until I found out that she hadn't bought even a single book for any of her classes. She *had* most of the books, but they were hand-me-downs from her older friends: glamorous postcolonial upperclassmen, who also took Lakshmi to New York to do clothes shopping at invitation-only sales and at the kind of consignment stores where rich women and teenagers offloaded once-worn couture, using the proceeds to buy each other's anxiety and ADHD medications. I had never heard of such goings-on, which Lakshmi spoke of as routine.

The skill of appearing to have money turned out to be something Lakshmi had learned from her father, a diplomat. She had grown up in palatial residences around the world where, attended by servants, chauffeurs, and gardeners, her parents had entertained on a lavish scale, without owning any of the things in their house.

All the Singaporean students, including Joanne, had the same scholarship: full tuition plus a stipend, in exchange for which they had to work for the Singaporean government for some number of years after graduation. Joanne cut her own hair, didn't like expensive clothes or makeup, and used liquid castile soap as shampoo. She used the stipend to buy a carbon road bike and a laptop with a built-in CD-ROM, treating these items with a kind of respectful ruefulness that seemed to embody her general attitude toward what the Singaporeans called their "bond." It was complicated, in Joanne's case, by the fact that her parents could technically buy her out, because her mother was an American citizen: a piece of information that we all knew, even me, but that her parents had apparently never discussed with Joanne.

The most famous Singaporean at Harvard, Percival, was a vermilion-haired classics major who organized seasonal Eleusinian Mysteries where they did psychedelics and roasted a piglet. Most non-Singaporean people didn't know that Percival was from Singapore. But he was often invoked by the other Singaporeans, as a symbol of what could happen because of your bond. In high school they had known him as a compliant, blazer-wearing math Olympian.

The Singaporean students' arrangement struck me at first as somehow extreme and archaic. But the more I learned about everyone's situation, the more it seemed that everyone had a "bond"; it was just less formal, and not legally enforced, and came from their parents and not a whole country. Riley had a full scholarship from the pharmaceutical company where her mother worked in marketing. Nobody else in her family had done particularly well in school, and Riley was the one who had to become a doctor.

It seemed related to the bond that Joanne volunteered ten hours a week teaching GED prep at an adult education program—the same one I had quit last year. Every weekday, she biked six miles to the housing project, returning in the same unruffled mood. When I asked her if the people there ever stressed her out, she just looked thoughtful and said, "Some of them can be a little bit tense."

In my case, volunteering had been my mother's idea. It was when I had mentioned getting a job. In her worldview, my getting a job was an insult—like accusing her of not providing for me. In high school, I had done my best to seem grateful, and to be grateful, because I knew how much more fortunate I was than the kids who *had* to work—

either because they were poor, or because their parents were the kind of rich people who thought it was harmful for their children to be spared any kind of hassle. It was usually the people I thought of as all-American who were like that—the white people, as my high school friend Clarissa called them. I had been surprised to learn that Clarissa, whose parents were from China, did not consider herself white. According to Clarissa, I wasn't white, either. But I asked my mother, and my mother had said, sounding scandalized, that of course we were white.

Non-poor parents who came from other countries, or who were Jewish, often didn't want their kids to have jobs. One rationale was that our earning power was so trivial that it wasn't worth the trouble it would cause for them. Leora's mother's attitude was: "I don't have time to pick you up from your fake job." Leora's mother always did find the most insulting way of phrasing anything. "I'm not going to listen to a ten-year-old," she would say, or "a seven-year-old" or "a twelve-year-old," in a voice that dismissed everything you said absolutely, with no grounds for appeal. That was one way I was more fortunate than Leora: my parents often solicited my opinion and, when they didn't, it didn't seem to be because of some principle they felt proud of. And yet I knew that Leora considered herself more fortunate than me, because she had brothers and sisters, and because she had never "been through anything like a divorce." But my parents were the only ones I knew who never acted like I owed them money for being alive, or talked about kids being "spoiled" or "selfish," or said that I had to be a doctor, or took other adults' side over mine. I was so grateful that sometimes I sat in my room and cried.

This year, I had decided to get a job. The highest-paying student job, Dorm Crew, was presented as a fun team-building experience, except that instead of going to the wilderness, you cleaned other kids' bathrooms. Last year, Priya and Joanne's Dorm Crew person was also a math teaching assistant, and had written problems for them on the mirror in dry-erase marker. Depending on their answers, he would leave a crying face or a smiley face, or, once, when they solved a particularly difficult problem, a dolphin-shaped bath bead.

Dorm Crew, which paid up to twelve dollars an hour, was only for federal work-study students, which meant your parents had to make under a certain amount of money for you to do it. Svetlana's roommate, Dolores, was on full scholarship, and had a work-study job washing dishes in one of the dining halls, so she could give her parents money to send to their parents. Some people spoke positively about Dorm Crew, but I never heard anyone say anything good about dishwashing, except that the hours were more flexible.

The best-paid job where you didn't actually have to do anything unpleasant was library check-out, and was also work-study. Non-work-study jobs started at four seventy-five an hour, and it wasn't like they were interesting. The interesting jobs were called internships, and were unpaid.

I got an off-campus job doing data entry for a gardening catalog. They gave me lists of addresses of people who might be interested in gardening, and I typed them on a computer. They paid by the number of addresses. When I typed as fast as I could, I made almost twenty dollars an hour. But then I started to get shooting pains in my wrists and hands, and when I went to the student health center, they said it was from typing, so I quit.

After that, I found an on-campus job posting at the Ukrainian Research Institute that wasn't work-study, but still somehow paid seven dollars an hour. At the interview, I tried really hard to show how motivated I was. "Your passion for Russian literature is quite inspiring, but you do know this is a Ukrainian research institute? And it's mostly office work," said the interviewer, Rob, who sounded like he was trying to dissuade me. But I talked about how much I loved office work and also the violinist Nathan Milstein, and in the end Rob said I could work there.

The Ukrainian Research Institute was in a wooden colonial house, with offices in the different rooms. About a third of the people who worked there were actually Ukrainian, and seemed always on the verge of being really upset. If anyone said "the Ukraine," instead of "Ukraine," or assumed that some word in Ukrainian was the same as in Russian, or asked whether a Ukrainian writer wrote in Russian, it was enough to push them over the edge. This kind of touchiness was familiar to me from Turkish people, and gave me a fond, protective feeling.

———

The futon in the common room was covered in the batik cloth that Priya draped over everything—as if it helped. Riley and Priya were at lab. I wasn't sure where Joanne was, but Joanne was so quiet, and so often asleep. As I was thinking admiringly of Joanne's ability to fall asleep anywhere, I saw to my astonishment that she was actually asleep under the table, a few feet away, in what I had thought was an empty sleeping bag.

When I checked my email, I found a forward from the president of the Turkish students' club. Do you feel like getting up at 8 on a Saturday, putting on your biggest smile, and looking like a constructive, sexually active, ethnically ambiguous member of the Harvard community? he had written. The forwarded message was an invitation from Crimson Key, the student group that gave guided tours of campus. They were trying to get different international and interracial students to greet some kind of visiting delegation, thereby making Harvard look more diverse than it would have if only Crimson Key people had showed up.

It occurred to me that the quality of emails from the Turkish club had risen dramatically since last year, when nobody said anything funny or interesting, or expressed any kind of distance from the people like Crimson Key. This, in combination with a positive impression I had of the Singaporean club, motivated me to try going to a meeting of the Turkish club.

Everyone in the Turkish club seemed to have gone to the same famous high school in Istanbul. All they talked about, other than their high school, was where in Boston you could get some particular kind of cheese. (You could get it at the Armenian store in Watertown.) Almost nobody said anything funny, unless you counted teasing each other about eating or drinking too much. In general, they seemed less like students than like miniature lame adults.

The only person I enjoyed talking to was the president, Şahin. He had gone to the same high school as the others, but seemed depressed, and said things that were funny, and didn't seem to care or even notice that my Turkish wasn't as good as everyone else's. When we talked, he just switched between Turkish and English, like he wasn't even noticing we were doing it. He was obsessed with birds, and later I often saw him striding around campus, wearing yellow sports headphones and glaring at the ground—because he was memorizing birdcalls, trying to get grant money to travel to the remote places where the most interesting birds congregated. Memorizing everything the birds said seemed like as much of a hassle for Şahin as learning Russian was for me. He was the only other Turkish person I had ever met who was actually interested in some specific field of knowledge, and who wasn't just automatically doing medicine, engineering, or the thing they called "management."

There were two grad students, Burcu and Ulaş, who sometimes came to the club meetings to circulate petitions about the Armenian genocide. They were really stressful people—not just about the petitions, but about everything. You could see exactly what their parents were like.

Most of the petitions cited two professors at Princeton who said that the massacre of Armenians in the Ottoman Empire had been part of a regional conflict involving pro-Russian Armenian groups, and wasn't technically a genocide. Sometimes, the petitions were addressed to the Holocaust Museum in Washington, urging them not to mention the Armenian genocide in different events or exhibits. Those petitions often worked, because there were enough people at the Holocaust Museum who didn't want to imply that anything else that had ever happened had been similar to the Holocaust. Other petitions were addressed to American legislators, to try to get them to not say that April 24 was Armenian Genocide Recognition Day. These were less effective, because there were more Armenian people who wanted a recognition day than there were Turkish people who didn't want one.

The Armenian genocide was something I had been hearing about from American people's parents since I was in elementary school. It was often the first thing they brought up: either a carpet they had bought, or, defiantly, "Jim's brother-in-law is Armenian," or "Our pediatrician is Greek." I had never heard any Turkish people say anything bad about Armenians, and I knew how much American people loved to talk about "ethnic hatreds," so I had always assumed it was just one of their fixations and didn't reflect anything real. It was a disappointment to learn that such petitions actually existed. It seemed churlish to lobby against a "recognition day" for a massacre, whether it had occurred genocidally, or in the course of what some people at Princeton considered to be a normal war. (What even differentiated a great and honorable war, where you were trying to secure some land by murdering people, from a shameful genocide, where you were trying to secure some land by murdering people?) On the other hand, when Ulaş talked about how the French and American governments were always trying to pass acts acknowledging genocides in other countries, but never called it a genocide about the Algerians or the American Indians, I felt an annoyance at the French and American governments that bordered on physical pain. Burcu and Ulaş sometimes tried to get Şahin to circulate their petitions for them, but he never did.

———

A famous Soviet bard died. All the Russian instructors were depressed. I saw Galina Fyodorovna crying in the photocopier room. The bard had been an emblem of the Moscow street culture of children, particularly on one famous street. In his honor, all the Russian students had to memorize poems by Pushkin. This made sense according to Russian people's logic, where everything always connected to Pushkin.

For our class, the thing we had to learn was a verse from *Eugene Onegin*. I was excited, because *Eugene Onegin* was the second Russian book I had ever read, in high school, right after *Anna Karenina*. It was written all in a kind of sonnet that Pushkin had invented, so it was really hard to translate. That was one of the main reasons to learn Russian: so you could actually read *Eugene Onegin*.

At some point, Vladimir Nabokov had gotten so mad at all the existing English translations of *Eugene Onegin* that he wrote his own, which was super-literal and didn't rhyme, and ruined his friendship with Edmund Wilson: a grown man whom people called "Bunny." That was the one I decided to read. My mother had a lot of Nabokov's novels, but she didn't have *Eugene Onegin*. I bought it myself at the Barnes & Noble on Route 22: one of the first places I drove to, in my mom's car, when I got my permit.

It was only because I had loved *Anna Karenina* that I had even wanted to read *Eugene Onegin*. Once I did, I realized the extent to which *Anna Karenina* had always been my mother's book, more than mine. The huge conflict in *Anna Karenina* was how Anna was torn between her lover and her child, and her husband was forcing her to choose between them. So, too, had my mother felt torn between her work and her love for her child, which her husband didn't believe in, and her boyfriend didn't understand. I knew she had compared Jerry to Vronsky and my father to Karenin. Almost all the women in *Anna Karenina* were mothers, and all of them had husbands or lovers—except that one girl, Varenka; but even with Varenka, Koznyshev almost proposed to her when they were picking mushrooms. Koznyshev had therefore at least contemplated having sex with Varenka. There were no women in that book with whom nobody thought about having sex.

Tatiana, the heroine of *Eugene Onegin*, wasn't a mother. She *had* a mother: a fretful, conventional, out-of-it person who limited her activities. Tatiana was a teenager, and lived in the provinces. She had no way of going anywhere, read novels all the time, and wasn't trying to have sex with anyone. Even when Eugene Onegin showed up—all she really wanted was to see him every now and then, and think about him, and keep reading her novels. It was only when she found out he was leaving that she went into despair, and wrote him a letter.

"Tatiana's letter" was famous in Russia—everyone knew it by heart. It was one of two passages we could memorize, for the bard's memorial service: either the first stanza of the book, or the beginning of Tatiana's letter. Most people, including Svetlana, chose the first stanza, because it was shorter, but I wanted to learn Tatiana's letter.

Svetlana was really good at memorizing. Her father had taught her something called "the method of loci." You pictured a route through a building, or among some buildings, and imagined yourself placing all the things you wanted to remember at different places—loci—along the route. Then, all you had to do to remember the things was to mentally retrace the route.

Svetlana suggested we map out an actual walk we could take, with stops that we would use to remember our stanzas.

"Like the Stations of the Cross?"

"That actually works really well, because there were fourteen Stations of the Cross, and there are fourteen lines in an Onegin stanza." We decided to start in the Yard, at the dorm where we had lived last year, and make our way toward the river.

It had been overcast all day, but we didn't get rained on until we got to our old dorm. We stood there for a moment, drinking it all in: the blank brick façade, the pointy gables. There was a feeling of rejection, knowing that our IDs wouldn't open the door anymore. New freshmen were going in and out. Some had clearly put a lot of thought into their clothes. Others seemed to have waterproofed their own persons as peremptorily as if they were lawn furniture.

The first line of Tatiana's letter—"I write to you—what would one more?"—was easy to remember, and to associate with this building, because that was where I had written to Ivan. The basic idea of the letter was how irretrievably it compromised her, just by existing. How, by writing it, she had put herself totally in Onegin's power, entrusted herself to his honor. She would never have done anything like that, she said, if things could have continued as they had been—if she could only see Onegin once a week, exchange a few words, and then "think and think about one thing" until their next meeting. I couldn't believe it said that: "think and think about one thing." That was all I had wanted, too.

Outside the Café Gato Rojo, in the grad student union, Svetlana had to memorize a line about Onegin's uncle being sick. Conveniently, Svetlana had once gotten really sick at the Gato Rojo, when she was meeting her French tutor. My line was about how I had exposed myself to being punished by Eugene Onegin's scorn. Well, I knew that

Ivan's girlfriend, Eunice, who was a grad student, held her office hours in the Gato Rojo; and the reason I knew it was that I had "fingered" her from online and her "plan" had her office hours. I felt scornful of *myself* for knowing that.

At the end of our walk, Svetlana headed back toward the T station to go to therapy. I sat on a bench and thought about Tatiana's letter to Onegin—about whether it counted as a success. On the one hand, they didn't end up together. And then there was a duel and a guy died. No, you couldn't say that the immediate outcomes had been positive. On the other hand, Pushkin himself loved the letter. He said he kept a copy of it, and read and reread it. Wasn't Pushkin's love, and the love of everyone who read *Eugene Onegin*, more important than Onegin acting like a loser?

Pushkin said that some readers would condemn Tatiana—they would call her impulsive or unseemly. But those readers weren't being truthful. What they really meant was that Tatiana wasn't strategic. She didn't know how to play games. "The coquette reasons coolly; Tatiana in dead earnest loves and unconditionally yields." I loved Tatiana, because she didn't hide what she felt, and I loved Pushkin for calling out the kind of people who conflated discretion and virtue. You still met people like that: people who acted as if admitting to any feelings of love, before you had gotten a man to buy you stuff, was a violation—not of pragmatism, or even of etiquette, but of morality. It meant you didn't have self-control, you couldn't delay gratification, you had failed the stupid marshmallow test. Ugh. I refused to believe that dissimulation was more virtuous than honesty. If there were rewards you got from lying, I didn't want them.

This was consonant with how women in my family talked about "our" shared character. In matters of love, we were too smart and honest to play games. We could only be happy with the kind of man who didn't need some huge charade. The men who needed a charade, though more numerous, weren't worth bothering with. Not only was it impossible for us to attract them, because we were constitutionally incapable, but they weren't worth attracting, they weren't capable of real love.

And yet, from an early age, I had seen women I was related to, like my aunts and my mother, prostrated by suffering because of men. "Prostrated by suffering" was the meaning I attached later to the Turkish phrases I half understood at the time: *kendini yerden yere attı*, or *başını taştan taşa vurdu*. A person "threw himself or herself [but let's face it, probably herself] from floor to floor," or "beat her head from one stone to another stone." The reason she behaved in this way was because a man had paid more attention to another woman—to the kind of woman who played games. And good riddance: clearly, the man had been intimidated by our intelligence and honesty.

The implication of "good riddance"—that love would switch off, like an electric light, once you realized the object of your love was dumb, or cowardly, or had bad taste—was not strictly borne out by observation. There were signs that it was, in fact, possible to suffer enormously over cowards with bad taste. But maybe such misfortunes only befell women of an earlier generation—women who were, as they themselves assured me, less fortunate and less smart than I was. It was a relief to find Pushkin corroborating what my relatives had always said: that it was better to be smart and honest than to play games.

On the whole, I thought, I had been right to write to Ivan. Just by typing some words on a computer, I had caused so many things to happen in the world—sleep to be lost, plane tickets to be bought, money to change hands. In a way, it had been a test of what a person could achieve just through writing. But there were also times when I worried that I had acted foolishly and without dignity. I thought of the ball near the beginning of *Anna Karenina*, when Kitty looked lovingly at Vronsky, who was already really into Anna: "and long afterwards, for several years after, that look, full of love, to which he made no response, cut her to the heart with an agony of shame." Kitty literally almost died of shame, and had to go to a German spa. Then she confided in Varenka, and Varenka said: "Why, what is there shameful? You didn't tell a man, who didn't care for you, that you loved him, did you?" And Kitty said of course not, she never *said* anything.

For some reason, what I thought of then was how my mother had told me that, at some point in the 1970s, my father had referred to *Anna Karenina* as a bourgeois novel about a fallen woman, and had expressed surprise that my mother should be interested in such a book. Was it possible that he had really said that? My parents sometimes remembered things differently from each other, and from me.

Once, when we were in middle school, my father had taken me and Leora to New York to see *Les Misérables*. In the car afterward, he had complained about the sentimentalization of motherhood—how motherhood, "mother love," was supposed to automatically make a character saintly, but in fact Fantine in *Les Misérables* was a prostitute and had dubious morality, and wasn't like Jean Valjean, who had stolen a loaf of bread to feed his family.

It had always been part of my identity to feel more objective than either of my parents—to be able to choose between their views, to retain the parts I found useful and discard the rest. On the one hand, I agreed that there was something annoying about the phrase "mother love," which felt related to the feeling I got when my mother talked about "her child." On the other hand, I recognized in my father's opinions about *Les Misérables* the kind of tendentious, impermeable, "prejudiced" discourse that a person had to ignore—the ignoring of which, indeed, was a cardinal skill of adult life. Wasn't the whole point of *Les Misérables*, and not a very subtle one, that Fantine being a prostitute wasn't that different from Jean Valjean stealing a loaf of bread to feed his family? And the way my father said "to feed his family" was at least as annoying as the way my mother said "my child."

On this, as on many issues, I concluded that, although neither of my parents was 100 percent right, I would, if pressed, agree more with my mother.

THE FOURTH WEEK

Over the weekend, Riley, Priya, Joanne, and I went shopping in Boston. At the Garment District, where they sold clothes for seventy-five cents a pound, I bought a burnt-orange corduroy shirt and a synthetic charmeuse wraparound skirt with huge purple flowers. We were shopping, it seemed, for "fabrics." I didn't totally get it: fabrics seemed like the one thing we had enough of. Nonetheless, at the textile store, I picked out a few yards of brown satin that seemed like it might work for making room dividers.

We spent the afternoon in Somerville chasing around a TV and VCR that a postdoc guy had said he would give to Priya. The level of coordination, the number of phone calls and changes of plan, made it feel more like a hostage negotiation than a voluntary exchange of property. It began to seem possible, then likely, that the VCR did not exist. It was a constant problem for Priya: men desperately, bald-facedly offering her things they didn't have. That was what it was to be beautiful.

Walking back from Somerville, we kept passing curbside piles of discarded household items. I pulled out a doormat that said I AM NOT YOUR DOORMAT.

"It's like it's capable of self-deception!" I enthused. Joanne asked in a kind voice if I wanted to take it home and have it be our doormat. I imagined seeing it every day, this protesting resentful doormat: we would crush its conception of itself, again and again, with our feet. I replaced the mat where I had found it, between a CD tower and part of a disassembled futon. A few blocks later, Riley found another doormat that had seven cats on it spelling WELCOME with their tails. It was clearly the correct doormat.

When we got back, one of Riley and Priya's premed friends, Lewis, was hanging around the entryway. I had been puzzled at first as to why this guy Lewis was always underfoot, but it turned out he was obsessed with Priya. He had told her that he wasn't sure whether most other guys would even find her attractive, but he couldn't get her out of his mind.

"What if he was the only guy who found me attractive?" Priya asked, her limpid eyes wide with horror.

Joanne left for a Singaporean club dinner. She asked me if I wanted to come, and I felt touched. But when the Singaporeans were all together, they started to speak Singlish and it took too much energy to try to follow the conversation.

I spent the next hour in Riley's and my bedroom, making a canopy above the top bunk by duct-taping the brown satin to the ceiling and then sticking thumbtacks in the duct tape. It came out really well. Now I could read in bed and feel like nobody was looking at me.

Back in the common room, Riley and Priya and Lewis had been joined by two other premed people: an approximately Lewis-like guy in a houndstooth pullover, and a girl who was as beautiful as Priya, though in a different way. Priya was sitting cross-legged on the floor, in frayed jeans and a scoop-neck jersey, her face framed adorably by flyaway hair; the other girl was perched on the edge of the futon, legs crossed, her white blouse and pencil skirt looking not just tailored but actually ironed. There was something familiar about her, though I couldn't put my finger on it.

Lewis was sitting right in the middle of the futon with his arms outstretched over the back, looking way more at home than I felt, even though I lived there. Most of his discourse consisted of alternately hostile or flattering remarks directed to or about Priya. Priya had made a bowl of Toll House cookie dough that everyone was passing around, digging in with cafeteria spoons. Only the girl with the ironed clothes declined to eat any cookie dough and, at the first pause in the conversation, immediately started talking about how she didn't know whether she was addicted to smoking. Everyone looked at her in puzzlement. She said that she smoked exactly one cigarette every day, alone, at sunset, on the roof of some particular building. "I don't know if I'm addicted, though," she said.

Riley told a story about her cousin who had quit smoking when his wife had a baby, and had gotten addicted to Nicorette, which was so expensive that he was always stashing wads of chewed-up Nicorette around the house for possible future use. It had all ended at the pediatric ER, when his two-year-old child had managed to stick its own testes together with about ten pieces of used Nicorette that it had pried off from the undersides of tables.

I told a story about how my dad had once worked in a lab at a VA hospital on the same floor with a guy who managed to get dogs addicted to cigarettes. There was a tracheostomy tube so the dogs *had* to inhale the smoke. At first the dogs hated smoking, but eventually they got addicted, and when the cigarettes were taken away, they howled, all day and all night. I didn't realize until I got to the end that it was a really depressing story. There was a pause.

"I don't know if I'm addicted, though," the girl said. She described her smoking ritual, minutely, though it was less that she imparted a lot of detail than that she used many words, identifying and re-identifying the details of time and place, as if they were inherently interesting and unique to her. She kept the cigarettes in a vintage cigarette case, in her underwear drawer. Lewis seemed to perk up when she mentioned underwear. It was while she was talking about what she did when it rained that I recognized her: she was Peter's friend, the one who had asked for Ivan's email address, and who had talked about the genius of Johannes Kepler.

I had mixed feelings about this beautiful nonsmoker. On the one hand, I despised her for talking so much and saying so little, and for seeming so unaware of Riley's expression. On the other hand, at least she was talking with enthusiasm about something that she liked to do, alone, just for the sake of having an experience, or thinking of herself a certain way.

She had returned now to the theme of not knowing whether she could call herself "a smoker." The point, she said, wasn't the cigarette itself, so much as . . . [the time of day, the cigarette case, the dresser].

I saw Priya look at Riley with stricken doelike eyes, and understood that Priya, too, was critical of the beautiful nonsmoker. I felt shocked, realizing that I had somehow grouped them together—because of their beauty, and because they seemed to inhabit a similar social persona: that of a magical fairy, inviting others to share in her bewilderment at her own mystery and specialness.

I had failed to draw a distinction between them that was evident, to Priya herself, as well as to Riley. It was true that, when Priya acted that way, she did it more subtly, with a greater awareness of other people's level of interest. Certainly Priya would never have droned on for so long. She would just drop a dreamy allusion to her love of steak tartare, or of neural networks, and it would float gracefully in the air for a moment before disappearing.

When I tuned back in to the conversation, I realized with an undertone of panic that that girl was still talking about how she smoked one cigarette every day. Why was this happening? Why were we all sitting here? She was reiterating how she had to be alone; how she had dealt in the past with the efforts of different people to join her. Then she returned, with sickening inevitability, to her inability to state whether or not she was addicted.

"Well," said Lewis, in his bantering tone, "the next time you go to the roof, do everything the same as usual, but don't light the cigarette. If you experience withdrawal, then you're addicted."

I stood up, more abruptly than I had intended. "I have to go," I blurted. Everyone looked at me, so I added: "I just remembered a book I have to read."

"Sometimes these things can't wait," Riley said in a reasonable tone that contrasted with my mode of being. We all laughed, and I was able to make my escape.

I hadn't really been planning to read a book, or had any plan at all, other than a vague idea of seeing what was playing at the film archive. The last screening was starting in two minutes, and it was a gender-transgressive docudrama about a prostitute in war-torn Belgrade who had a special way of bringing peace to the Balkans: "by acting as a kind of lightning rod for the erotic desires of violent men." Although I had some interest in war-torn Belgrade, I didn't want to show up alone, late, and out of breath, to a movie about violent sex.

I started walking in circles around the room, mechanically tidying my side, gathering together the scraps of fabric and tape, the receipts and plastic bags and flyers and pages of Russian homework. I found the used copy of *Nadja* I had just bought, and decided to go read it.

The street felt darker than usual. Every few yards, muffled music drifted out of dark or semi-dark windows. Small groups of people staggered by, the girls laughing hysterically and collapsing against the guys' chests. I knew that that was what a person was supposed to be doing, but I didn't know why, or how. I put on my Walkman. Listening to an all-Spanish album by Itzhak Perlman made me feel a shimmer of hope, as if life itself might be like those deadly violinistic showpieces: important, complex, to be performed with precision and flair.

The regular libraries closed early on Saturdays, so I headed to Mather, to use the house library. In the TV area, a bunch of guys were sitting tensely on a sofa, and then suddenly they all leaped to their feet and started pumping their fists and hooting.

"Yes! Yes! Yes!" one of them shouted.

I felt relieved when I got to the library: a soundless concrete cube, with a spiral staircase through the middle. There were only two other people there: one was listening to headphones with his eyes closed; the other twirled a pen between his fingers in an elaborate way while glaring into a giant textbook. Both were Asian. I felt a wave of kinship and admiration toward them, because of how they had opted out of what everyone else thought was cool.

The first line of *Nadja*—"Who am I?"—was just like I remembered it. The next pages were still unreadably boring. But this time, I kept going. If there was anything in there that could change my life, I wasn't going to let a few boring pages stand in my way.

On page 17, I felt a thrill of excitement at the mention of J. K. Huysmans: the author of *Against Nature*, the book from which I had learned about "living aesthetically." When you were trying to solve a mystery, and you came across a name you had encountered earlier in your investigation, it was a sign that you were on the right trail.

André Breton praised J. K. Huysmans for being different from the kind of conventional novelists—"those empiricists of the novel," he called them—who wasted their time trying to transform real people into fictional characters. I felt nonplussed. Wasn't that what a novelist's job *was*: transforming real people into fictional characters? But Breton seemed to actually be angry about it.

> Someone suggested to an author I know, in connection with a work of his . . . whose heroine might be too readily recognized, that he change at least the color of her hair. As a blonde, apparently, she might have avoided betraying a brunette. I do not regard such a thing as childish, I regard it as monstrous.

In these words, I caught a glimmer of some possibility of freedom. I realized that my inability to do what he was talking about—to disguise the people I knew and turn them into fictional "characters"—had been the biggest problem I had in writing, and thus in my plan of life. In some way it was a bigger problem than Ivan—or maybe Ivan was a part of that problem, which had predated him by many years.

I had wanted to become a novelist before I even knew how to read, back when I could only consume books by having them read to me, and none of them seemed long enough. They left too many questions unanswered, too many ramifications unexplored. My parents told me that I was expecting too much from *Frog and Toad Are Friends*: it wasn't a novel. In that way, I understood that a novel would explain all the things I still wanted to know, like why Toad was the way he was— why Toad was essentially unwell, and why Frog helped Toad, whether he really wanted Toad to get better, or whether he benefited in some way from Toad's unwellness.

I understood that novels, unlike children's books, were serious and important and that, just as my parents' job was to treat patients in a hospital, so, too, was it someone's job to write novels. Every civilized country had such people. They were in some way the very mark of civilization.

Once I learned how to write, I did it all the time, filling up one notebook after another, recording different things that people said, or that I had read in books. Adults would ask if I was writing a novel. I assumed that I was: that what I was writing was already somehow a novel, or that this kind of writing would someday naturally segue into novel-writing.

It wasn't until high school, when I took my first creative writing class, that I began to sense trouble. I realized, with shock, that I wasn't good at creative writing. I was good at grammar and arguing, at remembering things people said, and at making stressful situations seem funny. But it turned out these weren't the skills you needed in order to invent quirky people and give them arcs of desire. I already had my hands full writing about the people I actually knew, and all the things they said. That was what I needed writing *for*. Now I had to invent extra people and think of things for them to say?

It turned out that writing what you were already thinking about wasn't creative, or even writing. It was "navel-gazing." To be obsessed by your own life experience was childish, egotistical, unartistic, and worthy of contempt. I tried to get around the problem by ascribing my own thoughts and observations to a fictional character—one with a neutral, universal name, because I didn't want to seem like I was constantly harping on being Turkish. I didn't like books where the whole point seemed to be that the person was from some country, and they kept going on about the food. And yet, the things I was writing about somehow didn't make sense unless the people were from another country, and I didn't know enough about any other countries besides Turkey.

There was a creative writing workbook, with exercises. You had to fill out questionnaires about "your" characters, with their favorite food or color. I felt despair: what kind of person had a favorite color? Then I thought, OK: that was why you needed your imagination, to think of someone different from yourself. The words, "tacos, beige," written on a piece of looseleaf paper made me feel the foreclosing of every possibility of anything exciting ever happening to me in the rest of my life.

Nearly every exercise mentioned a diner in some capacity, as did many of the stories we read. Clearly there was a connection between creative writing and diners. It felt fortuitous, because I thought a lot about diners. That was when I was living with my paternal aunt, who actually worked in a diner, illegally. The diner was owned by a guy from Adana who hired only Turkish people without work permits. It seemed at first like he was doing them a favor, but then this became less clear. One of the line cooks, for example, got a kidney stone, which everyone said was the most painful thing in the world next to childbirth. (What if people said boys had to have two kidney stones by the time they were thirty—as the man my aunt eventually married, enabling her to leave the diner, had often told me about childbirth?) The diner owner paid for the cook's surgery and then, once he had him in his debt, tortured him in inventive ways, for example by making him prepare tripe soup. Tripe soup had a distinctive smell that made some people really sick, and the line cook was one of those people.

I recognized in this situation something narrative-rich, larger than me, appropriate for creative writing. But once I started trying to turn it into "short fiction," I felt rude, even traitorous. I had only met the diner owner a few times, and he had never done anything to me personally, and my aunt said sometimes that he wasn't so bad. He often sent her home with free chicken cacciatore, and I ate it, too.

Furthermore, I knew that the kidney stone and the tripe soup weren't, in themselves, a story; I couldn't just copy them down and call it creative writing. I had to identify the universal human situation they represented, and develop it, using my imagination. Probably the cook would have to take action: somehow break free, or cause some problem to the diner owner. And yet I had *seen* that cook, Serdar. He was so clearly the kind of person who, despite complaining constantly, was basically respectful and ineffective. The only decisive thing I had ever heard of him doing was punching a wall when he found out that his mom in Adana had cancer, and everyone else had known but had been hiding it from him, so he wouldn't go crazy. So, when he found out, he had to go crazy. He ended up in the emergency room with a broken hand. My dad had paid for it, because by then my whole family felt sorry for him.

I tried making Serdar the narrator, but it still seemed like I was patronizing him. I tried being the narrator myself, and saying I also worked at the diner. But it was too much the essence of who I was that I had never been made or allowed to work in a diner. I thought about asking my aunt for more details, but I felt too embarrassed. The diner represented just the kind of life problem that I was protected from and she was not.

The creative writing class ended, and theoretically I never had to read or write about diners again. But the seed of panic had been planted. My eyes had been opened to the dissimilarity between the kind of writing I was always doing, and an actual novel.

That was when the movie of *The Remains of the Day* came out, and my father bought all three of Kazuo Ishiguro's novels, and I read them, too. How compact, self-contained, and mysterious they were; how little they disclosed of *him*, whoever he was, an English-language writer with the name "Kazuo Ishiguro." How compassionate and imaginative of him to write novels about either super-English-sounding people living in a country house in England in the 1930s (who could not have been named Kazuo Ishiguro), or super-Japanese-sounding printmakers in Osaka in the 1940s (who could not have written a novel in English). Ishiguro wrote first-person, but the narrator was always "unreliable," i.e., crazy or ignorant, and different from the author. What discipline—what lack of pride! All I was ever trying to do when I wrote, I realized, was to show how much I saw and understood.

All my feelings of dauntedness were summed up by a quote on the cover of *An Artist of the Floating World*:

> Good writers abound—good novelists are very rare. Kazuo Ishiguro is . . . not only a good writer, but also a wonderful novelist.
>
> —THE NEW YORK TIMES BOOK REVIEW

It was what I had been counting on, in order to get out: my sense of being a good writer. My stomach sank with the knowledge of how wrong I had been.

———

The whole time everything had been happening with Ivan, I had always been writing about it in my notebook, or on the computer, and sometimes I wondered whether I would ever turn those pages into a novel. The thought made me feel ashamed. It felt shameful to be so unartistic and self-obsessed, to not want to invent richly fictional characters. It felt shameful to write a whole book about Ivan. What if he found out?

For some reason, I found myself remembering how my mother and I used to laugh about *Mommie Dearest*, a book written by Joan

Crawford's daughter, which neither of us had read, but which my mother often invoked, saying "Mommie Dearest" in a high-pitched voice, whenever she made me do anything.

Then I remembered another joke my mother used to make, when she did anything she thought was wrong, like telling a white lie over the phone, or unbuckling her seat belt while driving: "Don't put this in your novel." That, too, had always made me laugh, though there was an underlying assumption that was somehow troubling: that the disorder you experienced in your childhood was somehow to your credit, or capitalizable upon in later life—even though, or precisely because, it was a discredit to your mother. So your credit and your mother's credit were somehow at odds.

But why was I thinking about my mother now, when the subject was Ivan? Ugh: "Ivan." Telling anyone his name always felt like a betrayal—like I was *causing* the way they pronounced it, either incorrectly or with elaborate and ironic correctness, as if to imply that he was pretentious because he didn't say "Eye-van," the way literally nobody in the world except American people did. "When I like people immensely I never tell their names to anyone": I read that line in *The Picture of Dorian Gray*, and felt the sickening lurch of dishonor.

And yet—here was André Breton, saying just the opposite: "I insist on knowing the names, on being interested only in books left ajar, like doors; I will not go looking for keys." All the work-arounds I thought I had invented—turning two real people into one "fictional" "character," turning one real person into two characters, changing people's appearances and nationalities—he already knew about, and viewed as base tricks. He seemed proud of *not* changing anything, including himself.

Was that something it was OK to feel self-righteous about? Was it possible that the kind of book he was describing could somehow be better than the novels I already knew about—better than "psychological literature, with all its fictitious plots"? More pressingly: Was there a way that I could become a novelist, after all? Was it related to Huysmans and to the aesthetic life? What if I could use the aesthetic life as an algorithm to solve my two biggest problems: how to live, *and* how to write novels? In any real-life situation, I would pretend I was in a novel, and then do whatever I would want the person in the novel to do. Afterward, I would write it all down, and I would have written a novel, without having had to invent a bunch of fake characters and pretend to care about them.

Around page 20, Breton abruptly dropped the life-or-death subject of real people and novels, and launched, for some reason, into a minute description of some coincidences he and his friends had experienced. Why were other people's coincidences always so boring? Nadja herself didn't show up until page 64. "Suddenly, perhaps still ten feet away, I saw a young, poorly dressed woman walking toward me. . . ." I felt a thrill of recognition. So, being poorly dressed wasn't necessarily opposed to an aesthetic life, but could be consonant with it.

Once Nadja came in, there was something on almost every page that seemed like a clue. For example: Nadja got sick and couldn't afford a doctor, and she decided to cure herself through manual labor, by getting "a job in a bakery, and even in a pork-butcher's." This was clearly related to a story Ivan had told me multiple times, about his high school friend, whose Slovenian girlfriend moved to Budapest and ended up having to work at a meatpacking plant. Ivan had always spoken of the Slovenian girlfriend in a laughing and admiring tone. I had never understood why. I had been alone with this mystery. Finally, here was another data point, because clearly André Breton also thought it was somehow funny or admirable that Nadja worked at a pork-butcher's.

I started keeping a running record in my notebook of everything in *Nadja* that seemed related to any of my problems. Soon, all I wanted to be doing was to be working on this list. The rows of page numbers and quotes looked a little bit like *Pale Fire*: a novel where the first half was a poem, and the second half was an autobiographical commentary by the poet's mentally ill next-door neighbor. I wished I could write a book like that about *Nadja*, where I could explain each line, and how it applied in such a specific way to things that had happened in my life. I knew that nobody would want to read such a book; people would die of boredom. Why was it that science and history could be boring, but other books couldn't? When was the last time I had been so struck by anything in my "real" life as I was by the offhand disclosure that André Breton was married? Or by the even more offhand disclosure that Nadja had a *daughter*: "a child of whose existence she has informed me with so many precautions and whom she adores"? I read that line over and over; it changed everything. How old was the daughter, where, with whom? Why was Nadja wandering around Paris alone? I thought of my own mother, who adored me, and who had also fallen in love with a man who had eventually married someone else. Why did that happen to people? Was anyone even studying this stuff? Was anyone doing anything to fix it?

The Slavic department had a different atmosphere at night: like an airport, or like the past. A film projector had been set up for the bard's memorial service. A professor gave a speech thanking the language instructors for all their hard work, making it sound somehow pathetic. Like most of the literature professors, he was American. The language instructors were all from the former Soviet Union, and didn't have tenure, and weren't called "professor."

I recited Tatiana's letter too fast, but otherwise it went OK. A girl I didn't know read the same text but got stuck after four lines. I wondered if she was in love, and whether the guy was an idiot.

Five people in a row recited the stanza about Onegin's uncle. It was boring to hear the same thing over and over, until it was Svetlana's turn. How did she seem so much more alive than everyone else? Pushkin's jokes became funny again when she said them.

When Svetlana sat back down next to me, Matt, from the third-year class, sat in the empty seat on her other side, clapped her on the shoulder, and leaned over and said something to her, and her face turned pink.

We watched some black-and-white footage of the bard singing a song about Pushkin, whom he called "Alexander Sergeyevich," fitting the many syllables onto four or five notes, in a somehow poignant way. The song was called "All the Same, It's Sad," and was about how, notwithstanding the benefits that had accrued to humanity in the years since Pushkin's death, it was sad that we could no longer hang out with Alexander Sergeyevich. By the end, half the people in the room were crying. The saddest line was: "not even for a quarter of an hour."

There was a reception afterward, and Svetlana immediately took a glass of wine and started speaking Russian with the teachers and grad students. But I left early and went to the library to finish reading *Nadja*.

Nadja had money troubles. She was "resisting the threats of her landlord and his dreadful suggestions," and made "no secret of the means she would employ to obtain money for herself." Breton seemed to think she should have been making it a secret.

Well, at least that was one thing that had improved over the past seventy years. Girls weren't constantly being forced to become prostitutes. Prostitutes, of course, still existed, but some people liked being prostitutes and thought it was empowering, and it was un-feminist to think they were victims.

Were any people still forced to become prostitutes? When I thought about it, it seemed obvious that they were. Surely, though, it was less common than in the past. Literally every single old novel had someone in it who was forced to become a prostitute, whereas I had never heard of that happening to anyone I knew. I did know one girl who had posed for a "Women of the Ivy League" spread in *Playboy*. But modeling for *Playboy* to pay for Harvard was not the same as having sex with your landlord to not get evicted.

At some point, André Breton started to find Nadja annoying. It was hard to tell what exactly Nadja had done wrong. Had she complained too much about having to become a prostitute? Had she made too many puns? It was as if it had suddenly just already happened. "For some time, I had stopped understanding Nadja. Actually, perhaps we have never understood one another. . . ."

Ivan had said things like that: "maybe we never really understood each other, maybe we never had a real conversation." I thought this was absurd. But his viewpoint invalidated mine. If one person thought it was a conversation, and the other person thought it wasn't a conversation, the second person was right.

"I am judging a posteriori, and I merely speculate when I say it could not be otherwise," Breton wrote. That was what Ivan was doing: judging a posteriori, acting as if everything between us had run some inevitable course. How unjust it was, when people treated the actual as limiting proof of the possible! I felt that this was what I was fighting against, and always had been: the tyranny of the particular, arbitrary way that things happened to have turned out.

93

I hadn't expected *Nadja* to end well, but it still came as a shock when she went crazy and was committed to an insane asylum. Breton mentioned it in his usual offhand way ("I was told, several months ago, that Nadja was mad. . . ."), then launched into a mordant social critique of mental institutions, of how badly they treated poor people. He said it was because he hated psychiatry so much that he had never visited or inquired after Nadja. The book went on another twenty-five pages, and didn't mention Nadja at all. Then it ended. So did she get out? How was that not something people mentioned, when they said what the book was about?

I turned my copy over to reread the back cover: always a creepy experience once you had finished a book, like getting a message from a dead person. "*Nadja*, originally published in France in 1928, is the first and perhaps best Surrealist romance ever written," it said.

> The Nadja of the book is a girl, but, like Bertrand Russell's definition of electricity as "not so much a thing as a way things happen," Nadja is not so much a person as a way she makes people behave.

Just imagine being told that you weren't a person, but a way you made other people behave. "Well, I can't say I think much of the effect I'm having on *you*," I would say.

"That's what can happen when you fetishize an aesthetic life. It can make you irresponsible and destructive," Svetlana said later, about André Breton. "But people like that can invent a new style, and I can appreciate that."

"What should he have done when he met Nadja?" I asked. "If he wasn't being irresponsible and destructive."

She thought it over. "He could have tried to be a force of stability in her life, and avoided getting romantically involved with her."

I felt a pang. I hadn't wanted Ivan to be a force of stability in my life.

A recurring question in the ethics seminar was how to avoid ending up at something called the Repugnant Conclusion. The Repugnant Conclusion said that it was possible to justify decreasing a population's quality of life, if you made the population bigger. It was really hard not to get there. Even if you said something inoffensive-sounding, like, "I think we should do the most good for the most people," that meant that, if there were a million people whose lives were "well worth living," and you had the opportunity to transform them into a billion people whose lives were "barely worth living," you would be morally obligated to do it. There you were at the Repugnant Conclusion. The phrase "barely worth living" made a knot form in my stomach. In what country was it happening?

André Breton was both less smart and less kind than the ethics professor. Yet, what he was talking about felt more to the point. He wasn't coming up with rules for situations with implications we couldn't think of; he was interpreting things that had really happened. The really-happenedness was advertised on every page, with photographs. The fact that Breton had left his own shitty behavior in the story was, in a way, more proof of realness.

Nadja had the validity of constituting at least a tiny part of the way of the world. Part of the way of the world was that women had a tendency to go crazy. Men could bring out this tendency. But to blame the men was to take sides, to lose logic, to enter the craziness of the women—because the very content of the women's craziness was, in large part, the blameworthiness of the men.

In Russian conversation class, Irina Nikolaevna spoke so quickly, using so many unknown words, that I rarely had any idea what she was saying. But sometimes something shone like a gold ring at the bottom of the stream, and a sentence came to me with perfect clarity. Like this one: "Everything you want right now, everything you want so passionately and think you'll never get—you will get it someday." I accidentally met her eyes, and it felt like she was talking to me. "Yes, you will get it," she said, looking right at me, "but by that time, you won't want it anymore. That's how it happens."

My mind went into overdrive. Was she talking about Ivan? How much did she know? Ivan and I had both been in her class last year. Had she seen something between us? Had he *told* her something? I knew that he was fond of her—we both were, we had talked about it. Were they somehow in contact? Was that the kind of thing that happened? What was the kind of thing that happened? How was she so sure that she knew what it was—the kind of thing that happened? "You won't want it anymore": was it because Tatiana rejected Eugene Onegin at the end of *Eugene Onegin*? Was it possible that all Russian people were constantly thinking about *Eugene Onegin*?

Irina Nikolaevna couldn't possibly know what I wanted. And I would never not want it.

PART TWO

The Rest of the Fall Semester

OCTOBER

It was the golden time of year. Every day the leaves grew brighter, the air sharper, the grass more brilliant. The sunsets seemed to expand and melt and stretch for hours, and the brick façades glowed pink, and everything blue got bluer. How many perfect autumns did a person get? Why did I seem always to be in the wrong place, listening to the wrong music?

For Russian, we read a short story called "Rudolfio." It was about a sixteen-year-old girl named Io, who was in love with a twenty-eight-year-old married man. Io, who was whimsical, maintained that, when she and this man, Rudolf, were together, they formed a single entity: "Rudolfio." Rudolf laughed and said that Io was funny. Io talked a lot about "adults": how they only paid attention to each other, treating non-adults as subhuman. Rudolf loaned Io a copy of *The Little Prince* that he, a grown man, had for some reason.

One day, when Rudolf's wife was out, Io showed up at his house.

Her breasts resembled "little nests built by unknown birds to hatch their nestlings." Io asked Rudolf why he had gotten married so young, preventing them, Rudolfio, from getting married. Rudolf laughed. She was funny! Later, he felt "full of some kind of inexpressible, still not revealed melancholy, that was nonetheless existent in nature."

Rudolf went on a work trip without telling Io. When he got back, Rudolf wondered whether he felt *too* happy to see her.

"Did you go away and then come back?" Io asked. In Russian, that was one word. The verbs of motion were by far the worst part of learning Russian.

Io and Rudolf took a walk in a vacant lot full of garbage. Io asked Rudolf to kiss her. Rudolf kissed her on the cheek. "On the lips," Io said. But Rudolf replied: "Only the closest people kiss on the lips." Io slapped him in the face and ran away, through the garbage.

Io didn't come home that night. Her mother panicked and called Rudolf. Rudolf didn't know anything. Io turned up the next afternoon, and refused to speak. Rudolf went over. He found her sitting on her bed, facing the wall, mutely rocking back and forth. He said she had to tell him at least where she had been all night.

"Go to hell," Io said.

Rudolf nodded. Then he picked up his raincoat, turned around, and went to hell.

Up to then, I hadn't been impressed by the quality of the writing, but that ending blew me away. *He turned around, picked up his raincoat, and went to hell.*

In class, Irina Nikolaevna asked us whether Rudolf had loved Io. Everyone basically agreed that he hadn't.

"Maybe he loved her a little bit," said Julia.

"He didn't love her," said Gavriil, with certainty. "He was playing games."

"Did Rudolf love his wife?" Irina Nikolaevna asked.

Gavriil said yes. Julia said maybe. Svetlana said that Rudolf was a very conventional person who was attached to the institution of marriage but hadn't given it substantial thought. "Under such circumstances," she said, "speaking of love might not be to the point."

We learned the Russian verbs for "to marry," which were different for men and for women. A man "got wived *on* someone" (prepositional case), while a woman "went out husbanded *after* someone" (accusative case). Irina Nikolaevna illustrated the difference with stick-figures. Everyone laughed at the man *on* the woman.

We discussed the kissing scene in "Rudolfio"—how Io had been *hurt*, how Rudolf had *hurt* her. We discussed the difference between kissing on the cheek (prepositional singular) and on the lips (prepositional plural). Irina Nikolaevna asked each of us to describe the first time we kissed anyone on the lips.

Julia said she had kissed a boy in a playground when she was nine. Gavriil said he had kissed his girlfriend at a school dance when he was eleven. Svetlana said she had kissed her cousin's boyfriend in the zoo in Belgrade when she was thirteen.

I said, untruthfully, that I had kissed a boy at summer camp when I was fifteen.

"Fifteen, Sonya? Are you sure?" Irina Nikolaevna wrote "15" on the board. It turned out she thought I had to have been younger.

"Fifteen," I said firmly.

Irina Nikolaevna asked what the boy had been like. I said he played the mandolin, inviting follow-up questions about how and where he had played the mandolin.

"He played the mandolin everywhere—incessantly," I said.

"The Slavic department is so weird," Svetlana said, in the bathroom. "I'm feeling so much anxiety right now. I don't think when you learn other languages, you have to talk about your sexual history. It's funny because back when I was thirteen, I felt so bad about kissing my cousin's boyfriend. But it really came in handy today, because if it wasn't for that, I would never have kissed anyone. I was wondering what I would have said if I *hadn't* kissed anyone. Then I suddenly felt really worried about you! I know you never had a boyfriend either, and I didn't remember you mentioning kissing anyone. I actually almost turned around and told you, 'Selin, for once in your life, just don't tell the truth, OK?' But then you had mandolin boy up your sleeve! I was so relieved!"

"Mandolin boy saved the day," I agreed, looking in the mirror at the dark circles under my eyes. My hair resembled the nest of an unknown bird prepared to hatch its nestlings.

What had happened to Io, the night when she was away from home? Was it supposed to be understood that she had been raped? It felt like that was often what was supposed to be understood in short stories.

———

In the Chance class, we read an interview with John Cage where he said that the most profound music to him now was the honking of cars on Sixth Avenue. This was because he no longer "needed" the structure and overbearingness of "what we call music." "If something is boring after two minutes," Cage wrote, "try it for four . . . then eight. Then sixteen. Then thirty-two." I sighed. Only someone who was already old and famous could say something like that—that some randomly occurring garbage was the greatest art form. *I* couldn't go around being like, "Here's the sounds of Sixth Avenue. Oh, it doesn't sound interesting to you? Try it for thirty-two minutes." Nor did I want to.

Baudelaire said that walking in a crowd was an art that only poets were capable of. A fairy had to have bestowed something to him in the cradle. That's why he was able to enter freely into each man's personality. "For him alone everything is vacant."

If any poet tried to enter *my* personality like a vacant building . . . !

I asked the *I Ching* if I should drop the Chance class. I got Hexagram 6: "A cautious halt halfway brings good fortune. Going through to the end brings misfortune."

Svetlana bought the new R.E.M. album, *New Adventures in Hi-Fi*, and we listened to the whole thing in her room. How amazing it was when people who sounded so distinctive did something new. What would it be like to *be* them—to know why they were R.E.M.? One song had the line "I'd sooner chew my leg off": a subjective statement that nonetheless struck me as so cosmically true that I couldn't believe I had heard it correctly.

Svetlana had spent the evening in Scott's room, doing some wilderness-related paperwork. They listened to folk music, sipping chardonnay, and toasting their non-sexual love for one another. Scott, I learned, had to make parts of himself die in order to be in his relationship, because Jenna didn't appreciate "his music and his spirituality." What Svetlana felt for Scott, she said, wasn't a crush, but love. "A crush is about building up the self, and love is about giving from the self. For love, you have to have a self you're secure with, to give to the other person." I silently absorbed the implication that what I felt for Ivan was only a crush, because I didn't have a self I was secure with.

A poem in *Real Change* titled, incredibly, "And to think, she'd never been kissed." Was I losing my mind?

> Innocence tempted with the chance
> To feel the pleasures of the flesh
> Childhood stolen at twenty-three
> The minute his tongue met her breast

Childhood stolen at . . . twenty-three? How long had that person planned to, like, treasure her childhood? Yet I filed away the mention, as I always did, of any person who had been older than nineteen when they first kissed someone. Once, I had heard a writer on NPR say that he hadn't kissed anyone until he was twenty-five. But he had been gay and born in the 1940s.

The rest of the poem was about how regrets came later, but for now there was just "pleasure, pain, supposed love, / And just being in his arms."

What were the regrets that came later? Was it that she had thought he loved her, and then it turned out he didn't? It couldn't be that, again—could it? Was that what everything was about?

Juho invited me to High Table, which was the name of the weekly dinner for his fellowship, but was also the name of the table itself: several tables, actually, lined up end-to-end, on an elevated platform. People dressed as waiters were pouring wine. Some of the professors and tutors wore black robes. I couldn't believe stuff like this still went on, and in America: people in black robes sitting at a table that was like eight inches higher than the rest of the room, calling it "High Table."

I realized that I had based my idea of the other fellows in the society on Juho himself, assuming that they would in some way resemble him. This was not the case. He was clearly the youngest, by several years. His green jogging suit was unlike anything anyone else was wearing. One black-robed tutor, addressing him as "Yoo-hoo," asked in a forced, jovial tone, when Juho had last shaved. Juho said that he couldn't be certain but he thought it had been a Tuesday.

It was in some way to defend Juho that I made a special effort to talk to the other fellows, to ask about their projects—to prove that Juho and I inhabited the world as fully, and spoke about it as fluently, as anyone else there, and were just as entitled to an accounting of other people's activities.

The woman across from me said that she was trying to use a computer model of an extinct flute to reconstruct the music that had played during tragedies in Ancient Greece. "Tragic verse and music were inseparable for the Greeks, but today we have no idea what the music sounded like," she said, speaking with a British accent.

"What do *you* think it sounded like?" I was conscious of speaking in almost a flirtatious way, like Ivan would have. She had to be at least ten years older than me, but there was a hint of a smile or a spark in her eye that I sensed—or sensed that Ivan would have sensed—as some kind of potential.

"I think it sounded *terrifying*," she said.

I wanted to talk to her more, to find out more about her, but the guy next to her kept interrupting with a point he was trying to make about the area that a cow would graze if it was tied to a "movable fence."

I sawed at a piece of grilled asparagus. Didn't the very essence of a fence reside in the fact that it was stationary?

Riley had been to the SPCA, in an effort to procure a cat. Popular opinion held that a cat could be more easily concealed in overflow housing than in a regular dorm. I had never had a cat, didn't understand the point of cats, and had had a negative childhood experience with a dog. I was 60 percent sure that dog had ended up euthanized. Furthermore, I already had a troubling sense of being surrounded at all times by foreign intelligences. For these reasons, I felt no need to add any more sentient beings to our household. But Priya, Joanne, and especially Riley loved cats, and their love was more powerful than my indifference.

As it turned out, the SPCA wouldn't give you a cat unless you had a signed form from your landlord, stating that pets were allowed in your building. That was a problem, because pets *weren't* allowed in our building. Riley had a plan to get the form signed by one of the resident tutors, who she thought had a secret cat. The plan somehow backfired. After that, the tutor no longer returned our greetings in the hallway.

The radio in the Quincy kitchen was playing the new Alanis Morissette single, "Head over Feet." It was about having the maturity to want something good for you. I felt outraged. I had thought Alanis Morissette was there to remind us.

Now she was marveling at how "healthy" she felt, now that she had the ability to "want something rational." It was clear that the rational thing she wanted was some boring guy.

"You mean heels." I didn't realize I had said it out loud until Svetlana patted my arm.

"There, there," she said soothingly.

"'Head over feet' is, like, the customary way people are. It's the way of bipedalism."

"Well, Selin, I think that the problem-free grasp of idiomatic language isn't what we go to Alanis Morissette for."

We usually ate lunch in one of the meeting rooms off of the main dining hall—the smallest one, which was often empty. One wall was completely covered by a Mercator map of the world. Everything in the Arctic Circle was hugely magnified and prominent, like someone's giant grotesque forehead. The effect was especially pronounced on Franz Josef Land and Severnaya Zemlya.

We put down our trays and immediately started debating which poet we liked better: Anna Akhmatova or Marina Tsvetaeva. They were the most famous Russian women poets. Svetlana said she liked Tsvetaeva: objectively the cooler choice. I felt more similar to Akhmatova, so I defended her, but I wasn't happy about it.

Scott had invited Svetlana to a Halloween party and she couldn't decide what to go as. Sometimes, in the course of normal life, she wore her hair in two braids, and it made her look really different in a cute way, so that was a possible avenue. Svetlana said she was worried about infantilizing herself.

I tried to think of a competent, iconic person who had two braids. "Maybe like a Valkyrie with a Viking hat? From the opera?"

"I don't know . . . that might make me feel fat," Svetlana said, composing a forkful of cottage cheese and raw broccoli. One month into her diet, her face already seemed longer and more sculpted, her eyes more glittery.

The longer we talked about it, the more the Halloween costume seemed like a trap. If she went as anything that could be construed as sexy, Scott might tease her. But if she deliberately desexualized herself, that was also a kind of abasement.

Anna Akhmatova had a nose similar to mine. Her name was a pen name; she believed her great-grandmother was a descendant of a fifteenth-century khan named Akhmat. She became famous from writing a poem about pulling the left-hand glove onto her right hand. She wrote about partings and last words. One poem was called "Today

No Letter Was Delivered to Me." Sometimes she wrote about "him" or "my husband." Her real-life husband, also a famous poet, tried to kill himself. They suffered and got a divorce. Later, he was executed. Their son was arrested. Akhmatova joined the mass of mothers and wives waiting outside the prison gates, and wrote "Requiem": a political poem that circulated in samizdat and was considered to be a stark departure from her love lyrics. It, too, was full of stylized womanly suffering. At the end, she compared herself to Mary at the Crucifixion: "where the Mother stood in silence / nobody even dared look." Anything about suffering mothers gave me an oppressed feeling.

"How many times a day do you and Selin see each other?" Riley asked, the third time Svetlana and I ran into her on our way to and from each other's rooms.

"Do you think it's weird that we spend so much time together?" Svetlana asked me afterward. "It's almost like we're in a relationship."

"Hm . . ." I said, stalling. *Weren't* we in a relationship?

"This is how much time I would expect to spend with a boyfriend," Svetlana clarified.

"Oh, right," I said.

Valerie's older brother, who had just finished a math Ph.D. and now worked for the CIA, was coming to visit. Svetlana said she was going to figure out from him what the deal was with Ivan.

"What? No, don't do that," I said.

"Selin, we need to find out the truth. And you know all the math people know each other."

"He won't know anything useful, and if he did he wouldn't tell you. He'll just tell Ivan we're investigating him."

"Don't worry, I'll be very subtle."

"No, just don't."

We were headed to the language lab to watch a movie called *Moscow Does Not Believe in Tears*. Riley had thought the title was a joke, but it was really called that. It was about two girls who lived in a dormitory: a spunky blonde who was always thinking up schemes to catch rich husbands, and a tragic brunette who worked in a factory and wanted to become an engineer. The movie followed them for twenty years.

At some point the brunette, now in her forties, successful but alone, was on the metro, dressed in the crappy clothes she had worn to help someone renovate their dacha. A mechanic on the metro mistook her for a factory worker, and fell in love with her. Then, all her problems were over—until the mechanic found out she was actually an engineer. Then he got angry, ostensibly because she had deceived him, but really because he thought that men had to earn more than women. She looked at him, with her face full of different expressions, and instead of explaining all the reasons she was right, simply said: "Forgive me."

There was something so exciting about how submissively she said it—how different it was from if she had protested and reasoned. And it worked: he forgave her, in a way that was somehow intensely sexual, even though she was an attractive woman, and he looked like a pedantic thuggish elf. I was filled with the desire to say that to Ivan, and for him to forgive me.

———

Daylight Savings ended. Crossing the Quincy quad one afternoon, I made out what looked like four big light-colored stones. Then two of them stood up, trailing white tassels, and turned out to be Svetlana's blockmates, Danny and Josh.

"Hey, Selin! Were you planning on going into the building?" Josh asked in a weird, casual tone. I felt all four of the guys looking at me.

How could they all have gotten locked out at once? Then I saw that Josh was actually holding his ID card toward me, and I remembered it was Friday and they didn't use electricity.

"Oh, definitely," I said, swiping his card. The light turned green and I held open the door. For about the hundredth time, I felt impressed by how many different rules there were that a person could follow. This particular rule seemed pretty pointless, but maybe those guys knew something I didn't. They were talking cheerfully enough among themselves in the hallway, and the one whose name I didn't know called over his shoulder, "Thanks, Selin!"

Riley was sitting at the table in the common room putting on Chanel Vamp nail polish. Priya was doing a shoulder stand on the floor, while reading aloud from an expensive junior's clothing catalog that had been mailed to her by mistake. It was full of pictures of thirteen-year-old models posing sassily in three-hundred-dollar jumpers with daisies on the pockets. Priya was making fun of it, but it became clear that she was also planning to order a shirt.

Riley asked me to help her put the nail polish on her right hand. I felt pleased, because she so rarely asked for any kind of assistance. And right after I got to help some religious people open a door!

"It's hard to not get it in the crevasse," Riley said, about the place where the side of the nail met the finger. I had never heard the word "crevasse" used in that way.

"Moscow does not believe in tears," I told her, but I folded up a napkin and managed to get the nail polish out of the crevasse.

I told Riley and Priya about how Svetlana's blockmates had been sitting outside in the dark because they couldn't use a card reader after sundown. Priya said that once, in the Science Center, a random guy she had never seen before had yelled at her for not knowing that she was the one who had to call the elevator.

"Was that a Friday, though? I think that guy was just an asshole."

"That *is* another one of the world's major religions."

I said it didn't seem logical that a person should be prohibited from telling an elevator to come, but allowed to tell someone else to tell an elevator to come.

"It's not an argument you want to get into—believe me," Riley said. "All they do in high school is debate this stuff. They'll cream you." Apparently, Morris had asked an observant guy in their math section why he felt OK with sitting in a room with the lights on but not with turning on the lights himself. Over the next twenty minutes, the guy had proceeded to logically dismantle everything Morris said and thought and believed. Morris hadn't known what had hit him. "I mean, I did Model UN," he kept saying afterward. I couldn't help thinking it was wasteful for people with such good logic skills to spend so many years and so much energy learning to reconcile an old book with the way things were now. Couldn't a person just write a new book?

Joanne had just biked fifty miles to Lowell, Massachusetts, and back.

"Is there anything special in Lowell?" Riley asked.

Joanne looked thoughtful. "There probably is," she said, hanging her bike on its special rack.

Riley had given up on the SPCA and joined a Usenet group. I wasn't sure what that was, but it seemed to have connected her to the kind of people who often had a cat or two to unload, and weren't too picky about paperwork. Take this one guy, who crossbred domestic cats with servals. The servals had to be fed "whole live prey," so that was a no, but just as an example. Riley was explaining to me about the servals at lunch when our friend Jeremy asked if he could sit with us.

"We're about to leave," Riley said, though we had barely sat down. Jeremy pulled up a chair anyway, and started enthusing about *Gravity's Rainbow*.

Riley pushed back her chair. "I have lab," she said. "Selin, don't you have a Russian thing?"

I had just taken an enormous bite of peanut-butter sandwich. I wasn't like Riley, who always seemed able to leave a meal at any point, regardless of how much she had or hadn't eaten. Pushkin said that was the greatest good fortune: being able to leave the table before the wine was drained from the chalice. Not me; I was eating my sandwich. Riley lingered a moment, looking concerned, then left.

Jeremy segued to his other favorite topic, after Thomas Pynchon: his love for two girls named Diane. It was a subject I had never discouraged in the past, because I felt flattered that he was confiding in me, and because I thought it would be more interesting than listening to some random guy list all the famous professors he had taken classes with, which was another thing that often befell a person in the cafeteria. And yet—it somehow wasn't more interesting. The stories went on and on, full of details and coincidences.

I didn't know Diane W., but was acquainted with Diane H., who wore hoop earrings, tiered skirts, and Converse high-tops. Riley had once remarked of her, in an ironic voice, that she had had sex with four different guys we knew, including this one guy Ronnie, who sometimes lied about having read books when he hadn't. Riley was a feminist, so I knew that the reason she spoke ironically about Diane wasn't that she thought she was a slut. It was more complicated, and related to self-respect.

When I got back to our room, Riley was exchanging messages with a woman in Dorchester, whose obese Norwegian Forest Cat had sat, with near-lethal results, on her newborn baby. If Riley played her cards right, that could someday be our cat.

For my science Core class, I had to watch a movie about black holes. A theoretical physicist was explaining how we knew that black holes existed, even though we couldn't see them.

"Have you ever been to a ball?" he asked, speaking in a fond, sentimental voice. "Have you ever watched the young men dressed in their black evening tuxedos and the girls in their white dresses, whirling around in each other's arms, and the lights turn low and all you can see is the girls?"

I hadn't been to a ball, or to any formal dance. It was simultaneously disturbing and reassuring to hear the absolute, essential nature of this experience confirmed in cosmological terms.

The physicist said that the girl was an ordinary star, and the boy was a black hole. You couldn't see the boy, but the girl whirling around him was evidence that he existed, and was holding her in orbit. This seemed like corroboration of "The Seducer's Diary," where the seducer disappeared and Cordelia was going in circles. It seemed to me that the elements whirling around me in my own life were also somehow held in place by Ivan's absence, or were there because of him—to counterbalance a void.

Riley showed me how to use the "talk" command on Unix. All you had to do was type "talk," followed by the person's email address. If they accepted, the screen split horizontally. What you typed appeared in the top, and what they typed was in the bottom. You could see each other typing, thinking, backspacing. You could delete what you had just written and write something else—that could be a form of joke.

You could adopt the persona of someone who had displaced you by violent means, or you could pretend to be your own computer that had just achieved sentience.

When I tried typing "talk" and Ivan's Berkeley address, I got an error message.

Svetlana had interrogated Valerie's brother. Valerie's brother had been in some graduate math classes with Ivan. He said he seemed like a nice guy. Svetlana explained her mother's theory that Ivan was the devil incarnate. "I don't know anything about that," the brother said.

I emailed Ivan asking if we could do Unix talk. He wrote back saying that, although in principle he would like to talk to me, nonetheless in practical terms, not all the networks could connect to each other, and he wasn't sure it was possible in our case. Moreover, he didn't know if I was someone he could talk to right now, because he didn't know who I was. It is like there are many Selins and I don't know which one I will get. What if I meet the one who sees me as the devil?

I tried to write Ivan an email explaining what had happened: why Svetlana's mother had said he was the devil incarnate, how it was partly because of how he had appeared on the airplane to Paris, frightening me and Svetlana, and partly because of Svetlana's mother's attitude toward me, how she insisted on seeing me as a pathetic person, possibly because she was angry at the Ottoman occupation of Serbia, but also because she was envious of Svetlana and thus somehow envious of me; and why Svetlana might have elected to run her mother's remark by Valerie's brother, even though I had asked her not to. The thing with me and Ivan, I realized, had been hard, in its way, on Svetlana, had put stress on her project of self-improvement, and on her interaction with this guy, Scott. Trying to explain all the steps was boring and exhausting. I kept imagining Ivan getting bored, or not believing me, and it kept sounding like I was putting the blame on other people, like Svetlana and her mom. When I tried to put the blame on myself, it was also tedious and boring, and in the end I gave up trying to explain anything.

"This is mortifying," Svetlana said in the scalp care section of the CVS, picking up a delousing kit.

Halloween wasn't until next Thursday, but Scott's party had already happened. Svetlana ended up going as herself, having concluded that costumes were, on some level, opposed to human dignity. As a result—or perhaps coincidentally—a drunk person had clapped some kind of vintage hat on her head. At least three other people at the party had also gotten lice.

It occurred to me, not for the first time, how much simpler our lives would be if we could date each other. That delousing kit cost eleven dollars!

"Do you ever think it would be easier if we could go out with girls?" I said aloud.

Svetlana didn't answer right away. "I find most of the lesbians I know a bit intimidating," she said, finally. "And I don't really share their aesthetic sense—or they seem not to value aesthetics that much. I just don't think I'd fit in. Especially since I'm always lusting after boys."

That was something I thought about, too: the physical response I felt to Ivan, the dull electric jolt, some heavy, slow machinery starting to turn in my chest and between my legs. I had never felt those things with relation to a girl. On the other hand, I usually hadn't felt them in Ivan's presence, either; it was more when he wasn't there.

And how much was that physical feeling worth? Was it really enough to counterbalance all the disadvantages? You couldn't just talk to Ivan like he was a normal person; he didn't hear, or he didn't understand, or he went off somewhere and you couldn't find him. Also, all his friends thought I was crazy. Instead of dealing with those people, how much more fun and relaxing it would be to pet Svetlana's shining golden hair, to tell her how pretty she was and to watch her get more pretty, as she always did when someone complimented her. Her body wanted to be complimented, and I knew just what to tell her, so why couldn't I?

"But girls are more beautiful, and so much easier to sort of negotiate with. And the lust for boys never seems to work out well for me. So it just feels like girls are at least something to think about."

Again, Svetlana didn't answer right away. "I would feel squeamish with anything beyond kissing and playing with each other's breasts," she said after a moment.

I realized that I, too, had only been thinking about kissing and playing with each other's breasts. What else did lesbians even do? Other than oral sex, which was apparently horrible. The way people talked about it on sit-coms: "Does he like . . . deep-sea diving?" You had to be altruistic to do it—a generous lover.

That said, oral sex with a boy also seemed likely to be disgusting. Guys themselves seemed to think so. Wasn't that why they went around yelling "cocksucker" at people who cut them off in traffic?

"Do you not feel squeamish when you think about sex with a guy?" I asked.

"I do, but it feels exciting. The idea of being penetrated and dominated."

I recognized that the idea of being penetrated and dominated was exciting to me, too, though the mechanics, as well as the implications, were unclear and troubling. Also, why did we have to be excited by that? Why couldn't we be excited about something else?

But I knew I was being childish and unrealistic, and Svetlana was right. Love wasn't a slumber party with your best friend. Love was dangerous, violent, with an element of something repulsive; attraction had a permeable border with repulsion. Love had death in it, and madness. To try to escape those things was immature and anti-novelistic.

"Do you keep hearing that noise?" Riley asked. We were both up late studying.

"No," I said.

Riley paused her CD player. "*That*," she said. I still didn't hear anything. We had been listening to "Criminal" by Fiona Apple: Riley's favorite song. I got the sense that Riley thought that *she* was a criminal. I wasn't sure why. I couldn't see that she had done anything wrong. She had, however, gone to Catholic school.

I went back to reading *Fear and Trembling* for tutorial. Then Riley and I looked up at the same time: I had heard it, too. Riley pushed back her chair and went to investigate.

"Selin," Riley called, from the hallway. "It's for you."

I went out to join her. "Hello," said Juho, who was standing on the cat-themed doormat. "I saw that your lights were on, so I thought I would knock at your door. But I decided to space the knocks very far apart, and then decrease the interval, to see how close the knocks have to be together, before they are perceived as knocking."

Riley gave me a look. "I'll be inside," she said.

There was nowhere to talk in the apartment: Riley was studying in the bedroom, and Joanne was asleep in the common room. I grabbed my coat and headed to the stairwell. Juho followed me down to the lobby, at which point I noticed that his pants had a giant hole in one knee. Blood was running down his leg.

I went back upstairs for disinfectant and a Band-Aid. When I returned, Juho was sitting outside on the steps with his head tilted all the way back. That was when I understood that he was drunk. He rolled up the leg of his dress pants—the green sweatpants had been prohibited from High Table—but didn't seem to know what to do with the Band-Aid, and kept turning it over in his hands. He said he had been misinformed about the alcohol content of port. I put the Band-Aid on his leg myself, after dabbing the cut with alcohol. It must have stung, but he didn't say anything.

Juho explained the experimental protocol he had devised, about the door. He had knocked once, and then waited thirty seconds. Then he knocked again, and waited twenty-five seconds. He kept reducing the interval by five-second increments, until he got to fifteen. Then he went down by one-second increments. Riley had shown up when the knocks were twelve seconds apart.

"I was surprised by this result," he said. "I did not think that knocks that are twelve seconds apart will be perceived as knocking."

I said I didn't think Riley *had* perceived it as knocking.

"Ah," he said, a little sadly. "Then perhaps the experiment has been inconclusive."

I remembered that that was why he was here: to research, to do experiments. It was interesting to think that Harvard had underwritten the studies in knocking-perception that he had conducted on our door. What a stressful fellowship: how did a person know what to do? For the first time it occurred to me that maybe Juho *didn't* know; that maybe he was just like me, only even more so, wandering around the world in his institutionally non-sanctioned pants, incorrectly knocking on doors. But then I remembered that he had Ph.D.s in both chemistry and physics, meaning that he had some body of knowledge and accomplishment that I couldn't imagine having, and must be using it to make choices I didn't understand, either. When I looked over at him, he was staring at the sky with his usual peaceful expression—swaying slightly, but not seeming especially bothered by anything.

Fear and Trembling was about how Abraham was the greatest and most interesting person in human history, because when God told Abraham to go up to the top of some mountain and kill his son . . . well, Abraham immediately saddled up the donkeys. Kierkegaard speculated about how awkward the trip would have been—about what Abraham and Isaac could possibly have talked about.

Kierkegaard had published *Fear and Trembling* in 1843, the same year as *Either/Or*, under the name Johannes de silentio. De silentio meant "of silence." That was because the subject defied language, because it was so unsayable and paradoxical that Abraham had agreed to kill his own son. Abraham couldn't tell anyone anything. Nobody would have understood, or believed him about God, or believed that he didn't secretly want to kill his son.

In tutorial, we learned that *Fear and Trembling* illustrated the "teleological suspension of the ethical." Judith clearly liked this phrase. "But what do we think about this *teleological suspension of the ethical*?" she kept saying.

"Teleological suspension of the ethical" meant that it was OK to murder your kid, if God told you to. It meant believing that God loved you, even if he acted like he didn't; and believing that you loved your own kid, even if you acted like you didn't. After all, if everyone's behavior was visibly consistent with what their attitude was supposed to be, then faith would be unnecessary.

Why were religious people so obsessed with killing their own kids?

At dinner, Morris described a debate his Moral Reasoning class had had about Kant's categorical imperative. The idea of the categorical imperative was that moral rules were universal, with no exceptions. Lying, for example, was wrong—always, for everyone, under all circumstances. But what if an axe murderer knocked at your door and said, "Hello, sir, may I know where your children are so that I can murder them?" Were you morally justified to lie? Someone had actually asked Kant that, and Kant had said no. Morris's Moral Reasoning section had debated it for the whole hour.

I didn't see the point of debating how I would respond to an axe murderer saying something that an axe murderer would literally never say. More broadly, I mistrusted the project of trying to generalize a set of rules that would work in all circumstances. Surely, whatever rule anyone thought of, there would be some situations where it wouldn't work. I myself had often had the experience of being prevented, by my life situation, from following some rule that made sense for everyone else. When I explained it, people would laugh and say, "How could we have thought of that?"

Riley came back from Dorchester with a gigantic duffel bag containing Stanley: all twenty-six pounds of him. This was the culmination of a week of phone negotiations with Stanley's owner, Barbara, who had a neurological condition where she sometimes involuntarily said the word "speedboat."

Stanley was nine years old, neutered and declawed. He had terrible balance. Walking slowly and unenthusiastically around the apartment, he reminded me of a certain old man we had had to visit for some reason in Adana, who didn't reply when spoken to and barely seemed to register anything anyone said, including on the TV that was always on in the background. Stanley gave me the same bleak feeling—like whatever vitality had once been inside him had been snuffed out a long time ago. On the other hand, it was possible that Stanley did enjoy sitting on things, like keys and ID cards (and, as Riley pointed out, babies), because he seemed to go slightly out of his way to do it.

Stanley's most problematic feature was his habit of defecating on the carpet directly *next* to the litter box. Riley got a larger box and put it over the piece of carpet he favored. Once there was a box there, he shifted a few inches farther to the right.

"Moscow does not believe in tears," Riley said, and got out the carpet powder.

Priya started lighting incense to cover up the smell, creating the dense miasma of sandalwood and cat excreta that became characteristic of our apartment.

"Don't even get me started on *Fear and Trembling*," Svetlana said. "That book literally gave me a nervous breakdown freshman year."

"Really?"

"I didn't leave my room for a week. Valerie and Hedge brought me little bowls of food from the cafeteria. They must have thought I was a total freak."

"Where was I? Why didn't I bring you little bowls of food?"

"I don't remember. I felt really embarrassed about it. I probably felt too embarrassed to tell you, because I thought you'd think I was being self-important or lame. That's probably the worst part of having a Kierkegaard-related nervous breakdown."

The person Svetlana had eventually been able to talk to about *Fear and Trembling* had been Dave, whose preschool had featured a giant mural of Abraham about to murder Isaac, so he had been thinking about this stuff for years.

What kind of fucked-up preschool was that? I almost asked, before reflecting that such remarks were what made people not feel comfortable telling me about their Kierkegaard-related nervous breakdowns.

The black screen of my computer was filled up with green lines of text. Like fertile fields, like money, like the light that said go.

Message from TalkDaemon@playfair.stanford.edu at 20:54

talk: connection requested by ivanvar@playfair.stanford.edu

respond with: talk ivanvar@playfair.stanford.edu

Message from TalkDaemon@playfair.stanford.edu at 20:58

talk: connection requested by ivanvar@playfair.stanford.edu

respond with: talk ivanvar@playfair.stanford.edu

Message from TalkDaemon@playfair.stanford.edu at 21:01

talk: connection requested by ivanvar@playfair.stanford.edu

respond with: talk ivanvar@playfair.stanford.edu

It had to be Ivan trying to talk to me, from a Stanford email address. I knew he had had a summer job in a lab at Stanford once. The last request had come in almost an hour earlier. I hurriedly sat down and typed, talk ivanvar@playfair.stanford.edu.

The computer thought about it a few seconds, then said: [Your party is not logged on.]

I hastily emailed Ivan: Can we try again? There was no reply. Not that day, or the next.

On Saturday I woke up late. The first thing I did was check my email and finger Ivan's Stanford account. I didn't seriously think he would be logged on, since it wasn't even nine yet in California. But the computer started disgorging lines of text. He was using the account right now.

I requested a talk connection. One by one, new lines appeared on the screen.

[No connection yet]
[Waiting for your party to respond]
[Waiting for your party to respond]
[Connection established]

The screen split in two. My heart was pounding faster than the blinking cursor. I typed:

> Hello

And he replied:

>> hello

Happiness swept over me. Enemies didn't say hello. We were talking! There was a long pause, and then he typed:

>> who are you?

My heart seized up with fear, because it was as if he didn't know me, and everything had been erased, and nothing had been real—but then I remembered how he had written that he felt like there were many Selins, and I understood that he was asking which one he was talking to, and this filled me with a feeling of lightness and freedom, because he was letting me choose—he was asking me to choose. I typed:

> I am the soul in limbo.

There was a long pause.

>> do i know you?

I wondered how to answer. The cursor blinked implacably.

> I'm not sure.

Another pause.

>> why don't you want to tell me who you are?

> I do want to tell you.

>> who are you?

> Don't you know I would tell you if I could?

Pause.

>> who are you trying to talk to?

> To YOU. Not sure why it has to be so difficult

>> who do you think i am?

I wondered whether there was some way to tell him that the question came down to whom he haunted. More words appeared on the screen:

>> are you trying to talk to ivan?

I felt a sickening lurch. I typed:

> who is this?

The person replied:

>> are you celine?

I thought I was going to throw up.

> yes i'm selin. i'm trying to talk to ivan. who is this?

>> my name is zita.
>> ivan has 2 email accounts so he let me use this one

There was a knock on the doorframe and Riley came in. I felt so relieved to see her. "I've been doing Unix talk with someone for ten minutes and thought it was Ivan, but it turned out it's his ex-girlfriend!" I said.

"Wait, what?" She had been outdoors—there was a cushion of fall air around her. "Like, he left his account open, and she just started using it?"

"No, he has two email accounts, one at Berkeley and one at Stanford, and I think he gave her the Stanford one. So I was like 'talk to Ivan at this Stanford address,' and it connected me, but the person I was talking to was her."

"He gave her his account? He gave her the password? Why?"

"I don't know. I guess after they graduated she didn't have an email address anymore."

Riley had come to pick up a sweater and was standing there with just her arms in the sleeves. "So now she's using her ex's account and he can read her emails whenever he wants?"

"I don't know if he can read them. Maybe she changed the password."

Riley closed her eyes with a pained expression. "Have these people not heard of Hotmail?" She put on the sweater and came over to my desk. "How did you talk for ten minutes without noticing it wasn't him? Was she pretending to be him?"

"She wasn't pretending," I said. "She was like 'Who are you.' But I thought it was a metaphysical question."

"'The soul in limbo'?" Riley read over my shoulder.

"It's from a book," I said defensively.

Zita started typing again.

>> are you still there?

I hastily typed:

> whoops! sorry to bother you! this is very embarrassing.

I could feel Riley disapproving behind me. She was right, I knew I shouldn't be apologizing. "Want to come to brunch?" Riley said. "Oak and Lucas are downstairs."

New words appeared on the screen:

>> ivan talked about you a lot, so i almost feel i know you. he was
   so excited when he met you.

"You guys go ahead," I told Riley. "I'll probably be another few minutes."

"Well, I guess the soul in limbo knows best." I could hear her furrowing her eyebrows. And then I felt that she was gone.

>> i was actually wanting to talk to you. i thought i could explain
   some things about ivan.

> like what

>> i got the impression through peter that things are looking dark
   for you now. i think i know a bit what you're going through. i
   think i can help you to see more clearly.

I sat there for a while staring at the cursor, wondering whether "cursor" was related to a curse, and who had called it a "talk daemon." Then Zita was typing again:

>> would you be open to talking on the phone? i am not so fast a
   typist as you.

I imagined typing, "I have to go," and going to brunch. They wouldn't have sat down yet. Lucas would be waiting forever for a bagel to come out of the toaster. Oak would overfill the waffle iron and end up with a cauliflower-shaped waffle. Riley would make a correct waffle, eat two bites, and leave the rest.

One thing Riley had in common with Svetlana, and also, come to think of it, literally every other person I knew, was that she would advise me not to talk to Zita on the phone.

I see zero potential advantage in this conversation, I imagined my mother saying. I knew that she, like Riley, would find it strange and suspicious that Zita should be using Ivan's email address, and would be unable to conceive of any reason other than malice or insanity that she,

Ivan's ex-girlfriend, should want to talk to me. In fairness, I, too, had difficulty imagining what the reason could be. But that didn't mean it didn't exist.

Why was it that one's female relatives always said that, when a woman said or did anything inexplicable—that it was because of jealousy? If you pointed out, "But I, or you, did practically the same thing once, and *we* weren't jealous," they would say: "We're different from other people." This was true of women on my mother's side of the family, on my father's side of the family, *and* on my stepmother's side of the family: three different families, with otherwise different ways of looking at things. Yet they *all* thought that they were the only ones who weren't motivated by jealousy. Surely that meant that there were people all over who weren't motivated by jealousy. Why shouldn't Zita be one of them? After all, Ivan had liked her.

Anyway, even though all the women I could think of—Riley, Svetlana, my relatives—had, between them, lived a multitude of different lives and covered a lot of human experiences, they hadn't ever been in a situation just like this one.

Even as I was having these thoughts, I knew they were theoretical, because I was already definitely going to talk to Zita. When, on what basis had this decision been reached? I typed my phone number and hit return.

"Selin? This is Zita." She had a slight accent. Her voice sounded younger than I'd been expecting.

"Hey," I said. We both started laughing. We confirmed to each other that it was weird we were having this conversation, that our Unix session had been weird. This was a comfort. I realized that I had expected Zita to be like Ivan and Peter, because she knew them, and was their age, and was also probably Hungarian, but once we were talking I felt that her worldview and feelings were more aligned with mine than with theirs, because we were girls. For example, when something was weird, we were able to say so, and it felt a little less weird.

"So," she said.

"So," I said.

"I've really wanted to talk to you. Peter told me you were really upset with Ivan, and I think I understand. When Ivan told me about you last year, he was so excited. But I was a little worried, because I know how he can be."

I wondered whether Zita was going to try to impress me with how much better she knew Ivan—how she had always been watching from afar, worrying that I would be hurt.

At some point Ivan had asked Zita for "a woman's perspective." "If I ask someone for coffee, does it mean I like them, or only as a friend? If we go swimming, does it mean I like them, or only as a friend?" When he said he wanted to take me to Walden Pond on his motorcycle, she was worried, because she knew how romantic that was and how it would seem to me. "He said I didn't understand, that it wasn't like that with you. But afterwards he said, 'Zita, maybe you were right.'"

Zita said she wanted to help me. She wanted to help me understand.

To help me understand, Zita told me the story of her relationship with Ivan. Zita and Ivan had met in freshman year, at an orientation program for international students. Ivan had been to a special math high school, the kids there were very bright but didn't necessarily have great social skills. He had never had a girlfriend. Zita was different— very social, with a lot of boyfriends and friends, always getting involved. Already as a little girl she had been called an advocate, a social worker, she defended the weak, even when it meant picking a fight. It had been natural to her to help Ivan, who had seemed lost at Harvard. I wouldn't have recognized him. Zita was a year older than he was, so she was always taking the lead.

But things changed so fast in college. By the summer after sophomore year, their dynamic was different. She felt constrained. The thing that constrained her was Ivan's intellectual certainty, the way he already knew, and had known since childhood, that he would become a mathematician.

Zita wasn't like that. She was artistic, and liked to explore. She got really into Buddhism. She was at the divinity school now, studying Buddhism: that's why she didn't have her own email account. It wasn't clear to me whether nobody at divinity school had email, or whether it was only the ones studying Buddhism.

In junior year, Zita got a grant to study in Thailand. Ivan didn't want her to go. "We had a fight," she said proudly. She wound up at a temple north of Bangkok, getting up before dawn, meditating most of the day. For the first time in a year, maybe longer, she felt truly free. Meanwhile at Harvard, Ivan had started spending more time with Peter, who introduced him to Eunice. Peter and Eunice were both grad students. Peter was studying economics and Korean, and Eunice had been his Korean instructor.

Ivan and Eunice saw each other a few times with Peter. One day they met in the street and ended up having coffee and talking for three hours. They began to meet regularly, having passionate conversations about politics and history. There was an intellectual spark between them that hadn't existed with Zita.

"I'm very smart, in my own way," Zita said, "but I'm emotional more than intellectual. I care more about people and feelings than about ideas. With Ivan, we always talked about what I cared about, not what he cared about. I don't think I was very patient with him." After a moment she added, casually, "What were your conversations with Ivan like? Were they intellectual?"

I thought about my conversations with Ivan. "I don't know," I said. "I don't think so."

"But they must have been," she said.

I didn't know what to say so I just sat there until she started talking again.

Over spring break, Ivan had visited Zita in Thailand. They traveled to the south. She found a hut on the beach, for a few dollars a night. They could see the stars through the palm roof. Ivan and Zita had always told each other everything, so of course he told her all about Eunice. Zita didn't know how to feel. After all, the break had been her idea. She told Ivan she still loved him, and he said he still loved her, too. She knew he would give Eunice up if she asked him to. But then, he would always wonder. Zita told him he should follow his feelings, the way she had followed her impulse to go to Thailand. Ivan said he didn't know what his feelings were, or where they would lead. They agreed that this was the nature of feelings, and then they had sex in the hut in total darkness, listening to the crashing waves.

At the end of the break, Zita went back to the temple, and Ivan went back to Boston. Ivan wasn't sure if he was attracted to Eunice romantically or only intellectually. They had long, challenging conversations about history and abstract ideas. Then, the junior class had a formal dance on a bridge at sunrise, with an orchestra. Ivan invited Eunice. Their hands touched, and then they kissed. Zita's voice, as she told me these things, sounded affectionate or conspiratorial. "He fell in love," she said.

The next time Zita saw Ivan was over the summer, when they were both in Hungary. Ivan picked her up from the airport, in a car with his mother and all his sisters. The car was so crowded that Zita sat on Ivan's lap. "I'm very small," Zita explained.

Ivan's mother thought Zita shouldn't be sitting on Ivan's lap now, but Zita and Ivan laughed. The whole time they were in Budapest, they saw each other every day, like they always had, and Zita spent time with his mother and sisters, whom she loved. "My family isn't like that—we're all split apart. But I am a very affectionate person."

Ivan and Zita discussed the nature of love. Ivan asked Zita if she thought you could be in love with two people at the same time.

Zita said she didn't know—maybe you could.

Later, Ivan asked Eunice the same question. Eunice said: "No."

Zita spent the rest of the summer in Thailand, then flew straight to Boston in September. It was terrible to return from Bangkok to Boston—to such austerity and grayness and striving—and without Ivan, who was now getting serious about Eunice. In Budapest, everything had seemed possible. In Boston, this was not the case. Zita realized that Ivan had to choose. She told him that she had been wrong—that she needed him. Eunice became insecure and struck out at Ivan. All three of them were in hell.

At that point I heard the call-waiting tone. Zita, who couldn't hear anything, said that the situation might have been the hardest on Eunice. She wasn't a bad person, but was so highly driven, competitive, sure of what she wanted and how to get it. I recognized the way non-Asian women talked about Asian women. Zita seemed to think I was more like her than I was like Eunice. Was that because Zita and I weren't Asian, or because Zita and I were the ones who hadn't ended up with Ivan?

Something about the call-waiting tone sounded particularly insistent. I told Zita I would be right back, and pressed the receiver button.

"Selin?" It took me a second to place her: my own mother.

"Hey! Can I call you back? I'm on the other line."

"I'm in the hospital," my mother said, in a voice full of outrage and distress, and started to cry. "I just had my surgery."

I pressed the button again and told Zita that I had to go; my mother was calling from a hospital.

"Oh my goodness, right now? You must be so worried! Is she all right? What's the matter?"

"I don't know," I said. "I'd better go talk to her."

"Yes, of course. We can finish our conversation later. I'll leave you my number. You can call me anytime. Really, anytime, Selin." I wrote down her number.

My mother had just had a double mastectomy. She hadn't told me she had breast cancer. At some point she had mentioned a cyst, and the cyst had been a sort of allegory. She hadn't meant to tell me the truth. She was telling me now because she was relieved that the surgery had gone well. It sounded like the drugs hadn't worn off yet.

When I was ten, my father's sister in Turkey had also had breast cancer, and had moved in with my father and me, in New Jersey. That had been right at the time when my mother moved out.

I thought about my mother going to the doctor alone, getting the diagnosis alone, and going to surgery alone. I told her I would go back to New Jersey and stay with her. But she said emphatically that I couldn't miss school. My aunt was going to stay with her. I felt relieved. Then I felt guilty for feeling relieved. We talked for another ten minutes, until she said she felt tired.

It was past one in the afternoon and I was still wearing a nightgown. I made myself take a shower and wear clothes. Then it was two.

Zita picked up on the second ring. "Oh, I'm so happy you called. I was worried you wouldn't. How is your mother?"

"Well, it turns out she has cancer." As soon as I said it, I wanted to take it back. Zita asked a lot of questions about the diagnosis and treatment, whether my mother had been tested for the breast cancer gene, and when I was going to go home.

"It's fine," I said. "She's a doctor, she's a medical professor, so she's going to do a new hormone treatment, and my aunt is going to go stay with her."

"Oh, good," Zita said, still sounding anxious.

"Do you want to finish telling me your story?"

"Do you really want to hear about it now?"

"Yeah."

"Well . . . where were we?"

"It was really sad. You came back from Thailand and missed Ivan, and Eunice was a competitive person."

"Oh—you know, I don't want to say anything negative about Eunice. She was in a very tough situation. She was angry with me, but I was never angry with her. But for a while it was very tense."

Ivan had made a decision to be with Eunice, but now that he saw Zita suffering, he wanted to be there for her. That was the kind of person he was. But Eunice said he had to choose. For one day, Zita had thought Ivan was going to choose her. Ivan's mother had come to visit, and Eunice was cooking dinner for them. They were all in the kitchen, drinking wine—Ivan and his mother and Eunice. Then, Ivan had gone into the bedroom and telephoned Zita.

"While she was cooking for his mother," Zita said, with a hint of satisfaction.

Zita had gone through a period of not thinking clearly. That's why she thought she understood how I felt. She had been the same way in the spring. She had discussed the situation endlessly with her girlfriends and Peter, and had interrogated Ivan's math friends ("you can imagine how well that went"). She realized now she had been trying on some level to win Ivan back: not directly anymore, but socially, almost politically, through persuasion, because that had always been her strength.

She wanted to make everyone understand what was just, and to cause it to happen.

It had only been in the fall that she had fully understood and accepted that the rupture was final, and for the best; that it had originated, not when Ivan met Eunice, but when Zita went to Thailand, to become the person she really was. Once she realized that, she felt less sad. Of course, an ending was always sad, but to *not* end something that needed to end was even more sad.

Eunice, though not without her peculiarities, was right for Ivan. And Ivan was right for Eunice, in a way that he had not been right for Zita. This had been as difficult for Ivan to see as it had been for Zita. And this was what Zita wanted to tell me about Ivan: that he got into complicated situations sometimes, but it was because he had a big heart.

Thinking over the dates, I realized that the time when Zita had reached these conclusions was the time I had first met Ivan.

"So all the time you knew him, he was living with Eunice already," Zita said, excitedly. I remembered the tidiness of Ivan's dorm room, how he had talked about loaning it to a friend. I had never wondered why Ivan didn't have more stuff lying around, or where he stayed when he let other people use his room.

Zita asked how much Ivan had told me about what had happened. But why should he have told me, when I had never asked? I had found out about Eunice's existence, I told Zita, because we ran into her on the street.

"Oh my God. What did you say?"

"Nothing. I mean, I said 'Nice to meet you,'" I said.

"What did she say?"

"Nothing. She didn't say it was nice to meet me. She told Ivan he had to be home by nine."

"She must have been jealous," Zita said. "Of course, I hope she feels more secure now. I've moved on. I have a new boyfriend. I'm happy now."

"That's great," I said, recognizing the rule that, once you had a new boyfriend, you were happy.

Zita said that, since she had told me her whole story, now I had to tell her mine. I felt a wave of anxiety. Her story had had a beginning, a middle, and an end. Nothing between Ivan and me had happened that way. It hadn't made sense, the way her story had. Thinking it over, the thing that had made the least sense was how someone had tried to talk to me from the Stanford email account, two weeks earlier.

"That wasn't you, was it?" I asked Zita.

"No, of course not."

"So it really was Ivan?"

"No, that's impossible."

"Then who was it?"

"It can't have been anyone."

"But it happened."

"No, it couldn't have."

I felt lost then, because however cooperative we tried to be, and actually managed to be, we both trusted Ivan more than we trusted each other.

"So," Zita said. I felt that she wanted something—as was natural—in exchange for the story she had told me. "Did I change your mind?"

Sunlight slanted in the window, enabling one to individually appreciate all the dust particles on Riley's CD tower. What was a person supposed to do? Serdar, for instance, had punched a wall. But that had only caused other people more trouble and expense. I decided to mail my mother a present. We were always looking out for presents to mail each other, and I'd had my eye on a decorative candle shaped like the bust of Hippocrates. On the other hand, what good *was* a novelty candle? What good was the actual Hippocrates? Voices came from the hall. People were on their way to go eat or drink different things, before time passed and they had to eat or drink again. Surely there was more to life than just trying to avoid bad luck?

I thought longingly about jumping out a window—not our bedroom window, which was blocked by the bed and was only on the third floor and overlooked the turtle-shaped kiddie pool of a childcare center—but some other, higher window. For some reason, the image that came to my mind was of Peter explaining to someone in a quiet, serious voice that Selin's problems had been more serious than anyone had realized. No way, I thought. I was going to stick around and bury those people.

NOVEMBER

The crying started with songs, and movies. Then it was in bed. I kept a roll of toilet paper jammed between the top bunk and the wall, and stuffed the used wads of toilet paper back into the cardboard cylinder. When I had to blow my nose, I hid under the duvet, so Riley wouldn't hear. Once I got really congested like that, though, I apparently started snoring, because as soon as the misery let up even a little bit, I was jerked right back into it by the sensation of Riley jabbing my mattress from below. A person had to be in a state of unremitting misery, at risk of preventing others from sleeping.

When I woke up in the morning, there was a second or two when I felt light and free, unaware of any reason to feel upset. Then all my knowledge and memories rushed back and a weight descended on my sternum and the creaking started behind my eyes.

I increased my hours at the Ukrainian Research Institute. What a relief that there was a way of converting time into something so clear and quantifiable. Sit there for an hour, and that was seven dollars.

It turned out that a lot of things that people thought of as Russian were actually Ukrainian. Borscht, for example, and Gogol, whom Ukrainians called "Hohol." This made him sound merry, though he was rarely invoked in a merry way. It was regretted that he hadn't written in his mother tongue. Gogol's mother had had Gogol when she was sixteen.

It turned out that Ukrainians, just like Turkish people, and Russians, and many people in Hungary, considered their culture to be uniquely "torn between East and West." How many cultures *didn't* think that? I had once heard a Japanese person say it about Japan.

The microwave in the Ukrainian Institute was definitely haunted. Katya tried to microwave a cup of tea, and opened the door to find the teabag sitting *several inches away* from the cup of water.

The older Ukrainian women thought I was insensitive and annoying. Olha in particular hadn't thought life would have reduced her to this.

Once, when I was making tea, I made an extra cup for Olha, the way I had seen her make it, with milk and three bags of sugar. In my science Core class, I had seen a video of someone adding milk to tea, played in reverse, so the milk unswirled itself from the tea and streamed back up into the pitcher. Apparently, the laws of physics didn't differentiate between the past and the future, so a video played backward couldn't show you anything impossible. It wasn't impossible, but just very unlikely, for stirred milk to separate like that.

When I brought Olha the tea, I thought I saw some relaxation of the lines around her mouth and on her forehead. If a video of her face was played backward, the lines would disappear. Was that impossible in real life, or just extremely unlikely?

I typed a manuscript about how the Kievan Rus' was pre-Ukrainian and not pre-Russian. I transcribed a series of addresses by a Ukrainian ambassador. He never actually said anything—just invoked bilateral relations and geopolitical alignments, and made an occasional arch remark about "the clash of civilizations." Was that what it was to be a diplomat? How did anyone survive it?

Depositing a paycheck, I noticed, immediately produced some dissociation from whatever work you did: a job was a job. (Was that how the Holocaust had happened?)

One evening after I deposited my check, I stopped at the newspaper store in the square and bought a pack of cigarettes: Parliaments, the first brand that came to mind. I didn't want to stand there too long reading the different brands, in case the storekeeper got suspicious and asked for ID. I *had* ID—you only had to be eighteen—but any kind of dispute or challenge, however quickly resolved, would have ruined the smoothness of the transaction, which was somehow part of it—as was the box with the blue-and-navy panel, and the seal that resembled the Pan Am pilot badge, from back when people got specially dressed up to take airplanes, and armrests had built-in ashtrays.

I thought of the parliament building in Budapest: how suddenly it sprang into view across the river, how regally cakelike, just when you thought you were lost, and how strange to think that it still existed, now, in November, at what must have been—I checked my watch— two in the morning. Quite possibly there were people working there this minute, speaking Hungarian, steering the ship of state, emptying the wastebaskets.

"Matches?" the storekeeper asked, showing no interest in my age. I felt wonder at the matchbook: an actual little book, with a staple. For free. The thing Prometheus had paid for with his liver.

In the foyer of the library, it occurred to me to look for Zita's thesis. It wasn't on the shelves. So, she hadn't won a prize. Was that because she cared more about people and emotions than about abstract concepts?

I did find Zita's thesis in the online library catalog. The entry included the name of the temple where she had studied in Thailand. Following the same zombielike compulsion that had made me look up her thesis in the first place, I located an entry on the temple in an encyclopedia of Eastern religions. Apparently, the monks there were in conflict with most other Thai Buddhists, because of their belief that, when you reached nirvana, the thing you reached was "the true self." The others thought that nirvana meant reaching the "not-self." The words "controversy" and "dispute" were used several times. I felt surprised to learn that Buddhist monks were so argumentative.

On some level, it felt exciting to have a personal connection, however tenuous, to this material that was so far from my own experience. It seemed to be something I had achieved through writing.

Listening to my Walkman and smoking a cigarette by the river, I felt a kind of elevation in my chest, my eyes opened wider, I felt more alive.

There was something about crying so much, the way it made my body so limp and hot and shuddering, that made me feel closer to sex. Maybe there was a line where sex and total sadness touched—one of those surprising borders that turned out to exist, like the one between

Italy and Slovenia. Music, too, was adjacent. It was like Trieste, which was Italian and Slovenian and also somehow Austrian.

Music was the thing that made it the most clear what sex would be like. The feeling of different places being touched and resonating at the same time. Like sitting on a parapet with your eyes closed, feeling sunlight on your left eyelid and a breeze on your right forearm. Music was the only other thing that was layered like that, so that each new component changed the meaning of the whole. And so much building up and holding back—promising and withholding, and withholding, and withholding. You're going to die without it. You're never going to get it. You're going to die. Here it is.

At first, I didn't see the point of an orgasm. It seemed like an annoying abrupt spasm that interrupted things just when they were getting interesting. But gradually it started to take longer to get to, and to unfold into its own experience, and then it became this sought-after thing in the distance—like during the long periods in a symphony when nothing seemed to be happening, when it was just shifting textures, and then a glimmer of the soaring sought-after melody shone through—and the fact that you could glimpse it, even for a second, was a miracle that promised everything, that deferred everything to the future, and made living seem worthwhile.

I knew that what I had experienced was clitoral orgasm, which was immature and incomplete and somehow selfish and immoral, by comparison with a vaginal orgasm. The flickering, pulsing, agitated feeling I had sometimes afterward was proof. It wasn't real or right by yourself. But what was the man going to do—how was it going to work? I tried again to put in a tampon. ABSOLUTELY NO FUCKING WAY.

In music, the thing that made it work often wasn't the obvious delighting melody, but something somewhere further down—maybe not in any one of the components, but in the combination, the notes that proliferated and branched out and merged back together; the way they tensed against each other, and promised to resolve, and then went somewhere so unexpected and yet absolutely, in retrospect, necessary, that you had to replay it over and over, because remembering it wasn't the same.

The devastating line at the end of "The Seducer's Diary": "If I were a god I would do for her what Neptune did for a nymph: change her into a man." Would Ivan do that for me? YOU HAVE TO DO THAT FOR ME. The thought made me come, sobbing. The bathroom was the only place you could lock the door. I had the shower on, but was lying on a towel on the floor, so I could concentrate better. Riley rapped sharply on the door—she had to use the bathroom.

I had a recurring dream that I was in high school—stranded for at least the day, and probably every day for years. A question had come up about the validity of my diploma, and my mother had reenrolled me and paid the tuition. It wasn't that she really cared about the diploma; she was just excited about how I would finally get a really good education, I would really understand physics.

At some point in the dream, I was trying to explain to the principal that I didn't actually have to be there. I had come as a courtesy to my mother. I no longer needed the diploma. I didn't mention Harvard, because I knew it would enrage the principal, causing him to think that I was saying that I was too good to be there. The principal pointed out acidly that I was hardly doing anyone else a favor with my presence; there was a very real chance that I hadn't actually graduated, that I hadn't "earned" the credits I thought, and if he were me he would be very worried.

For some reason, the most painful part was knowing that the whole situation was my own doing. There was no longer any law that said I had to be at school. But the bus had shown up at seven in the morning and honked and honked, ever more insistently and expressively of the mounting anger of everyone who was being kept waiting—and I had gotten on. At the same time, I knew that, although nonattendance in high school was technically possible, and even expected, for most people in my position, it was somehow impossible for me, personally— because of who I was.

When I related this dream at brunch, it turned out that everyone except Priya had a high school nightmare. The one with the most similar dream to mine was Lucas. He, too, was our current age—the age where we were supposed to be in college—and a stressful part of the dream was the struggle to find somewhere in his old school where he could secretly try to keep up with his assignments for college. It was also his mother who had reenrolled him, saying that he would finally really learn math.

In tutorial, we did a unit on Freud. We read *Dora: An Analysis of a Case of Hysteria*. Her father brought Dora to see Freud, because she was coughing and choking, and because she had slapped the father's friend. Freud had to "take her history." The ability to take a history was something my mother often talked about: who had it, who didn't. It wasn't as simple as just asking the person.

"Patients often cannot give an ordered history of their lives," Freud wrote. The word "patient" made my stomach clench. I didn't want to become a doctor, but sometimes I worried it was the only way to avoid being a patient.

Freud said that the problem with Dora was that she was secretly in love with her father's friend, Herr K—the one she had slapped. She only thought that she hated him, because she was afraid of sex, and had repressed her own sexual desires.

Dora recounted to Freud how Herr K had ambushed her from behind a door and kissed her. Freud said that a normal virginal girl of fourteen would have felt a "healthy genital sensation" to learn that such an honorable and attractive man was in love with her. Instead, Dora had an unhealthy, choking response in her throat. This proved that Dora was also in love with her father, who was having an affair with K's wife. The choking was because she was jealous that K's wife got to have oral sex with Dora's father. (So oral sex involved your *throat*?)

Dora filled me with despair. What if someone told me that it was *my* sexual motives and frustration behind all my problems—my jealous and sexual love of my parents? I also felt demoralized by how far ahead of me Dora was, because she had attracted a man, and had been kissed by him when she was fourteen—whereas I had passed "sweet sixteen," and seventeen, and eighteen.

In class, we learned that there were two ways to interpret *Dora*: (1) Freud was right and Dora was in love with both her father and K; (2) Freud was an unreliable narrator who over-identified with K.

Reading *Dora* was supposed to teach us to read a text interpretively, the way Freud "read" Dora herself. "Interpretively" seemed to mean "with belligerence and hostility." Judith wanted us to see the text as a "performance" in which Freud, the "author," had to establish "authority," by marginalizing interpretations different from his own. We had to learn how discourses were taking power, how to identify a text's blindnesses and learn to take power and authority for ourselves. There was something depressing in this picture of everyone scrambling to grab power and authority over each other, before their own authority and power were grabbed.

Why did people still read Freud: because he had been right, or because he hadn't been right? What exactly had been wrong with Dora? The word "hysteria" was always spoken with irony, as if it was too backward and un-feminist to merit discussion. We learned that *hystera* was Greek for "uterus," and that Hippocrates believed that women's uteruses could become unmoored and wander around their bodies. This was clearly not correct.

Judith used an overhead projector to show us photographs from the clinic in Paris where hysteria was first documented. The doctor, Charcot, had asserted power over the women by documenting them. One woman was lying in bed with her arms outstretched, as if she had been crucified. Another was yawning angrily. Some women were having convulsions where they arched their backs. Some of them actually had epilepsy, strokes, or brain damage. Epilepsy, strokes, and brain damage were real. People still got them. But nobody got hysteria anymore. Apparently, the thing that had been giving people hysteria was repressive Victorian norms. We didn't have those norms anymore, so we didn't have hysteria, either.

Riley made me a tape of her Fiona Apple album. I initially mistrusted Fiona Apple, because of her belligerent, model-like beauty, because she was my age but sang in a scornful way about her ex-boyfriends, and because the lyrics sounded like she had been forced to use vocabulary words. But after I had listened to the album all the way through a few times, the janky grammar and word choices began to seem legitimate and necessary, and I understood that it was possible to look like that—glaring and tousled, with your limbs all in some artful pile—and also be good at something.

Fiona Apple's album made me more immediately depressed than any other music I remembered hearing. The most depressing songs were the ones with meandering arbitrary piano, that went from meandering to decisive and then back again. How did she know when to do that? The one that started "Days like this, I don't know what to do with myself" made me feel certain that I had spent my whole life not knowing what to do with myself—*all* day, and *all* night. "I wander the halls . . ." That was exactly it: not the streets, like a flâneur, but the halls. Oh, I knew just which halls.

The recordings I knew best were all classical, because of violin, and because my father only listened to classical music, so that was what we had at home. My mother had listened to American pop music, but only on the radio. I had thought of it as "radio music." For many years, I hadn't realized that it even came on records or tapes.

The essential qualities of radio music were: a tone of oracular truth; an appeal to "you"; an uncertainty as to whether you yourself were "you." Radio music was summed up by the woman with the sexless, sphinxlike voice who had traveled the world and the seven seas, and had found that everybody was looking for something. "Some of them want to use you; some of them want to be used by you": I recognized this to be absolutely true, without qualification—either despite, or because of, how it contradicted the logic of self-interest, in a way that would be revealed by adult life, and would be in some way its defining feature.

Tower Records was the least cool place to buy music, but the one where you were the most free from any expectation of knowing anything or talking to anyone. The cover art for the new Fugees album looked like the poster for *The Godfather*. What was more alienating: the album art that wasn't targeting me, or the album art that clearly was (Fiona Apple)?

The Fugees album had the cover of "Killing Me Softly": a song I had first heard in the spring, at a club in Boston. I had only gone to keep Lakshmi company, because Noor was DJ-ing. On the way to the T station, we had passed a few feet behind Ivan and Eunice. They were standing in a crowd, watching a guy play the guitar, and the sight of them had vaporized any thought I'd had of turning back. It became imperative to go forward, into whatever else there was.

Lakshmi had assured me, when I pointed it out, that the insufferability of clubs was widely acknowledged. Why else did I think everyone was on drugs the whole time? My reluctance to talk to the guy you had to talk to to get the drugs was exceeded only by my mistrust of the drugs themselves. If I messed up my brain, what else did I have? Why wasn't Lakshmi scared?

Noor hadn't been the one to play "Killing Me Softly" (or any other music that had words, or was recognizable in any other way). It had been the next DJ, the one who seemed like DJ-ing was his job. I immediately recognized it as an old song—the kind you heard as a kid, and knew that the world it came from and referred to was not only closed to you, but was one that in some sense you yourself had brought to an end, so that whatever it was really about was something that no longer existed, and that you could never have—except that now you *were* having it, because it had been transformed, uprooted, dragged into now, and some seemingly foreclosed possibility had opened up again.

Up to that moment, I had thought that the reason it was embarrassing to be in a club was because of not feeling anything, and having to go through the motions. But it turned out that feeling things—feeling so much—was even more embarrassing. Once you stripped away the music, the way I was always doing in my mind, to weigh the words and assess their meaning, "strumming my pain with his fingers" was unbearably embarrassing, like something you wrote in middle school. But when Lauryn Hill sang it, against a harmony that changed with each phrase, and changed, and changed, and changed again, so you didn't know where it was, or where you were—and the not-knowing was related to "his fingers," which were in turn so immediately connected to "your pain"—it was a feeling I couldn't believe I was having in public. Then, the song became *about that*, and "embarrassed by the

148

crowd" rhymed with how he found her letters "and read each one aloud." Her *letters*? Who even wrote letters anymore? Who, besides me and Tatiana? The idea of him reading my letters out loud. Of being fixed to the spot, praying that he would stop. The idea of being totally seen, but not pitied or stopped-at, of him relentlessly telling my whole life with his words. *My* life, with *his* words.

It had never occurred to me to buy a recording of "Killing Me Softly." Was that because the Fugees was hip-hop? "Killing Me Softly" had some of the features of hip-hop that I usually found alienating, like a man saying "Uh, uh," in the background. But the man, despite several false alarms, never did start rapping, and instead a girl sang an old song with beautiful harmonies. In relation to "Killing Me Softly," I was surely a poseur, the kind of coward to whom crossover albums were marketed or, worse yet, someone co-opting someone else's bad experience.

And yet, now, in the Tower Records, I understood that there was a sense in which "Killing Me Softly" was just a song—*it itself* wasn't the cursive font in which the titles were printed, which made me think of a tattoo, and caused me to feel sheltered and useless. I ended up buying the cassette single, because it was only two dollars, and because it seemed more honest about just being into the most popular song on the album.

Once I could listen to "Killing Me Softly" whenever I wanted, I was able to put together the whole story. Lauryn Hill heard about this guy who was a good singer, who "had a style." It was exciting to think that people at a certain level of competence knew about, and periodically checked up on, one another, and that her admiration of his competence was predicated on her own competence—which was, within the song, the only thing you heard. You didn't hear his skills, but her evocation of them; her turning them on you. (So, it was possible to make someone else feel that way: the way someone had made you feel.)

Insofar as those guys, Wyclef Jean and the others, were even there at all, it was just to set everything up for Lauryn Hill—for her to destroy everyone, with a display of technique that was unquestionable and brutal, like the end of chapter three in *Eugene Onegin*. They had queued up her entrance—"L, you know you got the lyrics"—the way Pushkin queued up Tatiana's letter, with the same pride and confidence. I recognized, in their solicitude, something that I had felt in emails with Ivan: the way he had made me feel my own competence, even saying once about the way that I wrote that I "had a style." I felt that he was right, I *did* have a style, in that sense, even if in the other sense—of living in an apartment in the right city, surrounded by the right things, wearing an interestingly heavy wristwatch that foregrounded my frail wrist—I did not. Somehow this thought made me feel worse, not better. Tears sprang to my eyes, and my heart filled with yearning.

For tutorial, we read part of *The Interpretation of Dreams*. It turned out that dreams were easy to interpret. They were all repressed desires. Did I secretly want to be back in high school?

Freud said that déjà vu in dreams was always about "the genitals of the dreamer's mother; there is indeed no other place about which one can assert with such conviction that one has been there once before." I felt relieved to think that this was not the case for me. My mom had gotten really sick when I was born—she had almost died—and I had been delivered a month early, by a C-section.

Apparently, a lot of children dreamed about murdering their siblings. Freud sounded like he was making fun of them: of the small boy "whose autocratic rule was upset, after lasting for fifteen months," by the birth of a sister; of the girl who dreamed that all her siblings and cousins grew wings and flew away, leaving "our little baby-killer" alone, as she wanted, with her parents. I felt thankful that I had never had a dream like that, and was reminded of all the adults who had observed of me, during my childhood, that I was an only child, that I must be "spoiled rotten," that I must love having my parents' attention all to myself. Leora had always said, whenever she wondered why she was one way and I was another: "My mother says it's because you're an *only child*. You're an *only child*." Later, in high school, the glee with which Clarissa asked, "Do you *miss* being an only child?" Whenever we played Truth or Dare. "How do you *really* feel about your step-mother and your half-brother?"

I kept starting emails to Ivan.

> Dear Ivan,
> Did you try to talk to me?

> Dear Ivan,
> I had a strange conversation with

> Dear Ivan,
> My general contempt for psychiatry is reason enough for my
> not yet having dared investigate what has become of Sonya.

> Thou, Nature,
> What do you want to dance about, you black hole? I have a cat
> now. Nothing happens that I don't want to tell you. The cat is
> in the box. The cat's poop, on the other hand . . .
> Are you dead, or aren't you?
> It is possible, in rare cases, to go to hell in your lifetime.
> Persephone's abduction to the underworld represents her function
> as the personification of vegetables. In spring they shoot forth

What? No.

> Moscow does not believe in tears.
>
> Sevastopol does not believe in earwax.
>
> Minsk does not believe in black bile.

It was like we didn't have the language between us to talk about anything normal.

> Dear Ivan,
>
> Olha at the Ukrainian Research Institute does not care for me.
>
> She did not think that her fate would have been so terrible. But
>
> she can't unstir the milk in her tea, so it looks like time is still just
>
> going one way.
>
> Now Hohol is in his sleigh, silver bells a-ringing, his sack full
>
> of dead souls for all the good children.
>
> When will we talk about genre theory?
>
> Please forgive me.
>
> Selin

Rob came in and, in my hurry to look like I was working, I accidentally hit Ctrl-S instead of Ctrl-D. I *sent* that?

For literature tutorial, we read part of *Swann's Way*, which was the first book of *Remembrance of Things Past*. Calling it that, instead of translating the title literally as *In Search of Lost Time*, was supposed to be a way of conveying Proust's universal status to an English-speaking audience, because "remembrance of things past" was a line from Shakespeare.

I thought *In Search of Lost Time* sounded exciting and detective-like, and *Remembrance of Things Past* sounded lame. "When to the sessions of sweet silent thought / I summon up remembrance of things past": I didn't like when people used "sweet" about non-sensory experiences. Why were we in my mouth all of a sudden? Nor did I believe poets when they went on about what a fun activity it was for them to call up old memories. It was like when old people said that all they had needed for entertainment was a stick and a piece of string, and it was their way of criticizing you for watching TV.

Something about the name "Proust" sounded fussy, and made me worry that he wouldn't have liked me. All I really knew about him was that he wrote wonderfully about childhood and about the French countryside. Why did the idea of the French countryside make me feel despairing? It looked OK in Van Gogh paintings. And that was where he had cut off his ear—so it had been intense. Ivan had asked me that once about New Jersey—whether it had been intense—making me realize that intensity was, indeed, what one valued in place. Childhood was somehow the opposite of intense.

Maybe that was my issue, and not the French countryside. I realized that I never had liked books about childhood—except, when *I* was a child, the kinds of books where the children themselves solved mysteries or had adventures. But books about childhood that were written for adults? "I misheard some word and thought it meant something else." "I mistakenly thought there was a relationship between two unrelated words or concepts." "I didn't understand this thing that I later found out was about sex." "I ate something delicious." "My mother looked like an angel." "I was unfairly punished."

Out of my three friends who had read *Swann's Way*, Leora said it was so boring that she could hear her own hair grow. Svetlana looked embarrassed and said it took some effort to get into, but eventually the rhythm was hypnotic. It turned out she had read all seven volumes.

"Proust is difficult, but not as difficult as Joyce," Lakshmi said. Mostly what she wanted to talk about was this freshman, Mia, who was friends with Noor, and who said that her favorite book was *Finnegans Wake*. Lakshmi asked if I thought a freshman could have read and understood *Finnegans Wake*.

"Who wants to understand *Finnegans Wake*, though?" I said.

"Yes, of course you're right," Lakshmi said immediately. Then she didn't say anything for a while. "I suppose it's possible that she did understand it, and she's really brilliant."

Svetlana had started doing meditation. I didn't *want* to think about my breath for twenty minutes.

I sometimes went with Svetlana to Pilates—even though the logistics of mat placement was deeply stressful, in a way that made me feel like I understood the primal conflicts for land that formed the basis of modern history. The room had a maximum occupancy of thirty, which might have been OK if everyone was just sitting there, but not if the idea was to make your body as long as possible and do sweeping motions with your limbs. Svetlana always made us get there early, to secure an advantageous position. Then the people who came later would try to crowd us out, inserting themselves between us, or directly in front of us, blocking our view—not apologetically, but with a self-righteous attitude. If you didn't defend your space like Svetlana did, sitting up extra straight and doing elaborate stretches, you got hemmed in and couldn't do the movements. People kept hitting you (or were you hitting them?) and giving you dirty looks.

One time, *I* was late to Pilates. Then I saw how everyone who had gotten there earlier was avoiding eye contact and doing stretches in the clear hope that I wouldn't sit near them, and would sit somewhere else. This felt unfair and hurtful: I had signed up on time, and had as much right to be there as they did. I had run all the way, and would have been early, except that I had been on the phone with my aunt, who wanted me to sign a piece of paper saying that I would be the adult guardian for my autistic cousin, David, after she and my uncle died. How confident the other people in the class seemed to be in the rights that had been conferred on them by being there first—which was really only a matter of luck, because their aunts hadn't happened to call just then. Where, exactly, did they want me to go? Did they want me to just not exist? Was that how the Israelis and Palestinians felt about each other?

I found myself looking to the instructor to arbitrate, but the instructor never did care about the fair allocation of space. She just said, "There's plenty of room for everyone." This was because of how flattered she felt by the number of people who came to the class, which she took as a personal compliment, rather than an indication of how stressed-out we were about our bodies. Every time a new person walked in the door, causing dread in everyone who was already there, the instructor seemed happier and more pleased with herself.

Her attitude reminded me of the tone in which my mother had sometimes relayed to me, when I was in high school, that someone or other at work had told her that she could still "have a child," or "have another child." She said it in a scoffing way at first, then added in a small voice that she supposed it *was* possible. I knew that she wasn't actually going to do it, and I shouldn't begrudge her the pleasure that the thought clearly gave her. But I couldn't help feeling panic. As matters stood, we never slept enough, and occasionally ran out of money. Why was it delightful to her to think about making things harder?

Dear Selin,

Olha has a difficult problem. It is no wonder that she is grouchy. You should try to be patient.

Of course I forgive you.

I don't know anything about genre theory, but I can learn.

Ivan

I hadn't expected Ivan to write back. It felt magical, like hearing from a dead person. I almost started to cry. Then I did "finger" and saw that Ivan was actually logged on to the Harvard network. He was physically here. Such relief—like some vital element had been restored to the atmosphere. He was finally here again, like last year, and he must have been planning to see me; that was why there had been hope and futurity in his tone. I wondered if I should write back to him, but I decided to wait for him to call, as I was sure that he would.

With the passage of time, this expectation came to strike me as insane. Of course he wasn't going to call. If he had hoped to see me, he would have told me he was coming. He was here to visit his girlfriend, to have sex with his girlfriend, to do any number of things and to see any number of people, but not me. I was literally the one person he would be least likely to want to see, out of everyone on the planet, including all the people he had never met.

All I wanted was to be unconscious—to be asleep—to experience that moment of freedom in the morning, right when you woke up. I always felt it was my fault for not managing to prolong it. But even in the moment when I was steeling myself to prolong it, I had already forgotten what it was that I was trying to ward off, and the effort of remembering would bring it all back.

I checked my watch. It was only four in the afternoon. How was I going to survive until bedtime? I wondered, not for the first time, whether it was possible to knock yourself unconscious by banging your head into a wall. But I knew that, if banging your head into a wall was a solution to the problem of consciousness, I would have heard about it by now. I decided to just go to the river and run until I got tired. (Was that what running *was*?)

When a song was about love, I felt the heavy gears start behind my eyes and in my sinuses. The songs that weren't about love seemed deliberately cryptic—almost frightening. Though I had hoped to run for two hours, I got a cramp after twenty minutes. I tried and failed to "power through." So: I wasn't even allowed to exhaust my body. I turned around and started to walk, blinking back tears as stronger, more admirable people ran or biked past me. Did they have the strength to run through their cramps, or were they so strong that they didn't get cramps?

When I got back to where I had started, I kept walking in the opposite direction. Walking didn't really change anything, the way running did, but time did continue to "pass" in the irreversible-seeming way that was attributable to the second law of thermodynamics. Soon, the sun had started to take itself elsewhere. At least one was vouchsafed that dignity: the passage from day to night, the illumination of the headlights that made human affairs resemble, to some slight extent, the cosmological formations that didn't have feelings or experience disgrace.

When I got home, Riley and Priya were getting ready to go to a party. Their premed friend Lewis was involved. The thought of the Lewis-clones in their drab pullovers, being witty and explanatory, expelling their robotic little laughs, was too dire to contemplate. Nor had I been invited. We exchanged jokes while they got dressed. By the time they left, it was almost nine. In only an hour, it would be a legitimate time to go to sleep. I could read in bed. I brushed my teeth and climbed into the top bunk and picked up *Swann's Way*.

"For a long time I went to bed early."

My eyes filled, I couldn't see, I couldn't breathe. For a *long time*?

It was actually disturbing, how much of *Swann's Way* was about trying to fall asleep. Some of it was interesting—like when he fell asleep reading and thought his body *was* the rivalry between François I and Charles V, because that's what he had been reading about. Or when he realized that his body could remember the furniture and configuration of all the other bedrooms he had slept in over his whole life. I felt somehow relieved to discover that I remembered the configuration of two bedrooms I had slept in in Ivan's parents' house—where the door and the window and the table were.

But I didn't like when Proust laid his cheeks "gently against the comfortable cheeks of my pillow, as plump and fresh as the cheeks of childhood." I wasn't into cheeks. Some people loved them. "Those *cheeks*!" women said, before they squeezed children's cheeks. My mother had used to speak gloatingly and enviously about my cheeks, always clarifying that hers weren't the same, she didn't have "baby fat." I had never liked it when she emphasized our differences. I had always wanted to look more like her.

Maybe the problem was childhood again. Falling asleep was interesting if you had the resources to confuse your own leg for a conflict between European kings, or to mentally review a space-time map of different bedroom furniture. But I didn't want to read about trying to fall asleep as a child. The part where his relatives got him a magic lantern: "They had indeed hit upon the idea, to distract me on the evenings when they found me looking too unhappy, of giving me a magic lantern. . . ." "Their" kindness—when "they" were the ones who had caused his problem.

The magic lantern reminded me of the shadow puppets on Turkish TV, and of the brass carousel on the piano in my Ankara grandmother's apartment. When you lit the candles, paper-thin brass angels turned slowly in a circle. How hard it was to describe, and how unrewarding. Yet there was a compulsion to describe it: the same compulsion clearly felt by many people to write vivid descriptions of things in their grandparents' houses. If I had to read about one more person's grandmother's sofa, about how it smelled like cough drops . . .

Proust's description of his grandmother herself was upsettingly sentimental—the way he went on about how much she loved them all, and disregarded herself. Her love and lack of self-regard were expressed in "a smile which, unlike those seen on the majority of human faces, bore no trace of irony save for herself, while for all of us kisses seemed to spring from her eyes." A grandmother's "love," her kisses: what did they mean? What was it to "love" a bunch of random people whom you maybe didn't understand at all—it seemed pretty clear that baby Proust was misunderstood by his grandparents—just because they were related to you? What was good about that: about a grandmother's "love" for you and disregard of herself? My Adana grandmother would stare into space, her eyes filled with tears. Once, I had suggested that she keep a diary: something I did, to keep from being bored and crying. "Ah, *maşallah*, my girl is always writing, ah ah, you write your diary. Me, what do I have to remember"—and her eyes swam tearfully.

"How I loved our church, and how clearly I can see it still!" Proust wrote, about a place where he had clearly been bored out of his mind. He described the "graceful Gothic arcades which crowded coquettishly" around a staircase—"like a row of grown-up sisters who, to hide him from the eyes of strangers, arrange themselves smilingly in front of a rustic, peevish and ill-dressed younger brother." The personification of the arcades reminded me of naps during which, to keep from dying of boredom, I used to hold my hand with the palm facing me and examine the fingernails which, seen upside-down or (in the case of the thumbnail) sideways, seemed to have different physiognomies and expressions. The index finger was a suppliant woman, with a big trembling smile; the middle finger, bigger and good-natured, a man, with a wider and less suppliant smile. On the ring finger, the white part of the nail had a different shape, giving it the brisk and ironical expression of my aunt Arzu (my mother's cousin), while the pinkie looked like a diminutive waiter: lithe and deferential. The thumb was genial and grinning, with a big jaw. In profile, the index fingers had an adoring expression. They could look up adoringly at each other, or look down shyly. The hours I had spent like that, making my fingers simper at each other. I would never write about that. It was enough I had wasted the time once. I would never waste more time by writing about it.

In tutorial, the part of *Swann's Way* that Judith talked the most about was the "good-night kiss," or the "bedtime kiss." The phrases were repulsive to me, as was the way Proust seemed to conflate his childhood love for his mother with romantic love between non-children. It was like when people joked knowingly about men who had "mommy issues"—it made falling in love seem babyish and unromantic. It was like my uncles who, whenever I had held one of my aunts' babies and the baby clutched at my chest—this was in middle school, before I had breasts—would laugh hysterically and say, "You're looking for something that isn't there."

The episode itself, about baby Proust's anguish on nights when his parents had dinner guests, was harrowing. I didn't like to admit it, but I was pretty sure that I had felt the same despair when my parents went to dinner parties. Being left at night for a party was so much worse than being left in the daytime for work; what was, for you, a cause of desperation, was for them an occasion for dress-up and celebration. But why did Proust have to keep thinking about it? Why couldn't he write a book about something else?

When I went home for Thanksgiving, my mother was funny and cool. Her new breasts stayed up by themselves, so she could throw out all her bras. She made an amazing meal as usual, from *The Silver Palate Cookbook*, and explained the new drug she was taking, how ingeniously it worked, by blocking estrogen from the hormone receptors on cancer cells.

A side effect of the drugs was that you got hot flashes and stopped having your period. You had to take the drug for five years, so, depending on how old you were when you started, your period might not come back. Of all the side effects of menopause, my mother seemed the most concerned about her voice deepening.

I thought about whether I would want to get implants, if I ever had to have my breasts removed. When my father's sister had stayed with us after her mastectomy, she had cried at dinner every night. One night, she said that she didn't feel like a woman anymore because she didn't have breasts. I didn't have breasts, and I didn't think it was a big deal. But I understood that it was a big deal, because my father, who usually tried to minimize my aunt's worries, fell silent and didn't tell her to stop crying. On the other hand, I still remembered how stressed-out Leora and I had been to start getting breasts, a year or two later. Was it possible to go back to that mental state?

In my former bedroom, I stared at all my old books. I took down my high school copy of *Eugene Onegin*. That was when I discovered or remembered something important, namely, that the guy I had first identified with Onegin had been, not Ivan, whom I hadn't met yet, but, rather, my violin teacher. How could I have forgotten that so completely? How could one person just replace another like that?

How much of everything had started with my violin teacher, who was Russian, and married, and had two children? He was the one to whom I had imagined writing a letter—the one I had imagined showing up, "like a grim shade." He really had resembled a grim shade, it was almost like that was the look he was going for. I thought this was funny—just like *Eugene Onegin* was funny. It was how funny Pushkin was about Onegin that made the whole thing seem benevolent and sparkling.

It wasn't like I hadn't seen my violin teacher's limitations. Clearly, there was something sketchy and undignified about him, something that didn't reflect well about how physically present and brooding he acted, how he called on the phone late at night to reschedule lessons, how he looked at me and touched my arm and took my violin and held it or played it or tuned it, forcing the pegs when they stuck. Also, even though private lessons were supposed to be covered by the music school tuition, he kept trying to get my mother to pay him extra, because he said he was so much better than all the other teachers. This stressed out my mom, and was unattractive, and made the whole thing now feel somehow shameful.

But he was so good at the violin, and the way he was good was so complicated and had so many things to notice. And he was working so hard, for that hour we spent together, every week, to make me better—listening so attentively, taking whatever I had played, and returning it, transformed and beautiful. At a time when all I thought about was escape or rescue—*he* had rescued me. He had rescued me from poor bow-direction-changing. I had been alone with the traumatic scratchiness of the change from up-bow to down-bow—and he had shown me how to control the pressure and speed, until you couldn't hear the change, and the sound just kept pouring like velvet.

Was it possible that, although I thought of Ivan as my first love, it had all happened already with my violin teacher? I hadn't written him a letter. But I had had the feelings that Tatiana had when she wrote to Onegin, that repeated when I wrote to Ivan: the feeling of having put myself in his power, entrusted myself to his honor, like I was falling, like I could die, but he would catch me . . . probably. I had felt it every week, in the drafty studio with the green wallpaper and the window overlooking Riverside Park.

And yet, the second time had blocked out the first time, and I didn't like to think that it hadn't been the first time.

That whole time, all of high school and also middle school, was something I didn't like to think about. It had been like prison. I knew it was wrong to compare my experience at a prep school in New Jersey to that of a disadvantaged person in an actual prison. Still, I compared it. Enforced idleness, arbitrary punishment, being trapped for hours among people crazed by hormones and boredom. . . . Some rewards went to the domineering, others to the servile. You couldn't *not* be in an unhealthy relationship to power.

The worst part was the school bus, because you couldn't get off, and the "American" boys did stuff like batting at the driver's head with their lacrosse sticks. The driver, Darnell, who was, in retrospect, gay, would utter theatrical protests, but didn't seem to view the situation as alterable in any way, and would just crank up the volume on his Queen tape. A sickening realization: driving on the highway, contrary to what adults were constantly saying, did *not* require total concentration, and Darnell was eminently capable of doing it while being hit on the head with a lacrosse stick. The next thought that came to me was the relieving one that, so long as they were occupied with Darnell, the lacrosse boys weren't persecuting me. I immediately felt ashamed. Later I saw a similar thought expressed in a Holocaust memoir, and felt better, and then felt worse.

The gap between Darnell's front teeth, together with the unselfconscious way he sang along with "Bohemian Rhapsody," reminded me of my youngest aunt, and made me feel close to him. The first ten times I heard "Bohemian Rhapsody," I didn't understand how it was a song, and felt that the others were justified in scoffing at it. But there eventually came a time when Darnell screamed, "Mama! I killed a man!" and I was moved to tears, feeling certain that I, too, had killed a man.

I wanted to do something for Darnell, but felt powerless against the lacrosse boys who, once I was brought to their attention in any way, would start snickering and droning to each other about how ugly I was. The one with disfiguring acne said that I was the ugliest girl in the school. His friend always took my part: "I just don't know. *The* ugliest?" They ended amicably, united in the consensus that it would be impossible for anyone to have sex with me.

I wrote a letter to the bus company, asking them to name Darnell Driver of the Month. It was something he always talked about: who had gotten Driver of the Month and how he hoped it would someday be him. Instead of making him Driver of the Month, they *gave* him the letter. He kept it tucked behind the sun visor and referred to it frequently, and I was so embarrassed I wished I had never written it.

That whole time, six years, I had always been in love with someone. It was the only thing that made it feasible to live that way, getting up at six and remaining conscious until late at night. It was like religion had been, for medieval people: it gave you the energy to face a life of injustice, powerlessness, and drudgery. The guys I was in love with always ignored me, but were never unkind. There was something abstract and gentle about the experience of being ignored—a feeling of being spared, a known impossibility of anything happening—that was consonant with my understanding of love. In theory, of course, I knew that love could be reciprocated. It was a thing that happened, often, to other people. But I was unlike other people in so many ways.

I knew that my mother, who was smarter than everyone else and also beautiful, had also never had a boyfriend in high school. Her sister said it was because she was too smart, she had seen through everyone, there hadn't been anyone worthy of her. That wasn't what my mother said. My mother said she had longed for a boyfriend and had listened to sad American songs and cried every night. "I'm so glad you're not like that. I'm so glad you don't care. You're so much smarter than I am. If I were you I would have been in love with one of those losers," she said. I often *was* in love with one of the losers, but I kept it to myself.

My mother's love life changed when she was seventeen and went to the top medical school in Turkey and met my father. So I always assumed that things would change for me, too, when I left high school. In the meantime, I experienced those guys' indifference as a benign, even beneficent force—one that supported me in the struggle to study and to get out.

There was a problem in it somewhere, because the point of getting out was to become a writer and write novels, and novels were all about that other kind of love—the kind where "something happened." But when had I not had to dismiss some concern about the disjuncture between literature and the way I was living my life? In middle school I had been troubled by Huckleberry Finn and Holden Caulfield, who didn't care about grades, and who had the courage to run away. Would they have despised me?

Over the weekend, my mother and I drove to New York to see a Picasso exhibit at the Museum of Modern Art. We strolled through slowly, arm in arm, reading the wall text aloud, and sharing our opinions. My mother would observe fondly, yet somehow begrudgingly, that a painting was beautiful; or sometimes, disapprovingly: "very ugly." Of a painting we only sort of liked, we would say, tolerantly, "He did his best"—literally, "he did what came from his hand": one of the many basic Turkish phrases that sounded, to me, like a world-weary witticism.

The exhibit was all portraits. The portraits "documented" Picasso's relationship with the women he was having sex with. Each woman was linked to a different style of painting, though the style sometimes preceded the woman who later embodied it. Fernande Olivier was Cubist. Olga Khokhlova was Neoclassical. Marie-Thérèse Walter was "surreal biomorphism," and Dora Maar was "anguished Expressionism."

The extent to which Picasso idealized or disfigured the women in his paintings was a test: not just of their physical beauty, but in some way of their human worth.

FRANÇOISE GILOT DOMINATED PICASSO'S AFFECTION FOR NEARLY A DECADE. GIFTED AS A PAINTER AND WRITER, GILOT FUNCTIONED AS HIS CO-EQUAL.

PICASSO'S DEPICTIONS OF HER AND THEIR TWO
CHILDREN, PALOMA AND CLAUDE, ARE AMONG HIS
MOST UNEQUIVOCALLY ADMIRING IMAGES.

How had Françoise succeeded? It wasn't just that she herself had been an artist. After all, Dora Maar had been a famous photographer, and she had failed. She had become "the Weeping Woman."

Green, jagged, screaming, Dora crammed into her mouth a handkerchief that resembled broken glass. Her body was crucified onto an armchair. Her face was woven into a basket. When Picasso left her for Françoise, who was twenty years younger than Dora (and forty years younger than Picasso), Dora was found naked in the stairwell of her apartment. She ended up in a sanatorium, getting electric shock therapy for three weeks. Lacan cured her, but she came out a Catholic, and didn't make any art for ten years.

What should a person's attitude be toward Picasso? As a child, I had felt bullied by him. In photographs, bald, aggressive, bull-like yet boyish, he had reminded me of Jerry. It was the boyishness that was sinister. I felt he was trying to take something that rightly belonged to children—one of the few things we had—and keep it for himself. The bullied feeling was connected to the way you had to choose between either the art teacher, who said that Picasso was a genius, or the kind of people who only liked photorealistic paintings of cars. I would side, under such circumstances, with Picasso, but I wasn't happy about it.

In high school, Picasso had seemed somewhat less threatening. Even though nothing in my external life had changed—even though my mother was still an elegant heroic woman, and I was an awkward overprivileged teenager with no power or independence or boyfriend—nonetheless there was a dimension, separate from perceptible reality, in which the balance had shifted. Love affairs no longer felt *only* like a power my parents had to menace me from a distance. They were a venue through which, if only hypothetically, I could be the one who was special—who could finally have someone on my side, apart from myself.

By then I was thinking more practically about how to become a writer, and I understood that a person had to appreciate Picasso—not all of him, but the part that was an artist. It was an intellectual exercise that made you feel proud of your open-mindedness and objectivity. You could note how he was an asshole, and hold it in part of your mind, and then, with the rest of your mind, appreciate how totally he had managed to express himself. If you were in favor of individualism, self-expression, and human achievement; if you believed it was admirable to stay alive and awake, to not be deadened and blinded by conventions; if you were generous, subtle, capable of complexity and nuance—capable, to put it differently, of forgiveness, and of surmounting your own grievances in the interest of "the human"—then you had to like Picasso.

The last portrait in the show was a crayon self-portrait: "a near-death mask, staring terrified and goggle-eyed into the abyss." The image of ninety-one-year-old Picasso goggling into the abyss, which was reproduced on the exhibit brochure, reminded me both of Jerry, and of Philip Roth, whose books Jerry had caused my mother to buy, and which I, too, had therefore read. Did it mean you were anti-Semitic if you didn't feel sorry for Philip Roth because shiksas didn't want to have sex with him?

Jerry had called my mom a shiksa, and had also often spoken of ice queens. My mother also began to refer to ice queens, and to wiseasses, and occasionally told me to not be a wiseass: a thing she had never said before she met Jerry. I understood that, although my mother was a shiksa, she was not an ice queen. I wasn't an ice queen, either, and never would be. But would I be a shiksa when I grew up?

Jerry called me "the kid," and said I was spoiled because I was allowed to read during dinner: a thing I only did when he was there, to avoid having to talk to him. Once, he told my mother at a restaurant— I heard him, even though I was reading—that she couldn't possibly understand how tenuous he felt in the world, knowing that the Holocaust could happen again any minute. He asked himself sometimes whether my mother would be the kind of person who would hide him from the Nazis, and he just wasn't sure.

When I compared his life—the multistory row house, the Italian sports car, the weekly squash game, the string quartet where he played a hundred-year-old violin, the two Harvard degrees and well-funded lab—to that of my mother, who had gone to med school at seventeen, autopsying dead drunkards in her gross anatomy class; who always got paid less than my father for doing the same amount of work, and now had two jobs and was constantly being berated by everyone; my mother, to whom colleagues routinely asked insane questions like whether she was personally acquainted with Yasser Arafat's wife, or whether women in Turkey were allowed to wear bathing suits—when I compared their lives, I wondered just what kind of protection this guy expected my mother to give him against the Nazis. Jerry eventually left my mother for one of the ice queens he had always complained about. Their wedding was on my mother's birthday.

My mother said I didn't seem well. In fact, tears were streaming down my face. "I'm fine," I assured her. "It's not related to anything." I had a belief that I had always cried this much. Hadn't we all laughed about it, when I was three? Adults would ask me what was the matter, and I would say I was "moved."

My mother said that I was incorrect; I had always had a tender heart, but I had not gone around like a stricken mask of tragedy. She talked about exciting work that was being done on antidepressants. "We have to find a maven," she said, and resolved to get me the name of someone who knew about psychopharmacology. It was just what I had thought I hadn't wanted—a referral to some guy—and yet, hearing her talk about it as if it was already decided, I felt relief.

"Won't it be expensive?" I asked.

"What? That is not an issue," she said, as if it was beneath consideration.

On the way to the train station, my mother said that she wasn't going to wash my sheets after I left. Sometimes, she said, she slept in my bed for one or two nights, because the bed still smelled like me. She smiled conspiratorially, and I felt my heart constrict.

DECEMBER

When I stopped by her room to pick her up to go jogging, Svetlana opened the door wearing just leggings and a sports bra.

"I hooked up with Matt," she said, indicating some red marks on her chest and shoulders. Was that hives? Who was Matt? Would I ever understand reality again? I felt relieved when Svetlana zipped up her fleece pullover. Maybe things would go back to normal. With some effort, I placed Matt—a genial, Dad-like dude who did a cappella. I used to see him at the Russian conversation table I had stopped going to, because the conversation was so boring.

Nothing went back to normal. Matt was now Svetlana's boyfriend. I felt the same shameful emotions I had experienced in the past, when my aunts, mother, and father, in pursuit of various "relationships," had brought more and more tedious people into our lives. Envy, jealousy, loneliness, despair—and also a kind of guilt, mixed with relief. Insofar as Svetlana and I had been in competition, to see whose worldview was better . . . that was over. She would never again be what she had been, not in my life, and not in her own. This boyfriend, or his successor, would restrict her activities, her thoughts. In a way, I had won, but it felt like defeat. How could she drop out of the race, when we had only just started? How had they gotten her so easily? Did they get every-one? Would they get me? Did I want them to?

There had been two guys at the Russian conversation table: Matt and Gavriil. I found Gavriil less off-putting than Matt. Was I supposed to date Gavriil? How were you supposed to know who to date?

Gavriil and I were partners to write a Russian skit. As soon as we had sat down, he told me he had started seeing this girl, Katie. I knew Katie: she did art history, spoke fluent French, and looked like an adorable puppet. She seemed just as friendly as Gavriil, *and* cooler and more conventionally attractive.

It became impossible to have a real conversation with Svetlana. On the plus side, Matt was good-natured and didn't have a self-esteem prob-lem, so you didn't have to deal with him blaming you for making him feel stupid. On the other hand, the minute you tried to talk about anything interesting, he would swiftly, good-naturedly, inexorably change the subject back to one of the three kinds of things he ever talked about.

Matt acted as if he enjoyed my company: a clear subterfuge to en-able him to interrupt me and Svetlana whenever we were alone. He greeted me in a collegial fashion, recruited me to join him in jokes on the principle of: "We all know what Svetlana is like." Then he would start kissing Svetlana's neck, causing me to feel like I was violating their privacy and embodying some kind of sterile bitterness.

Once, when Matt was traveling with the Chorduroys and Svetlana and I were talking the way we used to, Svetlana surprised me by saying: "This is the kind of conversation we can't have when Matt is around." I felt unutterable relief—finally, she had noticed that Matt wasn't fully capable of meaningful discourse!—followed by sinking horror: Svetlana had always known, and she didn't care.

Gavriil thought it was weird that last year my life had been so romantic and he and Svetlana hadn't had any adventures, but now he and Svetlana had romantic lives and I didn't. "Don't you think that's weird?" he asked.

Katie got sick and refused to eat anything but strawberries. Gavriil bought her strawberries, which she ended up puking, and which he cleaned up—because he loved her. He said in a fervent voice that he hoped that someday I would meet someone who would love me enough to clean up if I puked strawberries all over a bathtub.

Lucas and I were talking about books we thought were funny, and he mentioned *The Rachel Papers* by Martin Amis. My mother and I had both read *The Information* by Martin Amis, and hadn't enjoyed it. Lucas said that *The Rachel Papers* was funnier, and he thought I would like it. I was pleasantly surprised to learn that Lucas had any idea of me at all, let alone one that I could learn more about by reading a book.

The Rachel Papers was about a nineteen-year-old guy who wanted to conquer this girl, Rachel, who he thought was out of his league. Later, after they had sex, he decided that she wasn't smart enough and had a big nose. Her nose made an appearance every few pages. The narrator seemed to take its existence personally, as if it was deliberately flaunting itself to remind him of the low social status that prevented him from conquering someone with a better nose.

At one point, the nose added insult to injury by getting a pimple.

When I opened my eyes to the bubbling big boy inches from my lips, I really should have said: "Morning, beautiful." And seeing it half an hour later, matted with make-up, I really should have cried: "Oh look. You *haven't* got a spot on your nose!" And, that evening, when Rachel announced: "The curse is upon me" (misquoting "The Lady of Shalott"), my answer should really have been: "Surprise surprise. Listen, you've got it in italics right across your conk."

I reread the passage, trying to identify where Rachel had made her mistake. Definitely, she shouldn't have used concealer: it looked worse *and* it clogged your pores. And probably it was pretentious to quote "The Lady of Shalott" instead of just saying you had your period—especially if you didn't get the quote right. I looked up the correct quote—"The curse is *come* upon me," not "The curse is upon me"—and filed it away for future reference.

When I read the passage a third time, I understood that both the concealer and "The Lady of Shalott" were beside the point, since the narrator had become upset earlier, at the moment he first set eyes on the pimple. Maybe Rachel's real problem was that she hadn't figured out what product to use so she wouldn't get pimples. I had noticed an improvement in my own complexion after I started using seven-dollar pore-refining cleanser.

Later on the page, though, the narrator said something that implied that he believed that all people sometimes got pimples. So, the problem couldn't be getting the pimple, but reacting to it wrongly: failing to acknowledge it. Then it seemed to me that Rachel had participated in the genteel, life-denying hypocrisy, in the reluctance to speak frankly about menstruation or the body, that I had occasionally seen condemned in English novels. It seemed related to her refusal to give the narrator a blow job, even after he shoved his penis in her face ("almost up her nose"). She had owed him that—she had owed him to take the penis out of her nose and put it in her mouth—because he had been selfless enough to give *her* oral sex, even though it had been disgusting. ("It was too dark there (thank God) for me to be able to see what was right in front of my nose, just some kind of glistening pouch, redolent of oysters.")

At the end, the narrator got into Oxford, and dumped Rachel by writing her a letter. Rachel came over and cried, which made her nose look shiny. After she left, the narrator started writing a story from the perspective of a girl who was getting a PMS pimple. That was it—that was the whole book.

I tried to summarize my takeaways. "The curse is *come* upon me"; avoid concealer; be the writer.

Why had Lucas liked this book? It was, I supposed, good on a sentence level. (Was it, though? *Could* an oyster-redolent pouch glisten in the dark?) And didn't reading it make a person feel worse? Did it not make Lucas feel worse? Or was evoking a bad feeling somehow the artistic point? What if the only reason I *hadn't* liked the book was that I was a girl, and had a big nose—that it was a subject I was "sensitive" about, and I had a personal bias that I had to overcome if I wanted to appreciate the book objectively on its own terms, as Lucas had been able to do?

For some reason, I found myself thinking back to the time when I was twelve and went to stay with my mother for the weekend in Philadelphia, and found her face black and bruised and bandaged, as if she had been beaten. It turned out that Jerry had said that my mother would be "classically beautiful" if she had a different nose, and, when she laughed and said she couldn't afford a nose job, he had paid for it himself. Jerry was a short bald man with a visibly bad personality, and my mother was beautiful, and he had broken her face. Yet, my mother was happy with her new nose, and seemed to think of the whole episode as an example of something positive that Jerry had done. One of the things my father's lawyer had later said, when he was trying to prove that my mother was an unfit parent, was that she might force me to get plastic surgery. This statement somehow made me suspect that my father didn't like my nose. My mother always said that my nose was completely different from hers, and much more elegant. If her nose had been like mine, she would never have changed it. I wasn't sure if it was true, since I couldn't remember what her old nose had looked like, and none of the pictures from that time seemed to show her nose clearly.

Lakshmi said that, although Martin Amis had made some contributions to postmodern literature, *The Rachel Papers* was quite juvenile, and she wasn't surprised that I hadn't liked it. Lakshmi, whose nose resembled mine, said she wasn't against the idea of having work done someday. The conversation turned to Orlan, the conceptual artist whose art form was getting plastic surgeries based on famous paintings. She already had the forehead of the Mona Lisa and the chin of Botticelli's Venus, and looked terrifying. Apparently, one question people asked about Orlan was whether she was really an artist, or just a mentally ill person being exploited by surgeons.

I couldn't think at first who Orlan reminded me of, then realized it was the guy in *Against Nature*. Her project seemed theoretically cool, but in practice somehow gross and pointless.

Lakshmi explained that the point was to critique the male artistic convention of creating an ideal woman by recombining different parts of famous beauties. Orlan was showing how, if you took literally the things that were said by dumb men, you ended up at something gross and dangerous.

"Isn't that *literally* cutting off your nose to spite your face, though?" I asked. "Whose nose did she get, anyway?"

Lakshmi took a folded-up photocopy out of her handbag. She actually had an article about Orlan on her person. "A famous, unattributed School of Fontainebleau sculpture of Diana," she read. We both burst out laughing. I said I thought it would be more efficient to just ignore society and dumb men. Lakshmi said that, according to French feminist theory, you couldn't ignore the men, because their views on women were baked into culture at such a deep level. Just by using words, you were perpetuating their ideas, because they were the ones who had made up language.

"So what are you supposed to do? Not use words?"

"Well, they say that women have to make up their own language, and their own kind of writing, outside of the patriarchal hegemony."

I stared at her. "You're joking."

"No, not at all. It's called *écriture féminine.*"

I looked up "*écriture féminine*" in a dictionary of literary theory. The people who had thought it up apparently didn't like to define it, because definitions were part of Western phallogocentric rationalism. *Écriture féminine* wasn't the *opposite* of phallogocentrism, exactly, because the idea of opposites and binaries was also something men had come up with, in order to dominate and exploit nature. Rather, *écriture féminine* set out to shatter those binaries, opening up a new area of discourse, free play, and chaos. The idea of opening up a new language seemed exciting. On the other hand, I never had been a huge fan of free play or chaos. Nor did I feel like my main problem with other people or the external world was an excess of logic.

The more I read about *écriture féminine*, the less appealing it sounded. It was characterized, I learned, by textual disruptions, puns, etymologies, and slippery metaphors like milk, orgasm, menstrual blood, and the ocean. It worked by celebrating mother figures and the multiplicity of the feminine, defying the fetish of the sole "objective" God-father-author-truth, supplanting the unified phallus with "the two lips which embrace continually of the female sex." That was a quote from Luce Irigaray, who also noted that "collaboration" was etymologically related to "labia" and that women's lips were "always touching each other in 'collaboration.'"

What if I didn't want to collaborate that way? What if I wanted to use logic, by myself, in an "objective" way—without mothers or menstrual blood?

"A feminine textual body is recognized by the fact that it is always endless, without ending: there's no closure, it doesn't stop, and it's this that very often makes the feminine text difficult to read," wrote Hélène Cixous, in a sentence that could definitely have been shorter. I didn't get it: why did *we* have to write stuff that was hard to read and didn't have an ending, just because men were wrong?

At dinner, Oak said he had switched his major to Folklore and Mythology, which had the fewest requirements. I set out my views on the arbitrariness of departments, and on how there should be a department of love.

Ezra told a story about a kid in his computer science lecture class who had asked, about some algorithm—Ezra assumed the shrewd, hardhitting manner of someone unafraid to ask the tough questions—"But is it capable of love?"

Ezra's basketball friend, Wei, said that he had been teaching a section on the lambda calculus, and one freshman had hung around afterward, apparently yearning to get something off his chest, before finally blurting: "When do we learn about the lamb?" Wei spoke rarely, but always said something interesting.

Oak, who never seemed to have anything to do or anywhere to be, walked Priya and Riley and me back from dinner.

"Are you OK?" Riley asked Priya, who kept staring at the sky.

"I just can't tell if it's raining," she said.

"It could be Selin's Finnish friend doing a thought experiment," Riley said. That was what she always said now, whenever we weren't sure if something was really happening.

A note addressed to Riley was taped to our door. Riley's face lit up in a way I had only ever seen when cats were involved.

"Is that from Lucas?" Oak asked. Riley cast her eyes girlishly downward. "Riley likes Lucas!" said Oak. From the fact that Riley didn't contradict him, I understood that she not only liked Lucas, but felt confident that Lucas liked her, too.

I felt dumb for never having considered the possibility that Riley might eventually pair off with one of her guy friends. Now it seemed obvious. Obviously *all* the girls, whether they talked about it or not, were on the lookout for any reprieve from the hassle of not having a boyfriend: the way it exposed you to censure and nosiness.

This thing with the boyfriends—it wasn't a passing fad. Nothing would go back to how it had been. It would become more and more like the way it was. The stakes would get higher, the choices more limited. There were to be no exciting private discoveries of another person. Any option that occurred to you was bound to have occurred to others, embroiling you in a struggle—like the struggle between Zita and Eunice, which I had entered, without even realizing it. Lucas was funny, tall, polite, and didn't say or do gross things. He was such an obvious candidate. I reflected back on all the polite, kind things he

179

had ever said to me. Why had the thought never crossed my mind? It crossed my mind now, but I dismissed it, since Riley liked him.

My mother got me a referral to a psychiatrist in one of the gazillion teaching hospitals in Boston. You took the Red Line to Park Street and changed to the Green Line. The Red Line went underground and felt like a subway, but the Green Line came aboveground and started to feel like a streetcar.

In ancient times, this had been a charitable "lying-in hospital" for virtuous ladies of straitened means. The prostitutes had gone to a different hospital. The building was way more upscale than the one in Brooklyn where my mother worked. High over the street, busy-looking people in scrubs or white coats were clutching coffee cups, striding along a glassed-in walkway. The psychiatry department was in a basement and had no windows. It smelled like the hall outside my mom's lab. Was someone keeping rabbits down here?

The psychiatrist was thin, middle-aged, balding, and wore a white coat. He sat behind a desk in a leather executive chair. I sat in one of three less expensive chairs in front of the desk.

"What brings you here today," he said, with an expression devoid of curiosity.

"I think I'm depressed," I said.

"What makes you think that?"

"I can't stop crying."

He asked about my family's history of physical and mental illnesses. I realized that, although I felt that I knew my family's history, there were a lot of questions I couldn't answer. It was like looking in a drawer and finding it empty. I remembered that a great-aunt had killed herself, but why? A lot of people had cancer.

The psychiatrist looked at me sharply. "Who has cancer?"

I found that, notwithstanding my feeling that our house had constantly been full of people who had cancer, I couldn't name any of them, except my grandfather and aunt, and now my mother.

"Was the treatment *successful?*" he asked, about my aunt and my mother, sounding like he was criticizing me for not being sufficiently concerned.

He went down a list of routine questions: whether I had been dropped on the head as a child, had seizures, or received special messages from the radio or television; whether I was sexually active, did drugs, thought I would be better off dead, or planned to hurt myself or others.

I said "no" to everything, notwithstanding my wish, passionate at times, to be dead. It seemed clear that the only part he cared about was the plan—the plan to "hurt myself" (though it was really the opposite; it was a plan to stop being hurt). "Better off dead"—as if the whole point wasn't to opt out, once and for all, from the question of how to be well-off, or better-off.

But I didn't have a plan, I wasn't going to do it: partly because it would be the same thing as murdering my mother, and her sister, and then what would happen to my cousin; and partly out of fear that I would fail, and then people would say it had been a "cry for help." Which is exactly what it would be if I told this guy about it now.

"Did you like school?" asked the psychiatrist.

"No."

A look of displeasure flickered over his face. "Why not?"

The inexpressible twelve-year panorama of school rose before me. "It was basically torture," I said.

There was something he objected to, or didn't believe. "But you must have been a successful student," he said.

I couldn't think when I had last met a more unpleasant person. I wondered whether I was having resistance. Was he telling me things I had repressed for some reason? If I accepted them, would I feel better?

"I actually think most of the people in my family are depressed," I said at some point, realizing the truth of the statement only as I said it.

"Are they being *treated*?" the psychiatrist asked, making it sound like the lowest baseline of responsible behavior.

I told him that I thought my mother went to a psychiatrist. He asked for how long. At first, I was going to say that it had only been since the court made her move back to New Jersey. But then I remembered that, during the custody suit, she had asked a psychiatrist in Philadelphia to give her a character reference. So there had been a psychiatrist in Philadelphia. He had told my mother that the only thing he felt able to tell the court was that she had left one masochistic relationship with my father, to go straight into another masochistic relationship with Jerry.

"So your mother left your father and you. What was that like for you?" asked the psychiatrist, causing me to realize that, like most people, he was going to criticize and blame my mother, and my heart shut off to him completely. But I still sat there and answered the questions; I didn't get up and walk out. Was that because of social conventions? Or did part of me still hope that he knew something I didn't?

<hr/>

"It finally happened," Svetlana said. "I had sex with Matt. And afterwards I thought, today this really important step in my life has taken place. But how is it physically different than if yesterday I had just jammed in a banana?"

The dining hall seemed to have just gotten a shipment of particularly large and underripe bananas. Rigid and green-tinged, they were sharply curved at one end and less curved at the other, which gave them a smirky, jawlike aspect. To me, an apple had been the obvious choice. But Svetlana had taken a banana, and was holding it up now.

"It's *literally* the same thing," she said.

I eyed the banana, estimating its girth at about six times that of a tampon. And yet, Svetlana wasn't the kind of person who used "literally" to mean "figuratively."

As usual, she seemed to know what I was thinking. "It turns out Matt has a really big one," she said, in a tone of combined exasperation, humor, and pride.

"But, like . . ." I glanced—eloquently, I felt—at the banana.

"I know, I was so surprised. It's weird how you can't tell what size a guy is going to be."

"But how did you . . . How did it . . ."

"Well, it was excruciatingly painful, especially the first time. But after two or three times, it basically goes in. You don't *feel* like it's possible, but obviously your body's capacity is greater than your awareness of it. I mean, the circumference of a baby's head is thirty-five centimeters."

I felt a wave of despair.

Svetlana asked if I thought she looked different. I did. Her face seemed softer, rounder. She was wearing a white cardigan I didn't recognize, and the white seemed to hold a different meaning than it would have before.

Svetlana said that sex was different from what you expected—discontinuous from making out. It was something you couldn't imagine in advance and was clearly, like everything else, going to take practice. The only part that was already exciting and satisfying was being able to see Matt's desire—to have clear evidence of being so desired.

"As a woman, you can hide your desire from another person, or be unaware of it yourself," she said. I felt confused. Didn't men also conceal their desires from themselves and others? "But it's different for a guy," she continued, "because his desire has such a visual and tangible reality." Then I understood she was talking about an erection.

"Desire" seemed so metaphoric and wide-ranging, and an erection seemed so literal and specific. Was that really what desire was: the thing that was signified by an erection?

As if according to schedule, Gavriil told me he had had sex with Katie. He felt like he was good at sex, but worried that he couldn't know, and felt troubled by how much more mysterious sex was for women than it was for men.

"How so?" I asked.

"Well, for a guy, it's always the same. But for a woman . . . it's different every time."

I had no idea what he was talking about. "Do you mean, like, the *result* is different? Or the process?"

"That's just it!" he said.

The longer we talked, the more I felt like he was asking me for some kind of advice or information. It seemed almost like he was asking whether I thought Katie had had real orgasms, or whether she had been faking. But how could I know that?

Svetlana said that Katie was definitely faking orgasms. Even Svetlana, with her refusal to distort herself into acceptable forms, had felt a powerful compulsion to fake. Sex was radically different from making yourself come. What you had learned with yourself didn't translate. There were too many things to think about, and you weren't in control; you had to relinquish control. This was true even if you were on top. Therefore, you basically never had an orgasm. When Matt used his hand, it actually felt distracting, because penetration was such a different feeling from clitoral stimulation, and it took all a person's concentration to understand it. The two feelings did seem to converge somewhere, especially when you were lying on your stomach, so maybe that was the way it would eventually happen.

The impetus for faking was more complicated than it seemed. It wasn't *just* to relieve Matt's performance anxiety. It was also about Svetlana's anxiety. A guy's problem-free ability to orgasm from sex had something demoralizing about it. It could make you feel blocked, inadequate, and frigid. Svetlana knew she wasn't any of those things. There were moments when she felt a deep current flowing through her body, stronger than anything Matt could fathom, and she knew that when she tapped into it, it would flatten them both like a tidal wave. She was afraid of it, but she knew she had to get there, and *would* get there. But there were also moments when she felt despair, when it felt like it was always out of grasp, and she understood why they called it reaching for the brass ring. To fake it would be to give in to the despair, and that was something she was never going to do.

Riley disappeared for two weeks, because Lucas had his own room, and she was always staying in Mather. Then, one of Oak's geologists, Beau, got back together with his high school girlfriend, who went to a small liberal arts college where they encouraged people's personalities and didn't care whether they went to classes. That girl, Becca, basically moved into their suite and was always there, monitoring the guys' schedule, actually washing the towels. Becca was one of those people who either couldn't tell or didn't care that she was infuriating Riley, and had tried to give Riley pointers to help her be less negative. As a result, Riley stopped going to Mather, and Lucas started staying over in our room, sleeping with Riley in the bottom bunk. It was a situation we never discussed or acknowledged. We might all be talking companionably enough at an earlier stage in the evening, but, once everyone was in their beds, it was like we weren't aware of each other's existence. Riley and Lucas whispered between themselves, and I never did feel like I could just chime in with an observation about whatever I had just been reading.

After the psychiatrist, I always cried on the T. If you betrayed embarrassment or made a production of wiping your eyes, people stared, or asked if you were OK, or aggressively looked away in a way that made you feel guilty. But if you acted like nothing was happening, you floated on a magical cushion of invisibility. Maybe people didn't notice, or they thought you just had an eye problem.

It was always hard to reconstruct the conversation that had upset me so much. Only snippets stuck in my mind. Like when the psychiatrist asked: "Why are all these details so precious to you?"

"What do you mean?" I asked.

"What is so precious to you in this story with this Hungarian fellow? Why are you holding on to it?"

It reminded me of something I had read in Freud, about how misers hoarded gold the way children hoarded excrement. Was that what this guy was saying that I was doing? Was that what psychiatry was about? Was it related to toilet training? Did I have to think about toilet training? The word "precious" made me think of Gollum in *The Hobbit*, who represented all that was the most base in human nature. Why was "precious" bad? Why was it an insult for writing to be "precious"? Was it wrong to value things—to want to keep them? If so, how did I get free from it? If this guy was telling me to not value something, wasn't he obliged to offer me something better?

Later, I was back in that hospital basement, trying to describe my feeling of the world being a huge soul-crushing sex conspiracy that I didn't know how to be a part of. The psychiatrist looked at me dispassionately and said: "Do you think you are attractive to men?"

I gaped. Was he being cruel, or just dumb? I had told him that nobody had ever kissed me, or asked me out. And anyway, he himself could see me. Here I was. "No," I said.

Impatience flickered over his face. "Why not?"

I stared at him incredulously. How could he ask me to account for that? I had to experience it, *and* I had to explain it? Was he saying it was my fault?

At the T stop, I stared fixedly ahead, as tears streamed down my face, and my nasal passages shut down. Was this the "work" you had to do? Was I getting better?

My mother asked about therapy. I told her I cried a lot afterward and usually couldn't remember why, so maybe it was working.

"Hmm," my mother said, sounding unconvinced. "What does he say about meds?"

"Nothing."

"He hasn't mentioned anything?"

"No."

"Did you tell him about the crying?"

"Yeah."

"Next time, ask him about medication," she said.

I didn't say anything.

"Are you going to ask him?"

"But maybe he thinks I don't need it," I said. "Isn't it like you only need it if you have a chemical imbalance?" Surely, a brain was either chemically imbalanced, or it wasn't, and a trained professional could immediately tell the difference. Going to a psychiatrist couldn't be like going to a restaurant, where you told them what you wanted. And if it *was* like that—if antidepressants were something that wasn't objectively necessary, but was somehow optional . . .

"Sweetie, if it was optional to feel better, why would you not want to do it?" my mother asked.

"But then why don't we all just do recreational drugs?"

My mother explained the reasons that we didn't all just do recreational drugs. Street drugs were highly addictive, so that over time you had to keep upping the dose to get the same effect, and got sick if you couldn't get it. They affected the control centers of the brain, leading to hazardous behavior, and were unregulated, so we didn't know what was in them. They were illegal, meaning that if you bought them, you were continuing a system that led to poverty and wars, and you yourself could end up in jail. None of these things were true of antidepressants. I was filled with admiration for how good my mother was at explaining things.

My mother said that I was making this into a bigger deal than it was, because lots of people my age took antidepressants. My high school friend Shelly's boyfriend, Aidan, was now doing very well on Lexapro. This information, which had originated with Shelly's mother, was new to me.

Aidan, whose father was a proctologist in what my parents called "private practice," meaning that he cared about making money, had lived in a mansion in Watchung, and had been specially commended at our school for raising a hundred thousand dollars to protect elephants from ivory traders. He had always seemed so sure of himself— so sure of the wrongness of other people: of the elephant poachers, of the bands that were sellouts. It was true that once he had cried in front of the whole school, but it had been angrily, about the elephants. I had always thought of Aidan as being somehow spoiled and lacking in stamina, as not having real problems: if he had had real problems, how could he have been so upset about the elephants? Was it possible that Aidan had ever felt the way I felt now?

The possibility that lots of people my age were, unbeknownst to me, taking antidepressants made me think of the book *Prozac Nation*, which had come out when I was in high school. Anything with "nation" or "generation" in the title already seemed to be hectoring a person—about how "we as a nation" didn't, for example, "deal with our problems" anymore, choosing to just pop a pill. By "deal with our problems," they meant, "suck it up." I disliked people who said "suck it up." On the other hand, I also disliked laziness, and it had been impressed upon me many times that we were on a slippery slope to a situation where everyone was in an incubator being drugged to not think for themselves, like in *Brave New World*. I wasn't sure which of those two things the book was going to be—hectoring, or incubator—but either way I hadn't felt like reading it.

I knew that the author of the book, the girl who had taken Prozac, had gone to Harvard, and was viewed as the voice of a generation. Generation X: that was the people who were going around being alternative when I was in middle school. Her photograph was on the cover. Waiflike, with long, tousled hair, she bore a marked resemblance to Fiona Apple. At the time, I had found this all off-putting. But now I somehow wanted to know what the book said.

I found it in the library catalog—*Prozac Nation: Young and Depressed in America*. "In America" was also annoying, as if everything that happened to you was somehow about America. The library had two copies. Both were checked out. I ended up going to the basement to look up old book reviews. It felt dramatic to sit in the dark, spooling microfilm into the large, continually exhaling, annoyed-seeming machine. It was impossible to regulate the rate at which the weeks of the *New York Times* scrolled by, between screaming warp speed and barely moving.

Skimming the review, which was called "The Examined Life Is Not Worth Living Either," and which appeared in the same issue as the American invasion of Haiti, I remembered more clearly why I hadn't wanted to read the book when it came out. The author, Elizabeth Wurtzel, was described as a "precocious" person, who "had taken her first overdose" at age eleven, and started cutting herself at age twelve. Some of my mother's friends had daughters who were anorexic, or did drugs, or cut themselves with razors. My mother would relate their exploits to me, her face a mask of horror, wondering aloud what would she do if I was like that. As if I'd ever had time, even when I was twelve, to go around cutting myself with a razor. Anyway, I never had been able to understand how girls like that cared so little about worrying their parents.

It occurred to me now to wonder whether my consideration for my parents had been motivated by cowardice—by fear of having my freedom further curtailed, in ways that Elizabeth Wurtzel would not have tolerated. Surely she would have run away to do drugs with her cool friends. Was *that* why I felt animosity toward her: because she was braver and more resourceful than I was?

It wasn't a positive review. "Ms. Wurtzel spares us no detail about her life," Michiko Kakutani wrote. It was the same critique André Breton had leveled at Nadja: how she didn't hesitate to tell him all the vicissitudes of her life, "not omitting a single detail." (So: it was important to spare people details.)

For a person who supposedly didn't like complaining, Michiko Kakutani certainly complained a lot about Elizabeth Wurtzel's attitude toward her parents' divorce. At times, "Ms. Wurtzel's self-important whining" made Ms. Kakutani "want to shake the author, and remind her that there are far worse fates than growing up during the 70's in New York and going to Harvard."

I read another review, by a man named Walter Kirn. "The long moan begins with Wurtzel's parents, who split when she was 2." The complaint itself was "stretched with adjectival filler." Apparently, there was a link between the kind of self-indulgence that made people whine about their childhood, and the kind that made writers fail to "murder their darlings." Both came from not having enough problems: from dragging around slights that had happened when you were two, and padding them with adjectives.

Walter Kirn said that, by refusing to avoid self-indulgence, Elizabeth Wurtzel was turning her back on "the formal lesson of her hero Plath's poetry," which was that "hysteria has more impact when it's contained," and "sadness in art needs strict borders to press up against; otherwise, it's just a muddy overflow." It was a familiar, incontrovertible line of reasoning: you couldn't just dump everything on a page, because it wouldn't be art. Yet there was something newly troubling to me, as it had not been when I was in high school, in this story of a girl who had gone to Harvard, and was depressed because her parents were divorced, and had written a book that was widely critiqued as self-indulgent.

"I wanted to ask about antidepressants," I told the psychiatrist. To my surprise, he immediately asked if I wanted him to write me a prescription.

"I don't know," I said. "Would it help?"

"It might."

I stared at him. If he had known of something that might help me, then why hadn't he mentioned it? "Is there a downside to trying it?"

"As with any medication, there are side effects. The one most people worry about, especially women, is weight gain. But some people actually *lose* weight. Others don't encounter side effects at all." I had never before heard this man sound so interested in anything—especially when he said "some people actually *lose* weight."

I started taking half of the lowest adult dose of Zoloft every other day. A few days in, I was walking to the Ukrainian Research Institute while listening to "Cowboys," the B-side of the "Killing Me Softly" single. Most of the song was those guys rapping, but it didn't feel off-putting, partly because of the evocative background music, and partly because of the guys' attitude toward cowboys. When one of them said that *he* shot John Wayne—pushing him off the runaway train, like in the movie *Shane*—I laughed out loud. I had forgotten about *Shane*. My mother had rented it on video for me, because she had loved it as a child. I had stared in disbelief as a blond boy, who looked like one of the assholes from my school, ran around with a gun, pouting and bleating, "Shane! Shane!"—because he loved this grown man who went around shooting people. How, I remembered thinking, had my mother not seen that those people were losers? Pras and Young Zee saw it. "Me and that kid, uh, what's his name?" To think there were American people, men, who found cowboys as alienating and foreign as I did!

There was a part where Lauryn Hill rapped a verse, with her friend Rashia. The most interesting parts were about their own technical competence—their style. "My style is indeed one of the foulest," one of them said. "I inhale large clouds of smoke through my chalice." I had a thought that was so surprising that I stopped in my tracks. Was it possible that Zoloft would cause me to like rap music?

PART THREE

Spring Semester

JANUARY

Lakshmi and I were on a shuttle bus to Woods Hole. Who were these dour New Englanders? The shiksas and the ice queens, presumably, and their more numerous male counterparts. One of these he-shiksas, a balding man who looked exactly like my psychiatrist—was it possible he *was* my psychiatrist?—criticized me for talking too loudly. "You do realize that your voice is booming through the entire bus," he said.

Since it had been framed more as an observation than a request, I decided to counter it with one of my own. "It's a bus, not a library," I said.

"Selin!" Lakshmi whispered, seeming scandalized, but also laughing. I went back to the story I had been telling her in what I considered to be a normal speaking voice.

At first, I couldn't understand why nobody but me and Lakshmi wanted to sit on the outer deck. Then, the ferry started to move and we bowed our heads before the life-annihilating wind that gusted over the surface of the Atlantic. Lakshmi, undaunted, hunched over and somehow lit a cigarette inside her suede coat. When she stood up again the wind whipped the cigarette out of her hands and it *immediately* disappeared.

We had decided to spend intersession in Martha's Vineyard. I had made a reservation at a bed-and-breakfast, but Lakshmi turned out to have a categoric objection to bed-and-breakfasts and seemed surprised that I would even consider staying in one. She said we would surely find "a place to crash." Even when our one lead—some friends of Isabelle's parents—fell through, she was unfazed, saying that, once we got there, someone would invite us to stay with them. This made no sense to me. Neither of us knew anyone in Martha's Vineyard, so why would anyone invite us to stay with them? And, if they did, why would we do it?

"I just have a good feeling," Lakshmi said, as we disembarked the ferry. The thought of anyone having a good feeling in this obviously deserted place, where the lack of sentient life forms was compensated only by a bizarre excess of flagpoles, struck me as outrageous. Lakshmi said that in the worst case, we could spend the night somewhere that was open twenty-four hours, like an emergency room, and try again tomorrow.

It wasn't five yet but was almost completely dark. Only a few buildings had lights on. Lakshmi confidently strode past the first two—a bar and a hotel—and stopped at the third, a fitness club, where she struck up a conversation with two blond girls who came out toting squash rackets. Lakshmi asked about the fitness club and its hours, segueing to the question of places to stay. To my astonishment, the girls promptly invited us to stay with them.

Elsa and Malin were identical twins, though Malin was somehow prettier. They had come to Martha's Vineyard two summers ago, from

Uppsala, having heard how much money you could make, and had stuck around for the off-season, doing odd jobs, renting a house for almost nothing from a guy who had to pretend for some legal reason to live there, though he really lived somewhere else.

"Are men really into how you're twins?" Lakshmi asked.

"Oh, it's totally a fetish for some guys," Malin said.

"They're like, 'Swedish twins,'" Elsa said, meaningfully.

The understanding was that the twins could stay with us the next time they were in Boston.

"What do we do if they actually show up?" I whispered to Lakshmi, when we were finally alone, in the spare room with the giant lobster mural.

Lakshmi shrugged. "They can stay in our common rooms. You take Elsa, I'll take Malin." I couldn't help laughing. It was comical how Lakshmi liked Malin better.

Lakshmi was still in love with Noor, but had started dating Jon, a senior who wrote fiction and had a short story in almost every issue of the literary magazine. I had never successfully read one of his stories. Lakshmi said that Jon was too good-looking and smart for her. "I should probably dump him," she said. "If I wait too long, *I'll* get dumped."

Jon, who lived off-campus, had cooked dinner for her.

"Was it good?" I asked.

"It was fine." She dispassionately described the mushroom risotto, the Pinot Noir, the candles, and the vase of carnations.

I said it seemed like a lot of trouble to take, if he didn't actually like her.

"No, it's part of his whole thing."

"What thing?"

"Like, he stares into my eyes and says I'm a mysterious exotic beauty, and he can't decipher me. Guys must say stuff like that to you, too. You know: you're an exotic Eastern beauty, full of mystery."

197

They did not. "I kind of think you just *are* an exotic Eastern beauty full of mystery," I said.

"It's orientalist bullshit," Lakshmi said, tilting up her chin in a way that made her cheekbones stand out. Her mouth looked especially flowerlike and contemptuous and beautiful.

Malin offered to take us riding at the stables where she worked, if we helped her clean out the stalls. They thought I was joking when I said I didn't know how to ride a horse. Lakshmi borrowed an entire riding outfit, and looked like someone in a period drama.

Later, Malin and Elsa were in a panic—especially Elsa. Due to a misunderstanding with an architect they worked for, they had to immediately walk a dog, while collecting a large quantity of flat rocks from the beach. We all got into their used Volvo and drove across the island.

The architect's house was a long, low box made of wood and glass. Everything about it seemed evocative and expensive, except the dog, which looked less like a dog than like a panicked homunculus that had been crammed into an ill-fitting shaggy suit. Malin opened the glass sliding door and the dog sailed out over the dunes and started doing everything at once: peeing and frolicking and scrabbling in the sand. There was the ocean, like a recurring character you forgot about for long stretches.

Of the five big flat rocks that I lugged back to the house, I couldn't tell the difference between the two that met with Elsa's approval, and the three that didn't. Lakshmi seemed to view the unearthing of rocks as a matter outside her sphere of concern, and only dug halfheartedly with her toe in the sand. The crashing waves and the hiss of encroaching foam produced a meaningful, cinematic atmosphere.

That night, the twins had a double date with some local fetishists and said we could use their hot tub. They loaned us bikinis. I couldn't get my bikini top to stay put, so I just wore the bottom. Lakshmi's bikini fit her perfectly. Steam rose over the surface of the glowing blue. All around us was blackness. When had I last seen so many stars? Was this depressing, or was it fun?

The night we got back to campus, Matt was still on tour with the Chorduroys. Svetlana and I sat for three hours after dinner, addressing a wide range of questions. What was a Swedish twin fetish? Was the idea to have sex with both of them? Did they have sex with each other? I recognized the plausibility of Svetlana's hypothesis, which was that they didn't have sex with each other, but they did make out. Was that incest? Could an otherwise heterosexual person be attracted to their identical twin? Was narcissism good, bad, or neutral? Why was Narcissus a boy and not a girl? What role did personality and expectations play in determining a person's fate? Lakshmi had expected strangers to invite us to stay with them in Martha's Vineyard, and the expectation had come true. Neither Svetlana nor I would have expected such an outcome, or known how to bring it about.

Later, I was recounting a chili cook-off Malin and Elsa had brought us to. "So then Chili Con Blarney said to the Red Hot Chili Preppers," I began, but was laughing too hard to finish the story.

"You know, Selin," Svetlana said, "I think the Zoloft is definitely having a positive effect."

I felt shocked. Neither of us had mentioned the Zoloft, not since I told her I was taking it. I knew that Svetlana herself had declined to take anti-anxiety medications, saying that she wanted to understand her anxiety from the inside, not change it from the outside. But now she was looking at me with affection. "I missed this Selin," she said. It hadn't occurred to me that she had missed me, too.

I decided to try to take a creative writing class—less because I thought I would learn anything, than as a way to convert homework time into writing time.

There were two fiction classes. One was taught by a famous writer. You had to go to an introductory meeting, just to learn how to apply. I got there early, but all the seats in the auditorium were already taken. People were sitting on the steps and standing against the walls.

The famous writer, who wore a scarf wrapped around her head, said she didn't care for this business with the applications, but it had to be done to keep the numbers manageable. With this in mind, she had an assignment for us. She wanted us to write a description of our bed. "Quite a simple thing: your bed," she said, speaking slowly and clearly.

About a hundred people raised their hands. Could the bed be any bed we had ever slept in? What about a bed from history? What counted as a bed? Did it have to have legs? Looking mildly surprised, the writer said that she supposed we could write about anything that we considered a bed, though she had imagined us writing about the bed in which we ourselves usually woke in the morning.

"How long should it be?" someone asked.

Fatigue flickered over the writer's face. "It should be as long as it takes you to simply describe your bed."

The thought of writing anything about my bed—brimming with foam earplugs, overhung by the duct-taped "canopy," with a roll of toilet paper wedged against the wall—was deeply dispiriting. Nor was this feeling, on examination, specific to that bed. I didn't want to describe *any* furniture. I didn't want to describe my bedroom, or anyone else's bedroom, or my childhood home, or a place I knew well. I wanted to write a book about interpersonal relations and the human condition.

Looking at the writer, at her face that emanated a kind of humane but blocked-off weariness, I felt a profound conviction that she herself couldn't possibly want to read like a hundred descriptions of what was, essentially, the same dorm-issue bed. Of her many books, I had read only her first novel, set in a former British colony, based on her own childhood, which had sounded so much more difficult than mine that I had felt guilty and ashamed. Now she had to hear about my bed?

I ended up applying to the other fiction class. It was taught by an American man who wasn't famous. There was no introductory meeting—you just had to drop off a writing sample about whatever you wanted.

Lakshmi said that the problem with Jon was that eventually he was going to want to have sex. I wasn't sure why it was a problem.

"But I'm going to be a virgin when I get married," Lakshmi said.

I was astounded. Of course I knew that some people were specifically planning not to have premarital sex, but Lakshmi hadn't struck me as one of them. "But what about Noor?" I asked.

"Nothing ever happened with Noor," she said.

I frowned, wondering if there was any way to ask her whether that had been the plan, or if the plan had been something else. "So you don't think you have to know you're sexually compatible with someone, before you decide to get married?" That wasn't the right question, either. I didn't know how to ask about what I wanted to know, which was what rules she was following, and with what expectations, and how she had come up with the rules and the expectations.

"But I'm having an arranged marriage." Lakshmi seemed even more surprised by my surprise than I was by this new information. She said it wasn't new. "You knew about my sister," she pointed out. This was true: Lakshmi's older sister had married the son of a family friend, in a big wedding with fireworks and a white horse. But almost the first thing Lakshmi had ever told me about her sister was that she "wasn't an intellectual." It wasn't the same as not being intelligent; she was brilliant at entertaining and decorating and fashion, and a person really had to be smart to be good at those things. But she didn't care about books. To me, it made sense that someone who cared more about entertaining than about books might have an arranged marriage. But Lakshmi said that it wasn't related to your interests. Everyone in her whole extended family had had an arranged marriage. It wasn't something you thought about doing, or not doing. Marriage *was* arranged marriage.

"What if you don't want to get married?"

"But I do want to. I think living alone is really difficult, especially for a woman. I admire people who do it, but it's not for me. Anyway, I want to have children."

Feeling increasingly like the idiot friend from an American after-school special, I asked if she didn't want to choose her husband, to marry for love.

Lakshmi said that dating and romance were fun when you were young, but that freedom of choice in love was an illusion, and caused only pain. Sartre had explained this: to choose was to be never secure, to be always in flux—to be, for a woman, as Simone de Beauvoir had shown, in a kind of nonexistence. Maybe Sartre had been happy, but Simone de Beauvoir hadn't. And even if she had been, it wasn't for Lakshmi.

Furthermore, when it came to choice, Lakshmi's father valued her so highly that he would demand more for her than she could ever demand for herself. He called her a rare pearl, a priceless rose—she couldn't repeat the overblown way he talked about her. Her sister was the beauty of the family, taking after their mother, but Lakshmi's father thought that Lakshmi, too, was beautiful, in a more idiosyncratic way, *and* she would have a Harvard degree, and she sang. (I learned this with surprise, I had never heard Lakshmi sing.) And the great advantage of an arranged marriage was that your husband was committing, not to you personally, but to the institution of marriage—to his whole family, as well as to yours. That took a lot of pressure off your looks, which wouldn't last forever, and off the rest of you, too, because whose personality was enchanting enough to keep a man interested for sixty years?

Lakshmi's father sometimes joked about women who married for love: how much they must value themselves, to think they were more attractive than the sum total of all other women—to think they were enough, without the institution of marriage, to keep a man faithful to them. He teased Lakshmi, asking if she thought of herself that way.

I felt a wave of gratitude toward my parents, who would never have thought or said anything like that about me. On the other hand . . . that didn't mean it wasn't true.

At the last minute, I went with Svetlana to a Pilates class. Lying in a sea of Lycra-clad girls all doing pelvic bridges, synchronously imitating the instructor's huffing, rhythmic breathing, made it hard not to think about childbirth. For some reason, the person who came to my mind was my parents' friends' daughter, Dilek. When I was in middle school, Dilek had gotten engaged to a balding Turkish economist, a man who had what he called a "sarcastic sense of humor." My father said in a fervent voice that Dilek finally seemed happy and stable, that she had finally found someone who really cared about her.

Dilek's pregnancy, even more than her wedding, was met by everyone in our families with a kind of tearful celebratory relief, like the end of some agonizing period of worry. The baby, Erol, was "difficult," meaning that he screamed for twelve hours a day, sometimes sobbing until he vomited. It was pointed out, somehow humorously, that Dilek, too, had been a difficult baby, and had tortured her mother by screaming and crying and vomiting.

When I asked why it was good that Dilek had had a baby, I was told: "But if she hadn't had Erol, we wouldn't have Erol." I didn't have anything against Erol; he was a baby. But hadn't everyone gotten along fine without him? My mother said that *Dilek* hadn't gotten along fine. She had wanted Erol, she had missed him. When I brought up Dilek dropping out of her Ph.D. program, it was pointed out that Dilek had always quit things, ever since she was a little girl. My aunts said that she hadn't really wanted a career, or she would have managed to have one anyway, like my mother. My mother was often cited as evidence that it was possible to have both a well-adjusted child and a career. To imply otherwise was small-minded, even sexist.

Nobody acted like the suffering of Dilek or the baby, which was clear to anyone who spent even five minutes with them, had invalidated in any way the celebratory view taken of her marriage and pregnancy.

Now the Pilates instructor was talking about closing our rib cages. I often couldn't tell if the things she said about ribs were literal or figurative.

It was a strange thing how people acted as if having a kid was the best thing that could happen to anyone, even though actual parents seemed to experience most of their children's actual childhoods as an annoyance, which they compensated for by bossing them around. People with kids had to go to work every day, at boring, reliable jobs. On the plus side, work was an acceptable way to escape your children, without seeming to want to. The children, having no such escape, lived through long stretches of boredom and powerlessness, punctuated by occasional treats that they overvalued and freaked out over because the rest of their lives were so empty.

Why was it important to keep doing that? Some people, usually men, talked about genetic programming, and said we couldn't deny our nature. This was supposed to be scientific. I didn't see how obeying our nature was scientific, since it was also our nature to die from smallpox and to be unable to fly.

Religious people were the only ones who said openly that having kids was the purpose of life—something you did because God told you to, and because you had to outnumber people in other religions. That at least made sense, though it did seem sort of antisocial. But what if you weren't religious? I had heard some secularist people talk about a civic duty to keep pace with the religious people—to outnumber them in elections. But weren't there more direct ways to affect the outcome of elections, other than physically birthing people who would vote the same way as you?

My grandmother's housekeeper had told me that the reason I should have children was so they would take care of me when I was old. But I thought I would rather pay a preexisting person to take care of me—as indeed seemed to be normal for educated people—rather than creating a whole new person and making them do it for free.

My parents said that the real reason to have children was love: the unforeseeable, unimaginable way you "fell in love" with your baby. This wasn't a satisfying answer, since it involved imagining something that you apparently couldn't understand until it happened to you. I also didn't see what there was to prevent a person from "falling in love" with something other than their own baby. Furthermore, whenever parents talked about "love," some part of my brain switched off. They had their story, and they were sticking to it. The story was that they loved us with a love that we were incapable of understanding, and the reason things were the way they were was because they loved us so much.

In the end, I thought the most likely explanation was that most of the people in the world just didn't know they were allowed not to have kids. Either that, or they were too unimaginative to think of anything else to do, or too beaten-down to do whatever it was they thought of. That had been a big reason why I had wanted so much to get into Harvard: I'd been sure it would be full of fortunate, resourceful, courageous people who had some better-conceived plan for life that I could learn about. It was a great disappointment to find that, even at Harvard, most people's plan was to have children and amass money for them. You would be talking to someone who seemed like they viewed the world as a place of free movement and the exchange of ideas, and then it would turn out they were in a huge hurry to get everything interesting over with while they were young.

"Hey, Selin," said a blond guy with a pouty expression, at the first meeting of the creative writing class. I recognized him, after a moment, as Lakshmi's new suitor, Joey. Jon really had broken up with her, as she had predicted. I didn't see a huge difference between Joey and Jon: both were seniors, wrote short stories, and had blond hair. Lakshmi said I was crazy: Jon was smarter, more confident, had a better body, dressed better—and hadn't I seen his eyes?

The next time I ran into Jon, I made a point of looking at his eyes. He *immediately* looked back at me with eyes that were piercingly blue and seemed to be shooting light out of them. "Oh, sorry!" I said, and quickly looked away.

Gavriil asked whether I thought that women liked Jon better than Joey, because Jon was a jerk to women, and Joey was a nice guy. I felt irritated, understanding that it was girls' responsibility to disinterestedly award ourselves to nice guys—to guys whom other guys agreed were nice, because our opinion couldn't be trusted. What, if any, was the connection between the rising wave of annoyance that I felt, and the mental image of Joey's pouty, self-conscious facial expression? Was that expression something he could control, or was it just what his face was like?

Every week in creative writing, we read two short stories: one by an actual writer, and another by one of us. The published stories were usually OK, but everything we wrote was awful. Why did we have to talk about it? All the suggestions felt random and performative. It was like we were all looking at a malformed sweater and saying, *Maybe it would be better if it was a different color, or if it was actually made of ice.*

The most interesting part of class was when the teacher, Leonard, talked about what it was like to be a writer. I had never met a professional writer before, apart from my parents' endocrinologist friend who wrote spy novels under a pseudonym.

Leonard said that being a writer meant that you lived your life on the outside looking in. Whenever Leonard went to people's houses, the men would be in the living room, talking about football, or the stock market. Leonard couldn't survive five minutes in there; he always ended up in the kitchen with the women. They were the ones talking about stuff he actually cared about: gossip, basically, about real or fictional people. Women were kind, so they never kicked him out, though he had no kitchen skills, beyond chopping things and opening jars.

I, like all the girls and most of the boys in the class, smiled at this description—at how the women tolerated Leonard, despite his incompetence. But my smile felt a little mechanical. Why were the women always in the kitchen, and what was it that Leonard had forfeited by being with them? Why was he a writer, and they weren't, when they cared about the same things? Why wasn't he better at cooking? Why was there something exciting about the brutishness of the men who only talked about sports and money?

"You never know who has what it takes," Leonard said, once. "You'll be surprised later by who makes it." In Leonard's first year of grad school, one of his classmates had written a perfect short story, about two guys in prison who trained fighting spiders. There had been no doubt in anyone's mind that he, the author of the story about the spiders, would be the one to become a famous writer. Yet, the next three years had gone by without that guy writing anything that good again, and he still hadn't written a book. In a lot of ways, being a writer was about endurance more than talent.

Writers, Leonard said, were not normal people. As a writer, you were never totally present. You were always thinking of how you would put a thing into words. You were constantly putting yourself on the line, and constantly being rejected. You betrayed the only people who really loved you. For this reason, the most honest advice anyone gave about becoming a writer was that, if you were capable of doing absolutely anything else, you should do that thing instead.

I didn't get it. Wasn't everyone capable of doing something else? How was that a test of whether you should be a writer?

From the way he talked, it was clear that Leonard considered himself to be a failure. Yet he had published two novels that could be found in bookstores, and was teaching at Harvard. Why did he act as if those things didn't count?

A cool dude called Marlon, who had sideburns, wrote a story about a cool dude called Marvin, who sat on different sofas and at some point drank some beer.

Leonard said, kindly: "I think what we need to know about this story is whether—and I don't say this at all in a spirit of dismissiveness—

but whether it's a story about not being able to get laid. Because if it is, that's fine, but we need to *know* that that's what it is."

Was that what *my* story was about?

Leonard assigned us to read "My First Goose" by Isaac Babel. All the surface markers—the type, the layout, the tone with which Leonard had mentioned it—indicated that it was a great and important story. The narrator, an intellectual, had been sent to join a Cossack military regiment. The Cossacks weren't intellectuals. In this way, if in no other, they resembled Lakshmi's sister. A Cossack soldier with long blond hair and "a wonderful Ryazan face" defaced the narrator's suitcase and started farting at him. Other Cossack soldiers also made fart jokes. The narrator tried to read a copy of the newspaper *Pravda*, but was too distracted by the farting Cossacks, so he ordered the landlady to bring him something to eat.

The landlady, whose farm had been requisitioned, looked at the narrator with dripping, half-blind eyes and said that she wanted to hang herself. The narrator responded by seizing and murdering a goose, and ordering her to roast it. After that, the Cossacks called the narrator "brother," and they all fell asleep together in a hayloft.

There were many things I could relate to in the story. I had spent a lot of my formative years trying to concentrate on what I was reading, while surrounded by blond boys with amazing faces who were farting at me. But I didn't see why the narrator had to murder a goose or be so rude to a disabled person. Was it because I knew that, no matter how rude I was and no matter how many geese I murdered, the respect and camaraderie of the towheaded farters would always be turned against me; that I—my name, my appearance, my being—was part of what sustained that camaraderie?

I knew that, by having these negative feelings, I was being simple and simplistic—that the story was being more complex, and thus more "human," than I was. The closing lines were about the narrator having nightmares that night: proof that the story wasn't endorsing his actions, any more than it was judging them. Great literature didn't judge. It described complex individuals who were neither good nor bad. Oh, I knew how to get an A in English just as well as the next person.

Lakshmi had ended things with Joey.

"What did you tell him?" I asked.

"The truth. That he wasn't attractive enough or interesting enough. I tried to be more diplomatic at first. But he kept asking, 'Why, why.'" She imitated an American intonation when she said "Why," in a way that was funny to me, even though I also talked like that.

"What did he say?"

"He *cried*," she shot back. There was something funny about her unquestioning, righteous-seeming anger, its immediacy and abruptness. And yet, since early childhood, it had always been a part of my identity that I was the only person who didn't laugh when someone tripped on a banana peel. The only other people who didn't laugh were the openmouthed people who never laughed at anything. Yet there was something about Joey's expression, its combination of sensitivity and hurt and lack of imagination, that made me feel less sorry for him than I wanted to.

I knew that Svetlana thought that I deceived myself—that I pretended to feel pity for people, when I actually felt contempt. Ivan had said something like that, too. "I guess you're going to feel sorry for the dog." What had Ivan been accusing me of, that time with the dog? Being excessively sorry? Pretending to be sorrier than I was? Indulging in empty sorriness-feeling without backing it up with action? Ivan was the kind of person who thought it was funny when someone tripped on a banana peel. In this, I felt certain that he was incorrect.

"Poor Joey," I said aloud.

"He doesn't really care about me, just about his own idea of himself," Lakshmi said, opening a new and painful line of thought. *Did Joey care more about his idea of himself than he did about the actual Lakshmi? Who was the actual Lakshmi—other than someone who didn't care much for Joey? What would Joey act like if he really cared about her? Did Joey's pursuit of Lakshmi betray some fundamental misunderstanding of who she was? Had I missed the point of Ivan? Did I care more about my idea of myself than I did about him?*

FEBRUARY

I went to a party that Lakshmi organized at the literary magazine. She was greeting people at the door, smiling dazzlingly through fake eyelashes.

"You came! And what's this?" She touched the velvety material of my skirt. "Finally you're wearing something that shows your body."

My aunt had bought me the skirt and matching top over winter break, from the DKNY section in Bloomingdale's. They were made of some velvety, lush, yet drapey and elastic material, soft to the touch, reminding me of my childhood toy koala, Tombik, whose white fluffy ears I had thought of, again and again, as "perfect for crying into." Usually, when clothes were attractive in such a superficial way—by being so soft, or sparkling, or having a built-in hood—they ended up looking stupid, in a particular way that made you see that you had been duped. But this time it wasn't like that. The two pieces were so sinuously and gently clingy, without being tight. The way the skirt hung looked intentional, almost sentient. The cost for the two items, over three hundred dollars, had struck me as obscene—how was a person allowed to have something like that? Seeing the garments hanging in Riley's and my closet made me feel sorrowful and moved almost to tears—how soft they were, how full of comfort, what a sign of the love that my family had always given me.

Someone had put on an Ella Fitzgerald CD. It produced a grown-up, New York–like, somehow Christmassy atmosphere that felt at odds with who Ella Fitzgerald was. She herself surely hadn't inhabited such spaces, at least not until she became a famous singer. That meant, too, that the prison that she was always singing about, in that elegant delighted tone, between the devil and the deep blue sea—she wasn't in it, and hadn't been in it, she had been in a different one, and so you were alone in an experience that she couldn't be having, simply by virtue of the shimmering, silvery voice that could not but have utterly transformed the life of any person who sang like that.

Surveying the room, I was surprised to see Şahin from the Turkish students' club, standing near the window, talking to a fair-haired guy.

"Oh, so I actually know a literature person," Şahin said, when I went over. "This isn't really my scene." He had to lean over for me to hear him. I had never stood so close to him before, and hadn't realized how tall he was. His friend was also well over six feet. It was pleasant to stand beside them, to feel like the smallest and most delicate person. They were drinking to Şahin getting a grant to study Antarctic seabirds. He had to hurry because the winter here was the summer there. They made some joke I didn't hear, repeating the word "icepick."

"I don't know that I've ever seen an icepick," I said, producing much mirth. Şahin brought me a glass of wine. We drank to some kind of petrel. "So what else is new with birds?" I asked. Şahin explained that someone in China had identified an unknown bird and named it after Confucius. Someone else had discovered that dinosaurs had had feathers. This was true, not just of avian dinosaurs, but of some other dinosaurs.

That reminded me of a Woody Allen line, about how "the thing with feathers" turned out not to be Hope, but was actually his, Woody Allen's, nephew. I didn't have positive feelings about Woody Allen, whose movies so often included scenes of men my parents' age having remedial conversations about "free will," or dating catatonic-seeming teenagers. Yet I now found it humorous that his nephew, like both the avian and non-avian dinosaurs, had feathers. Was it the wine that helped a person appreciate things uncritically?

Was that why Ivan had always been trying to get me to drink? Definitely, it was easier to think of things to say. In the past, my goal in conversation had been to accurately represent the things that I thought, and to deploy these thoughts in relation to the things that other people said, while exercising caution to not betray ignorant or antisocial ideas, and the whole thing had been so much to think about that in the end I usually hadn't said anything at all. Svetlana had pointed out that, if I actually listened to other people, instead of worrying so much about what I was going to say, I would notice that everyone was saying all kinds of antisocial, ignorant, or irrelevant things, which were often just a posture they were trying out, as opposed to a reflection of their essential personality, which was probably a thing that didn't even exist. I hadn't believed her, but she was right: nobody was actually answering anything anyone else had said, and people were *constantly* betraying antisocial ideas.

Şahin's friend brought me another glass of wine. How easy and pleasant it was to stand there with them, saying whatever random, irrelevant stuff came to mind. The two guys looked amused, and occasionally contributed their own random, irrelevant observations— though their general attitude was one of being impressed that I could think of so many more of them. It was implicit that it was girls' role to think of such things, and their role to view them as amusing. I felt that I understood for the first time, because I was able to participate in it, the persona inhabited by Priya and the beautiful nonsmoker.

It turned out that I could ask the guys whatever questions I thought of, and they would answer. I asked Şahin's friend where his accent was from, and he said Poland. I asked about the public transportation system in Warsaw: whether it was on the honor system to buy a ticket, whether there were inspectors like in Budapest, whether he had ever run away, or talked himself out of a fine. He smiled evasively and said that it was possible that something like that might have happened. He said you could ride a tram for free if you had fought in the Warsaw Uprising, or if your mother had given birth to you on another tram.

Later we were at another party in a dorm. Why did all parties sound and smell the same, even though the component people were different? It was as if all the different individuals came together and formed the eternal entity Party Person. This reminded me of *Voltron*, a cartoon about five space pilots who were supposed to defend the universe. In every episode, they got into a terrible predicament, where the one who was a girl was always about to have to become a sex slave and carry fruit on her head. At the last minute, they would remember to merge their five rockets, thereby forming Voltron: a gigantic unbeatable robot-man with rocket-arms and rocket-legs. It was unclear why they didn't become Voltron earlier.

"It's probably their selfish American individualism," Şahin said.

I was impressed by this evidence that he had been following my long story about Voltron. On the other hand, I was pretty sure *Voltron* hadn't been an American show. Then again—maybe that was why their selfish individualism didn't work better.

I asked whether there was anything in a gin and tonic besides gin and tonic. Şahin's friend said that the beauty of a gin and tonic lay precisely in its simplicity. The conversation turned to quinine. Şahin said that birds could get malaria; it happened to native Hawaiian songbirds.

"So get a grant to go to Hawaii and make them tiny gin and tonics," Şahin's friend said, handing out another round.

I watched the people moving around the room in different configurations. What were they even doing? Not exactly dancing, or talking. They were "partying." People talked about it as if it was an honorable, prestigious activity. Massive Attack was playing at a loud volume. I felt like there was something behind all the people that I could almost make out—something moving. I could almost see Voltron in the background, raising his giant arm.

Tea lights perched on the rim of a claw-footed bathtub. The sink had two faucets. One tap ran scaldingly hot; the other, numbingly cold. The bathroom door opened, and Şahin's friend came in. I felt embarrassed to realize I hadn't locked the door. I said I was just leaving. I turned off the cold faucet; the other was now too hot to touch. But Şahin's friend walked right up to me, looked down at my face with a speculative, almost affectionate expression, and kissed me. It felt slow and easy and endless and immediate. For something that had seemed so impossible for so long to happen so effortlessly, like a row of cards falling over, and falling, and falling . . .

I remembered some advice I had read in *Seventeen* magazine, when I had pneumonia and my mother had therefore gotten me *Seventeen* magazine, about what to do with your hands When He Kissed You. It said to put one hand on his neck and the other on his chest. The hand on the chest let you feel how strong and sexy he was, but also gave you "control."

I put my hand on his chest, to feel how strong and sexy he was—somehow unexpectedly solid, like a statue, though also, of course, alive. He smelled faintly and intoxicatingly of aftershave, and of sweat, which didn't make sense, because the smell of sweat was usually repulsive. With my other hand, barely daring to touch the back of his neck, I felt the place where his buzz cut started. It felt so tender and dear and alive—so full of life. What an amazing thing a neck was, the way all the blood in a human body had to pass through it, and how easy that made it to kill someone, and this easiness of killing a man also felt dear and close to my heart.

He put his hands on my waist, moving them over the soft fabric of my skirt, and slid one hand under the waistband—first over my underwear, then under it. When I felt his hand on my skin, I felt a wave of panic and pushed lightly with my hand on his chest. Right away, he took his hand out of my underwear—just like *Seventeen* magazine had implied that he would. How amazing that it was possible to communicate like that. He touched my face, tilted my chin up, and the angle changed and got deeper. My own hair felt silky against my neck. He stepped back and looked down at me again. There was something new in his expression, something lazy and proprietary.

We went back outside and stood in a circle with Şahin and some other people, "dancing." This lasted a long time. Şahin's friend danced for a while with a short girl who was wearing a silver dress. Then somehow he and I were facing each other, there were no people between us, and then he was standing closer and brushed his hand against my leg, and touched my waist, and kissed me again. "Shall we get out of here?" he said in a suave, euphemistic-sounding tone. I nodded. I *always* wanted to get out of here, and nobody ever asked. I didn't understand where we would go, or whether Şahin would come, and, if not, what we would tell him.

"Get your coat," he said. I was looking through the enormous pile of coats when I became aware of Şahin standing next to me.

"What's new," he said in Turkish.

"Everything's good," I replied, pulling out a coat and trying to figure out if it was mine.

"You don't have to jump," he said.

"To jump?" I repeated.

He nodded emphatically. "You don't have to jump. I'm here."

I didn't understand what he was saying. His friend came back, took my coat out of my hands, and helped me put it on.

The cold was breathtaking. Şahin's friend and I were walking toward the river. Our hands brushed against each other, and then he took my hand in his, which felt warm and smooth. Why wasn't it possible to hold hands all the time? I suddenly remembered that, in grade school, Leora and I would routinely walk down the hallway holding hands. When had that stopped seeming normal?

It felt wonderful to walk next to someone so tall and strong. As soon as I had the thought, I remembered that that was what my mother said about walking next to me, and it always made me feel stressed-out. What if I made this guy feel that way? I looked at him. He didn't seem especially stressed-out. Maybe it was OK, since I wasn't his mother.

I didn't understand why he was slowing down in front of some random iron gate. "Here's where I live," he murmured. It hadn't occurred to me that we were going to where he lived. We went through the gate, under a clock tower, across a courtyard, into a brick entryway, up several flights of steps. In one deft movement, he unlocked and opened the door and flicked on a sallow overhead light. When he leaned in to kiss me, it was like sliding back into the water on one of those long days at the beach, where you just get out so you can go back in again.

At some point, he said he would be right back, and disappeared into the bathroom. I remained standing, contemplating a pile of outdoor equipment that was leaning against the wall. When I had looked at it for a while—it had spikes—I walked around the room, which was minimally furnished with a sofa and a coffee table. The sofa, when one sat on it, had an organic, swamplike quality. There was a journal lying on the coffee table. I opened it to a random page. "Depolarization-induced slowing of Ca2+ channel deactivation in squid neurons." It seemed to be a sign about how big the world was—how full of unknown processes.

Şahin's friend came out of the bathroom, went over to where we had been standing, and seemed surprised that I wasn't there. His eyes swept the room without seeing me. Maybe I had sunk too far into the sofa. In his bemused yet tolerant expression, I felt like I could see his whole attitude toward girls. They could be anywhere! He actually opened the closet and looked inside, like maybe I would be sitting in there thinking about my period.

"Over here," I said.

He seemed slightly annoyed, like it was unfair of me to expect him to guess that I would do something like sit on the sofa. This despite the hallowed traditional nature of sofa-sitting. But maybe I had imagined it, because then he was saying, again in the suave voice: "I was afraid I had lost you." We started kissing again. How smooth, how easy it felt. Suddenly, I started worrying that it was *too* easy, that I was being too passive and was failing to be interesting or express my personality. Magazines always said stuff like that: "Don't just lie there." I tried to think of different things I could do. There didn't seem to be that many things. He started to laugh. "Maybe go a little easy with the tongue," he said.

I felt encouraged: so you could request pointers. "Does a person have to be interesting?" I asked. He didn't answer.

"Just relax," he said finally. I never had liked being told to relax.

In his bedroom, the bottom bunk had been removed to make a loft, but there was no desk or dresser underneath—just empty space. With nothing there to step on, it was unclear how to get into the top bunk.

"I like this fabric," he said, fingering it for a moment before pulling my top over my head: something I hadn't experienced since age six. How strange that *this* was like *that*—that the most adult thing was in some way like being a child. When he tossed the garment onto the floor, I resisted the urge to pick it up and fold it. I felt a pang of regret and embarrassment that this was all happening with these clothes that were a gift from my aunt. She had been happy to get them for me because they were appealing and attractive . . . and thus, in some sense made for a guy to be taking them off and dropping them on the floor? It was my uncle who had a job and made money, and gave it to my aunt. You need to stop thinking about this. Şahin's friend reached behind my back to undo my bra. "It opens from the front," I said, just as he undid the bra—from the back. He found the hidden zipper and the skirt fell to the ground with a soft whoosh. I stepped out of it and hastily picked it up and draped it on a chair.

His shirt had disappeared. How were his arms and chest so strong? I reached a clearer understanding of why a man's body was exciting: not just in itself, but because of how it made *you* feel, how slender and pliant.

It turned out that the way you got into the bed was by climbing on top of the desk and sort of jumping. Why would a person choose to live this way? His pillowcase was black with a white skull. The sound of his belt buckle caused something to happen between my legs. How did my legs know? I thought about "the walls have ears," and then "the legs have ears," and about how it was supposed to be sexual when Shakespeare talked about pouring poison into an ear.

"Is something funny?" he murmured.

I started to explain, but he didn't seem that interested. How radical to feel so much of a person's skin—not with one's hand but with one's body. I had never seen eyes that color up close: grayish blue with hazel flecks. He put his hand between my legs, pushing aside my underwear. This time, I let him.

"Ah, Jesus." His voice had some kind of regret in it, like something was somehow going to get him in trouble. The feeling of being able to get him in trouble was breathtaking.

I was trying to run through the possibilities at the same rate as external developments. I knew that the first time you had sex was supposed to be with someone special who cared about you. I also knew that, even if it wasn't your first time having sex in your whole life, you weren't supposed to do it with any particular person on a first date. Since I had never had sex before, and hadn't been on even one date with this guy, indications were I should not let him have sex with me, if that was what he was trying to do, on this, our zero date.

On the other hand, Svetlana had done everything the way you were supposed to, and none of it had sounded appealing. Even Svetlana herself hadn't seemed that enthused about it. Furthermore, supposing I did want to follow that route—who knew whether or when the opportunity would arise? Special, caring guys, the kind who were always talking about respecting women, never did seem interested in me. Frankly, I wasn't their number-one fan, either.

The more I thought about it, the less I understood why the duration of my current condition—this indignity and stuckness, the feeling of being somehow tied to Ivan—should depend on my ability to find some doofus who would tell me I was special. I already knew I was special. So what did I need the doofus for?

Insofar as this guy, whose hand was now completely inside my underwear, touching me in a way that was contiguous with, yet different from—more agitating, more erratic than—the way I touched myself, I had lost my train of thought. Where was I? OK: insofar as he didn't seem to think I was special, and seemed to be engaging with me only as a girl, as a woman, as a member of the category he pursued because of what he was—it felt euphoric and freeing, it was one of the most exciting things that had ever happened to me.

Then he moved his hand farther back and did something that made me freeze with pain and terror, and I realized that, as often happened, all my thinking had been beside the point. I couldn't "decide" to go further, any more than you could decide to bend your elbow in the opposite direction.

"I'm not very experienced," I blurted.

"That's fine," he said, and withdrew his hand. It was weird how some things you said seemed to have no meaning to him, while others had a recognized meaning that he immediately responded to.

"I'll show you what you can do," he said in the suave voice.

So, here was the thing everyone kept talking about: his "desire," that was tangible and real. Was it really in some way about me? He put his hand around mine. I had often heard the term "hand job." This was clearly it. And here was another thing I had heard about: the gap between the signifier and signified. Where the term "hand job" sounded generic, mechanical, and tough, the act itself felt specific, organic, tender, and sort of gross. The skin was so soft and mobile. An eyeless creature was going in and out of its cowl. I couldn't imagine putting it in my body—how it would fit, or what the point would be.

He released my hand, so I could do it by myself, but it turned out I wasn't doing it right. He demonstrated: more vigorous, more rhythmic, harder, slower. At first, I wanted to do a good job, but I soon grew demoralized. It felt like I was missing too much information. Couldn't he do a better job himself? What was the point of delegating it to someone who would do a worse job? A twinge of pain shot through my palm. What if I got repetitive strain injury again, like with the gardening catalog?

As I was wondering how to diplomatically phrase my concerns, the thing happened that I had often seen symbolized in movies by geysers or fountains or a lawn irrigation system. But this was such a helpless little spurt, it seemed so young, like a new spring plant. I couldn't help feeling touched. He pulled a Kleenex from a box wedged between the bed frame and the wall. Kleenex, not toilet paper: a class act, I thought, because part of me was always generating a commentary.

I was worried that I was going to have to try to sleep here, in the narrow bunk with the single, sinister pillow, but it became clear that this wasn't expected. He helped me pick up my clothes, watched me get dressed, kissed me, touched my waist again. I was sorry when he removed his hand and stopped kissing me. Why did everyone's favorite part have to be something different?

I woke up early and went running. It was the first day all year that made it possible to imagine what spring would be like. Sunlight sparkled off the river. Crew boats sliced through the current like long stick-insects. Everything looked new and freshly painted. The old paint jobs looked freshly chipped.

It was only afterward, when I had taken a shower and was getting dressed, that a great column of malaise crashed over my head, causing me to understand that it was not possible to outrun a hangover.

When I woke up again several hours later, my headache was gone, though it also felt like I had died and nothing was real. The weather was the same, but more so. On my way to the library—I didn't know where else to go—I ran into Gavriil, who suggested taking a walk. We walked around for two hours, soaking in the balmy sunlight.

I hadn't planned to say anything about the previous night, but he talked so much about Katie that I ended up telling him I had met a guy and gone home with him.

"How old was he?" Gavriil asked.

I could answer that, because he had mentioned his birthday. "Twenty-three," I said. Gavriil said the whole thing sounded sketchy. He looked into my eyes and held my hand and said he thought I should be with someone who really cared about me.

At dinner, Riley asked if I was "seeing someone."

"No," I said.

She frowned slightly. "Adam mentioned that he saw you with someone at a party."

"That's true, but I just met him at the party," I said, trying to remember who Adam was. "Is he friends with Adam?"

"Adam doesn't know him well, but he said he thinks he's a really nice guy. He's older, right?" I recognized in Riley the same curiosity I had always seen in my aunts, about whom I was going to date.

In line at the dishwashing window, a guy was describing his recruitment interview with McKinsey. They didn't ask you about facts, but invited you to solve puzzles. The puzzles were about the mysteries of mass production: how M&Ms were made, how toothpaste got into tubes. "They want to see how you think," he said, in a venomous tone.

After dinner, I still felt like walking. I set out along the river toward MIT, listening to the Tom Waits tape that had the song "Innocent When You Dream" on it. The bellowing sentimentality made me laugh, yet I still felt moved. The longing of someone who was no longer innocent, for the time when he *had* been innocent—the idea of getting a reprieve, in dreams, from non-innocence, or from any other aspect of the present—made me think I was going to cry, although I never actually cried anymore. It felt like my eyes had physically dried up. Previously, I had believed that the sadness came first, and tears were a result, but the reality was clearly more complicated, because once the tears didn't come, the sadness somehow bottomed out, became shallower. What if the way Zoloft worked was just by dehydrating you?

Hulking buildings flanked the river. Some were dark and warehouse-like, others brilliantly lit. The moon had risen, and planes and satellites blinked inscrutably. I felt it was the time for stocktaking: for looking back at what I had learned about the aesthetic life.

In its simplest form, the aesthetic life involved seducing and abandoning young girls and making them go crazy. This was what I had learned from books. There was a problem of application: what did you do if you *were* a young girl? Nadja had been a girl, and had tried to live an aesthetic life. That had involved *her* being seduced and abandoned and going crazy. But that had been then. What were you supposed to do now: seduce and abandon men? Was that what feminism had made possible? Something about the idea didn't feel aesthetic. Just think of the angry, complaining men. Maybe you, too, were supposed to be seducing and abandoning young girls: was *that* what feminism had made possible? But what would you do with the young girls? And wouldn't it put you in a losing competition against men?

Maybe it was OK to just "ruin" men more broadly: not the way men ruined girls, by driving them out of society into convents or mental institutions, but, rather, by getting them to pay for things, as had happened even in the days of Kierkegaard. I saw no percentage in driving another human being into a mental institution; but with money, a person could travel, or write books. A person could live an aesthetic life.

Where did you draw the line between trying to make a particular person fall in love with you and give you money, and trying to get money out of the world more generally?

The next song on the Tom Waits album was called "I'll Be Gone." In the verses, Tom Waits was enumerating different things he was going to do tonight: cut the hearts from pharaohs, drink a thousand shipwrecks, paint a sheet across his bed. The chorus was: "And in the morning I'll be gone." A rooster crowed. It made me think of the line in "The Seducer's Diary," where the seducer was up late, plotting Cordelia's ruin, thinking about how sad it all was, and a cock crowed, and he said that maybe Cordelia heard it, too—but she would think it was the coming of a new day.

Tom Waits had gotten more and more worked up, and was now just shouting random-sounding phrases: "Eight hundred pounds of nitro!" "I have a French companion!" "I'll Be Gone" seemed in some way like an antidote to the feeling summed up by the new Cranberries single, "When You're Gone": its syrupy fifties doo-wop harmonies reproducing, again and again, the dreamy, layered awfulness of everything without you. How could I work it so that *I* would be gone?

Some key seemed to reside in the phrase "leaving the country." "I'm leaving the country." "I'll have to leave the country." Hadn't international travel been, in some sense, the yardstick that Ivan used to measure human worth—even though, in most other ways, he had seemed to look down on rich people? Later, in Hungary, other people had asked the same question—"What other countries have you been to?"—in the same tone; implying that leaving the country wasn't a sign of privilege, but a kind of accomplishment.

What was the relationship between leaving the country and an aesthetic life? What was it about America in particular that seemed to make one's life unaesthetic? Did it just seem that way to me? Didn't everyone in the world think that American people were babies? For most of my childhood, I was the only child in the American chapter of my family, and the only American person in any part of my family, and there had been no very clear distinction between my Americanness and my childishness: the way my parents had to carry my peanut butter and Flintstones vitamins in a suitcase, and other children had to be warned not to make fun of me for not knowing about things. (My cousin Evren still complained about that: how I had cried about everything, and she had been blamed.) Wasn't that how people in other countries viewed *all* American people—with their innocence, their Disney, their inability to drive stick shift? With the way they were protected—the way *I* was protected—from so much of the "reality" that happened elsewhere?

I had previously been looking down on the people who were already panicked about the summer, frantically applying to work at Merrill Lynch or to build houses in Tanzania. I now realized that I had been wrong: I had to start panicking, too. Somehow, I had to get someone to pay for me to leave the country.

What was the relationship between leaving the country, ruining people, falling in love, and having sex? There clearly was one. It was starting to occur to me that, when it came to having sex, I had mistaken an emergency measure for a sustainable policy. But the emergency had been childhood itself, and sex was the thing that made you not a child. It was the thing that made your childhood finally end.

I had thought that an aesthetic life would be more like a string of adventures than like a coming-of-age novel, or the life-cycle of a frog, where there was a grand progression ending with "maturity" and the ability to procreate. But it was impossible to imagine an aesthetic life, or any life, without falling in love. Without love, knowledge itself became a hassle; became bullying and imposition. "My country." "Learn about my country." Being in love was the only thing that made you *want* to learn about a person's country, or about anything else outside your experience. Falling in love was the essential feature of a novel. The Russian word for "novel," *roman*, could also mean "love affair." A "love affair" implied sex, at least the question of sex.

What was the relationship between falling in love and having sex? Even in middle school, I had known that it was related to "being in love" that my underwear would get wet, that I had dreams about being pregnant, that I wanted to look up "orgasm" in a dictionary. But I hadn't thought any further than that. It had never been the most pressing problem—especially since nobody had shown any signs of wanting to have sex with me. Now, multiple variables had changed. First, the emergency was over and I didn't have to be a child anymore. It was time to become a writer, and understand the human condition. Second, hadn't that guy, Şahin's friend, who had been, in retrospect, handsome—hadn't he wanted to have sex with me? I went over the whole interaction again in my mind, and couldn't think of any other interpretation.

If falling in love was the only way to learn anything, and if falling in love was in some way *about* sex, could the fact that I hadn't "had" sex explain why I seemed to myself not to have really learned anything—why I seemed not to have really learned anything about, for example, Hungary—why everything I did learn felt somehow incomplete and beside the point? Was it sex—"having" sex—that would restore to me the sense of my life as a story?

Should I have done it with that guy, when the opportunity presented itself? Should I do it now? How would I go about it? Would he still want to? Inconveniently, I seemed not to have retained his name. Şahin had introduced us, but we both had foreign names, the kind you needed to hear a couple of times. It began to seem inauspicious that he hadn't asked me to repeat my name. On the other hand, maybe he had missed the right moment, and had planned to ask Şahin later. Once this possibility occurred to me, I felt sure that it was going to happen: he would find out my name, and contact me in some way.

MARCH

The most well-established way to get someone to pay for you to go overseas was to be a researcher-writer for *Let's Go*. Every year, they sent like a hundred people around the world, to update the previous year's guidebook. On my application, I put Russia as my first choice, followed by Argentina and Spain.

Meanwhile, at the student employment office, I found a summer job posting from a Peruvian frozen food manufacturer who was starting a partnership with a Moscow supermarket chain, and wanted to hire an English speaker who also knew either Russian or Spanish. It was unclear what the job entailed, but I felt excited to apply, because I had studied both Russian *and* Spanish.

Radcliffe College turned out to give special travel grants for women. At first, it seemed unfair to try to gain a financial advantage from being "a woman," when things were so much easier for me than they had been for my mother and aunts. On the other hand, it was becoming increasingly clear that literally nothing was fair. The people who had said that throughout one's childhood hadn't just been joking around, or trying to whitewash their own personal lack of integrity. So, I went ahead and applied for a grant in the amount of the tuition for an accredited summer study program in St. Petersburg.

I hadn't heard anything from Şahin's friend, so I decided to ask Şahin what his name was. Şahin somehow didn't seem thrilled, but he told me. The name, Przemysław, was one I didn't know how to pronounce. One of the Iris Murdoch novels that my mother and I liked had a character in it whom everyone called the Count, not because he was a count, but because he had a Polish name that none of the English people could say. "That's a dog's breakfast of a name," one of his schoolteachers told him kindly. I remembered "dog's breakfast" and "kindly," and another line that said: "By now it had fully dawned upon the Count how irredeemably Polish he was doomed to be." Was that a problem Przemysław had?

There were only two Przemysławs in the whole university database, and one of them was in the dental school. I carefully composed an email to the other Przemysław, asking if he wanted to get a coffee. He wrote back right away. To be honest, I don't really drink coffee.

It turned out there was always a party somewhere. You could go to one every night if you wanted. You didn't have to know the people who lived there. At one party I ran into Ham, a guy who had been in the Constructed Worlds class last year. His hair was longer now, and green. I could tell from how he hugged me that I could go home with him if I wanted to. I walked around the room, drinking warm beer from a Solo cup. Everyone was obsessively drinking this beer, which came out of a keg. I had never seen a keg before. It looked comically literal. I went back to where Ham was standing and stood close to him.

Sure enough, within two minutes, he put his arm around me and asked if I wanted to leave. Had it always been this easy, and I just hadn't noticed?

Armies of tiny painted lead figures, belonging to different tribes or races, were stationed on every surface of his dorm room. The drawers of the dresser were pulled out to varying extents and covered with green felt, so they made terraces, and there was a war happening on the terrace. Clearing a platoon of militarized trolls from the bed, Ham talked about his girlfriend in Anchorage, who had an eating disorder. He said he had always been attracted to me in Constructed Worlds, a class that had literally no normal people in it. I told him I had never had sex before. He said there were lots of other things we could do. So I didn't technically have sex with him, either. He had a huge cock, terrifying, curved upward, like a horn.

At another party, I drank two rum and Cokes and became violently ill. I hadn't thrown up since childhood. It was even worse than I remembered. The host, a guy I barely knew, seemed really worried, and left his own party to walk me home.

"I didn't think you would even come," he kept saying.

I woke up the next day feeling sicker than I could remember having felt in my entire life. I dragged myself to brunch and barely recognized Juho when he sat across from me. "I hope I am not being rude, but you look terrible," he said.

His eyes were alight with the informativeness of someone who had clearly had a lot of hangovers in his life, and held a Ph.D. in chemistry. I told him what had happened, and asked how it was possible to feel like this after only two drinks, when I had drunk more than that in the past without getting sick.

Juho explained that there was a lot that we didn't understand about how alcohol worked on the brain, but that different people were affected differently by the compounds that accompanied the production of ethanol, which, in turn, could interact differently with carbonation, sugar, and caffeine. Dark liquors like rum had more compounds than vodka, because they weren't distilled so many times, and cheap rum was distilled less than expensive rum. In the end, there were so many factors that you would probably never know why you got sick one time and not another, but a good idea was to drink lots of water and avoid cheap booze.

"Interestingly, the effects of a hangover seem to be the same as mild alcohol withdrawal, so you feel better if you drink more. I do have some vodka in my room," Juho said.

"Oh my God, *no*."

Juho told me about how some people in Iceland treated hangovers by eating specially putrefied shark meat that had been buried for a long time in sand.

"OK, I never want to talk or think about this ever again, but how long do they bury it?"

"Well, a few months, I think."

We had adopted, in our conversation, the universally humorous attitude toward alcohol—toward people throwing up, and blacking out, and being hung over. And yet . . . it felt like you were dying. Of course, you weren't really dying. Was that the source of the humor: the disjuncture between how serious it felt and how trivial it really was?

I remembered now that, in the fall, a guy at MIT had died of alcohol poisoning while pledging a fraternity. At the time, I had dismissed this as a story about a guy who was so dumb that he drank until he died. Now, it looked different. After all, I had been dumb enough to drink until I threw up. That was because it had come up on me by surprise. So maybe that frat guy had been surprised. More broadly, why was it considered laudable, sociable, and funny to do this thing that often made a person feel like they were dying, and occasionally actually did induce death?

Of course, you couldn't have a party without alcohol; I understood this now. I understood the reason. The reason was that people were intolerable. But wasn't there any way around that? Juho was talking about different research into alcoholism that people were doing in Finland. Why was nobody researching the more direct issue of how to make people less intolerable?

"It might be a case of having to reduce a big problem we can't solve to a smaller problem that we can solve," Juho said.

One Sunday afternoon, Oak and I went to the film archive to see a restored print of *Ivan the Terrible*. Afterward, we walked around the arts building. When the cleaning crew had left, we went back into the dark screening room and sat on the floor—it was interesting to see the screen from such a different angle—talking in a desultory way about beards. At some point, I wondered if Oak was going to kiss me, and he did. He wasn't someone I had just met, and we hadn't been drinking. Was that why it felt somehow more cognitively demanding than usual? Was this "something rational"? Was he going to be my boyfriend now? He started to unbutton my jeans, but I said, truthfully, that I had my period, and shortly thereafter we dusted ourselves off and went to dinner with Riley and the others.

When we were all saying goodbye, I stayed behind a moment next to Oak, and he briefly held my hand, but otherwise nothing was different from usual.

At another party, I encountered a guy who combined such a grotesque gnawing, prying way of kissing, with such a tedious, smirking, and knowing attitude, that I couldn't go through with it. The guy had the same accent as Lakshmi, whom he was talking about in a presumptuous and avuncular way. The party was at a distant residence, so then I had to stand fifteen minutes in the freezing cold at a shuttle stop, feigning grave illness and trying to prevent the guy from gnawing on my neck.

In the past, when I had heard girls talk about different guys being good or bad at kissing, I had assumed, without consciously disbelieving them, that they had somehow been exaggerating: conflating whatever good or bad feelings they had about a guy with his imagined technique. Kissing had just seemed like a thing a person couldn't be especially good or bad at. I saw now how mistaken I had been.

All the next week, I kept running into the gnawing guy. He kept smirking at me from corners and making insinuating remarks.

I emailed the Count again. OK, forget the coffee, I wrote. There's this other thing I need you to help me out with. I tried to explain it really clearly, so he wouldn't misunderstand, because I wasn't sure how good a reader he was. After I hit Ctrl-S, I started doing my Russian homework. I had done three exercises when the phone started to ring.

His voice was deeper than I remembered. It was exciting to hear him slightly mispronounce my name.

"Selin was on the phone with a *boy*," Riley said, after I had hung up. I forced a smile. How had she known? The whole conversation had lasted like a minute. It must have been the tone of my voice.

The next three days were among the most peaceful I had ever experienced. I didn't think about what was going to happen. It was settled, so I could finally *stop* thinking about it.

On the evening of the third day, I went running, took a shower, and stared at my half of the closet. Did a person get dressed up? In the end, I put on jeans and the burnt-orange corduroy shirt from the Garment

District. As I was about to leave, I realized I had misplaced my keys. I looked for ten minutes before finding them in the most obvious place: under Stanley. When I picked him up, he actually turned and looked at me. His yellow eyes with the black almond-shaped pupils: what was behind them? He turned away to stare at the wall.

The clocks had just been turned forward. It was five past seven. The branches stood stark and bare against the glowing sky, but here and there the streetlights picked out the tiniest buds starting to show. It had rained earlier, and the pavement still sounded wet when a car drove by. I could smell everything: the rain, the asphalt, the tires, the damp soil, the tree bark, the barely visible new leaves. To see life—to see what it really was.

At first I was reflexively hurrying, because I was "late." But then I thought better of it. He wasn't going anywhere. I should take my time, see as much as I could before the window closed again.

"I was really surprised when I got your email," said the Count. "Nobody ever wrote anything like that to me before."

"No?" I glanced around the room. He was looking at me in an amused, ironic way.

"I think we can both keep a secret," he said, in a suggestive tone.

What did that mean? I wasn't allowed to tell anyone? "Mm," I said, noncommittally. Out of the corner of my eye, I noticed a three-pack of condoms and a partially flattened tube of K-Y jelly. What had it been used for? When had it been acquired? How had the jelly gotten into the tube? I thought about the huge factories and the giant machines and the millions of dollars, the molds that shaped and crimped the molten plastic, the hiring of engineers and consultants, the deployment of some of those consultants to college cafeterias, to ask people how different colloidal substances got into tubes—because they wanted to see the way you think.

"You don't have anything to drink, do you?" I said aloud.

"You mean alcohol? No, sorry. Are you nervous?" A mocking note had entered his voice. That felt deadly. I had to do something to change it. Willing myself to look into his eyes, I picked up his hand—it felt like the most forward thing I had ever done—and placed it on my chest, on what I thought was my heart, though I felt momentarily confused about left and right. But did it matter, wasn't my whole rib cage pounding? It worked. He was serious again.

"We don't have to do anything you don't want to do," he said.

"I know," I said.

He moved his hand farther down. "We'll take it very slowly."

And then it was like slipping back into the water again after lying on hot sand, and knowing you were going to go back and forth like that, between the beach and the sea, until the sun burned up and sank into the water. I felt simultaneously calm and excited, in a way that felt somehow inhalable—I wanted to inhale it. There was a brief jolt when he unbuttoned my jeans—wasn't he being a bit overliteral?—but, once I recovered, it wasn't unpleasant to be wearing fewer clothes.

A series of expressions moved across his face. I knew that his feelings couldn't be the same as mine, but they seemed, at least in that moment, to be equally numerous. How close I felt to him, and I felt him feel it, too, and I thought: Would it have killed him to have coffee first? We went through the bizarre ordeal of climbing onto his bed.

I understood the point of faking an orgasm. Clearly, he wasn't going to stop what he was doing until something changed. But it wasn't quite right, and I didn't know how to direct him. It was like hearing a sound in the forest and not knowing which way it was; and, even if I had known the direction, it would have taken too long to get there—it seemed to be taking longer, lately—and I would have worried that he was bored or uncomfortable, and even if I could have known that he wasn't bored or uncomfortable, *I* wouldn't have been able to bear such intensity and tension without knowing how and when and whether it was going to end. It was increasingly imperative for there to be some achieved or manufactured climax—not just so that he would stop, but so that he would feel as masterful and gentle and adept as we both needed him to be, and so that I would feel as responsive and released and grateful as we needed *me* to be—and I heard myself uttering sounds that I hadn't known I was capable of producing: the kind of soft cries that conveyed, in movies, that what was happening was si-multaneously against a person's will or judgment, but was also what they most wanted. My breath caught in my throat, I experienced a convulsion that both was and was not my own doing. What even *was* fake?

He half laughed, and moved his hand farther back. "God, you're so wet." I didn't understand what he meant, until he showed me. Then I felt my heart also melt.

He sat up and I heard the condom wrapper tear. I sat up, too, to see better. How was it all rolled up like that? How big was the machine that did that? How was he going to get it on? What did it feel like?

"You look fascinated," he said, with a hint of dissatisfaction.

"Why wouldn't I be?"

He didn't say anything, but once his hands were free again, and he was above me, I felt that his preferred state had been restored. The preferred state was for me not to be fascinated. It was for me not to be thinking about the condom factory, wondering why they called it Tro-jan when the Trojan horse was a story *about* permeability, about how the Greeks swarmed out and foiled the Trojans, who had believed themselves to be protected—and in the moment that he pushed me onto my back I realized, with elation, that I could prefer that state, too, that I didn't *need* to be thinking about those things. It was the opposite of "they want to see the way you think." There was nothing to do but to look up at him, to reinforce our shared awareness of his greater strength. What good fortune, that the thing he wanted was something I was so eminently capable of wanting—that my desires overlapped, or could overlap, with the concrete social reality. I felt my body adjusting to the concrete social reality.

"You're sure you want to do this?"

I nodded.

"I think I need you to say it."

"I want to."

Unimaginable pain shot through my body. I cried out in a different way than I had before, and understood that *this* was truly involuntary and thus not-fake—because it was an extension of how every fiber of my being was saying that this was something that was not supposed to be happening.

"Try to relax," he murmured.

I took a deep breath and closed my eyes. At first, I thought the relaxing was working. Then it really started—the pain. I willed myself to relax *into* it. It intensified and grew until it was bigger than the tallest building, looming over and around me.

"Do you want me to stop?"

"*No.*" The thought of having to go through this again later—because we didn't do it right the first time—was unbearable.

He applied more lube. I saw blood on the condom. That made me feel reassured. So something was finally happening.

It went on happening. He told me again to relax. "You have to let me," he said. I thought about *letting him*. It got so much more intense that

I was sure it must be done, or almost done. This proved not to be the case.

"I'm barely inside," he said. I detected a note of panic in his voice.

"Is there always this much blood?" I asked.

"I don't know," he said tensely.

"What was it like your first time? Was she more experienced?"

"You could say that," he said, in an ironic tone, implying that she had been a prostitute.

He tried not to show that he was upset when blood got on his skull pillow. There was something exciting about the specificity of his reaction—how precisely it delineated what he was like: considerate enough to try to hide that he was upset, but not considerate enough to try harder, or to not be upset. Then he seemed to regain control of himself. That, too, was sexy: to see him conquer something, even himself. "We might have to try something a little unorthodox," he said, in his suave, amused voice, helping me down from the bed. He pushed his computer to one side of his desk. Was he going to somehow use his computer? Then he laid me on my back on the desk, where the computer had been, and drew my legs up against his chest.

My head kept hitting the window and I could see outside to the river, to Ivan's old dorm.

Walking down the damp street, I felt both wide awake and unprecedentedly still. For the first time I could remember, I didn't feel guilty about not working. It felt like I was finally off the clock.

According to my watch, three hours had passed. My memory seemed to be missing some time. At some point, he had said something about his roommate, and asked if I wanted to take a shower. Taking stock of the situation, I realized there was nothing I needed so much as a shower.

It was like a foreign country, nothing in there but an almost empty thing of Head & Shoulders, radically unlike the shower that I shared with three girls, where you were always having to make room for the rain-forest shaving gel between the custard-apple shampoo and the apricot exfoliant. The towel, too, was different. Coarse, gray, in no way objectively superior to our towels—to the contrary—it nonetheless emanated a kind of protective strength that gave me a longing feeling. What would it be like if that was your towel? As a child, you learned that all the soft, colorful things were for girls, and at that time I had felt lucky. But this coarse gray towel . . . had I been duped?

At some earlier point, he had gone to the bathroom, and I had been standing in front of the desk. I saw his pants with the heavy belt, the heavy fabric, everything heavier than my clothes, crumpled almost violently on the floor. I felt a desire to fold them, feeling like it was a good thing I could do for him, something that might even put us on more even terms. I had picked them up, shaken and smoothed them out, and was draping them over the back of the chair when he came back in—and then I saw from his face that I had done something wrong, I wasn't supposed to fold his pants.

Had it been before or after then that, surveying the scene of carnage, I had said, in my most sparkling voice, "So this is what the big deal is about?"

"No!" He actually sounded worried that I thought that. I felt touched, though also disappointed that he didn't appreciate what I thought had been a really funny joke. "It isn't usually like this," he said. "You'll see later."

"Will I?" I said. The words seemed to turn electric, like a battle line, live with the mortal danger that somehow surrounded the question of whether I would see him again.

People said you had to be careful whom you lost your virginity to, because you would become attached, you would want to do it again, you would never get over it. Indeed, even though it had been one of the most painful experiences of my life, still what I felt toward him was something like gratitude, and a feeling of submission that was hard to differentiate from desire—because you had to submit *to* something.

I thought of a bus shelter ad I had once seen, for Virgin Atlantic (why was there a whole airline named after that?): YOU NEVER FORGET YOUR FIRST TIME. They said you never forgot your first time, but they didn't say whether the other person forgot your first time. Mentally reviewing the way I had looked in the bathroom mirror, my face tearstained, my legs and body smeared with blood and K-Y jelly, I thought it was possible that he would remember.

The dining hall soda dispensers were glowing in the dark. I drank a glass of Gatorade, followed by a glass of water. How had I gotten here? I made out a solitary figure in the dark, typing on a laptop. Was that Juho?

"Ah, I was hoping I would see you," Juho said, when I went over. "I am always forgetting to give you this." After unzipping his giant backpack, he handed me something plastic and crinkly: a bag of the Finnish candy called Turkish peppers. These tarry black lozenges tasted powerfully of licorice and salt, and gave you a feeling of having inhaled swimming-pool water. I wasn't sure what was Turkish about them, or why they were considered desirable, yet I already wanted another one.

We sat in the dark, sucking on the briny candies, talking about Juho's winter break. In the winter in Helsinki, the sun didn't rise until past nine, and set before four, so almost the whole time was twilight and darkness. You spent all day in this twinkling, glowing landscape—because the electric lights reflected off the snow—going between different cafés to listen to really specific kinds of music and drink incredibly strong coffee. Every home had its own sauna and, even though the national cuisine was based on hunting and fishing, it was still easier to be a vegan in Helsinki than it was at Harvard; a person wasn't always eating marinara sauce. Juho had never been away for so long, and understood now that he had been depressed.

I told him that I had been depressed, too, but felt better after taking antidepressants. Juho said that he was glad I felt better, but that drugs weren't the right solution for him, because in his case the depression was a natural reaction of his body to not procreating.

I thought I hadn't heard him correctly. "To not . . . procreating?"

"Yes. As you know, we are genetically programmed to reproduce, and if we don't do what our bodies are programmed to do, we can expect to feel useless and sad." Once he finished his fellowship, he continued, he was planning to return to Finland and have children, so he wouldn't be depressed.

I thought back to the many people I had seen in the course of life who had seemed more depressed after they had produced children. "But what about postpartum depression?" I asked.

"I think it is hormonal. Like feeling depressed after orgasm. It might be related to suddenly getting something you were deprived of. But it isn't a permanent condition."

"But being a parent . . ." It was hard to put into words. "How can you handle that much responsibility if you're already depressed?"

"Well, you're assuming that a lack of responsibilities makes a person happy, and vice versa. I think this is a very American assumption. You have relatively few responsibilities now. Are you happy? Maybe you would feel happier if you had more responsibilities."

The next morning, the angles of my face in the mirror looked different—more sympathetic. I was still bleeding. The blood was bright red, not like during my period. But the amount didn't seem particularly worrisome, so I just put on a pantyliner and went to Russian. We were learning past participles. Grammatically, the emphasis was less on doing the thing than on having done it.

"Your hair looks nice today," Svetlana said.

For the first time, I felt grateful for Matt's presence at lunch, because I didn't have to think about whether to tell Svetlana about last night. I did keep thinking about it, on a loop in my head, but it actually made it easier to nominally participate in the conversation that Matt and Svetlana were having, which involved something somebody had said about stem cells.

It went on like that all day: the previous night replaying over and over, seeming to confer a kind of weighted legitimacy onto all the routine, boring parts of the day, making me feel like I was in a movie. Why was it that, when you got to a routine or boring scene in a movie, you didn't panic or despair? In a movie, the number, duration, and meaning of scenes were determined in advance. You just had to wait it out. Theoretically, I supposed, this was true of real life—certainly, the number and duration of scenes weren't infinite—but there was always the chance it would just end without anything meaningful happening at all.

Lakshmi was hosting another party, this one with a theme, and was worried that people wouldn't dress correctly. The theme was sadomasochism.

"You know, S&M," Lakshmi said. "Bustiers, fishnets." Lakshmi had clearly lost her mind.

I thought about not going, but this would have upset Lakshmi, and presented me with the problem of how to physically dispose of myself. The libraries would be closed or empty, because of the weekend. In my current condition, I was unable to work unless I was surrounded by other people who also appeared to be working.

"You dressed . . . somewhat appropriately!" Lakshmi said, leaning in to kiss me on the cheek. I had put on Very Vamp lipstick and was wearing black lace tights with a floral pattern. Lakshmi seemed critical of the tights, until she saw they had seams on the back. Seams were apparently sadistic, or masochistic. Lakshmi was wearing a black leather choker with silver spikes, a fitted strappy top, a tiny vinyl skirt, and stiletto heels.

Some people, like Lakshmi, looked cool or interesting in their sado-masochistic outfits, but most did not. One particularly tedious editor had a plastic ball strapped in his mouth, but kept taking it out to talk, so then he just had this saliva-covered ball hanging around his neck. A couple of first-year girls were wearing black lace bras with nothing on top, and looked sad and pauperlike. A literature major whom I knew slightly was walking her lame boyfriend around on a leash. The tough-talking heiress to a British grocery-chain fortune, who wrote microfiction where people made jokes about cancer, was wearing skintight leather pants that looked too expensive, and thus also somehow sad.

I felt relieved to see Oak, who was wearing a black turtleneck and had what Svetlana called his demented Nureyev expression. His hair was sticking straight up and he seemed particularly distractible. At one point we were talking about Russian formalism, and then he had disappeared. I found him in the next room, playing with Lakshmi's riding crop. Lakshmi rolled her eyes. "It's not *for* you," she said.

He looked at her boldly. "Why not?"

"Because you're not interesting enough or sufficiently good-looking," she said.

A couple of bystanders laughed uncomfortably. Oak's eyes widened. "Come on," I said, dragging him toward the stairs. "Let's go have a cigarette."

"Why would she say that?"

"Because all people do is reject and disappoint each other," I said.

He shook his head vehemently. "No, this is completely different."

We stood in the window where people smoked cigarettes and I said things to try to cheer Oak up.

"You're always very sweet," Oak said, playing with a pair of handcuffs that he had apparently had in his pocket.

"Are those real?" I asked.

The next thing I knew, Oak had handcuffed me to Jeremy, our most exhausting friend, who had come over to borrow a cigarette, and who was even now talking about how Michel Foucault's interest in bondage was related to his critique of penal institutions.

"Give me the key," I told Oak.

"I don't have it," he said. Before my eyes, he took a small key from his pocket, leaned over the window, dropped it out, and wandered off. I stared in disbelief. Had I done something to offend him?

"Well, I hope you're a masochist about stairs, because now we're going downstairs," I told Jeremy, in an attempt to say something sadomasochism-themed that would cause us to go down the stairs.

"Let's have a drink first, OK?" he said. "It's been a long week."

"Key first, drink later," I said.

"I'm going to get you some wine."

"You're going to *get* me some wine? While I what: stand here and wait for you?" We were both laughing by then, and had drifted over to where the wine was.

"Cheers," he said, pouring with one hand.

"Cheers," I conceded, feeling that it *had* been a long week.

"You know," he said, "I've always had a bit of a crush on you."

The clear dishonesty filled me with outrage. "What about the Dianes?"

"I think I'm finally over the Dianes," he said. "It's a huge step for me."

"Tell me more," I said, taking advantage of his long answer to subtly drag us toward the stairs.

"You're really not into me at all, are you," Jeremy said.

"I'm sorry," I said.

"It's because you're in area studies."

"What?"

"There's always a fetish involved. You don't even want to look at me because I'm not Eastern European."

Although I felt confident that I would have found Jeremy exhausting no matter where he was from, it was nonetheless true that I *had* been only half listening to him, while thinking about Ivan and the Count, both of whom were Eastern European. This made me feel bad about myself. I forced myself to look at Jeremy. He had great hair and was wearing a cool T-shirt. On the other hand, he was one of the guys you sometimes met who held some kind of principled position against exercise, and this was manifest in his physique and comportment. Why didn't he feel like he constantly had to go running or starve himself, in order to earn the right to impinge on other people's attention, the way Svetlana and I did? Now he was tracing a finger along the underside of my forearm. "The skin over here is fine, but really just fair to middling. But here, close to the wrist—this is *sublime*."

I felt a stab of annoyance. Had I requested a comparative skin evaluation? I pointed out that the skin on the underside of his forearm, too, was smooth and soft. "That's the human arm," I said.

"You don't have to tell me. I have silky, girlish skin. I'm not some huge Yugoslavian guy."

I glanced around for somewhere to put out my cigarette.

"That's the first thing I've said that made you pay attention. You immediately looked around the room. You're like 'Where is the huge Yugoslavian guy?' Well, I accept that I'm not some Yugoslavian stallion. I accept that I can't look at you from across the room with eyes that say, 'You know you vant to fuck me.'"

"Maybe *you're* the one looking for a huge Yugoslavian guy. Did it ever occur to you that your interest in me might be transferential?" Even as I was saying it, I felt ashamed by the inadequacy and childishness of this, the first comeback I had thought of. But Jeremy was beaming rapturously.

"Touché!" he said.

"What?"

"Touché! You always speak ironically, and yet you're so sincere. *You* are the only one who can prevent me from my self-absorbed flights of bathos."

"I'm a busy woman. I don't have time to prevent you from flights of bathos."

"I know! You're just as self-absorbed as I am! That's why we're perfect for each other!"

Something powerful jolted through my body. At first I couldn't tell what had happened. Then I saw the Count standing in the doorway, wearing a shearling jacket. Our eyes met, and he raised his eyebrows and nodded slightly. Then there were people between us. When I caught sight of him again, he was heading right toward me. I felt my body change—everything felt like it was melting and running down, like rain on a window—like it was getting ready for something to be jammed in there again—like he owned me in some way.

"How's it going," he said.

"Hey," I said.

His eyes seemed to pass over Jeremy without seeing him. "Are you here with someone?" he asked, in a meaningful tone. This struck me as absurd.

"No," I said, equally absurdly. I saw him notice the handcuffs. "Well, someone handcuffed us together," I said.

His expression changed—that mockery entered into it. "Looks like you're having a good time," he said, briefly gripping my shoulder, and disappeared again into the crowd.

"Who the *fuck* was that," Jeremy said.

"What do people ever do but torture each other?" I asked Jeremy.

For the first time, his eyes met mine, and it was as if some curtain had gone up and I was seeing him, the actual person, for the first time. I felt relief and promise, like maybe this was the beginning of our real relationship. But the curtain came down again almost immediately, everything went back to how it had been, and I understood that what had been revealed to me at this sadomasochism-themed party was the true face of all parties: how they were all, in one way or another, sadomasochism-themed.

"You do know that handcuffs all have a standard key," said a guy wearing a green open-fronted bodysuit. (Was that sadism, or was it masochism?) "There isn't," he continued in an expostulatory tone, "a *different key* for every pair of handcuffs."

If that was true, then all we had to do was find someone else with handcuffs and ask for their key. I scanned the room and noticed two diminutive guys handcuffed to each other, wreathed in smiles. I dragged Jeremy over to them. They seemed eager to help. The one with sideburns produced a tiny key with one tooth. It fit perfectly.

How could a key even be a key if they were all the same? Wasn't the point that each key was different? I tried to think it through, on the way to the bathroom. Was it related to whether your goal was to keep out many different people, or keep in one person?

For a while, I had been dimly aware of something squishing under my right foot. In the privacy of a wooden stall, I realized that blood had soaked through the pantyliner, dripped down my leg and under the lace stockings, and pooled in my shoe.

The bleeding stopped the next day. I felt relieved: if it had lasted any longer, I would have felt like I had to go to the student health center, which was always degrading. At the same time, I felt sorry and anxious, like I was back on the clock again—like some exemption was over.

APRIL

Once, on an impulse, I picked up the phone and dialed the Count's number, but nobody answered. I left a message. A couple of days later, when I was walking back from dinner, I heard the whirring of a bicycle chain and someone said, "Hey, Selin," and it was him. I was walking uphill and he was coasting down. He raised his hand cordially, but without slowing.

One way of looking at it was that now I had feelings about *another* guy who wanted nothing to do with me. It was, of course, an outcome I had anticipated; but insofar as I had given it any thought, I had seen it as an improvement on the status quo, reasoning that it would feel more bearable and legitimate if the guy was someone I'd actually had sex with. It had been a comfort to imagine a future in which I wasn't constantly thinking about Ivan—even if it meant just subbing him out for a guy with a worse personality.

In fact I had been right: it *did* feel, by comparison, more bearable and legitimate. Yet to say that I was on any objective level enjoying myself would have been an overstatement.

In creative writing, we read Chekhov's "The Lady with the Little Dog." It was about a married man nearing forty, who had an affair at a summer resort with a married woman half his age. (So, she was my age.) She went everywhere with a little dog. After they had sex for the first time, she cried and said that she had "fallen," and "the Evil One" had tempted her. Then, the man despised her and felt bored. In general, he looked down on women, and thought of them as "the lower race," even though he always needed to have one of them around and was always having affairs with them and then forgetting about them.

At the end of the summer, the man went back to Moscow. At first, he enjoyed wearing a fur coat and going to parties. But time passed, and he couldn't stop thinking about the "lady with the little dog." That was how he thought of this person who was nineteen.

Eventually, the man went to the crappy province where the lady lived, tracked her down to the depressing theater where she was attending an opening night, and realized that, despite her ordinary, even vulgar, clothes and accessories, she was, for him, the most important person in the world. When he cornered her during the intermission, she implored him to go away, and told him that she had never been happy, and never would be happy, but that she would come to him in Moscow.

There was much I didn't understand in this story. Did the man like having an affair with the lady? If so, why didn't he think she was special? If she wasn't special, why was he unable to forget her? I also felt confused by his attitude toward his children. The part where he was walking his daughter to school, explaining weather formations, all the while thinking of how he wanted to go to a hotel and have sex with his girlfriend: that was something I felt that I had always known. But the part where it said, "He was sick of his children, sick of the bank"—lumping his children together with his job—that was somehow shocking.

In class, everyone talked about how subtle and understated Chekhov was, because he didn't idealize the characters, and made it clear that the protagonist was a cad. They discussed whether it was a "redemption" that he was able to feel love for a woman who was banal and wore a gray dress.

I wondered whether I was having a defensive response to the story, because I hadn't acted the way the lady had when they had sex. I hadn't felt that "the Evil One" had tempted me, or that I had "fallen." Nor was I holding my breath for the Count to be "redeemed" by realizing he couldn't live without me.

Someone said that "The Lady with the Little Dog" broke all the rules of storytelling, because there was no climax or resolution. Leonard said that maybe that was what was so wonderful about Chekhov: how he was, in a wonderful way, boring. Was that true? Did I agree? Fundamentally, I liked Leonard. It didn't feel like he secretly hated us, or was trying to be mean. Yet almost everything he said caused me pain.

"Selin? Any thoughts?" Leonard asked.

I didn't know how to ask what I wanted to know: namely, what was wrong with Leonard, and what had been wrong with Chekhov, and why they seemed so unhappy, and made us unhappy, too. Instead, I talked about my favorite line in the story: the one where the guy realized that all parties were the same. You were always just stuck in a room while drunk people said the same things over and over, "as if you were sitting in a madhouse or a prison."

"That's such a great description of what unrequited love feels like," Leonard agreed. I had never heard anyone say the word "unrequited," and hadn't realized it was pronounced that way, or that it was something Leonard had experienced. "Or not necessarily unrequited, but just not going the way you want it to." Gazing into the distance, Leonard talked about "a wrongness underlying the machinery," and everything he said was true.

My mom forwarded me an email from Jerry. Can you explain to me the meaning of this missive? I hadn't realized that she and Jerry exchanged emails. I knew that he did sometimes call my mother, to complain that his wife, the shiksa ice queen, didn't know how to appreciate a good meal. Her ideal dinner was a bowl of cereal on the treadmill with *The New England Journal of Medicine.*

Subject: Fw: Fw: Fw: Fw: Fw: Fw: More Evidence the World Is Full of Idiots

* Police in Wichita, Kansas, arrested a 22-year-old man at an airport hotel after he tried to pass two counterfeit $16 bills.

* A bus carrying five passengers was hit by a car in St. Louis, but by the time police arrived on the scene, fourteen pedestrians had boarded the bus and had begun to complain of whiplash injuries.

* Police in Radnor, Pennsylvania, interrogated a suspect by placing a metal colander on his head and connecting it with wires to a photocopy machine. The message "He's lying" was placed in the copier, and police pressed the copy button each time they thought the suspect wasn't telling the truth. Believing the "lie detector" was working, the suspect confessed. . . .

I had gotten this email before. It had annoyed me with its self-congratulatory, pro-police tone. The thing with the photocopy machine sounded illegal.

It's a joke email forward, losers send them. I've gotten it like 4 times, I typed furiously. I don't know why he would send it to you. I guess to prove how cool he is.

After I hit Ctrl-S, I realized I had managed to send the reply, not, as I had intended, to my mother, but to Jerry. My heart seized up. But why? What did I care whether Jerry knew that I thought he was a loser? Didn't he already know?

The microwave at the Ukrainian Research Institute had started spontaneously turning on and microwaving invisible items. Katya said she had heard the microwave actually speaking Ukrainian.

"Reciting Shevchenko?" Rob asked dubiously.

Someone said it was possible for a microwave to pick up AM radio.

Dear Ivan, I typed, when I was supposed to be working.

It's hard to believe it's already spring. There was a blizzard on April 1 so all the tulips fell down and died—or so we thought. "April Fool's, assholes!" Now there are all these undead tulips all over the place.

I've been working really hard to do what you said, to move on and forget about you. It is necessary, and therefore possible.

I'm doing better than I was before, when I was so scared and upset. I didn't realize until afterwards how afraid I was! It was like there was something jamming the door, and I couldn't get out, and I was really starting to panic.

In the end, I realized that one way to move it would be sex. I wrote an email to a guy I met at a party. I'm not sure if this was, in itself, a good thing or a bad thing.

Did you ever read in Russian formalism about the "knight's move"? The theory is that change or innovation never goes in a straight line. That's why it's always surprising, and sometimes feels almost backwards.

There is a wrongness underlying the machinery. The microwave is not supposed to recite Shevchenko!

But where there is undeath, there is hope.

Selin

Malin and Elsa were visiting Boston. Elsa stayed one night with me, until Riley's glares, in combination with the bouquet of cat effluvia and sandalwood, drove her to Lakshmi's.

"It's fine, don't worry about it," Lakshmi told me, barely even looking annoyed. She was busy planning a trip to New York with Isabelle and Noor, whose investment-banker friend, the owner of a SoHo loft, was vacationing in Monaco.

I got called to an interview for *Let's Go*. "So you're in second-year Russian," said the Russia editor. "Do you think you know enough to bribe an official?"

"I can learn it," I said. "I mean, I already learned like seventeen lines from *Eugene Onegin*, so . . ." I trailed off, confident in my reasoning that, whatever you had to say to bribe someone, it was surely less than seventeen lines. The mention of *Eugene Onegin* clearly left a negative impression on the editor. "The greater part of this job is thinking on your feet," he said. "I'll tell you what. Why don't you try to bribe me right now."

Trying not to seem flustered, I removed the entire cash contents of my combination keychain-wallet—four dollars—and waved them at the editor's face. "You want four dollars?" I asked in Russian.

"OK, see, you can't wave money around like that," he said, adding that I had used the genitive plural for "dollars," but "four" actually took genitive singular.

That was when the Turkey editor, whom I hadn't noticed in the room at first, jumped into the conversation, asking a lot of questions about how well I spoke Turkish, what citizenship I held, where my parents were from, what other cities I had been to, and how much I knew about Central Anatolia.

Not this again with the nervous breakdowns, I thought, because I knew Let's Go had a problem where they sent American people to Turkey and they kept having nervous breakdowns. The last guy had been beaten up by a pimp in Konya and fake-befriended by a reporter from *Rolling Stone*, who turned out to be gathering material for an exposé.

The editor started explaining about the nervous breakdowns. It turned out that I had been conflating two different guys: one who had a nervous breakdown in Konya, and another who had been befriended by a reporter in Istanbul and *then* had a nervous breakdown. A third American guy had gone to Central Anatolia last year, and had also had a nervous breakdown. The upshot was that Let's Go wasn't sending anyone to Central Anatolia who didn't speak Turkish, but I could go, if I wanted to.

Joey's story in creative writing class was about a kid in high school "losing his virginity," a phrase that sounded weird to me when used

257

about boys. The narrator was lying on top of his girlfriend on an old sofa, and the girlfriend started to writhe and moan and cry out, and the narrator felt upset: he, too, wanted to writhe and scream, and felt it was unfair that only the girl was allowed to behave that way.

I felt nonplussed. Could it be true that guys also wanted to moan and cry out—to have their lack of control over the proceedings be an object of interest, and not of contempt? But just think if *everyone* was moaning and crying! And for him to begrudge his girlfriend . . .

No, it couldn't be that all guys felt that way. Maybe it was just Joey. Was that why Lakshmi despised him?

I went to an off-campus party with Riley and Priya, and the Count was there. I felt him trying to avoid me—from one room to another. At first I thought I was imagining it, but it was definitely true.

Also present was the guy who had loaned me his handcuff key at the S&M party. He had seemed nice at the time, but now he was speaking in an affected voice, repeatedly telling Riley and me to make out.

"If your mother language is your mother tongue, why isn't your mother country your mother cunt?" some other guy was saying.

All around us, people were ironically doing Jell-O shots. There was a giant abstract painting on the wall that I knew someone would eventually compare to a vagina.

Riley and I had declined the Jell-O shots, so it became a project for some people to get us to do Jell-O shots.

"Let's just get it over with," I told her. She shrugged and we clicked together the tiny cups.

"Kiss! Kiss!" chanted the handcuff guy. Riley kissed him on the cheek. The ironic people had clearly messed up the Jell-O, which hadn't gelled at all.

Looking for the bathroom, I passed the Count, who was standing by the doorway next to a tall guy with puffy hair. "That could be the clit," he was saying. They were looking at the painting that I had known someone would compare to a vagina.

The next day at brunch, Priya was talking about how the Count had tried to hit on her. She didn't know he was the Count. "That slutty guy with the impossible name," she said. "He was hitting on the other two Southeast Asian girls, and then he came up to *me* and was like . . ."

Riley interrupted her, ostentatiously changing the subject—to be considerate of me. I realized that, although I hadn't felt implicated or hurt by Priya's characterization of the Count as a slutty guy who made unwelcome advances to women of Southeast Asian descent, I did feel hurt by Riley's assumption that I would or should feel implicated.

"It was just so gross," Priya said.

The night I met him, the Count had been dancing up close with a short girl in a silver dress. Had she rejected him? *Was* he gross? On some level, I knew, it was a subjective evaluation. Yet the way Priya said it, in combination with Riley's response, made it seem objective. On the other hand, Priya's reality was different from mine. She had many more opportunities than I did, so of course she evaluated them differently.

———

"My life is ruined," Lakshmi said in a dead-sounding voice. It was Sunday afternoon. She should still have been in New York.

It had started after lunch on Friday, when Isabelle had picked up Lakshmi in the BMW. Mia, the freshman who loved *Finnegans Wake*, had somehow already been in the back seat, pretending to be humble about impinging on their trip. They were picking Noor up next. Lakshmi understood that any seating configuration—either Noor with Isabelle in the front and Lakshmi and Mia in the back, or Lakshmi in

259

the front and Noor and Mia in the back—would be insufferable. For a while, after the rest stop, Mia sat with Isabelle in the front, and even then, alone in the back with Noor, Lakshmi felt his energy directed like sunlight at Mia.

It went on like that all afternoon, through the parking and a key-related mishap. Finally, when they were drinking beers on the roof and watching the sunset, Mia said something that betrayed a confusion between Baudelaire and Baudrillard. Noor downplayed the error, and Lakshmi added, "Yeah, what's a hundred years' difference?" Noor froze Lakshmi out the whole night and, when she confronted him, he told her he hadn't known she could be cruel.

Lakshmi had left for Boston alone at daybreak on a secret bus from Chinatown that she somehow knew about. When she got back, the phone was ringing. It was Joey. He had been calling for weeks and she had always refused to see him. But this time she felt too exhausted to argue and agreed to meet for a drink.

The last thing Lakshmi remembered was Joey bringing her a second tequila.

The whole time she was telling the story, I was trying to figure out which was the terrible part. At first, I thought it was the unjustness of Noor saying Lakshmi was cruel, after he had been torturing her all day. But that wasn't it. The terrible part was waking up in the morning in a bed next to Joey.

"I'm probably not a virgin anymore," Lakshmi choked, when she saw I didn't understand. A tear glittered in her eyelashes, and another rolled down her face. I had never seen such sparse, reluctant, angry-looking tears.

"But how do you know?"

"There was evidence."

"You mean—blood?"

"No, but there wouldn't have been. Not with all the horseback riding." She acted like it was obvious what the evidence was, but I still didn't get it. It had been a condom. Joey said he had put it on before he realized Lakshmi was passed out, and then had taken it off again without doing anything. Lakshmi didn't believe him. She said she had permanently forfeited her claim to her father's love—the love of the only person in the world who truly valued her.

Lakshmi was my friend, so I was on her side. Yet for some reason my mind was working to figure out what she had done wrong. Had she been "using" Joey, to make herself feel less badly about Noor? On the other hand, wasn't that what you were supposed to do: give up on the bad boy you liked, and maturely, self-respectingly accept the attentions of a less charismatic guy who had proven his essential goodness by wanting to be with you? Wasn't that the plot of 40 percent of romantic comedies? Wasn't it what Alanis Morissette had finally done?

———

In the bookstore, I picked up a book I had seen many times, and had never once thought of reading: *The Rules: Time-Tested Secrets for Capturing the Heart of Mr. Right.*

The Rules were basically to do the exact opposite of everything I did. You could never tell a man that you loved him, or show that you liked him, or initiate sex, or agree to have sex. The Rules closely corresponded to the list of things that Tatiana didn't do, in *Eugene Onegin.*

> She does not say: Let us defer;
> thereby we shall augment love's value . . .
> let us first prick vainglory
> with hope; then with perplexity

harass a heart, and then

revive it with a jealous fire. . . .

That was it—that was the Rules.

Eugene Onegin didn't contradict the Rules, but rather confirmed them—because Tatiana didn't get Eugene Onegin. A person who had followed the Rules *would* have gotten Eugene Onegin. This was proven by how Tatiana herself basically got Eugene Onegin later, after she was married and had no use for him. Then, he threw himself at her feet, imploring her to have an affair with him and lie to people and ruin her life.

That was the essence of the Rules: to treat the man you were interested in just like the man you *weren't* interested in. You could never stop pretending you weren't interested, not even after you were married. That was Rule 26. If at any turn, anything you did seemed like your idea, it was a huge turnoff. This was because of "biology." ("Biologically, he's the aggressor.")

How decisively the Rules sliced through the endless debate I had been a party to all my life, over the words and deeds of people's boyfriends. "You might wonder, 'Is his behavior the result of bad upbringing or something in his past?' Maybe. But we believe it's because you didn't do the Rules." So it wasn't that my mother and aunts were wrong; the men's behavior probably *was* the result of some incident in their past that had left them incapable of receiving, acknowledging, or valuing genuine love. But it did you no good to know it, or to discuss it, let alone to ingeniously reconstruct what the incident had been. The only thing that did you good—because it hacked the man's brain and made him act the way a person who loved you would act—was for you to pretend that you didn't truly care about anything except your hair.

According to the Rules, being obsessed with your hair wasn't shallow or antisocial. *Neglecting* your hair was antisocial, because it made other people feel like losers if they hung out with you. So was cutting your hair short, because it didn't help men to feel more manly. It didn't matter whether you looked better with short hair. In general, it didn't matter what you, in particular, were like. Rule 1, "Be a Creature Unlike Any Other," made it sound like you were going to get some points for not being exactly the same as everyone else, but it turned out to mean the opposite. Basically, all your actual qualities and achievements were pointless and boring, and your real value lay in the mysterious unspoken essence that made every woman "a creature unlike any other." The book repeatedly said that "smart, educated women" were the worst at doing the Rules—because they thought their fancy degrees entitled them to display their personalities. They always got their comeuppance, and were "heartbroken."

Nothing in *The Rules* was news, exactly: the eternal defeat of non-lame women, the worthlessness of their "honesty," the way they so often ended up marrying lame guys whom they had initially rejected as tedious. It wasn't that I hadn't known these things, but that at some point, without realizing it, I had persuaded myself that I was different— that *my* honesty and non-lameness wouldn't be punished like that, because I had some special skill, some self-sufficiency, an ability to be alone. I always *had* been alone, when every other person in my family had insisted on having someone around to have sex with.

It was shocking to see Ivan's name in my in-box, even though, or maybe because, it was no longer the white-hot one, being somehow less activated than the longer Polish name pertaining to the Count. But I felt its latent power: how it could start again, how the wire was still live.

Selin,

Sometimes I don't understand you at all. Why can't you do
anything like a normal person? When I see how you behave it
makes me feel quite helpless. I used to wonder this last year:
how could you be so graceful in writing and so clumsy in life?

I stared at the screen. Why was he acting as if I had complained to him?
I hadn't complained to him. Who was he to tell me I didn't do anything
like a normal person? Who was he all of a sudden: Mr. Normal? If you
want to get laid, he continued, don't write emails. You have to . . .

What was it now—advice? He was talking about creating a mood
of uncertainty. The man shouldn't know whether he was allowed to
touch my hand. There was no wrongness underlying the machinery. In
fact, if you did it right, it was amazing how well the machinery worked.

The crassness of if you want to get laid, the vulgar interpretation of
the machinery were both uncharacteristic and upsetting. It felt like
some spell had been broken—like he was finally telling me something
he had refused to talk about before. Because, although he had never
previously accounted for himself, for what had and hadn't happened
between him and me, he now seemed to be answering the question I
had been so careful, this time, not to ask.

Man, you really screwed it up with me big time. Never tell a guy
you love him until he tells you seven times first. Otherwise, you
are playing a losing game. Even if he was thinking about saying
he loves you, he can't now, you have destroyed the mystery.

I realized that, although I had often felt hurt by things Ivan had said
or written, I had never before felt that he was deliberately trying to
hurt me. Was it possible that what I had written had hurt *him* in some
unprecedented way? Was it possible that was why I had written it—to

hurt him? As I had been hurt, and hurt, and hurt, for two hours, on the skull pillow and on the desk?

I thought about the Rules, and how I had felt they didn't apply to me. All that time, when I had been telling myself that I wasn't dependent on other people, hadn't I been holding on to the contradictory conviction that someday I would—in the very phrase, heavy with significance, used by my mother and aunts—"meet someone": someone as different from the tedious guy who wanted to marry you, as from the tedious guy who didn't want to marry you?

Now Ivan himself had told me, apparently in a moment of anger— did that mean it was more or less likely to be true?—that I had ruined everything by basically not doing the Rules. So maybe Ivan *was* the guy who didn't want to marry you, whom you had to trick every day for the rest of your life.

> Anyway, there are mountains of oedipal phobias between us,
> when towards me you seem like a little sister. Moreover, you
> somehow remind me of my mother.

There it was again: the hard glitter of revelation. When I thought about all his little sisters, the part about a little sister made sense. The mention of his mother, though, felt gratuitous and foreign. Wasn't it older women who reminded people of their mothers? How could I be both: like a little sister, and like his mother?

I thought back to Ivan's mother, trying to remember what she was like. At some point, she had shown me a faded chart they had once used, to apportion household chores, back when Ivan and his four sisters still lived at home—a grid indicating whose turn it was to make the cocoa at breakfast. Why did thinking about that make me feel sad? Her tone had been cheerful, and her general bearing one of brisk competence. Surely, if she had been sad, it wouldn't have been anything she would have betrayed in front of me, a hapless teen stranger.

I thought again of the Rules—of Rule 3, about the first date: "Avoid staring romantically into his eyes." Rule 10, about "Dates 4 through Commitment Time": "Act independent so that he doesn't feel that you're expecting him to take care of you." Weren't they somehow the rules that one wished one's mother would follow? Of course, there was no reason for her to follow them; you couldn't, you wouldn't avoid her, the way men avoided you. "Avoid staring romantically into his eyes." Was it possible that I had made Ivan feel the way I sometimes felt about my mother?

MAY

Juho said he had to ask me for advice about dating: a concept he considered to be specifically American. In Juho's world, I counted as both an American and a dating expert.

Juho had been prevailed upon to visit Wellesley on the bus known as the Fuck Truck. At the ensuing dance, Juho, who considered the music to be unsuitable for dancing, struck up a conversation with a girl who also wasn't dancing, and who described herself as a very shy person who normally spent her every waking moment putting on plays in an all-women Shakespeare group. This girl had now invited Juho to return to Wellesley to see her play Polonius.

Was this a date? What was the difference between going on a date and dating? Should Juho go? Would I come?

I said I thought he should go, by himself, in case it *was* a date; if it wasn't, he would have seen *Hamlet*. It was a sentence I could imagine my mother saying, judiciously: *In the worst case, you saw Hamlet*. It worked. I could see Juho was pleased. He asked again if I didn't want to come. I pointed out that I had already seen *Hamlet*. But it did seem odd that Juho would now have been twice to a women's college, and I had never been to one.

I found myself remembering my summer-camp friend, Jordan, who was my age, but already a junior at Smith. (She had applied to colleges a year early, because she lived in Kansas and hated her father, and Smith had given her a full scholarship.) My mother hadn't been crazy about Jordan, whom she had met when she picked me up from summer camp. Jordan was even taller than I was, she made her own clothes (mostly out of other, pre-existing clothes), and had a tattoo of half a snail, because it had gotten interrupted. She published a comics zine and was half Chinese. Whenever my mother pointed out someone she thought I should be friends with, it was always some American girl with a French braid.

On the last night of camp, Jordan and I stayed up talking the whole night, because we didn't know if we would ever see each other again. We had been right: we never had seen each other again. My mother had said that I seemed unnaturally excited, asked repeatedly if I was doing drugs, and ironically tried to give me Valium so I would sleep in the car. I had never felt so awake, and didn't want to stop feeling that way.

All the next year, Jordan and I exchanged letters, handwritten on the biggest pieces of paper we could find: brown bags, wrapping paper, continuous-feed printer paper. When my mother saw one of Jordan's long, scroll-like letters, she said she thought Jordan seemed mentally unstable, and asked whether she was a lesbian.

Once, when my mother and I were watching *Law & Order* on a Friday night, my mother had asked whether I was a lesbian: otherwise why was I here with her, instead of out on a date? It seemed sort of rude, but I answered as politely as I could. She wasn't satisfied by anything I said, until I pointed out that, if I *had* been a lesbian, I would have told her already. Then she clearly felt relieved—"You would, right? We have no secrets, right?"—and we could go back to watching the district attorneys prosecute the offenders.

Last year, when I got to college, Jordan and I had sometimes exchanged emails. Jordan wrote increasingly about her housemates, two of whom were mysteriously in love with the third, Pepper, who was snotty and insufferable. After six months or so, Jordan said that she and Pepper had kissed, and that now she, too, loved Pepper. I didn't get it. How could Jordan love a human being named Pepper? *Was* Jordan a lesbian? Was that something my mother had been right about? At camp, Jordan and I had talked for hours about crushes we had on guys.

It hadn't occurred to me to apply to women's colleges. In high school, I had noticed how classes, already intolerable, became exponentially worse whenever the boys weren't there. Even the girls who were smart seemed to care less than usual about making good points. This was especially the case when the teacher was also a woman. Anyway, I didn't want to be "nurtured" in an "environment" that was set up for me to "excel." I wanted to do whatever was the most real and rigorous. Obviously, everything would be set up for boys. So what? I would work ten times harder than they did, and everyone would eventually acknowledge I was doing a better job.

The more Juho told me about Lara, the girl from Wellesley, the less she corresponded to any of the stereotypes I had heard of. She was Mexican and had grown up in Mexico City, but her mom was from England, so she had a British accent. She had three brothers, was obsessed with theater, had acted since she was little, but was pathologically shy. Hearing about what a specific person she was, it occurred to me that Wellesley must be full of all different kinds of people, just like Harvard was, only they were all girls. That made it seem exciting. But clearly they missed the boys, and had to bring them over on some kind of a bus.

Radcliffe sent a letter offering me a travel grant, but for less than half the study-abroad tuition. The Peruvian frozen food guy emailed saying I could work for him, pending my submission of a "full-body photograph." The Let's Go Turkey editor, Sean, kept calling on the phone with ideas to expand the coverage of Central Anatolia. But I had gone to Ankara every summer of my life, so how did Central Anatolia count as travel?

As I was walking by the Science Center, staring at the ground, I ran into Peter, who asked about my summer plans. I told him about the deficient Russia grant, the visually oriented frozen food supplier, and the Central Anatolian itinerary that gave American people a nervous breakdown. I had meant it as a funny story about how all the options had something wrong with them, but Peter seemed to understand it differently. He asked if I had ever traveled alone in Turkey, and said what an incredible experience it would be, and seemed to take it as a given that I was going to go to both Turkey and Russia.

"I don't know if it's really enough money to go to Russia, though."

"Why, how much is the grant?"

When I said twelve hundred dollars, Peter laughed and said that the study-abroad programs overcharged by orders of magnitude. More economical arrangements could be made privately, with greater benefit to local hosts. Moreover, everyone in every country wanted free labor: all I had to do was find someone with an interesting job and offer to make them coffee, and that would be an internship, and I would learn just as much as from a three-thousand-dollar American program.

Struck by Peter's way of viewing things, by the way he made the world sound so manageable and small and large at the same time, I wondered aloud whether I should try to work something out with the frozen food guy. Wouldn't it be pleasing in a narrative way for everything to tie together like that? Peter laughed, but with a slightly concerned expression, and said he was going to put me in touch with one of his friends.

<hr>

I hadn't had a clear mental picture of Juho's new girlfriend, Lara, and realized that I had almost expected her to look blurry. Of course, she turned out to have a normal level of material reality, with gray eyes, dimples, and tangled-looking hair that was gold and brown mixed together. She was wearing ill-cut boxy overalls that somehow managed to look both cool and flattering.

Why was that the thing you had to do when you saw a girl: to prosecute whether and in what way she was beautiful—as Lara, I realized, was? With guys, some of them were physically repellent or appealing, but a lot of them initially presented as neutral, and there wasn't that immediate, urgent-feeling cognitive puzzle to slot them in, as there was with literally every female person, including one's own self, in windows and storefronts. Sometimes it seemed to me that I looked interesting, mysterious, and sculptural. Other times I thought that I didn't look *like* anything, that nothing matched together or corresponded to anything or had any kind of grace or proportion or meaning, that the posture was deformed and hateful, like a sign of laziness or obsequiousness or some other personality flaw.

The second most striking thing about Lara, after her beauty, was her eagerness to be liked: not the overeagerness that drove a person away, but a radiant, Bambi-like hope, that seemed, in this instance, to be specially directed at me—as if I were a particular friend of Juho's whom she needed to love her. (So, she loved Juho.)

Juho read a Spanish textbook and listened to Spanish cassettes in his sleep. Over spring break, he went to Mexico City with Lara, and when he came back, he could speak Spanish. Lara was going to take a Finnish immersion class over the summer. How quickly it had all happened! Juho and I had been friends for months, but it would never have been a plan for us to go to different countries and learn languages because of each other.

Juho had told Lara that, if they were going to think about staying together for more than a year, she would have to learn Finnish and develop her own relationship to the culture, because he had to move back to Helsinki after his fellowship. He had seen too many Finnish people return from overseas with non-Finnish-speaking partners, and the partners ended up totally dependent, and everyone got depressed. After Lara graduated, she was supposed to spend six whole months alone in Helsinki. That way she could see if she liked Helsinki enough to live there—for itself, and not because of Juho.

"Where will you be?" I asked.

"Somewhere else. Or even in Helsinki. We just wouldn't be in contact."

I felt relieved to learn that there was some logic, after all, behind who ended up with whom, because this plan sounded crazy to me, and yet I could imagine a person different from me thinking it would be fun. Clearly, Lara was such a person, and that was why she and Juho were together.

At dinner the next week, Juho said he had to ask me for advice. He was worried about Lara, because they had spent the weekend together and at some point she had started crying uncontrollably. I asked what had been happening right before the crying. Juho said they had been talking about the six months she was going to spend alone in Helsinki after graduation. I said that maybe Lara didn't want to spend six months alone in Helsinki. Juho said that couldn't be the case, because they had discussed the plan at length and Lara had agreed that it was reasonable.

"It could be the kind of plan that seems reasonable when you talk about it, but if you have to actually do it, it makes you sad," I said. "I could imagine feeling that way."

"You?" Juho exclaimed. "But you lived in a Hungarian village!"

That was true. I had stayed with random people, tried to learn Hungarian, and hadn't talked to Ivan for weeks. But most of that hadn't been Ivan's idea. Definitely, he had never said that I had to learn Hungarian, or wasn't allowed to talk to him.

What if he had? On the one hand, it might have been nice for my study of Hungarian to be a recognized, legitimate project, and not something weird I was doing in secret. On the other, when I tried to imagine living in Budapest for six months and knowing that Ivan was there, but wasn't talking to me, on purpose . . . well, it felt at least as bad as my actual situation.

I went to the Café Gato Rojo to meet Peter's friend Seongho. He was wearing a suit and carrying a briefcase, and told me about the self-directed program of study he had undertaken in Moscow last year, having suddenly realized, in the course of his dissertation research into Korean Communist factions, that he urgently needed to be able to read Russian. He slid a piece of paper across the table. On it were the long telephone numbers pertaining to some geneticists who had rented him a room in the outer suburbs, and to a literature graduate student who had taught him enough grammar to read Communist newspapers. There was also the pager number of a guy named Igor in Queens who would, for two hundred dollars, get you a visa invitation letter.

Was it possible that everything was so . . . not easy, exactly, since it sounded like kind of a pain, but so feasible? Seongho made all his problems sound funny. He said he would vouch for me to the geneticists, and would tell them I wasn't an axe murderer. (How could he know that?)

I started trying to think of people in Moscow whose job I could learn about by making their coffee. I remembered an English-language Russian literary journal I had occasionally attempted to read. I found it in the library. There on the copyright page was an editor's email address, ending, thrillingly, with "msk.su." I took the journal into a carrel, determined to read it from cover to cover.

From the first few pages, I got a depressed, hopeless feeling that reminded me of why I had never previously succeeded in reading this journal. "Serdiuk realized what it was that had suddenly brought the singer Polyp Pigdick to mind," I read. I flipped forward to another story. Someone called Vic the Snot-Faced Drooler was commenting on a woman with "four tits, two backsides, and a plait of hair as thick as your fist."

Yet, for some reason, this, in a story by a third author, struck me as funny:

> "Why are you wearing a gas mask?" asked Pissoff. "Have you got a leak from the gas oven?"
>
> "And why do you limp on both legs?" Karmalyutov answered his question with a question. "Are you an old sea wolf?"

I sent the editor an email, enthusing about Pissoff and Karmalyutov, asking whether, since I was going to be in Moscow in August—how bold it felt—there was any work I could do to further their interests. She wrote back, asking me to pass out flyers about her journal to different famous professors at Harvard. I replied, implying that I might not be able to pass out flyers if she didn't also think of something for me to do in Moscow, and she said she would think it over.

Priya was also doing Let's Go, in Nepal. We went together to the women's self-defense training session. A giant ex-convict wearing a space suit pretended to mug you. That was his job, now. It was demonstrated to us how we should knee him in the balls while screaming, "No."

The ex-convict spoke with professional pride about the unconscious processes according to which criminals chose their targets. He cited a study where several violent offenders were shown a video of people walking through a shopping mall, and independently identified the same marks. It wasn't the wealthiest-looking people, but those who seemed to lack self-confidence or alertness.

Priya knew a lot of Let's Go lore, because one of her admirers was a law student, and those were the people who handled most of the legal claims. According to Priya's law student, the last time Let's Go had "sent a single woman" to Turkey, she had been sexually assaulted, and had tried to file a negligence claim against her editor. Was that true? Definitely, people were always trying to sue Let's Go, but it was usually for libel.

Part of Let's Go training was learning to write in a special tone. The tone was called "witty and irreverent," and was also employed in *The Unofficial Guide to Life at Harvard*, a book that was freely distributed to undergraduates and that we had all read many times—at least I apparently had, because whole sentences, mostly from restaurant write-ups, seemed to have been burned into my memory. Lines like, "The Fishery serves up huge portions of fresh but mediocre fish to a family-oriented clientele," impressed me with their judicious apportionment of strengths and weaknesses, as did the writers' easy conversance with social types I had never heard of ("chatty alterna-folk," "relaxed Gen-X waitrons").

Each researcher-writer was assigned three Boston-area businesses to write about for next year's *Unofficial Guide*. Mine were Vintage Treasures, Bob's Muffler Repair, and Dr. Stoat's Comics Vault, all in Coolidge Corner. It was satisfying to have a reason to go to a neighborhood I rarely visited, and Bob was nice, saying he could give students a 10 percent discount on mufflers. Still, it was hard to think of anything witty or irreverent to say about any of these places, since most Harvard students didn't have cars or buy antiques and, even at Dr. Stoat's Comics Vault, the median age seemed to be forty-five. Who were those grown men, paying good money for figurines and trading cards: a commodity about which I didn't even know enough to say if it was a "large selection"? The figure of Ham came to my mind. Was Dr. Stoat known to him? It seemed likely. I hadn't had any interaction with Ham since that party.

Back at home, I reread the restaurant section of *The Unofficial Guide* from beginning to end. It seemed to encapsulate a specific worldview, almost a specific persona: one you came to inhabit as you were reading. Just as, when you read a nineteenth-century novel, you entered into the persona of a nineteenth-century Christian male member of the propertied classes, so, too, when you read the restaurant reviews, did you become a person whose lifestyle required constant infusions of coffee, which couldn't be burned or mediocre or purveyed by a nationwide chain; a person who held the rich in contempt and considered "overpriced" and "overrated" to be the worst insults, yet who could, under the right circumstances, identify and appreciate a memorable venison pastrami. You were continually engaged in destroying yourself in an inevitable, prestigious, yet shameful way, hinted at in sentences like: "That (crabless) crab rangoon will go great with the hangover you're going to have tomorrow." And how powerfully the phrase "(crabless) crab rangoon" summed up the disconnect between the way things were described, and the way they actually were. By a similar operation, the write-up of Wholesome Fresh moved me almost to tears.

276

Supposedly open 24 hours, Wholesome Fresh offers pretty much everything your heart desires. Hearty sandwiches. Hot dishes. Sushi. Chocolate Sauce. Paprika. Napkins.

There it was, finally on display: the gap between the idea that Wholesome Fresh promulgated about itself, in a naïve or sinister way, and what it felt like to actually be there. What a relief to see it articulated!

How alone a person was normally, walking down a street, trying to choose between different businesses. It wasn't the most glamorous part of life, or the one that was most often discussed, but it was so constant, like a heartbeat, like the waves: the question of where and how to spend the money that had been wrung from the world at such cost. Nobody really talked about it, except the advertisements, but the advertisements weren't trying to tell the truth; the advertisements said simply that Wholesome Fresh *was* Wholesome Fresh. In some way it seemed to me that *The Unofficial Guide* was the most truthful book, more so than *Either/Or*—because it was describing the exact concrete situations you were in, specific to time and place, and was updated every year.

I met Sean, the Turkey editor, to go over my itinerary. Heavyset, with glasses and pockmarked skin, Sean had a pleasantly conspiratorial, over-caffeinated demeanor, like a newspaper editor in a movie. He openly disparaged Let's Go's existing Turkey coverage, acting as if we both knew that any sane traveler would prefer to use the Lonely Planet guides, which were written by actual travel writers: the kind of people who lived in other countries and called themselves "expats." (Were my parents expats? Somehow, it felt like only British and Australian people were expats, just like only Russian and Polish nobles were émigrés.)

At the same time, the fact that Let's Go relied on clueless students who were sent out for a few weeks every summer was, in a way, its selling point—one in which Sean himself seemed to believe. Let's Go didn't have enough money to pay real researchers, and the travelers didn't have any money, either, so *Let's Go* was the only realistic guide.

My itinerary was Central Anatolia, the Mediterranean coast, and North Cyprus, which Turkey considered to be a part of Turkey, though nobody else thought that. The assignment packet contained marked-up photocopies of the relevant pages from last year's edition, along with a list of new places to add.

My mother said that the itinerary was impossible: nobody could go to so many places in seven weeks, nor was there any need for them to do so. What tourist had ever thought of visiting two-thirds of these places?

"Well, they're supposed to be 'off the beaten path,'" I said.

"There's a reason why nobody beat a path there," replied my mother. After consulting my aunt Arzu, she sent me a revised itinerary. More than half of the stops had been removed. As compensation, she had added two stops on the Black Sea, where we had "connections." But the other researcher, a Turkish grad student, was doing the Black Sea. I couldn't just decide to go there. My mother said that was exactly what I had to do. I felt deep fatigue at the vastly differing worldviews of my mother and Let's Go.

The places my mother was the most adamant about my not visiting were North Cyprus, a site of previous violent disputes, and Hatay, on the Syrian border. My mother wept and said there was no reason for me to go there, there was no advantage and she forbade it.

My father said that North Cyprus was supposed to be beautiful, and maybe I could take my cousin Evren. He didn't have anything bad to say about Hatay, either; it was only a couple of hours from Adana, which was also on my itinerary. I could pick up Evren from Adana and we could go to Cyprus together. When he described it, it almost sounded fun.

PART FOUR

Summer

JUNE

In my heart I didn't see the need for a backpack. Wouldn't I be better off with a suitcase? Especially now that suitcases all had wheels. People never even talked about that anymore, and acted as if it had always been that way. Yet, all through my childhood, everyone had been yelling, "You'll hurt your back!" and wrenching suitcases out of each other's hands, in an effort to personally be the one who hurt their back.

In the end, I bought the least backpack-like backpack: it was all black and "convertible," meaning the straps could be hidden, causing it to resemble a giant misshapen duffel bag. If you unzipped another zipper, part of it fell off and turned out to be a detachable daypack.

Many people watched with interest as I dragged this item off the conveyor at the Ankara baggage claim. I unzipped the straps, worked them over my shoulders and, ignoring the openmouthed stares of a family of six, trudged to the taxi line.

Lemon cologne, leatherette seat covers, and that smell when you opened the cab window—what even was it? Tar? Cigarettes? Some kind of trees? What was so exciting about just recognizing things, almost regardless of what the things were? The unlit hall at my grandmother's building, the stone floor and stairs that always seemed to be in the process of being washed by someone suffering from back pain. Even now, they were darkened and damp and smelled like mud, because dust here wasn't allowed to be dust, but was flooded with water. Whenever anyone went away, everyone else cried, and dumped out a pot of water on the stone stairs—so they would "come back quickly like water." That was another time when the stairs and floor were wet.

My grandmother opened the door, skinny and Muppet-like, with her giant grin and her booming voice. "Selin, my beautiful girl! Welcome, welcome! Mercy, what's on her back!"

The hulking carved wardrobes and cupboards and sideboards; crystal ashtrays, embroidered cloths, stacked bezique counters, decks of cards that my aunts knew how to shuffle and manipulate with terrifying expertness and an absent expression. The polite, urgent speech of newscasters, coming from the wooden television console. The indescribable smell, soapy yet human. The framed photograph of Atatürk wearing a fur hat. The oil painting of my grandmother when she was young, with an expression she still had now, skeptical and amused and imperious.

"Ah! Ah! Getting old is a great misfortune!" My grandmother sat down and smiled into my face, leaning forward and listing everything that was hurting, which included her kidneys and some things I didn't understand. As always, she alluded to a nail that doctors had put in her back.

A paralyzing wave of tenderness. Was it possible she was happy? Her big smile, her shouting, "Sit down, be comfortable, you're in your own house now, shall I put on the tea?"

Soon it was time to face a problem I had tried not to think about: the problem of sleep. Nothing else had ever been like the sleeplessness of Ankara. Sleep evaded and evaded you, and by the time it came it wasn't a blessing but a curse. Now, the more you slept, the more you were eating into the next day, destroying what was left of it with depressingness, sealing the doom of the next night.

When I was little, I couldn't understand what was happening—why we had to suffer like that. It was explained to me that this was a normal part of travel, called jet lag. My mother offered me Valium, telling me not to put it in my novel. Once, though, the Valium had left me feeling even more fatigued and hopeless, yet still unable to fall asleep, so after that I didn't take it anymore.

Instead I read, finishing all the books I had brought in the first two or three nights, reading them over and over for the rest of the summer. I still remembered large sections of those books, which were about American children who got leukemia or were obsessed with babysitting. There was an English series, too, about some small children in Cornwall who were somehow delegated to save humanity by discovering King Arthur's grail: a task clearly exceeding their strength and abilities. This went on for several depressing and yet insufficiently numerous volumes.

The English children always did encounter Magic, or seemed about to. The girl in *The Secret Garden* knew about Magic "because she was born in India where there are fakirs." This was confusing, because my grandmother often talked about "fakir." This was the Turkish word for poor person, and was uttered in a tone full of pity, regret, and sentiment. My grandmother's house was known as a place where anything might disappear and turn out to have been given to the fakir. My mother was still upset that he had gotten her bicycle, at some point in the 1950s.

How hard I had tried to like those trips to Ankara, to feel that something interesting was happening—and not that I had been stricken somehow from the register of the living. It was something I had never admitted, and could only bring myself to think now that I was here without my mother. It would be ungrateful and traitorous to think that it had been depressing; yet I had been depressed. I could barely form the words to myself, feeling how much my mother would disbelieve me, and would say I was doing "revisionism."

Was I doing revisionism? Had it actually been wonderful? Of course, it had. Ankara had always been a place of treats: beautiful golden rings and trinkets, new clothes, quilted robes, red slippers, chocolate-covered orange rind, candied chestnuts, pale golden apricots and grapes. My grandmother always made marvelous jam: sour cherry, Seville orange, wild strawberry. My mother took me on special outings, just the two of us. The Flamingo Patisserie had the best lemonade. My mother would debate ordering profiteroles. I encouraged her: I always wanted it to be a special day, a day when my mother finally got a treat. And I felt pleasantly disinterested to say, about the profiteroles, "Why don't you have one," since I didn't particularly like them myself. My indifference to cream and puff pastry was spoken of admiringly by my mother and aunts. But my mother almost never did order profiteroles.

Near the Flamingo Patisserie was the Paşabahçe glassware shop, where we would admire the *çeşm-i bülbül* carafes, the extravagantly gilded and specifically shaped glasses for Turkish tea, *rakı*, champagne, and cognac: the gilt sets blending, in my mind, with the elaborate collections of personal effects on display at Atatürk's mausoleum, which we also visited sometimes, in a taxi, though not as frequently as—when we had gotten up early enough—the Hittite Museum.

The best part of the Hittite Museum was when my mother read from the stone tablets with hieroglyphs. One was about a goat who lost his clothes, and took a vest from somebody's clothesline. Another involved a bird who was studying to be a plumber. On some level, I knew that my mother was inventing the stories, and not reading them, but on another level—when she pointed out the glyphs of the Two Crossed Monkey Wrenches and the Broken Faucet—I knew she was reading them. When we came to another tablet on the other side of the hall, by which time I had all but forgotten the goat, my mother said, thoughtfully: "Ah, of course—this one is about the goat's neighbor."

The goat's neighbor had hung his laundry on a clothesline and, just when he had been looking forward to wearing his nice clean vest . . . !

If anyone else had been telling the story, the neighbor would have been angry. In my mother's version, it was a gentle and delightful mystery. Where was the vest? Had the bird flown off with it? But the bird didn't like clothes; they interfered with the plumbing. The goat, on the other hand: hadn't he complimented that vest a few too many times? "Well, I think I'll just have a few words with the goat." By then we would both be helpless with laughter.

So—I had been wrong to think it had been bad. The thought of how I had wronged my mother caused me so much pain that I started racking my mind for counter-evidence. And it hadn't *all* been like the Hittite Museum; usually we woke up too late to get anywhere before it closed, because I wasn't the only one with trouble sleeping; it was even worse for my mother, who often drifted off only after daybreak. The living room doors with their brass handles and frosted glass panes remained closed until the mid-afternoon sun shone directly and depressingly through the front-facing windows. The terror of waking her—the terror of her strained voice.

Other times, visitors prevented us from leaving. Heavily made-up women sat for hours on the sofa, drinking tea. They refused the tea, with a pained expression, but my mother or grandmother or aunt insisted, and then they drank it with a pained expression, while "conversing." This entailed relaying to each other the varyingly dismaying or witty remarks that had been made to them by other people, inserting "he said" or "she said" between almost every other word: "And then, she said, Şenay, she said, you, she said, don't, she said, understand anything." Sometimes, there were long stretches when nobody said anything but "ah, ah, ah," or, "really."

I started to go into a cycle, like the one in "The Seducer's Diary" where Cordelia kept arguing one way and the other over whether anything bad had happened to her. It couldn't have been depressing, because my mother had worked so hard to make it not be depressing. And yet— was it possible that how hard my mother worked was part of why it had been depressing?

I knew how vigilantly my mother had protected me from the things that had depressed her as a child—like having to kiss the old people's hands on holidays. She had thought their hands were gross, and felt insulted to have to kiss them, but they made her do it. My mother said that that had been wrong. She said that children were people, whose dignity and privacy were worthy of respect. She was the only person I had ever met or heard of who thought or said anything like that.

It was explained to the other relatives that Selin wasn't going to kiss anyone's hands. "Fine, fine, let Selin not kiss," they would say, in the voice of someone humoring my mother in how she spoiled me. I always knew that this way in which I was disappointing people and making a spectacle of myself was a favor bestowed upon me by my mother, who was sparing me a bad experience that she had not been spared, and I felt guilty toward everyone: toward my mother for not appreciating how she always defended and protected me, toward the old people whose hands I didn't kiss, and toward my cousins who *did* have to kiss the old people's hands.

Arzu's son Murat was four years older than me, and obsessed with knives. Insofar as I existed in his consciousness, it seemed to be as a source of annoyance, because I was taller than he was, though I was younger and a girl. Murat became convinced that the secret to my unnatural height lay in the Flintstones chewable multivitamins that my mother dispensed to me out of her suitcase. My mother immediately began sharing the Flintstones vitamins with Murat, and after that she always mailed or brought him his own supply. The effect on his psyche when, after taking the vitamins for a whole year, he didn't surpass me in height . . . Arzu said the reason I was so tall was because the chicken in America was full of estrogen. This angered my mother.

But why was I still thinking about that, now that I was long past the age where anyone could expect me to kiss their hand? Maybe my father was right and I tended to "dwell" on imagined slights and bad feelings from the past.

My grandmother was reading the newspaper in bed, in the small side room where she usually slept, still drinking tea, which she said didn't keep her awake. As usual, I had been given the master bedroom. I took a shower in the bathtub that coughed when you turned it on, changed into shorts and a T-shirt, and sat up in bed to read the Central Anatolia and Ankara parts of *Let's Go*.

It was incredible to see *that guy*, the *Unofficial Guide* person, invoking the neighborhoods of Ankara: a place that had always felt somehow un-described to me, because so few of the people I knew had ever been there, except the people who were actually from there, and who didn't feel a particular need to describe it. The places that *Let's Go* recommended were preceded by the thumbs-up logo, which was also the apostrophe in *Let's Go* on the cover, and which made me feel badly about myself, because I had never gone hitchhiking. Only one site in Ankara had a thumbs-up: the Museum of Anatolian Civilizations. What relief I felt when, reading the description, I understood that it was the place my mother called the Hittite Museum! So, we had been right to like it—and they had been right to identify it as having value.

At the top, *Let's Go* said that Ankara wasn't worth a special trip, if you didn't have a reason to go, because it was so much less interesting than Istanbul. The comparison struck me as strange. They were totally different cities. Nothing about them was the same. I decided I would make the coverage of Ankara more positive. I woke up at ten the next morning, realizing that I had actually been asleep.

How long had it been since I had thought of Fatma or Berrak, the two women who helped my grandmother at home? Fatma lived outside the city, and came once a week. She had a large sculptural face set in an expression of kindness, and acted like a relative. I did my laundry in secret, hiding the clothes afterward, so she wouldn't iron them; but she found them and ironed them anyway, even the T-shirts and underwear. Why did I want to cry when I saw those perfectly stacked squares?

Berrak, who came every day, was skinny with a lopsided grin, and looked like a teenager, though she was in her twenties, and was married to the doorman. She lived downstairs. My grandmother ordered Berrak around without saying please or thank you, like she was always already annoyed at her. Why was Berrak viewed with skepticism? It might have been because of her political views, which she shared with the doorman, who was a Marxist, and also religious—not privately, like my grandmother, but in a way that was critical of secularism and of the United States.

On the other hand, it could have been less about politics than about her tendency to say unpleasant things. Once, Berrak had spoken in my mother's presence of "the kind of woman who has gotten to be fifty years old but doesn't own any property."

"Isn't it kind of funny that she's a Marxist, but despises people who don't . . . own property?" I asked.

"It's very funny," my mother said, not laughing at all.

On another occasion, Berrak had hung wet sheets over the tops of the doors to dry. "Remind me why that's not a good thing to do?" I said thoughtfully, as though I had simply forgotten. My mother and aunts stared at me with identical sorrowful expressions. A door, it was pointed out to me, wasn't designed as a load-bearing element; that wasn't part of the great plan for doors, they weren't made for people to ride on, but simply to exist on their hinges, regulating access to rooms. When they had done that, they had done enough, without also carrying the weight of great dripping wet sheets. And what possible reason could there be, what possible benefit to be derived from rejecting the hallowed product of human ingenuity that was the clothesline?

"So, they wrote a book about Turkey, and they sent you to fix the mistakes?" I heard in my grandmother's voice the family partisanship that would have made her swear up and down that of course I could fix any kind of book, as well as mild skepticism about the possible value of this particular book.

I spent the first two days with my grandmother in the living room where she passed most of her time, sitting with her knees doubled up in her green armchair, smoking Marlboros, drinking glass after glass of tea, solving the crossword puzzle, getting mad at the neologisms. Modern Turkish had only been around for sixty years, so it was still changing. Arabic and Persian loanwords were periodically replaced with equivalents that were supposed to be more Turkish, but were sometimes just made up. It was annoying to older people. No sooner had my grandmother come to accept *simge*, a bogus word for "symbol," than she had to put up with the brazen foisting upon the public of *imge*, for "image."

My grandmother often spoke in proverbs that I didn't understand. I was used to tuning them out. Now it occurred to me that, if this had been a "foreign" country—if it had been Russia—I would have been trying to learn the proverbs. I started writing them down. Some featured my old friend, the fakir. "The fakir chicken lays eggs one at a time": that was about not being in a hurry, and seemed somehow directed at me. Another saying, "The egg didn't like its shell," was used for people who tried to distance themselves from where they came from, or who disrespected their parents.

I did some fact-checking, using the rotary phone next to my grandmother's armchair. My grandmother insisted on evacuating the armchair for the occasion, and sat across from me on the sofa, beaming at me and commenting on my grammar. I planned out the sentences in advance. "Good day, might it be possible for me to request some information regarding . . ." My grandmother said approvingly that I wasn't like most young girls, who said "ehh" all the time, and said "thing" when they couldn't think of a word. Yes: they sounded normal, and I didn't.

At my mother's urging, my grandmother and I went out to buy a cell phone for me to carry around. I couldn't buy a phone by myself; it had to be registered with a citizenship card. My own citizenship card didn't have a photograph. This was normal for children, but at age fifteen you were supposed to have one put in. The customs officers still let you in, with a U.S. passport and a faceless Turkish citizenship card. But, once you were there, you couldn't buy a telephone.

How elegant my grandmother looked, with her pumps and matching handbag. We picked out an Ericsson phone the size of a loaf of bread.

My grandmother shouted at me how much she loved me and how she would miss me when I was gone. Tears sprang to her eyes because of how differently her life had turned out than she thought: everyone was in America, she had only two grandchildren, there were some questions of communication, which she never specified, but she probably meant that I spoke Turkish imperfectly, and my cousin David didn't speak Turkish at all. My grandmother always quickly added how much she loved David and me: how much she loved looking at pictures of us, and thinking about us. She was grinning broadly the whole time she said these things, like it was all delightful. "Ah! Ah! How I will look for you when you're gone!"

My grandmother seemed shocked and upset when, on the third day, I actually left the house, though I had told her repeatedly that this would happen. I had set the alarm for eight-thirty, feeling terror that it would jerk me into the state of despair and exhaustion where I couldn't do the things I was supposed to, and that I would fail and have a nervous breakdown. But once I had managed to calm my grandmother and remove myself from the house, everything was easier than I had anticipated. The taxi driver already knew how to get to the bus station. Once you got there, it was basically people's job to answer your questions about bus schedules. You didn't have to explain anything, or account for anything, or manifest love. If anyone got annoyed at you, they couldn't cry, or scream at you, or accuse you of offending them, and at any point you could just leave. It was totally different from being in your family.

I bought an olive roll and tea at a pastry counter, and tried to separate the euphoria of freedom, which seemed legitimate, from the satisfaction that my bill came out to less than a dollar, which felt suspect.

How satisfying it was to go to an address in last year's edition, and find that the building, location, and hours were either already correct, or, better yet, slightly incorrect but easily correctable. This was the most exciting part: learning that the truth was something that really could be verified, and put in a book.

Sometimes, an address or landmark in the book would turn out not to exist. At first, this gave me a sinking feeling. But when I made inquiries, I almost always found an older person who was happy to explain. The street had two different names, or the bus route had changed because of the new metro. I was even complimented for noticing: "Most people in this neighborhood don't remember that it was like that, but you remember." I would explain about *Let's Go*, and more than once I was told that Americans did things right, they actually checked things, not like here in Turkey where we just hoped for the best.

I felt excited when I saw a plaque outside the Hittite Museum, announcing that it had won the 1997 European Museum of the Year Award from the Council of Europe. Then I felt troubled. What was it about being here that made a person feel relief at such things? "The Council of Europe"? It was one of my core beliefs that real worth was independent of what some European or American people happened to have heard of. And yet . . . what *was* value, if it wasn't conferred by some people? A daunting thought: How would I eventually root out from my mind all the beliefs that I hated?

A famous eight-thousand-year-old fertility goddess sat on a throne, her pendulous breasts hanging down almost from her neck, her stomach flopping over her thighs, her face—what there was of it—blurry and stupid-looking, because her face didn't matter. Something was falling between her legs. I knew that feminists liked it when societies worshipped mothers. Why didn't I want to look at her?

The Bronze Age girl known as the Hasanoğlan figurine was about ten inches tall, made mostly of silver. Her face, a hammered gold mask, wore an expression of great sadness. Gold sashes crossed her silver body and gold bands encircled her ankles. There was something sexy about the ankle-bands. I could tell she wasn't empowering. The way her arms were clasped around her made her seem either cold or afraid, and she was too thin. But she was beautiful—lithe, doll-like, eminently portable. You wanted to move her through the world. In that sense, she seemed exciting and free.

Someone had made a life-sized diorama of a Neolithic household, modeled on ruins found near Ankara. Five eyeless clay bull-heads of varying sizes were arranged on the whitewashed walls. An electric fire glowed in a white fireplace. In the middle of the white floor, a shallow circular pit contained two human skeletons in fetal position. The scene looked like a puzzle, a murder mystery. At the same time, it had a tidy, self-contained quality that reminded me of my grandmother's apartment.

When Arzu's cousin Şenay saw my backpack, she stared openmouthed. "But surely you can't carry that on your back."

"That's what I said!" my grandmother exclaimed, immediately adding, in my defense: "But she carries it! My strong girl, *maşallah*, she carries everything."

I put on the backpack, so they could see.

"Truly, she carries it," Aunt Şenay murmured. "But, Selin, can you walk? Tell me that."

I took a few steps around the living room. Şenay was staring at me with admiration and dismay. "Everything on her back like a *yörük*," she said, alluding to an Anatolian nomadic people.

"*Hamal, hamal*, she's become a *hamal*," said Aunt Arzu, when she saw the backpack. *Hamal* were the street porters you still sometimes saw lugging three-hundred-pound loads up and down hills. Later, in an anthropological museum, I saw some Ottoman saddle-packs that the street porters wore under their loads. They really did look like my backpack.

My biggest problem was "nightlife." You couldn't check it by phone, because nobody there answered the phones. Even if they did, they couldn't give you a witty, irreverent description of the atmosphere or the clientele.

"What research can you do in a bar?" Arzu asked, with a pained expression.

But clearly bars were just where I did have to do research, not just for Let's Go, but so I would understand the human condition. The longer I lived, the more evident it became that going out and getting drunk were the things people cared the most about. They thought you were putting on an act if you said you were more interested in anything else. Even *Let's Go*, which was written by people who supposedly cared about human achievement, was always implying that museums were somewhere you went to seem high-minded, and that the thing that was actually important and desirable was knowing which were the right bars and clubs.

Nothing that Arzu said contradicted the central importance of bars and clubs. It was just that, for her, the important thing was to keep me from going. There was nobody who thought bars and clubs didn't matter. Even when I was little, there was a point at family dinners when

294

someone invariably made the joke: "So, what now? To the disco-theque?" And, laughing: "Selin is going to the discotheque."

The joke had been . . . what? That I wasn't allowed to go to the discotheque? That I didn't want to go to the discotheque? That I didn't know about the discotheque—I had never seen its giant mirrored face winking at me in its significance?

Later, I was wandering around an enormous warehouse-like building called No Parking, trying to figure out whether it was a bar or a club, and who the people were. "Club kids," "grim politicos," "well-heeled socialites"?

I felt a tap on my shoulder. "Excuse me, miss," said a man in a suit, "but your car is outside."

"You have the wrong person," I said. "I'm not expecting a car."

"Forgive me, Miss Selin," he said with a little smile, sending a chill down my spine, "but the car was sent precisely for you, by a lady who gave a very detailed description." As he said "detailed," he glanced sur-reptitiously up and down my person, as if admiring how correct the description had been.

I followed him outside. Another man in a suit was standing beside a parked car. I understood who the second man was: an employee of MİT, the central Turkish intelligence agency, which was where Arzu worked.

I had felt I was being followed, but hadn't believed it. I burst into tears.

"My arm won't reach that far. Do you know this expression?" Arzu asked. Like there was any knowledge involved. "If something hap-pens," Arzu said urgently. I was familiar with this way of talking about my life as a liability to older people. The way my mother would say, her face transfigured with horror, that she dreamed I had been raped, and thought it had been a sign that in real life I was in trouble and had needed her.

I kept telling my grandmother I was going to leave, and she kept not believing me and saying I could go another day. Finally I just left, early one morning, leaving a note. I didn't specify my destination. Nonetheless, when I got off the bus in Tokat, I was personally greeted by a civil servant with the state hydraulic works.

The subject of Tokat had been a long discussion with my mother, who said there couldn't possibly be anything to see there. Tokat hadn't been in last year's *Let's Go*. Sean had given me a half page of research, with a quote from Strabo's *Geography*: "There on account of the multitude of prostitutes, outsiders resort in great numbers and keep holiday." Tokat province, on the way to Zile, had apparently been where Julius Caesar had said, "*Veni, vidi, vici,*" after killing a lot of people. It didn't sound like a huge Tokat endorsement from Julius Caesar.

The civil servant, Arif bey, insisted that I stay at his house. His wife made a bed for me on the sofa. The houseplants were wearing crocheted outfits. Arif bey was interested in my Walkman. When he saw I wasn't listening to Turkish music, he tried to give me all his Sezen Aksu tapes. "She is our sparrow," he explained in a voice full of sentiment.

Sezen Aksu's songs started out promisingly, but eventually she always started doing the thing where it just sounded like she was wailing with histrionic grief and trying to make other people feel badly. I knew from music theory class that, when Middle Eastern music sounded like wailing, or like it was out of tune, it was because our ears—my ears—had been desensitized by the conventions of Western music. The Middle Eastern scale had twenty-four tones per octave and was actually more true and real than the twelve-tone version that European people had invented to make a piano work. But I still didn't like to listen to more than one or two Sezen Aksu songs in a row.

For the next few towns, I was met at the station by government employees. In Kayseri, Turkey's *pastırma* capital, an actual colonel from the army showed up at my hostel and took me to dinner at a military restaurant. He told me three different times how I probably didn't realize how lucky I was to study at Harvard University—how many Turkish kids would cut off their ears to have such an opportunity. At some point, he asked what I was studying, and when I said Russian literature, he almost had a heart attack. I kept forgetting that Turkish army people were still mad about . . . the Crimean War?

In the hostel library, which had mostly English books, I found a 1950s introduction to Turkey, published by the U.S. Army. It basically said that Russia and the Ottomans had always been at war. "When the Ottomans lost Hungary in 1699"—so, Hungary was involved—Russia renewed its attempt to seize the Turkish Straits, so they could get to the Mediterranean.

> Russia's age-old ambition for conquest is, of course, familiar to all of us. She is still at it. She has been at Turkey's throat for nearly 400 years, and this knowledge will enable you to understand why every Turkish schoolboy hates Russia. You will meet many Turks who have had relatives and ancestors killed in wars with Russia. Other Turkish people have not forgotten that it was Czar Nicholas I of Russia who sneeringly referred to Turkey as "the sick man of Europe."

Of course I knew the line about the sick man, but hadn't realized that it had been said by a Russian person, or that this remark in particular had "given rise" to "the Eastern Question." The Eastern Question, too, was something I had heard of: like "the Woman Question," it turned up in nineteenth-century novels. The Eastern Question was essentially, "How do we divide up all the Ottomans' stuff?" It wasn't so different from the Woman Question, which was about whether women could have jobs and money. The things some people considered a "question." If you read stuff like that all your life, it *would* make you hate Russia.

———

Cappadocia was famous, but it was hard to tell what it was, even from photographs. The photographs often showed an unnatural number of hot-air balloons, maybe fifty hot-air balloons, suspended at various heights over what was generally described as a "surreal moonscape" or a "fairytale landscape." I thought there had to be some relationship between the hot-air balloons and the moonscape, but it seemed there wasn't. Someone had just decided that a balloon was the easiest way to see everything.

Cappadocia was the ancient name for a region that now extended into three or four modern Turkish provinces, each with its own city. The whole region was on a high volcanic plateau that had been eroded into ridges, valleys, pinnacles, and weird formations, including "fairy chimneys." Fairy chimneys sounded ethereal, but were actually massive stone pillars or cones, hundreds of feet tall, each with a huge boulder perched on top. The wind sculpted them that way.

When I was little, my mother and aunt had tried to describe the fairy chimneys to me. My mother had eventually said that the thing a fairy chimney most resembled was a penis. "Very true," my aunt had said, nodding judiciously. At that time I had never seen a penis.

In many places, the rock formations were riddled with holes: portals to thousands of dwellings, churches, and monasteries that had been carved there by ancient people. It was another confusing thing about Cappadocia: the sculpted-looking rocks had gotten that way through erosion; the holes, which looked like the result of some obscure natural process, weren't—unless you counted ancient people hiding to be a natural process. In some places, they had carved out whole interconnected villages: multilevel cities that accommodated up to ten thousand people, with stables for horses. People had been hiding in Cappadocia since the fourth century BC. Early Christians had hidden there from the Romans—Peter wrote about them in the Bible.

Today, Cappadocia was a famous tourist destination. Nobody thought it was weird or dangerous for me to go there, so I wasn't followed. I got a room in a pension in a 150-year-old Greek Ottoman mansion. The proprietor, a middle-aged woman with a cool haircut, showed me to a huge room overlooking a rose garden. I had noticed, with surprise, that I was often received warmly at pensions. In restaurants, they were sorry that you weren't more people, or a man, but pensions were different.

"Welcome, welcome, welcome," said one proprietor, using a lot of different phrases that meant "welcome." "You're very welcome here." He seemed barely able to contain his excitement, and finally said, in a confiding tone: "A lady traveling by herself is our favorite customer."

"Really? Why?"

"Ladies never break anything."

"Do other people . . . break things?"

"Of course they do. Men, families. Immediately something gets broken. The property value decreases."

"What do they break?" I asked, feeling worried. His pension was starting to sound kind of fragile.

"What *don't* they break. They break the windows. They smash through the walls. Things you wouldn't even imagine. Whereas a nice, well-brought-up lady"—he inclined his head deferentially—"can stay ten years in a room and it looks exactly the same as when she came there! The property value doesn't change at all!"

I felt relieved, because I was sure I would manage not to break the windows, and it was pleasant to receive what was clearly intended as a compliment. At the same time, there was something disquieting in the image of a well-brought-up lady staying ten years in a room without leaving a visible trace.

Then I was in the intercity bus station trying to figure out how to get a local bus to Ahmetpaşa, a village that Sean had told me to visit, because it supposedly had some undervalued ancient grottoes. The guys who worked for the intercity bus lines stared at me like I was insane. Some of them told me with an aggrieved expression about the many tourist bus companies that would take me to see far more interesting and famous sites.

"I have to go to Ahmetpaşa," I kept saying. "I work for a book."

This had been going on for ten minutes when a station employee said, in a cheerful tone: "Ahmetpaşa? Not a problem, I'll drive you there. When are we leaving?"

He looked to be in his twenties, with a lively expression. I couldn't tell if he was joking—not that it mattered, since I had to take the bus. That was the only reason they gave jobs like this to students with no skills: because if someone said to ride a night bus for seventeen hours while eating a tripe sandwich, we would do it, and write down how much it cost.

He said there was no bus. I objected. How else did people go to and from the village? I must have made a grammar mistake, because he immediately switched to the strident, officious-sounding English spoken by tourism workers. It was really depressing. Who had taught them to talk like that? What knowing, pedagogic haranguers were they imitating?

"From here, you must go two hours. You must go two buses." He held up two fingers.

"Splendid," I said energetically in Turkish, using one of my grandmother's favorite Ottoman words. "The more torture I live through, the more beneficial."

"I am sorry?" he said in English.

"This book I work for is for Americans. If their life is too easy, they worry that they're missing the authentic essence of Turkish existence. That's why they want to go to Ahmetpaşa."

"Yes?" He seemed to think it over. "I propose it to you like this," he said in Turkish, and it was like his whole personality changed and became once again courteous and humorous. "Let's say we put you on a bus to Ahmetpaşa. In two hours, you'll travel seven kilometers. You'll see all the things there are to see in Ahmetpaşa—one by one, you'll see all of them. Will you see the authentic essence of Turkish existence? This I don't know, you'll have to judge. You'll find it's enough torture for one day. By that time, I'll be done with work, I'll come pick you up and we'll have dinner. What do you say?"

"If you help me find the bus, I'll be very grateful," I said.

"And dinner?"

"Well, I don't think so. But I can think about it on the bus."

"Terrific!" He beamed, sitting back in his chair. "All I want is for you to think about it. You've made me very happy."

"So which is the bus to Ahmetpaşa?"

"What? Oh, right. I have no idea. Velih bey!"

An older man shuffled over with a cane. "Yes, Mesut," he said. "As you command, Mesut. You see, when Mesut calls, I come right away, in a manner of speaking, as my ability permits, and I'll tell you why

301

that is. It's because I know some very important business is waiting for me. Other people will call you over for some nonsense, but with Mesut you never regret getting up out of your comfortable chair."

"Velih bey, I've disrupted your comfort, and now you're making me bashful."

"Not at all, son. Tell me how it's my honor to help you."

"Velih bey, listen! This young lady has to get to Ahmetpaşa on a bus. You see, the young lady is a researcher, and there's something she has to research in Ahmetpaşa, and this can only be accomplished by going there on a bus."

"On a bus? But there is no bus. If she changes buses . . . it's two hours."

Mesut explained about how the bus was part of the research. Velih listened closely, then called a messenger to ask a guy they knew who lived in the village next to Ahmetpaşa. Another messenger was sent to bring tea. Everyone now called me "miss," and acted like it was not just reasonable but also important for me to get to Ahmetpaşa.

"A researcher!" Velih said, while we waited for the messengers. "How nice."

"You and I should do some research one of these days," Mesut told him.

"Very true. You and I live here all our lives and don't do research. Then from America they come and research all kinds of things."

"Even in Ahmetpaşa, they research something."

"And rightly. Isn't there something to be researched, in every corner of God's creation? Isn't that what you've found, miss, in your travels?"

Mesut escorted me to the local bus and told the driver to leave me at a place in the road where I could flag down the bus to Ahmetpaşa. I asked the name of the place in the road, so I could write it down. The driver told me the name of a nearby creek. I copied it in my notebook—so that someday other people could have the same experience as me.

The second bus deposited me in a square with an Atatürk statue and a general store. There was no sign of any ancient hidden grottoes. Well, there wouldn't be, would there? But when I went into the store to buy a cherry juice, the storekeeper asked if I had come to see the churches, and called a boy to show me the way. The boy, who seemed used to being ordered around, set off at once in a businesslike manner, walking quickly, and then more quickly, until we were basically jogging.

I gradually understood that the reason we were walking so fast was to outpace two fornicating dogs, who were somehow following us. They would go at it for a few seconds, and then stagger along after us, and then start again.

"Are those your dogs?" the boy asked finally. When I said they weren't, he threw a rock at them, and they ran away, with embarrassed expressions.

When we got back from the grottoes, the guy from the bus station, Mesut, was standing in front of the Atatürk monument, by a parked white Opel—the same model that Ivan's mother drove. His face lit up. "Selin!"

"You took too much trouble," I said. It hadn't occurred to me that he would be able to find me so easily. I told him I had been planning to take the bus. The minute I said that, it sounded absurd. The idea of taking the bus was to assert one's independence, and to not get into a car with a strange man. But wasn't one dependent on the bus—wasn't the bus full of men?

I got in the car. We drove half an hour to a city I had thought of as being far away, because it took forever to get there by bus. The sun set and the moon rose. Mesut parked on a side street behind a restaurant. I hadn't really looked at him before, but I was able to watch him as he was exchanging greetings with like every single person who worked in the restaurant. I saw that he was shorter than me, and somehow looked more alive than everyone else.

We sat on the roof under a grape arbor. Tavern-style Ottoman music was playing. Mesut ordered two glasses of wine, took out a pack of cigarettes, offered me one, smoked half a cigarette, then said cigarettes were bad for the health and threw his out. He didn't drink most of his wine, either.

"So, Selin," he said. "Tell me."

"What should I tell you?"

"About your researches."

I told him about the grottoes, about the boy who had shown me around. We had walked four kilometers and climbed up and down rocks. The boy had known all the easiest places to climb, and had held my hand at a difficult point, and told me what he said were the names and ages of all the churches, though I wasn't convinced he had the Greek names quite right. I hadn't known whether to give him money afterward and had tried to buy him cookies, but he had said he had to go home for dinner.

"He was a good kid," Mesut said. "He did well. He could tell you were a good person, too. Good people always find each other."

Was that true? It was too bad there wasn't a club you could join, the way there were for different religions, ethnicities, and nationalities, all of which comprised both assholes and non-assholes. How evenly they seemed to be distributed. What was it based on?

Everything was delicious—the salad with sumac, the fresh bread, the harsh wine.

"Now, you tell me," I said.

"What shall I tell you?" He sat up straighter.

"About your childhood."

"My childhood passed very happily on the Black Sea," he said immediately. His mother had died when he was a baby, so he didn't remember her and had never been sad. The closest person to him, his older sister, Elmas, was now married to a wonderful man, so he never saw her or talked to her anymore. His favorite thing to do as a child had been catching fish, with his hands: that's how many fish there had been then. He used to put them in a bucket and sell them. It seemed to me that Mesut's life was more real than mine, though how could anyone's life be any more real than anyone else's?

I said I had to go back to the pension, to write up the day's copy. He proposed a scenic route back. I said OK. After two weeks of local buses that stopped every twenty feet to pick someone up, it was pleasant to move so freely, without a giant slow bus-butt dragging behind us.

The steep road ended suddenly at a precipice. Spread out beneath us were "fairy chimneys" like giant creatures gathered in the moonlight. What would this place have looked like, "then"? Where were we, what did everything mean, why was it like this? His bearing, when he kissed me, was daring and deferential—like he wanted to see how far he could get through charm and diplomacy. His heartbeat: was I feeling it or hearing it? In Turkish, you could "hear" a smell. Why did aftershave always feel like it was hacking your brain?

"What a beautiful girl you are," he said, with a kind of ache or awe in his voice, that made me think about how someday I would be old or dead or both, and the transience of all things, of the car, the moonlight, the volcanic rock that was eroding and the stars that were shooting by, made the world seem at once more important and less important, until finally the concept of "important" itself faded away like an expiring firework that glittered against the sky.

He reclined my seat and started to climb over the gearshift box.

"No, don't do that," I said.

"Why?"

"I don't want to."

"Why?"

"Because I don't."

"Why? It would be really nice with you. I can tell," he said. "I could tell when I saw you in the bus station." (What?)

"No, impossible."

"But why?"

I hadn't initially considered "why" as an actual question but, as the exchange dragged on, I turned it over in my mind. Wasn't it that thing related to self-worth? I thought of an episode of *Sex and the City*, when Samantha got stood up in a restaurant, by a real-estate tycoon, and started crying, right in front of "the Pakistani busboy." Carrie called him that in the voice-over, though he looked to be in his forties. At the coat check, the Pakistani busboy kissed Samantha—"Samantha let the Pakistani busboy kiss her; after all, he'd been so sweet and attentive with the bread"—and suggested they leave together. Samantha hesitated, then recovered her self-respect just in time to give him a big tip and leave with her head held high. Yes, that was it: you were supposed to remember that you were better than him. But why were you supposed to be better than him?

"I just don't," I said, and I heard my voice break.

"Don't worry about it," Mesut said promptly. "Let's do something else. Why don't we go to the thermal springs?"

At the thermal springs, as at the restaurant, Mesut seemed to enjoy a large acquaintance. A guy showed us to a steam-clouded yellow stone room with a rectangular pool. Wearing only our underwear, we lowered ourselves into the warm water, which was metallic and sulfurous and felt unusually buoyant.

We kissed for a long time. Eventually, when he pushed aside my underwear and slid his fingers in, I felt a jolt that seemed to promise something. It felt like a message coming through a wall. It felt like an important lead in the case.

His erection looked different from the Count's—its expression was somehow more optimistic and alert. It occurred to me that the Count might not have been circumcised. But what even was circumcision? Of course I knew that it was the cutting off of the "foreskin," which was "a flap of skin." But even when you knew that, how much did you really know?

I was scared at first that everything would be just the same as the first time, and we would mess up the bed in the hotel run by Mesut's friend, which was where we had ended up. Then it seemed to go in really easily, so I thought maybe it had already happened and I wouldn't have any more problems. Later, though, it turned out that it hadn't been in all the way, and it became like the first time. So nothing had changed.

"It's OK, we can stop here," Mesut said, and went back to where it didn't hurt. He stroked my hair, told me my body was even more beautiful than he had imagined. Then, after a while, he started pushing again.

With the Count, I had thought that that repetitive motion was related to how it was my first time: that it was about breaking through something and, once he got through, that would be when we would do whatever it was that sex was.

Now, I was starting to get the feeling that the in-and-out motion *was* sex—that there wasn't anything else after that. I mentally reviewed the sex scenes I had seen in movies. Either the people were comically bouncing, or, if it was serious, they were slowly rising and falling. When someone was being raped, you just saw the man's jabbing butt. OK: now I knew what was happening on the other side. It was him poking it in and taking it out, over and over. That's what sex was. I tried to assimilate this new information—to accord it its correct importance.

Later, he dropped me off at the pension. I walked through the moonlit garden, went up the stone staircase, took a shower, and wrote copy until I fell asleep, with the feeling of leading "a full life."

After the first five or six times, it barely hurt anymore. But then at some point, when we were talking, I laughed at something implausible-sounding—"But how could that possibly be!"—and, out of real or simulated anger, he pushed in deeper, and the blinding jolt made me realize that before that he had been going gently, and the thought made my soul feel like it was opening wider.

It did start to feel less pointless, the more you did it. The point wasn't what I had thought it was going to be; it didn't immediately resolve or answer any preexisting need or question on my part. It didn't automatically make sense, as I had expected, given its universal and canonical status. It was, rather, its own super-specific thing, like the taste of some particular kind of wine.

The moments, isolated at first, when I started to feel like I understood it—like I understood why it was desirable, how to appreciate it, and how to draw it out—reminded me of the first time I managed to follow a Shakespeare play, and understood not only what all those people were talking about, but why their mode of speech was considered admirable. How all the things that went unspoken in a real conversation—because they were secret, or because nobody had realized them, or put them into words—had been translated into a measured multi-syllabic torrent that unfurled so ceaselessly from the actors.

Yes: understanding the point of sex felt just like understanding the point of Shakespeare. And weren't the two related? The animus I had previously felt . . . not toward Shakespeare himself—what had he ever done except write some plays?—but toward the story that was told about his universal humanity, its virtuosic expression through earthy ribald wordplay, such that Shakespeare said "nothing" and meant a vagina, or said "O" and meant a vagina, or said "country matters" and meant a vagina.

Sometimes, when I caught that glimmer of promise, I tried to touch myself to see if I could have an orgasm. It never quite worked. Afterward, when Mesut had gone into that weird trance, I wondered if I should get up and go to the bathroom and try to do it by myself in peace. But it always felt like more hassle than it was worth. I concluded that having an orgasm must not have been the point, and that *not* having had one wasn't the reason for the vague unsatisfied feeling I had sometimes. The reason must have been something else.

I moved from the pension to Mesut's friend's hotel. Mesut's friend had overgrown curly hair, bushy eyebrows, and a comically perplexed expression, like he didn't understand why or how he had ended up running this hotel, which had so much beige carpeting and, on top of everything else, beetles. The beetles were extraordinarily shiny, large, and black, with a slow, wobbly gait. I never saw such beetles anywhere else, either before or after.

Mesut didn't like to be seen leaving in the morning, so at sunrise he jumped out the window into some bushes. When I told my mother how Mesut jumped out the window, she said he was married. I said I didn't see how that was possible.

"I'm positive," she said.

"Are you married?" I asked Mesut later.

"What?" He started to laugh. "How could I be married?"

"When are you going to get married?"

He laughed again and didn't say anything. "You and I will get married someday," he said finally.

Why did I feel a wave of elation? It was like my brain knew to strive toward freedom, but my body had another plan. Or was the elation the part that was real, while the rest of it—the idea that you couldn't get married before you finished college, that you had to marry someone who had been to college and spoke English—was somehow fake?

I could tell Mesut was smart, because he wasn't always repeating himself, and he always understood what I was trying to say, even when I didn't know the right words. Once, when one of the guys at the bus station expressed skepticism about my knowledge of the provinces around Ankara, Mesut laughed and said: "You should believe her, she knows." He said it in such a funny way that everyone laughed, and nobody was offended.

I got lost for two hours in "the Valley of Love." At first it seemed impossible to believe that the rock formations were naturally shaped that way. Then again, actual penises were shaped like that, so maybe that was just nature's MO. I climbed up a steep slope, thinking it was the way out, and then I was too scared to climb back down. Far above me, on a different plane of existence, like in a Dutch painting, a man with a donkey was walking along the edge of an orchard. The man waved. I waved back. The giant Ericsson phone in my bag started to ring. It was my great-aunt Bahriye.

"Who is this?" she demanded, though she was the one who had called.

"Hello, Auntie Bahriye, this is Selin."

"Who? Selin? The gardener's daughter?" She sounded outraged. It took a long time for me to explain who I was. She said that the gardener's daughter, Selin, was only eight years old, but always getting into things that weren't her business, so it would have been just like her to figure out how to make phone calls.

Eventually, a German couple with hiking gear helped me out of the valley. The girl held my hand. Afterward I tried to buy them lunch at a restaurant that I liked, but they paid for my lunch when I wasn't looking. I went to a café to revise the day's pages.

"Take a left on the dirt road at the onyx factory, walk about 400m, descend on the right . . ." The directions hadn't worked for me, but was that the fault of the directions? Did I have a better suggestion?

Mesut turned out to be religious. He kept asking about my relationship with Islam. I said it was respectful but distant. He gave me an illustrated booklet for women, about how to do ritual ablutions, and demonstrated how to wash your ears.

I had a headscarf that I carried in my daypack, for going to holy sites. Mesut asked to see what it looked like.

"Not like that," he said, and then he tied it himself much more expertly, wrapping and tucking the ends several times, so that it covered all my hair and also the lower part of my face.

"Wow, this is great!" I said, turning in front of the mirror. I looked like a different person. "I'm just going to go around like this from now on."

Mesut looked uneasy. "Take that thing off," he said.

One night, Mesut spoke to me shortly. At the thought of how differently he had spoken to me such a short time ago, I felt so desolate that I thought it must surely be wrong for me to stay there in that hotel. I packed my daypack with clothes for two days and took a four-hour bus ride to a town near a valley where you could hike to see some more thousand-year-old underground frescoes. I checked into a hostel, left my bag, and set out for the trailhead. The cell phone started to ring.

When I told Mesut where I was, and said I was spending the night, his voice changed, he said he would come and get me after work. "But it's four hours away," I said.

"What? No it's not, in a car it's barely an hour."

It wasn't dark yet when he came. He said he had never been to this town before. "So show me what's here," he said. And I showed him.

Mesut said it was only important to wear a condom at the end. I told him this wasn't true, but I couldn't tell if he believed me.

Once, in the middle, he said he had taken the condom off when I wasn't looking.

"How could you!" I said, pushing him away, and burst into tears.

"How upset you are," he said, in a voice of wonder, and showed me that he had been joking.

Later, I found a package insert in the Durex box, written in polite Turkish: "Entering a vagina without wearing a condom must not be done. Entering the vagina, even before orgasm, may be a cause of pregnancy." I cut out that part of the insert, together with an illustrative diagram, and made a collage inside a greeting card with an Ottoman miniature on the front. The miniature showed a world with many levels and balconies and terraces, among which men with doll-like faces and pillowy bodies were kneeling under a starry sky.

When Mesut opened the card, I was worried for a moment that he was offended, but then he burst out laughing and said that I was an awake one, and that he would keep this card always as a reminder.

Once, because I felt grateful and because I didn't want to make any mistakes, I tried to give him a blow job.

"What are you doing!" Mesut exclaimed. He said it was unclean and made me swear that I would never ever do anything like that again with anyone for the rest of my life.

"OK, I promise," I said finally. He made me promise never to do anal, either. I wondered whether those things were considered worse than having sex when you weren't married.

Pubic hair, it turned out, was also un-Muslim. There was a hadith about it. The subject seemed to make Mesut really anxious. His feelings were so much stronger than mine that one day, in the shower, I shaved everything off. Had anything I had ever done in my whole life delighted anyone so much as that one act of depilation delighted Mesut?

"So what do you think about love?" I asked Mesut in a casual tone.

"Love is to get caught on something," he said readily. "It's to be unable to forget."

I postponed my departure date a couple of times. Mesut said he would put me on the best bus: a Mercedes.

On the way to the station, Mesut said how lucky he was to have met someone like me, to have spent this time together. He printed my ticket at the counter. Outside, dusk was falling. Only one bus was lit up. Mesut greeted the driver and porters, and stowed my backpack under the bus. How present and alive he was, how strong and substantial. Yet this was itself a form of limitation. An inextricable aspect of his strength and solidity was that he existed, not everywhere, but in a particular place. Unlike my feelings, which were dimensionless and followed me wherever I went, he was person-sized and staying here.

The heavy gears creaked into motion behind my eyes and in my chest. I felt just like I had for the whole fall. I couldn't imagine how I had lived like that. At the same time, I felt lucky to feel it again—to be here again. It was as if some portal had swung open. Weeping, a powerful physical process that was normally out of the question, became a constant possibility. This seemed to prove the material reality of thoughts and feelings.

Mesut got on the bus with me. I had a row of seats to myself, at the front, so I could see out the giant windshield. You could see a lot, because the bus was so high up. Mesut gave me a gift-wrapped packet and said to open it later, and touched my face to brush away a tear, and it was unbearable that he was being so kind, and that this moment was already compromised by being the last one, and presenting so few possibilities. Now he was conveying good wishes to people in my family and saying complimentary things about Adana. More time passed. Eventually, he turned and went down the steps, and the doors closed behind him, and all the people around me were strangers.

The driver watched me in the mirror, and said I was clearly a good person to be so sad. I must have really liked Mesut, and it was true that Mesut was a good kid, but now I had nothing to worry about because he, the driver, knew what he was doing, and the trip to Adana would be so smooth and devoid of incident that we would be there before I had time to be uncomfortable.

I opened the gift Mesut had given me. It was a cassette. I put it in my Walkman, worried that it would be the kind of despairing "arabesque" music that Mesut liked to listen to. But it was upbeat Americanized pop music, with a drum machine that sounded like Turkish hand drums, and synthesizers that sounded like a lute, and the first song was called "This Girl Will Be the Death of Me." It was a comical song. Tears streamed down my face.

Why this intensity of grief—almost worse than it had been with Ivan? Was it because I hadn't known, with Ivan, that I was seeing him for the last time, and had still believed in a future where things would go back to how they had been? Certainly I didn't think that now. How would I ever be back in Cappadocia, why? Mesut had promised to visit me, but the possibility seemed unlikely, and not entirely appealing. We would have to deal with all his ideas about America, and his way of speaking English, and what would we even do: eat Thai-style chicken wraps at The Wrap? I tried to remember the insulting name of the Thai-style chicken wrap. The name was "Thai Me Up." I felt my face contort with sorrow. I would never again climb into Mesut's white Opel, we would never drive around the phallogocentric columns in which Byzantine people had hidden, we wouldn't drink astringent wine on that roof, or go to the hotel and have sex for hours. Was that what was so painful: that nobody had ever come so close to me— nobody had ever seen me, and come right up to me, and kept going, and looked into my eyes so seriously, with so little fear?

JULY

In Adana, I was immediately absorbed into my family. It was important for me to meet every powerful man we knew. They weren't actually so numerous, but each meeting seemed to last forever. Lackeys
brought tea. The powerful men kept jocularly threatening to make
someone make you a Turkish coffee, using the potentially infinite verb
construction that also existed in Finnish. At some point, they tried to
mention all the old people in your family by name.

My cousin Evren was on summer break from medical school in Istanbul. She had gotten in a year early. Now that she had left Adana and
was studying at a famous and beautiful university, she seemed more
relaxed than before, and I felt less guilty.

 When I had visited Adana as a child, I had spent every day with
Evren. Evren was always at our grandparents' house, because her
father—my aunt's husband—drank, and had once thrown my aunt
down the stairs when she was pregnant.

At the playground, Evren always wanted me to tell the other children, the boys, that I was from America. It was never something I felt like doing: hunting down strange boys, to tell them about America. Wasn't that what I had earned, by always being different in America: the right to be the same, here? But what had Evren earned by being the one whose parents weren't doctors in America?

When the boys said they didn't believe me, Evren would get angry. The boys seemed to expect this, and to be surprised that I wasn't angry. "We don't believe you," they kept saying, as if waiting for me to freak out.

Evren and I had never taken a trip together just the two of us, and it was exciting to be headed to North Cyprus. We took a four-hour bus ride to the port where the ferries departed, but that was as far as we got, because it turned out you needed government ID to get on the boat. My passport was in Ankara, and I had only student ID and my faceless citizenship card. We made some calls from my giant cell phone. An intervention was effected by one of the powerful men I had drunk tea with. After that, everyone was really polite to us. I was allowed on the boat, though Evren wasn't—because she hadn't brought any ID at all. We were both crying. Evren wanted me to go back to Adana with her, but I was already two days behind in my itinerary.

Feeling the traitorousness and guilt that had so rarely left me since Evren and I were children, I got on the boat alone. I wasn't entirely surprised when, four hours later, arriving in Kyrenia with my faceless ID, I was promptly hustled back onto the boat and sent back to Turkey. Clearly, I was going to live the rest of my life like that, going back and forth. But the Turkish customs officers seemed to take it as a personal affront to them that I hadn't been admitted into Cyprus. They printed me a special pass and said that if I hurried I could get the last boat back.

The ferry wasn't actually running anymore, but some of the crew were heading back for the night. The hatchet-faced captain, who hadn't previously addressed me or acknowledged me in any way, said that I could sit with him on the upper deck. I wasn't sure that I wanted to sit with him, but it was clear from how everyone else acted that this was a great privilege. In the glass-enclosed cabin with the steering apparatus, I was shown to a leather command chair next to the captain's, high above the sea that unfurled before us like some magical shimmering fabric. The sun was sinking into the horizon, and gold and purple seemed to pour infinitely out of the clouds.

The taxi driver who took me to the old harbor told me the story of his life, and started to cry. He had been evacuated from the south, with all the ethnic Turks, when the island was partitioned in 1974. He swore that the north was a shithole, the places he had left were ten times more beautiful, with trees and flowers that didn't exist here. Was that possible? The south was literally a fifteen-minute drive away, and it was hard to imagine anywhere more beautiful than this.

At Let's Go, the fact that you couldn't travel between North and South Cyprus was spoken of with humor. It was part of the aura of provincial quaintness that surrounded so many of other countries' problems, especially those related to "ancient ethnic conflicts." America's position, moderating between these groups of unreasonable people, was inherently comical. Like: the Turks and the Greeks "hated" each other, yet both were NATO allies. What a funny, delicate position for America!

The Kurdish conflict was taken more seriously, maybe because Kurdish people had militant separatists who did suicide bombings, not just in Turkey but sometimes in Western Europe.

Why were there so many such people: people who preferred to kill themselves and others, rather than just join some country? In some cases, it seemed like the country itself was keeping them out. Other times, it seemed like the separatists just didn't want to join.

I found myself remembering one of the final projects that someone had made in Constructed Worlds class last year: a wooden box full of garbage—a broken piece of ornamental ironwork, a stained green satin square, an old wooden pen with a rusty nib—accompanied by a short story. The story was about a little girl who lived in a fantastic realm and who had to mine some kind of ore all day, and whose mother often told her: "Our people were not always slaves." One day, the girl challenged her mother. The mother's eyes flashed with rage. She wordlessly went to a closet, took down a wooden box, and removed, one by one, the priceless artifacts of her people: the curiously molded amulet, the scrap from the princess's dress that had been used to tie the hero's wound, the rusted pen that had signed the treaty that had been violated. If the little girl ever forgot those things, then she would have helped to murder her ancestors.

I knew that Leora believed something like that, and thought she had to learn her ancestors' languages, translate their books, and memorialize how they had been murdered. But Atatürk said: "There are many countries, but there is only one civilization. For a nation to progress, it needs to join in this one and only civilization." If that was true, then you weren't betraying your ancestors just by speaking whatever language published the most books, and trying to write new books that were different from the old ones.

When my mother was six and found out about England—about the existence of England—she said she wished she had been born in England, and my grandfather flew into a terrifying rage: the kind he didn't have anymore by the time I was born, because of his heart.

All over Turkey there were painted signs that said, HOW HAPPY IS

THE ONE WHO SAYS "I AM A TURK": another quote from Atatürk. If my grandfather had been happy to be a Turk, why had he shouted at my mother?

On my weekly phone call with Sean, I tried to ask about separatists. Sean let out a bark of laughter. "Above my pay grade!" Well, I was getting paid even less than he was.

————

After Antakya, which turned out to be the same thing as Antioch, I started working my way back west along the Mediterranean. Now it was no longer government officials but, rather, pension owners who met me at the bus station. Addressing me by name, they vied to grab my backpack, hustle me into their cars, and shout about the tourism sector. These encounters were stressful and disconcerting. Still, if I had to choose, I preferred the hoteliers to their counterparts in the government or the army. At least the hotel people thought my job was real. They had heard of Let's Go and thought it was important. They didn't, of course, believe in it in the same way that Let's Go itself did—in "our" objectivity. They thought I could write whatever I wanted, and withhold or grant infinite business according to my caprices. The idea of an allegiance to "the reader" made no sense to them. What difference was it to the foreigners what hotel they stayed in? The other hotel had a better breakfast? But the reason it had a better breakfast was because more people stayed there, so they could buy more different kinds of cheese, and could make eggs to order, instead of just boiling them. If more people came here then we would have a big fresh breakfast here every day, too, with even more things! (Then they would list all the things they would have for breakfast.) So now will you write it in the book?

At first, it seemed to me that I had been deposited into an easily resolved misunderstanding, one I could help straighten out, because of my conversance with different cultures. I saw, for example, that the Turkish word *turistik* had a positive connotation, implying things that Turkish people valued, like air-conditioning and an international clientele. I was excited, at first, to tell some of the sadder and more intellectual-seeming hostel owners—to explain that the particular kind of tourists who used books like *Let's Go* didn't like the word "tourist." But the only thing these explanations conveyed was my "good-heartedness" and possible willingness to have sex with them.

I eventually gave up trying to explain anything to anyone. It did no good. Everyone was too afraid. The Turkish people were afraid of missing some "opportunity" represented by the tourists, of being taken advantage of and left with nothing. The tourists were afraid of missing some "authentic" experience, of being exploited for their money and left with nothing. What the tourists really wanted was never to pay for anything, because they were good people. I had noticed this in myself: how I always hoped to be given things for free, as a reward for not being a total asshole. It was, I saw, a specious hope, one I would potentially outgrow when I was older and had more money. But Let's Go acted like not paying for things wasn't just advantageous, but noble. Conversely, to "pay the tourist price" wasn't just to lose money, but to capitulate to panderers: to fail to support the truly deserving and authentic. The way you supported the deserving and authentic was apparently by paying them less.

How much of not wanting to be "a tourist" came down to stinginess? At some point, *Let's Go* pointed out that you could bypass the "swarms of tourists" that crammed Istanbul and the beaches, by not going to Istanbul or the beach; instead you could backpack around small villages, enjoying "countless cups of *çay* offered by people who take pride in their tradition of hospitality." I thought it looked stupid when they put *çay* in italics, as if there wasn't an exact synonym: tea. More to the point, what was so great about that tea? Why was it necessarily better than the burnt coffee at Au Bon Pain? Because it was free?

Let's Go said to avoid restaurants that had a view, because they served "overpriced, overrated food"—but what did overpriced even mean? A building with a view cost more to rent, so didn't the food there actually cost more? My mother wouldn't *want* to pay less to go somewhere without a view. It always felt like *Let's Go* was criticizing my mother. They kept telling you to go to "cheap dives." But the cheap dives were often full of poor and unhappy men, who tried to compensate for their lack of power by dominating women. Was I shallow and elitist for wanting to avoid them?

Whenever anything made me feel badly, my standard procedure was to recount it to myself as a story in which everyone was at least a little bit right, and some people were kind or humorous, and their kindness and humor redeemed everything, and recognizing it redeemed *me*. Then I felt humane and objective. But *was* I humane and objective? What if I was being like Let's Go, when they acted as if everyone else's problems were comical and sectarian—like an English novel, where the guy who had been to Eton was always finding himself in a dashed fix? It was as if even trying to narrate all the different sides put you more on the side of Let's Go and of English novels—because they were the ones who thought about narrating the different sides and being "objective." It made me remember the last chapter of *Either/Or*: "The Edifying in the Thought That Against God We Are Always in the Wrong." In relation to travel, too, I felt, we were always in the wrong.

On the roof of the hostel in Side, a German girl, having heard me speak Turkish, demanded to see me belly dance.

"I'm from New Jersey," I said.

"Oh, forget it then," she said, turning her back as fast as she could, like it might have been contagious.

I was sitting on the roof drinking wine and working on copy, trying to make everything sound magical and inexpensive—and a gray puppy frolicked up to me. I hadn't paid it anything. The tears that were closer to me now, because of Mesut, filled my eyes. The puppy turned out to pertain to a vacationing Turkish family.

"What's its name?" I asked.

Everyone started laughing: the puppy's name was a mildly sexual double entendre. The father of the family, a retired schoolteacher, had twinkling eyes and a kind expression. He spoke politely, asking about my work and all the things I had seen, and I felt relief, because I knew he wouldn't ask me to belly dance or to write about his friend's hotel.

But, the next evening, when I went to the roof, the father was there alone, and asked me a lot of questions about my sex life, and whether I had sex with Christians, and the next day he gave me a typed report to give to the American government, about how the murder of the Armenians hadn't been centrally coordinated, and shouldn't count as a genocide.

Then I was sitting in a parked bus in the bus station, looking out the open window. Outside the next bus, a white-haired man in safari clothes was thronged by young Turkish guys. "Please. Please. Hello." They seemed friendly, and desirous of helping the man with his luggage, but there was something scary about their mechanical pronunciation of "please"—like it wasn't language, but just a sound you repeated, to get money.

The white-haired man, who had an English accent and bore a distant resemblance to my ethics professor, spoke politely at first, but seemed to be getting anxious. One of the younger men slapped him jovially on the back, as if to imply what a good time they were all having.

"Please don't touch me," the English man said, several times, but the younger men didn't pay attention, they kept rollicking around him. I felt sorry and called in Turkish, "He doesn't want help, he says not to touch him."

One of the men turned to me with a chilling look of contempt. "We speak English, too," he said. Then they all left off persecuting the English man and started calling to me, in horribly accented English, "Can I touch you?" and, in Turkish, other, worse things, and I realized that they hated me. Because I spoke with an accent, because I was taking the part of the foreign man, because I was interfering in their attempt to get money, because I myself had enough money to come to another country, and because I was a girl.

When I looked back at the white-haired man, who was now fussing over his suitcase, I felt I had misjudged his expression. He didn't look professorial or educated. He looked like another dumb, unkind, greedy person, trying to get away with something.

In Anamur, Turkey's principal area of banana production, a tall, intense-looking hostel worker offered to drive me to the ancient city of Anemurium. It was on a deserted beach. When we got there, he wanted to have sex. Why did this keep happening? It was weird that there were only two options: yes or no. Which was active, which was passive? What would I want to happen in a book? What was it that it said in that one particular book? "Only connect"?

I was stuck with that guy for days. His name was Volkan. He left the hostel and followed me to the next town, acting like my boyfriend. It was easier, in some ways, to have a guy with you. Interactions with other people tended to go more smoothly. And yet, nearly everything the guy himself said was insane. We drank wine, smoked cigarettes, and had screaming arguments in the street. It felt somehow important and universal to be arguing in such a way with a man.

"Do you think I'm a difficult person to get along with?" Volkan asked once.

"Yes," I said. "What about me?"

I had only asked out of a sense of fairness, but to my surprise, he thought about it and said: "No, not really, you're easier than most people."

I offered to pay for the buses and taxis, but Volkan insisted that we hitchhike. He flagged down a car, hustled me in, and told the driver that we were both students at Harvard University. The driver glanced at us in the rearview mirror and didn't say anything.

Afterward, Volkan yelled at me for half an hour because he said the driver hadn't believed him. It was my fault for not having said: "Yes, we met at Harvard University." At least now I had tried hitchhiking.

I tried not to betray the bottomless insecurity and dread I felt when Volkan had trouble maintaining an erection.

"I'm not a machine!" he shouted.

Volkan didn't like it if I touched myself while we were having sex. "Why don't you just have sex by yourself then!" he shouted.

Volkan was constantly talking about anal sex: about how much more pleasurable it was for women, and how they loved it more than vaginal sex. Sometimes he said this in English, in the pedagogic tourism voice, mispronouncing "vagina." When I told him the right way to say it, he continued to say it wrong, and said, "This is how I say it."

Finally, to shut him up, I said we could do anal sex. He used sunscreen as lubricant. When I told him it burned, he almost died laughing. He didn't want to stop, but then I kicked him.

Once, when we were walking somewhere, a shoeshine boy looked at us. For the next half hour, Volkan kept asking which of us I thought the boy had been looking at: him or me.

Volkan talked a lot about gay people. He said he had been raped as a teenager by a German archaeologist. I wondered if that was true. Who could know? Wasn't that what *Rashomon* was about: how you could never know if a person had actually been raped?

"Your hand is so soft," Volkan said, "it's obvious it has only ever held a pen." I felt annoyed. Who was he all of a sudden: a coal miner?

"Your hand is also soft," I said.

"Really?" He seemed pleased.

At dinner, Volkan told me about a girl he knew who had sex with a fire hydrant.

"Is that so," I said.

Then he laughed for five minutes at how gullible I was, because I hadn't shouted at him that he was lying.

On the one hand, I wasn't bored, and we were having sex every day. It was a relief to feel that I wasn't leading a sterile, life-denying existence, only learning the things that were in books, ignorant of the real world. My complexion looked better than it had at school.

But after three days, it was too much; I realized I would rather be sterile and have dull skin and live in peace. In the afternoon, when

Volkan fell asleep, I packed my bag, locked him in the hotel room from the outside, and went to the bus station. My heart was pounding. I tried to act like nothing was out of the ordinary. There was only one guy on duty at the station. He had seen me with Volkan, and had joked around with Volkan, and when I said I needed one bus ticket, not two, he just laughed and wouldn't sell me a ticket, or say anything else, or acknowledge anything I said. I went back to the hotel, unlocked the door with the key I had hidden in a flower planter, and pretended nothing had happened. But the next morning I went back to the station and it was busier, and a different guy sold me a ticket to Konya.

In Konya, I walked into one of the restaurants mentioned in *Let's Go*, and tried to sit down. Four men rushed to my table with looks of alarm.

"Miss, allow us to welcome you to the family section where you will be more comfortable," one of them said.

"I'm not here with my family, it's just me," I said.

"But you can't sit here!" one young guy screamed.

The oldest of the men stepped forward. "We call it the family section, miss, but in fact it's where we welcome all ladies."

"Ladies can't sit here?" I asked, looking around and realizing that everyone else was a man.

"You'll see for yourself, the family room is nicer."

It did have newer floors, and air-conditioning. My entrance with a phalanx of waiters produced a small sensation. The local specialty, Konya *kebap*, was true to its description: "a chunk of oven-roasted mutton."

It took Volkan less than twenty-four hours to show up in Konya. The woman at the hotel desk had said it would be OK for a friend to join me, but she took one look at Volkan and started screaming. She had assumed that my friend was a lady. She hadn't expected something like this from me. Her eyes filled with tears and her voice shook.

I apologized, explaining that I hadn't meant to upset her, that Volkan would stay somewhere else, and I would leave in the morning. But she said that I was no longer welcome there even for the night.

Then Volkan and I were standing in the street in the middle of the night. He said that I had been wrong to not describe him as my husband. We went to another hotel and said we were married. The guy behind the desk asked to see our citizenship cards, both of which said "unmarried." Volkan gave him some extra money, and then he said we could stay one night. Now I had seen how to bribe someone.

"He's leaving tomorrow anyway," I told the receptionist.

In fact, the guy who was covering for Volkan at work got appendicitis, and Volkan really did have to go back to Anamur.

Konya turned out to be a stop on the pilgrimage to Mecca. The main sites were all religious. The most famous one was Rumi's mausoleum. Rumi had founded the Mevlevi order of dervishes, and had written lyrical ecstatic poems about mystical union, or maybe about wine. I never had been into transcendental states that defied the limits of language, or anything else that defied the limits of language.

The mausoleum was crowded with pilgrims, mostly men. I wore a scarf and stood to one side. There were sixty tombs, pertaining to Rumi and his family and friends. Each dead person's status was indicated by the size of the casket, whether it had a turban, and what color the turban was.

In the adjoining museum, I learned about Rumi's life: how he had grown up in a religious family, become a cleric, taught in a madrasa, and lived quietly with his wife and four children. Suddenly, at age thirty-seven, he met a wandering dervish named Shams. That was "the decisive moment of his life." Shams asked Rumi a question. Rumi fell on his face. Rumi answered the question, and then Shams fell on *his* face. Shams and Rumi became inseparable, spending every moment in a realm of pure conversation, not eating or drinking. This went on for a year and a half, annoying Rumi's family and the people at the madrasa.

One day, Shams disappeared. Rumi went crazy and became a poet. He listened to music and whirled around for hours. That's why dervishes did that. Rumi tracked Shams down to Damascus and got him to come back. Shams and Rumi fell at each other's feet, and "no one knew who was lover and who the beloved." The whole thing started up again: the mystical discourse, and everyone freaking out. At some point in the never-ending conversation, Shams was called to the back door, and went to see who it was, and nobody ever saw him again.

Rumi went searching for Shams. He made it as far as Damascus, where he had a revelation: he and Shams were the same person. All the time he had been looking for Shams, he was looking for himself. In fact, *Shams was the one writing Rumi's poems.* From then on, Rumi signed his poems with Shams's name.

It wasn't what I expected from a life of a saint. He started out conventional, religious, and law-abiding—and *then* he became consumed by love, and was alienated from his family and community, and went mad and wrote poetry? It was like St. Augustine backward. This was somehow exciting.

I went to the bookstore to read some of Rumi's poems. I tried the Turkish translations first, feeling they would be somehow closer to the original. I knew that Rumi had written in Persian, but he had at least spoken Turkish. Anyway, Turkish, unlike English, had a lot of Persian words. But the only Turkish editions in the store, aside from an expensive shrink-wrapped multivolume set that would never have fit in my backpack, were flimsy booklets full of typos, where the cover art was a rainbow-colored whirling dervish, or a photograph of a dew-covered rose.

I picked up an English translation: one that seemed correctly book-sized, with a professionally designed cover, an introduction, and hundreds of pages of couplets organized into different categories.

> In dreams, and even awake,
> you will hear the beloved screaming at you.

Was it possible that Rumi was funny?

Reading in English was so much easier and more fun, and yet I felt dissatisfied, as if I was failing to capitalize on some advantage I had from "being" Turkish—one that would compensate for the hassle of having a name and appearance that had always required explanation. It had, I realized, been a real disappointment to get to Turkey and to discover that my name and appearance still required constant explanation— maybe even more so than in America. People heard my accent, and saw what I was wearing, and doing, and it didn't make sense, or fit with my ID card.

I realized, too, that, even though I had known that Rumi had written in Persian, I had still thought that he somehow "was" Turkish, or also wrote in Turkish. Was that itself a part of Turkish culture: the belief that a thing was Turkish, or had some connection to Turkey, even if nobody else thought that? Turkish people thought that Turkish and Hungarian were related, but Hungarian people didn't think that.

I skimmed a pamphlet published by a Turkish historical association, explaining that Rumi considered himself to be an ethnic Turk, and wrote in Persian only as a literary convention. It quoted a line from a poem: "I am that Turk who does not know Persian." The pamphlet was contradicted by a book in English that had more regular formatting, included more different quotes, and pointed out that the line about not knowing Persian was itself written in Persian, and was therefore a metaphor or paradox. Rumi hadn't been attached to the idea of people being from different countries, and generally invoked Turkishness in order to destabilize it. "I am a Turk one minute and a Tajik the next," he had written. And: "I called you a Turk, but I did so to confuse the onlookers."

I bought the English edition. The translator, Coleman Barks, was apparently from Chattanooga, Tennessee, and didn't speak Persian. Yet his book had some of the only true-seeming descriptions of spring that I had ever seen.

> The ground turns green. A drum begins.
> Commentaries on the heart arrive in seven volumes.

That was clearly correct. So was this one:

> Spring, and no one can be still,
> with all the messages coming through.

And I had never heard anyone describe so accurately the difference between last year and this year:

> Last year, I admired wines.
> This, I'm wandering inside the red world.

Sometimes, as I was reading, I felt worried that Coleman Barks had made everything up. How could a thirteenth-century person have written such things?

> If you want what visible reality
> can give, you are an employee.

On the other hand, why *couldn't* Rumi have said that? What was the thing they didn't have back then? Visible reality? Employees?

It seemed strange that Rumi had been married twice, and had children, but they hadn't been the most important people in his life. Some random guy had been more important. Did that mean he was gay, or would have been gay if it had been allowed? Or did it mean that there was some different way that I hadn't heard of for one person to be important to another?

> You are not the bride or the groom.
> You do not fit in a house with a family.

Was it possible to be like that—to not be the bride or the groom, to not fit in a house with a family? What happened to you, then? Everyone said that Shams had probably been murdered, with the involvement of Rumi's son.

Antalya

As I was staggering around the edge of the Antalya bus station, an unusually handsome young man stood up from a railing he had been leaning against.

"Shall I help with your bag?" he said.

He looked like a movie actor, like someone on an ancient vase: lithe, muscular, with high cheekbones and cropped hair that showed his elegantly shaped head and neck. The cartoon Martian on his T-shirt brought out the green of his eyes. I must have given him the backpack, because then he was carrying it, walking ahead of me in an easy loose-limbed way. I followed him to a small hostel with a weedy garden. He said it was owned by his cousin.

"I see you've met Koray," said the cousin, who was short and square, with military posture and an outdoor tan. "He's actually a good kid," he added, as if I had suggested otherwise. The cousin had worked for five years on a Russian ship, and knew about Pushkin. The hostel was nothing special, but it was cheap and clean, and my bag was there. Koray offered to come back in the evening and show me the nightlife.

We went first to a beer garden, where Koray bought me an Efes and told me a story about a German pig. I was pretty sure I wasn't understanding him right—maybe he was speaking some regional dialect. It sounded like the pig worked for the traffic police in Hamburg, actually directing traffic in some capacity. Koray spoke a little contemptuously of the pig, even though it sounded smart. A light shone in his eyes, now scornful, now laughing. He leaned over and kissed me—a long, slow kiss.

The biggest nightclub was outdoors, abutting the sea, with multiple dance floors arranged among ruins, and huge speakers that resembled missile launchers. Women were running around screaming, wearing almost no clothes. It became clear that I was supposed to pay our cover. "But I don't have that," I said, laughing: it was almost forty dollars, my whole daily allowance. To my surprise, Koray seized my arm in the viselike grip of an insane person and marched me down an unlit side street, to an ATM. "Get the money," he said.

"I didn't bring my card," I said.

"Don't lie to me—I can tell," he said.

I was so surprised that I put my ATM card into the machine and entered the PIN. The transaction menu came up in English.

"Oh no, my account is empty," I said. "It says I won't get paid again till tomorrow."

Koray leaned over and looked at the screen. "It does?" he said. "But then how are we going to get into the club?"

That was when I realized he was mentally—unwell, disabled? I wasn't sure what to call it, or how to think of it. Looking back, it wasn't that there hadn't been signs. But that whole time he had been talking about the German pig, he had seemed so noble. Why had I assumed that the problem was with my Turkish—that the problem was with me? That was something girls did. On the other hand . . . wasn't the problem with me, by definition? After all, *I* was the one having the problem.

"I'm actually really sleepy. I think I'm going to go home," I said.

"No, you're not," he said. "I won't let you." He was holding my upper arm. I thought about jerking away, or screaming, but couldn't think of how. It felt as if it required some specialized knowledge. The enormous cell phone hadn't fit in my pocket, so I had left it at the hostel.

"I'm really sleepy," I said again. "I want to go back."

He looked searchingly into my face. "You're not," he said. "I told you not to lie. Come on, I know a hotel." He laughed. "There are beds in a hotel!"

Did I secretly want to have sex with him? Dora had thought she didn't want to have sex with Herr K, and hadn't it made her sick? With Koray, I had kissed him, and thought he was handsome. And I had already done it with three people, so what did one more matter? True, he might have had a mental disability. But wasn't it shallow and elitist and somehow snottily feminine to hold that against him? A guy wouldn't care about something like that—about a girl turning out to be incapable of reasoned discourse. Why did I insist on blocking myself against the marrow of life? Wasn't this—this, being outside, here, negotiating with a handsome, possibly disabled mugger—wasn't this, the cigarette butts and melon guts in the gutter, the faint smell of horses, the sickening pulse of bass from the clubs—wasn't this what life was?

"Do you have condoms?" I asked.

"No, don't worry, there's no need."

"What do you mean, there's no need?"

"There's no need for anything like that."

I stopped walking. "If we don't have condoms I'm not going to a hotel, I'm not going anywhere, I'm going to stand right here and create a scene," I said, to my own surprise.

He looked worried and annoyed. So, I was allowed to make demands. We walked up and down the streets until we found an open pharmacy. I walked in alone, past the baby formula and pacifiers, the French and German anti-aging creams. Condoms were always behind the counter—you had to ask. Once, a pharmacist had tried to upsell me ribbed condoms. "They're more pleasurable for women," he explained, with a lewd expression.

"It doesn't have to be pleasurable, just let me not get sick," I shot back, quoting my grandmother, who, if you took her to a restaurant and asked her how her dish was, would say: "Just let me not get poisoned."

I looked through the glass door of the pharmacy onto the street. Koray was standing outside, right in front of the door. The back of his neck looked strong and innocent.

The pharmacist stood up. He was heavyset, with bags under his eyes, and was wearing a white coat. I mentally composed the request for condoms, but instead the words that came out were: "Is there another door?"

"What?"

335

"A back door, maybe, that I can go out. I'm experiencing a problem with the person outside."

The pharmacist glanced out the glass door. "That's the only door," he said, in an annoyed way that suggested that he didn't want to help me—that he didn't think I deserved help.

"Can I use the phone, then? I want to call the police." Even as I said it, I started to feel worried about what I could possibly tell the police, but it turned out not to matter, because what the pharmacist said was: "There's no phone." It was an incredible, unforeseen degree of treachery.

"How can there be no phone in a pharmacy?"

"It's broken." He said it like he didn't care if I believed him—like he wanted me *not* to believe him. I paid for a three-pack of condoms and left.

"*Selamün aleyküm*," said the guy at the hotel, shaking Koray's hand in a manly way. It was the kind of hotel Let's Go didn't write about, even though it was "off the beaten path" and there weren't any tourists.

"Will the young lady be paying?" he asked. It was like four dollars.

"Unfortunately, I don't have that," I said. "I think I'm going to go home." I noticed a songbird in a cage behind the desk. Was that a sign of kindness, or the opposite?

Koray stood in my way. "That's for a whole night," he told the hotel guy in a petulant voice, "but we only need half of one night."

"You must have half," the hotel guy told me.

"She has it, I saw it!" Koray said.

I gave the hotel guy the equivalent of a dollar seventy-five, and he and Koray both seemed really happy.

Koray's face was red and distorted and squinty, his expression no longer noble, he looked like an infant, like he was having a fit. He went through all three condoms—not by putting them on and then saying there was something wrong with them and throwing them in the toilet, like Volkan, but actually using each one, laboriously, all the way to the end. "OK, give me another," he said, after he had thrown the third, sodden and heavy, onto the floor. I said there weren't any, and started getting dressed. He pulled me back and said, sounding bewildered, "It's as if you won't do sex anymore, now that there aren't any condoms."

Something shifted and it was suddenly instinctive to shove his face away with my hand, jump up, and lock myself in the bathroom. He rattled the knob and banged on the door, but not in a way that suggested he was going to break it down. I felt ashamed by how easy it had been to get away. The banging went on for a while. Someone downstairs started throwing what sounded like shoes at the ceiling. I sat on the toilet, feeling strangely calm, thinking of the engraving on the philosophy building at school: WHAT IS MAN THAT THOU ART MINDFUL OF HIM.

The banging stopped, and so did the shoes. I waited a few minutes, then cracked the door open. Koray was sprawled on the bed, like he had been shot, but his chest was rising and falling in a regular, peaceful way.

When I got back to the hostel, nobody was at the front desk. I went to my room, took a shower, and packed my bag, so I could leave first thing in the morning. I woke up before dawn and had to go to the bathroom. That was when I discovered that I was unable to urinate. Subsequently, it hurt to sit down, and then it also hurt if I didn't sit down. I had heard enough about urinary tract infections from my mother to wonder if I had one. When I checked my watch, it wasn't yet eleven in New Jersey, so I called her. I explained the situation. She said it was definitely a urinary tract infection. She didn't sound worried, or angry. She said that Antalya had a good hospital, that I should go straight to the ER and tell the attending physician that my parents were also physicians. He would give me a prescription, I would feel better in no time, and I should call her afterward no matter what time it was. I hung up, filled with relief.

The only other people in the ER waiting room were a half-asleep woman in a headscarf, and a little boy who was lying on his stomach on a chair, repetitively snorting mucus up his nose with a hocking sound. The boy kept trying to make eye contact with me. I picked up a magazine and pretended to read an article about how to feed your baby a diet based on its horoscope, but really I was just waiting for the next hocking sound. I understood that the boy understood that I was unable to ignore him and was pleased, and was trying to snort more loudly and more particularly in my direction.

When I told the doctor that my parents were also doctors, he acted like it was the greatest news he had heard in his life. He believed every-thing I said, didn't act like I was trying to steal medicine, didn't make me take off my clothes, wrote me a prescription, and explained how to get it filled. The whole thing cost five dollars. I couldn't believe how much easier it was than going to the student health center.

When I told Koray's cousin that I was checking out early, he acted like I was leaving him after twenty years of marriage.

"Nothing happened, my plans changed," I kept saying. Again and again, in an impassioned voice, he asked where he had gone wrong, how he could make it up to me. We went back and forth like that a few times.

"Did my cousin do something?" he suddenly asked, taking me by surprise.

"Is your cousin a half-wit?" I blurted, without having planned to. I didn't know how to say mentally disabled.

A series of expressions passed over the cousin's face. "What did he do," he said.

"Nothing, forget it."

"What did he do?"

"Nothing, my plans changed."

"You can talk to me. You have to talk to me. Look into my eyes. Look into my eyes, Selin. Am I a half-wit?"

Without meaning to, I looked into his eyes. What I saw—it was above my pay grade. I went out to get a taxi.

AUGUST

The village of Olympos was an archaeological site, so construction was prohibited, and the hostel rooms were all in treehouses or shipping containers. At Gökhan's Treehouse Pension, a cute girl ran up and greeted me like I was her best friend.

"Now we can have a talk," she said.

"What are we going to talk about?" I asked, smiling.

"My big brother." She launched into a description of how handsome her brother was and how many girlfriends he had. They were beautiful, with well-developed figures, and came from all different countries. They always wanted to see him, but he never had time, because he was the manager of the whole pension.

"How nice," I said. The smile with which I had been acknowledging her cuteness was still fixed on my face. Then, the brother appeared. He was wearing Terminator sunglasses and resembled a potato.

"What a coincidence!" gushed the girl. The brother and I shook hands, after which he stepped a few feet away, apparently to organize some brochures.

"Don't you think my brother is the most unbelievably handsome and sexy man you've ever seen?" the girl asked. The brother was standing maybe five feet away. It was like we were in a play and the convention we were observing was that he couldn't hear anything we were saying. I looked more closely at the girl, trying to figure out how old she was. Her face was radiant and transfigured, apparently at the prospect of her brother's sex appeal. "You must be right," I said, which was my default Turkish response to crazy people. "You're very right" worked better than "You must be right," but I couldn't always bring myself to say it. There were cases where it seemed like a violation of the social contract, because didn't we both know that her brother resembled a potato?

"I'm just going to go stop by my room," I said.

"Of course, of course," said the brother, breaking the fourth wall. "Please make yourself comfortable. I'll be waiting here."

I didn't get it. Wasn't he running a hostel? What about all his girlfriends?

Backpackers were everywhere, with their bandannas and wilted flowers, their two-liter soda bottles filled with tap water, their one-liter water bottles that had been turned into bongs. Some were playing volleyball, shouting and cheering in a way that seemed unrealistic. A large pasty guy in madras shorts lay in a hammock. Other people with similar physiques and clothing were lolling on low cushioned benches. I had always thought of myself as someone who didn't judge people for dressing informally. And yet—how could those people wallow like that, in shorts, reading *The Alchemist*?

I took my time climbing the ladder: one of the few occasions when

I was glad to have a backpack, rather than a suitcase. The neatly made bed and folded towels, the wall hooks and the crate for you to put your bag on, all contributed to a feeling that you had everything you needed. Seen from the little window, filtered through the leaves, the scene on the ground looked less squalid. Some treehouse-related feeling of pride and seclusion, familiar from childhood, washed over me. Was it because adults didn't like to climb ladders? Maybe it was because a tree-house was a house you could have a claim to as a child—because you had built it, or you could plausibly have built it. For once you weren't in debt to an unfathomable world built by expensive machinery.

The brother, Alp, looked crestfallen when I said I had to go to the beach. "But I don't know how to swim," he said, or had I misheard him? "But you'll be back in the evening for dinner," he continued, speaking now in a smiling, conspiratorial voice. "You'll see the special air we have here. How indescribably social, how lively, with genuine, sincere conversations, and high-spirited jokes and witticisms. People come here for one night, and then they stay for a week. Look, here are some Australians who have been here for three weeks!"

"Alp, my man!" The Australian guy high-fived Alp, while his girl-friend watched with amused tolerance. "Alp is *very* social," she said to me. I resolved to stay out past dinner. I didn't have to be back until nine, to catch a minibus that took people to see the Chimaera: a perpetual flame that came out of some rocks, believed by ancient people to be the breath of an actual Chimaera. According to *Let's Go*, it was because of the perpetual flame that Olympos had been founded as a temple to Hephaestus, god of blacksmiths. I didn't totally get it: Didn't the flame have to be either the breath of the Chimaera, or the fire of Hephaestus's forge? How could it be both? How would I know which it was? Was I supposed to be able to tell, by looking?

The sea gradated, over the course of a meter or two, from perfectly transparent to violently blue green. If you kept swimming parallel to the shore, you could see the ruins: half-excavated Roman and Byzantine arches, towering above the water, dripping with vines and magenta flowers that resembled insane gaping faces.

There was a demographic bifurcation where the local-seeming guys, the ones with the deepest tan, weren't swimming, and were only wading in the shallows. The people swimming seemed to be Turkish and foreign tourists.

I swam out to a big flat rock where some people were sitting. A tanned guy with a missing tooth edged next to me and complimented my swimming. He said that most people didn't like swimming but he liked it. I smiled politely, avoiding eye contact. Then he put his arm around me and stuck his tongue in my mouth. I immediately felt guilty: Why would I allow some people to do this, and not others? Just because he was poor, and missing a tooth? It was certainly food for thought, as I slid back into the water and breaststroked away as fast as I could, which was not fast, so, when I heard the guy jump in after me, I felt sure that he would catch up. Yet, when I looked back, he was dog-paddling in such a strange, furious way that he was barely moving forward at all.

"How are you able to swim so fast? Are you a professional swimmer?" he called, sounding dismayed.

Alp sidled up to me while I was waiting for the minibus. I pretended I had forgotten something in the treehouse. This time, he followed me up and stood blocking the ladder, talking about how much we had in common. He could tell I was very intelligent. Other people cared only about external appearances, but for him intelligence was even more important.

"I do have to get the minibus, though," I said.

"There's lots of time, they're always running late. Do you know what's the really striking thing? Despite your intelligence, you aren't cold. I can tell you have a warm heart—a soft heart." Suddenly, his tongue was pressing into my mouth.

"Stop, what are you doing?"

He stared into my eyes. "Who sent you here to drive me insane?"

"I need to go to the bus."

"But the bus already came and left."

I thought he was joking, but he wasn't; it turned out to have left five minutes ago.

"You did something very wrong," I said, trying to pick out the right words to express anger. "You knew I had to go to the bus, and you prevented me. How could you do that?"

"Don't be upset, it's not important. You'll see the burning rock to-morrow." He grabbed my waist.

I hit his hand away. "Tomorrow I won't be here. I have to see it tonight, for my job. Isn't there some other way I can get there?"

He looked genuinely confused. "Why do you want to see it so much? It's boring. Look, I can describe it to you. There's some rocks. Between the rocks, a little flame comes out. It doesn't look like anything."

There was something destabilizing about this description of the Chimaera, with its unmistakable ring of truth. A moment ago, I had thought that I really had to see it. Why? Why did anyone have to see anything?

The cute girl said that I must be really grateful to her, because she had introduced me to her brother. She asked if I knew about Converse high-tops. When I said I did, she asked me to mail her a red pair in a size thirty-seven. "You're going to send them, right? You're going to send me red Converse high-tops?"

Back in Antalya, I sent off my last batch of copy. I hadn't skipped anything in my itinerary, nor had I had a nervous breakdown. Failure had not, of course, been conclusively eluded. My flight to Moscow was in three days. There, I would have to locate the geneticists, whose address included, troublingly, a street number, a "corpus" number, a building number, *and* an apartment number. I would then have to persuade that journal editor, who seemed to not know what an intern was, that I was her intern. Even so, one stage in my journey had been completed, without dishonor.

On the bus, a porter was handing out tiny cakes. It was wonderful to be eating a prepackaged cake full of candied fruit—an experience it would never have occurred to me to seek out—while watching the glittering Mediterranean being shunted away behind the thick windows, replaced by the mountains and the steppe. Dusk began to fall, and I turned on my seat light and took out my new book: *The Portrait of a Lady*, chosen somewhat perfunctorily from the one shelf of English-language books—all discount paperback "classics"—at the bookstore in Antalya.

It opened at an English estate, where some rich people were drinking afternoon tea—I was drinking tea, too, by now, the porter had handed it out—and making witty remarks. How comfortable it was to read about comfortable people! The main character showed up: Isabel, an American, somebody's niece. Everyone found her incredibly interesting, and she got to play with a cute dog. . . .

When I looked up again, almost two hours had passed. I looked out the window. At first, all I could see was blackness, and my reflection.

But when I looked more closely into my own face, I could see through it to a whole world: black mountains standing out against a glowing deep blue sky, with striated gray clouds, and stars scattered between the clouds. Some distance from the road, a long bright blue tent was lit up from inside, and near the tent was a bonfire, and I thought I could make out the shape of a horse.

I couldn't believe how relevant and applicable *The Portrait of a Lady* was to my life—way more so than *Against Nature*. The main character, Isabel, was my age, American, and lively. Only some people thought she was beautiful. The work of art she was creating was her own character: how she acted, how she was, how other people saw her. From this perspective, the aesthetic wasn't really the opposite of the ethical. The way Isabel wanted to be, and act, and seem, was generous and brave. Her main goal was to avoid meanness, jealousy, and cruelty— not because God said they weren't permitted, but because who even wanted to be like that?

Isabel's rich tubercular cousin Ralph, who was too sick to live aesthetically himself, realized that he could still have an aesthetic life just by observing Isabel. It was a great comfort to me that Ralph found Isabel as interesting as Isabel did—that Isabel wasn't the only one who found herself interesting. At some point, Henry James said that that was the only thing keeping Ralph alive: he hadn't yet seen enough of what Isabel would do. Isabel, then, was like Shahrazade, with whom I had always identified, and who used stories to postpone the moment of death. (Wasn't that what I had done, when I had written to Ivan: kept myself alive for another day?) In Isabel's case, the death she postponed wasn't her own, but Ralph's, and she was living the stories, rather than narrating them. But as she lived them, they *were* narrated. They became the book you were reading right now.

Isabel's friend Henrietta showed up, wanting Isabel to marry a square-jawed American who charismatically ran his father's cotton factory. Henrietta was blond, and said it was everyone's duty to get married, and accused Isabel of acting "like the heroine of an immoral novel." But Isabel didn't want to marry anyone: not the cotton guy, and not the handsome English lord who also almost immediately proposed to her. Lots of people were shocked when she rejected the lord. Isabel herself felt afraid, recognizing how she had raised the stakes. Now she had to do something even more spectacular.

Ralph persuaded his dying father to leave Isabel a fortune, so she would never have to get married, and he could see what she did instead. So Isabel became rich. And then she was *really* scared. A large fortune meant freedom, and one had to put it to good use—or what shame, what dishonor! And so one had always to be thinking.

"One must always be thinking," Isabel told Ralph. "I am not sure it's not a greater happiness to be powerless." And Ralph replied: "For weak people I have no doubt it's a greater happiness." It was a confirmation of my own idea of strength—of my determination to be strong.

Isabel's values made sense to me. She wasn't interested in ruining destitute women, or electroplating a tortoise. She wanted to fathom the human condition. She valued reading, travel, and relationships with radically different people: the kinds of people who didn't necessarily get the point of each other. At some point, Ralph asked what Isabel saw in Henrietta, and Isabel said that she liked people to be different from each other, and that, if a person struck her in a certain way, she liked them. I, too, had friends who found each other annoying and incomprehensible, and some of them really could be annoying, but they all struck me in a certain way—and that was why I liked them, that was why I loved them. Isabel said that was "the supreme good fortune": to be in a better position for appreciating other people than they were for appreciating you.

Thinking of the people who populated my life, who acted, spoke, and viewed the world so differently—Mesut, Juho, Lakshmi, Riley, and all the others—I recognized how important it was for me that I could understand them all, at least a little bit, and better than they could understand each other. Was that what a novel *was*: a plane where you could finally juxtapose all the different people, mediating between them and weighing their views?

The Ankara airport felt similar to a bus station, with its tea stands and goldsmiths, and the international and domestic flights listed on the same panel. But my connecting flight was through Istanbul, with its miles of duty-free shopping and hermetically glassed-in terminals. I had checked the convertible backpack and was carrying my army surplus bag, which now contained *The Portrait of a Lady*, my Walkman, and a family-sized package of hazelnut wafers.

I was flying Turkish Airlines. The attendants were Turkish, as were the brands of juice and mineral water. The Russian safety announcements were played from a recording. Nobody near me seemed to be paying attention. Nothing I was doing felt like a process that would end with a person being in Russia.

Things weren't going well for Isabel. She had ended up marrying some kind of a dilettante, to help him buy antiques. She lived in a palace, had a salon, and was unhappy—just like Tatiana at the end of *Eugene Onegin*. How strange that that had happened to both of them. Where had they gone wrong?

But *had* they definitely gone wrong? Hadn't their lives been great, in a way, furnishing the plots of great books? And yet . . . what good had that done them? *They* hadn't known that their lives were actually the plot of *The Portrait of a Lady* or *Eugene Onegin*. If they had, they could have written the books themselves. Maybe that was their failure, or their misfortune: they hadn't been able to recognize and write the books.

Near the beginning of *The Portrait of a Lady*, there was mention of an aunt who kept telling people that Isabel was writing a book. In fact, Henry James said, Isabel was not and never had been writing a book. She "had no desire to be an authoress," "no talent for expression," and "none of the consciousness of genius," having only "a general idea that people were right when they treated her as if she were rather superior." It was one of the few places where Henry James was mean about Isabel.

Well, it made sense. If she could write a book, he would be out of a job. That's why Madame Bovary had to be too dumb and banal to write *Madame Bovary*: so Flaubert could have a great humane moment where he said he *was* Madame Bovary. But I wasn't dumb or banal, and I lived in the future. Nobody was going to trick me into marrying some loser, and even if they did, I would write the goddamn book myself.

Isabel, who had had the experiences, hadn't written a book; Henry James, who had written the book, hadn't had the experiences. He had had different experiences, and those, for some reason, he hadn't written about.

I turned to the preface, which I had skipped at first, because it was written in the convoluted, embarrassing style that Henry James had apparently adopted in his old age. It did seem to be about what I wanted to know—about where the book had come from. He had, he said, written it in Italy. (He didn't specify how he had gotten to Italy, and had enough time and money left to write a whole book.) The first part that had come to him had been Isabel herself: a free-floating character, with no setting, circumstances, or plot. I didn't get how you could have a person without circumstances. But apparently Turgenev had told Henry James that that was how *his* novels started: with the hovering vision of some person who was empty and beseeching, and the thing an artist had to do was to make up their circumstances.

"As for the origin of one's wind-blown germs themselves," wrote Henry James—he kept calling Isabel a "germ"—"who shall say, as you ask, where *they* come from?" I felt excited, because that *was* what I had been asking. But he didn't really answer. First, he said, "Isn't it all we can say that they come from every quarter of heaven." Then, he said, "One could answer such a question beautifully, doubtless, if one could do so subtle, if not so monstrous, a thing as to write the history of the growth of one's imagination."

That was exciting again—especially since he went on to say that, if you *did* do that subtle and monstrous thing, you would definitely find what you had been looking for. It would be there, in some circumstance of your real life. (So Isabel had come from his real life?) But it became clear that he was speaking only theoretically: in practical terms he thought that that kind of reconstruction or excavation was impossible, or somehow not worth trying, or not worth thinking about.

Instead, he changed the subject to what an insignificant person Isabel was, and how weird it was that "this slight 'personality,' the mere slim shade of an intelligent but presumptuous girl," should be "endowed with the high attributes of a Subject." He marveled at "how absolutely, how inordinately, the Isabel Archers, and even much smaller female fry, insist on mattering," and acted as if he was some kind of visionary for even thinking of writing a whole book about someone like that.

I started to feel the combined annoyance and exhilaration that sometimes came over me on airplanes. You could tell that Henry James wasn't actually dumb, or a jerk. So how didn't he realize he was sounding like a jerk? More importantly, if the situation of a young girl whose fate wasn't decided yet was so wonderfully and paradoxically interesting, then didn't I have a big advantage by being such a person?

Nowhere in the preface did Henry James say why he hadn't found his *own* life interesting enough to write about. I tried to remember what I knew about Henry James's life. I was pretty sure I had read that he was gay. Probably being gay had been illegal, and he had been ashamed. So his problem, like Isabel's, was that he had been born too soon. That was sad, but it didn't really change anything. Like, for whatever reason, Henry James had had to do stuff like find a "wind-blown germ" and then forget how he had found it, so he wouldn't feel like he was stealing. But I was more fortunate. I was going to remember, or discover, where everything came from. I was going to do the subtle, monstrous thing where you figured out what you were doing, and why.

I loved Henry James again, when he wrote about trying to dramatize Isabel's life, even when there seemed to be no drama. He described a scene where the only "action" was that Isabel sat in a chair by a burned-out fire. In her mind she was recognizing all the machinations that had been whirling around her, remembering tiny details that she thought she had forgotten, and that now acquired new significance. Even though she never got up out of the chair and nobody else came into the room, Henry James had wanted that scene to be "as 'interesting' as the surprise of a caravan or the identification of a pirate." And it had been. All the scenes where Isabel sat in a chair and realized things were amazing.

There was one line that I had copied into my notebook:

Now that she was in the secret, now that she knew something that so much concerned her, and the eclipse of which had made life resemble an attempt to play whist with an imperfect pack of cards, the truth of things, their mutual relations, their meaning, and for the most part their horror, rose before her with a kind of architectural vastness.

It was how I had felt when I was sitting in a dark classroom after watching *The Usual Suspects*, or after reading *Either/Or*, when all the different things that Ivan had said and written had come flooding back to me, assuming a new shape, bigger than I had suspected. It was happening again now: some pieces of some larger story that I could barely make out were flying into new positions, and I was remembering things I had forgotten, and putting them together differently, and all while I was sitting still and not going anywhere or doing anything— though in another way I was hurtling north at five hundred miles an hour.

At the lost baggage counter in Sheremetyevo-2, I was shown a laminated page with pictures of different suitcases and backpacks. None looked much like my convertible backpack, which had vanished at some stage of the journey. Pointing to the closest approximation, I wrote out, in the fake-seeming Cyrillic cursive that I had only ever used in Russian class, the geneticists' convoluted address. The man at the counter glanced at the paper and said fine, the bag would be brought there tomorrow. Was that a possible outcome? I had no idea. But there was nothing more I could do here: the longer I lingered, hoping for some extra assurance, the more distinctly I felt the last ambient goodwill whooshing out of the room, like sand from an hourglass. I went out the only way there was, into the arrivals hall.

The smells, the colors, the people's flat and wary faces, were radically unfamiliar—as if the plastic and the cigarettes and the light bulbs and the clothes had a different chemical makeup, and the people had eaten different food, and their clothes had been made in different factories, and the distance that separated them from my own existence was determined not just spatially, by things like biogeography and regional trade blocs, but also somehow by time.

The lighting, the air quality, the heavy bronze sculpted ceiling that seemed about to fall on our heads: all lent the immediate surroundings the hazy amber cast of a 1970s photograph. The structures themselves—the bronze panels, the black numberless clock, the pillars that resembled the skyscrapers on the cover of *The Fountainhead*— seemed to connote a bygone futurism, the projection of a historical reality different from the one that had, to my knowledge, actually come to pass. That was what Russia had done: taken a fork in the road to a different future. For all my life there had been another world, and no one had come out, and no one had gone in—until one day the borders turned out to be fictitious, the insurmountable barrier became nothing but a pack of cards, so that now you could walk right through the looking glass, into the world of backward N's and R's.

With only my messenger bag, feeling light as a soul, I got into a Lada taxi and told the driver the address.

"OK," he said, and started driving.

So it was true. There really was a whole country where people spoke the language from *Eugene Onegin*, the recombined components of which now rose up around me, on highway signs and license plates, on the sides of the prehistoric, post-historic, exhaust-spewing trucks. And I had willed myself into it. In the past, I had been in one country or another because of other people: my parents, Svetlana, Ivan, Sean. But I was in Russia because I had looked at the literatures of the world and made a choice. Nobody had especially wanted me to come— indeed, the customs officer who stamped my passport had left a distinct impression of wishing me to be elsewhere—yet here I was. It was like when Isabel managed not to marry the guy with the cotton mills, and it was her first taste of victory—because "she had done what she preferred."

Was this the decisive moment of my life? It felt as if the gap that had dogged me all my days was knitting together before my eyes—so that, from this point on, my life would be as coherent and meaningful as my favorite books. At the same time, I had a powerful sense of having escaped something: of having finally stepped outside the script.

NOTES ON SOURCES

The poem "We Masses Don't Want Tofu" (p. 23) is by Ruth A. Fox, and appears in *Real Change*, vol. 4, no. 13 (August, 1997). The poems "We Live in a World," by Sprite (p. 23); "Hate," by Anonymous (p. 23); and "And to think, she'd never been kissed," by SGZ (p. 104), all appear in *Real Change*, vol. 3, no. 9 (September, 1996), as does an advice column similar to the one Selin reads on pp. 40–41. (In the original, letters by Single in Seattle and Annoyed on the Ave. are answered by Nancy, Frank, and Candi.)

Real Change is the Seattle-based sister publication of *Spare Change*, the Boston-area street paper that Selin would actually have been reading. The two papers were founded by Tim Harris in 1992 and 1994. *Real Change* has a search-able digital archive going back to the 1990s: https://www.realchangenews.org/archive.

The reading list for Chance is inspired by a syllabus kindly shared by Miryam Sas, who taught a class by this name at Harvard in 1996.

The phrase "promiscuous sexual conquest of Goneril and Regan," which Selin reads in the synopsis of *King Lear* in the liquor store, is from Jeffrey R. Wilson, "Edmund's Bastardy," in "Stigma in Shakespeare": https://wilson.fas.harvard.edu/stigma-in-shakespeare/edmund%E2%80%99s-bastardy.

For an account of the debate over the level of inclusion of the Armenian genocide in the United States Holocaust Memorial Museum (very tangentially evoked on pp. 69–71), see Edward Linenthal, "The Boundaries of Inclusion: Armenians and Gypsies," in *Preserving Memory: The Struggle to Create America's Holocaust Museum* (Columbia University Press, 2001).

The phrase "by acting as a kind of lightning rod for the erotic desires of violent men" on p. 82 is from the write-up of Želimir Žilnik's *The Marble Ass* (1995) on the Berlinale website: https://www.berlinale.de/en/archive/jahresarchive/2016/02 _programm_2016/02_filmdatenblatt_2016_201602952.html#tab=filmStills.

The quotes from the song "And All the Same, It's Sad" are from "The Past Can't Be Reversed" ("Byloe Nel'zia Vorotit'," 1964), by Bulat Okudzhava (1924–1997), a pioneer of Russian "author's songs." You can see Okudzhava perform this song on YouTube: https://www.youtube.com/watch?v=o1xrTnXQmRQ.

The phrase "the Repugnant Conclusion" is from Derek Parfit's *Reasons and Persons* (Oxford University Press, 1986), as are most of the ideas attributed to Selin's ethics professor.

"Rudol'fio," by Valentin Rasputin (1937–2005), is quoted in my own awkward translation from the text on Biblioteka Serann: http://www.serann.ru/text/ru dolfio-9522. A more elegant translation by Helen Burlingame appears in *The Kenyon Review*, vol. 5, no. 3 (Summer, 1983).

The John Cage quote about listening to something boring for thirty-two minutes is from *Silence: Lectures on Music and Writing* (Wesleyan University Press, 1961). The quote about the traffic on Sixth Avenue appears in *ArtLark*, "John Cage's Music of Chance and Change" (Sept. 5, 2020): https://artlark.org/2020 /09/05/john-cages-music-of-chance-and-change/.

The comparison of tuxedo-wearing boys to black holes is made by the physicist John Wheeler in Errol Morris's documentary *A Brief History of Time* (Triton Pictures, 1991).

The quote from the Picasso exhibit about Françoise Gilot is taken from the brochure written by Patterson Sims for the show *Picasso and Portraiture* (MOMA, 1996). "Staring terrified and goggle-eyed into the abyss" is from the *New York Times* review of that show by Michael Kimmelman ("Picasso Again, Still Surprising," April 26, 1996).

The Luce Irigaray quote about the two lips that embrace continually appears in the discussion of *écriture féminine* in Patricia Waugh, *Literary Theory and Criticism: An Oxford Guide* (Oxford University Press, 2006). The Hélène Cixous quote is from "Castration or Decapitation?" (which, unlike Selin, I think is brilliant), trans. Annette Kuhn, *Signs*, vol. 7, no. 1 (Autumn, 1981).

The email forward about the world being full of idiots appears on an anonymous Tripod website titled "Jokes," last updated in June 2001 and still accessible as of August 23, 2021: https://wbenton.tripod.com/humor/Jokeindex076.html.

Most of the quotes from *Swann's Way* are from the 1992 Modern Library Edition (trans. C. K. Scott Moncrieff and Terence Kilmartin, rev. D. J. Enright). However, the quote about the magic lantern ("They had indeed hit upon the idea . . .") is from Lydia Davis's translation (Penguin, 2002).

The Iris Murdoch novel with the Count (his irremediable Polishness, etc.) is *Nuns and Soldiers* (1980).

The quotes from the English-language Russian literary journal on p. 274 appear in *Glas: New Russian Writing*, issue 14 (1997), eds. Natasha Perova and Arch Tait. Vic the Snot-Faced Drooler is from Genrikh Sapgir, "Mind Power," trans. Andrew Bromfield; Polyp Pigdick is from Victor Pelevin, "The Black Bagel," trans. Arch Tait; Pissoff and Karmalyutov are from Valery Ronshin, "Cloudy Days," trans. Edmund Glentworth.

The *Sex and the City* episode where Samantha lets the Pakistani busboy kiss her is "They Shoot Single People, Don't They?," season 4, episode 2 (June, 1999).

Most of the quotes from *The Unofficial Guide to Life at Harvard* are drawn, with slight modifications, from *The Unofficial Guide to Life at Harvard, 1995–96*, eds. Jeremy Faro and Natasha Leland (Harvard Student Agencies, 1995). The write-up of Wholesome Fresh is from the Unofficial Guide website: https://www.theunofficialguide.net/articles/top-five-late-night-eats.

The *Let's Go* quotes are a composite based on the 1997 edition of *Let's Go, Greece & Turkey* (ed. Eti Brachna Bonn), the 1998 edition of *Let's Go, Greece & Turkey* (eds. Patrick K. Lyons and Ziad W. Munson), and the 2003 edition of *Let's Go, Turkey* (eds. Ben Davis and Allison Melia), all published by St. Martin's Press.

The quote about Russian-Ottoman relations is from *A Pocket Guide to Turkey* (Department of the Army, Washington, D.C., 1953): https://archive.org/details/ldpd_11150008_000.

The translated Atatürk quotes on pp. 319–320 appear in Ayşe Zarakol, *After Defeat: How the East Learned to Live with the West* (Cambridge University Press, 2010).

The Rumi quotes about Turkishness, as well as the argument about Rumi's non-nationalistic worldview, are from Talat Sait Halman, "Mevlana and the Illusions of Nationalism," in the *Mawlana Rumi Review* (Nov. 6, 2015): http://www.jstor.org/stable/26810313.

The other Rumi quotes on pp. 330–332 are from the following poems, translated by Coleman Barks and published by HarperCollins: "On Gambling" and "Burnt Kabob" in *The Essential Rumi* (1995); "Dark Sweetness" in *A Year with Rumi* (2006); and "Disciplines," "Trees," and "You Are As You Are" in *The Big Red Book* (2010).

The quotes from *The Portrait of a Lady* are from the original 1881 version—not the New York Edition, which Henry James revised twenty-five years later. (The 1881 version is the one I read at age twenty, and those are the quotes that stuck with me.) The preface, however, is from the New York Edition, so it wouldn't normally be in the same volume with the 1881 text, as it is in Selin's imaginary copy. Most editions you come across now will have the New York text, but a few, like Signet Classics (2007), use the earlier version. You can find all the prefaces in Henry James, *The Art of the Novel* (Scribner, 1937).

Although it isn't directly quoted, I would also like to cite Adrienne Rich's 1980 essay, "Compulsory Heterosexuality and Lesbian Existence," which I first read in 2017, and which enabled me to reconstruct some of the heteronormative forces that operated on me in the 1990s (preventing me from being attracted, at that time, to texts with titles like "Compulsory Heterosexuality and Lesbian Existence"). One goal of this book was to dramatize those forces. Rich's essay appears in *Blood, Bread, and Poetry* (Norton, 1986).

Lastly, a bibliographic update on *The Idiot*. At the time *The Idiot* came out, I didn't have any authorship information about "The Story of Vera" (the inspiration for "Nina in Siberia," a beginning Russian-language text that Selin and Ivan read together). Since then, it has been brought to my attention that most of "Vera" was written by Michael Henry Heim in 1967, when he was a first-year Russian teaching assistant at Harvard. Heim went on to become the translator of, among other works, Milan Kundera's *The Unbearable Lightness of Being* and *The Book of Laughter and Forgetting*: two more books that Selin and Ivan read. I'm grateful to Charles Sabatos for pointing out this coincidence, and for directing me to the mention of "the Vera stories" in Henning Andersen's essay "My

Friend Mike," in *The Man Between: Michael Henry Heim and a Life in Translation*, eds. Esther Allen, Sean Cotter, and Russell Scott Valentino (Open Letter Books, 2014).

Other Works Quoted

Anna Akhmatova, "Requiem," in *Selected Poems*, trans. Richard McKane (Penguin, 1969).

Martin Amis, *The Rachel Papers* (Vintage International, 1992).

Fiona Apple, "Sullen Girl," *Tidal* (Sony, 1996).

Charles Baudelaire, "Don Juan in Hell," in *The Flowers of Evil*, trans. Keith Waldrop (Wesleyan University Press, 2006).

André Breton, *Nadja*, trans. Richard Howard (Grove Press, 1960).

Anton Chekhov, "The Lady with the Little Dog," trans. Richard Pevear and Larissa Volokhonsky, in Cathy Popkin, ed., *Selected Stories* (Norton Critical Editions, 2014).

Eurythmics, "Sweet Dreams (Are Made of This)," *Sweet Dreams (Are Made of This)*, (RCA, 1983).

Ellen Fein and Sherrie Schneider, *The Rules* (Warner Books, 1995).

Sigmund Freud, *Dora: An Analysis of a Case of Hysteria* (Touchstone, 1997); *The Interpretation of Dreams*, trans. James Strachey (Basic Books, 2010).

Fugees, "Killing Me Softly" and "Cowboys," *The Score* (Columbia Records, 1996).

Johann Wolfgang von Goethe, *The Sorrows of Young Werther*, trans. R. D. Boylan, ed. Nathan Haskell Dole, Project Gutenberg, https://www.gutenberg.org/files /2527/2527-h/2527-h.htm.

The I Ching or Book of Changes, trans. Richard Wilhelm and Cary F. Baynes (Bollingen Series XIX, Princeton University Press, 1977).

Michiko Kakutani, "The Examined Life Is Not Worth Living Either," *New York Times*, September 20, 1994.

Søren Kierkegaard, *Either/Or: A Fragment of Life,* trans. Alastair Hannay (Penguin Classics, 1992).

Walter Kirn, "For White Girls Who Have Considered Suicide," *New York,* September 5, 1993.

Alexander Pushkin, *Eugene Onegin: A Novel in Verse*, trans. Vladimir Nabokov (Bollingen Series LXXII, Princeton University Press, 1990).

R.E.M., "Bittersweet Me," *New Adventures in Hi-Fi* (Warner Bros., 1996).

Tom Waits, "I'll Be Gone," *Frank's Wild Years* (Island Records, 1987).

Oscar Wilde, *The Picture of Dorian Gray,* Project Gutenberg, https://www.gutenberg.org/files/174/174-h/174-h.htm.